Quail Creek Villa

SHE KNEW

Someone, something, some presence, was in that room. It was in there *now*.

Rebecca pushed the door open, the feeling of dread now giving way to something else: a mixture of both fear and attraction, polar opposites both tangling with each other, like the needle on a compass spinning wildly out of control.

The door went wide. She stepped in expecting to see someone.

But instead she saw no one.

Didn't see. But knew he was there.

"Ronny?" she asked.

No movement. But there was this unbanishable sense of a presence. A presence that she somehow thought she recognized. Something familiar, as familiar as a kiss from a lover. And her sense of being watched was as keen as it had ever been.

I'm near, Rebecca. Very near.

MORE FROM BEST-SELLING AUTHOR
NOEL HYND!

CEMETERY
of
ANGELS

NOEL HYND

PINNACLE BOOKS
KENSINGTON PUBLISHING CORP.

The author gratefully acknowledges permission from his friend, James DePreist, Music Director and Conductor of the Oregon Symphony Orchestra, for permission to reprint BOTTOM-LINERS BEWARE, from his volume of poetry, *The Distant Siren*, © 1989 by James DePreist.

Readers can reach Noel Hynd at: NHy1212@AOL.com.

PINNACLE BOOKS are published by

Kensington Publishing Corp.
850 Third Avenue
New York, NY 10022

Pinnacle and the P logo Reg. U.S. Pat. & TM Off.

First Kensington Printing: August, 1995

First Pinnacle Books Printing: May, 1996

Printed in the United States of America

10 9 8 7 6 5 4 3 2 1

BOTTOM-LINERS BEWARE:
there's
      another

set
 of
 books

—James DePreist

PART ONE

I

i

Rebecca Moore would never forget the face of the man who had wanted her dead.

The first time anyone tried to murder her was late on a February afternoon in 1994. And the incident came up out of nowhere, as if it had risen conspiratorially out of the nether precincts of the earth, regions of the earth that were as dark and cold as the wintry afternoon in Connecticut.

It began in a supermarket parking lot in the town of Fairfield. Rebecca had done a day's worth of grocery shopping and was anxious to arrive home. Already there was snow and ice on the ground. But more—and a generous belt of it—was predicted for later that evening.

As was the case on most days, she was to make dinner for the "three guys" currently in her life, as she affectionately called them.

The three: Bill was her husband, stepfather to her children. Patrick, seven, was her son. The third "guy" was Karen, five. At that moment her husband, a free-lance architect, should have been home with the kids. The "three amigos" were waiting for her.

As she unlocked the rear door of her Dodge Caravan, a pair

of headlights swept around the dark parking lot. The lights, and the fast creeping shadows they cast, caused her to look up. Almost simultaneously, she felt a pair of eyes upon her. She had always felt that she had a keen sixth sense, a sense of being watched—an instinct about an extra presence whenever one was there. And she felt it now, intertwined with a shiver.

The headlights belonged to a woman in a Mercedes. The Benz parked and the woman stepped out. But Rebecca's antenna was primed. Her eyes kept working.

Turning, looking around, she scanned past the parked cars. Then, finding nothing, she searched further, looking under the supermarket's sign and the variety store's billboard. When she finally found the source of her anxiety, a surge of fear coursed through her.

A man was watching her from only fifty feet away.

He was sitting in the driver's seat of a big wrecker of a car, an old Lincoln that was battered but looked otherwise as sturdy as a Hum-Vee. But it wasn't the vehicle or its condition that frightened her. What riveted her was the sheer menace on his face.

As a reporter for a suburban newspaper called *WestPress,* she had known a few criminals in her day. She had even, in her impetuous early twenties, loved and slept with a free-spirited young man who would eventually go to jail for selling an ounce of window box hashish to a narc.

But that had been different. Her reporting assignments had taken her into all sorts of stories, so she had known more people who had gone to jail than she would have cared to. Yet most of the criminals whom she had known personally were physically harmless: tax cheats, recreational druggies, and swindlers. And the young man to whom she had been a lover had actually been quite tender.

But the man in the car was pure threat. He was there to devour her. From somewhere came a horrible image: a vision of this man tearing off her clothing and attacking her flesh with his mouth.

Her heart quickened. She knew he was watching her. Her only question was, had he also been waiting for her?

Instinct again: Something told her he was there for her.

She sneaked a second look, trying to pick up the details.

He was very pale-skinned and his head was shaved. He wore dark wraparound sunglasses—they looked like razor shades. He looked like he would be tall—maybe six-two, six-three—if he stepped out of the Lincoln. And worst of all, sunglasses or not, his line of vision was fixed on her.

At first she tried to dismiss him as some sort of petty crook. Then, as she shoved the first of three shopping bags into her van, she shivered again as she thought of him as a potential rapist.

Turning to continue unloading from her shopping cart, she took a longer look at him. She held him in her gaze for several seconds, as if to try to convince him (and herself) that she wasn't afraid.

It didn't work. Their eyes locked. But at least she got some of his details.

He was wearing a leather jacket over a bare chest, odd attire for a raw February afternoon. There were some chains—gold ones, she thought—around his neck. His features were sharp, and he reminded her of a hungry feral predator looking for a lamb.

And then another thought came to her. It was not an attractive one:

This man, she thought, was something far worse than anything she could imagine or anything she had ever faced before. There was something genuinely horrible surrounding him.

A malevolent aura? A threat of violence that surpassed even the physical threat? Something creepy bordering on the supernatural? All of those things?

Yes, she decided. All of those things.

Rebecca felt herself break a fearful sweat under her coat, sweater, and jeans. She felt perspiration form at her neck and drift between her breasts. She suddenly saw herself as very female and very vulnerable.

This is what a werewolf looks like, she found herself thinking. The words, the thoughts, formed almost by themselves. *Or a vampire. Or some sort of half-human monster beast that is going to kill me, strip my body, and exsanguinate me. I will be found battered, sexually ravished, and naked in the snow. My body will be violated, I will be mutilated, all the life and blood will be drained from me and—*

God damn it! she thought to herself. All of a sudden, she couldn't even control the drift of her own thoughts.

As she entertained that idea, he turned over the ignition in his car. She hurriedly pushed the second grocery bag into her own car. She glanced back again. Through those hostile shades, through a streaked car windshield, he continued to stare.

She took her eyes off the man and pushed the third bag of groceries into the van. Then she looked at him again.

Definitely, she told herself. He was there to stalk her. The entire night was now the color of his dark eyes. He was there for one thing: her.

What to do?

What was Rebecca Moore, suburban wife and mother, reporter for a suburban weekly, to do?

She tried to stay calm. She told herself: You are smart. You are wily. You have been around a bit. You are not going to be intimidated by a thug.

And, oh yes. One other thing that she acknowledged to herself: Might as well admit it. You are not just scared. You are terrified. She begged her composure not to desert her. She had to stay calm. She knew that her life would depend on it.

His car, the ignition running now, was positioned between

her and the supermarket. Between her and the nearest telephone. Something told her that if she tried to walk back to the store, the man with the shaved head would hit her with his car and kill her.

She looked for his license plate.

None on the front bumper.

Mentally, she cursed the pointy-headed state bureaucrats up in Windsor Locks. Several years earlier they had taken away the front plates and made any vehicle in the state fifty percent more difficult to identify.

She broke a bigger sweat. Then she made a decision.

She was only two miles from her home, two miles from the house where her family waited. She would leave the parking lot quickly and get out of the area. If she were lucky, she would elude him, then she'd call the town police. But her first impulse was to get out of there as fast as possible.

She slammed her van closed. She turned on the ignition of her car. She waited. The old Lincoln made no effort to move.

Rebecca reached to the backseat. Her son Patrick had left a child-size baseball bat in the car. Child-size or not, it was made out of wood and Rebecca, at age thirty-two, knew she could still pack a wallop when she swung it.

She had played soccer and run track at the University of Maryland a decade earlier. She had kept in shape ever since— aerobics, the Nautilus at the health club twice a week, three-mile runs four mornings a week, and the occasional game of tennis when time permitted.

So help me, she told herself, *if he comes anywhere close, I'll bash his—*

This thought was interrupted by a second one.

Fact of life: a strong man could always overpower a strong woman. And what if he had a weapon? The best defense was always the defense of that most noble of beasts, the rabbit.

Swift flight. Run like hell.

She put her Dodge in reverse. She eased out of the parking place.

Yeah! Run like hell!

"Make one move with your car, Buddy," she whispered aloud, her heart thumping in her chest, "and I'm hitting this accelerator so *fucking* fast—"

She backed up and turned toward the exit which led out onto the Post Road.

Where are the police? she found herself thinking. *Where are the police? Never when you need them. Never when you need them.*

She drove evenly, watching her rearview mirror the whole time. The darkness of a late winter afternoon closed in on the bare parking lot. Snow was piled near the light standards. And the bald man in the car didn't move.

Rebecca Moore relaxed very slightly.

She breathed more easily. She mildly scolded herself for becoming so upset. For *imagining* herself in danger. After all, what had this strange man even *done?* His face was pointed in her direction. That was all.

But she was still alarmed. Her instincts had kicked in mightily. And her instincts had rarely lied to her.

Rebecca's Caravan arrived at the exit. The Lincoln made no move. She heaved a big-time sigh of relief. She watched for a break in traffic, glancing repeatedly in her rearview mirror as she waited.

A few seconds later, she had a break. She turned left, exiting the parking lot. And as soon as she committed herself to driving in a specific direction, Rebecca heard a screech of tires.

She looked in the mirror and let out a short scream. Goose bumps surged across her entire body. She saw her worst fears realized: The man had turned his car sharply. He was following her.

She hit her accelerator.

Her wheels screeched on the asphalt. She followed the Post Road for several blocks and watched in the rearview mirror. The Lincoln darted out of the parking lot and was in pursuit.

She made a flash decision. She didn't want to lead him directly home. And she saw no place where she could stop for help. So she turned sharply when she came to Tremont Lane, a winding road which cut through a patch of woods. It was in the general direction of her house.

She hoped she could lose the man if she floored the accelerator on winding Tremont.

She hit her gas pedal hard. But almost immediately, she knew that she had erred. The roads were slick. There had been some melting during the day and now what had melted was frozen. It was impossible to move quickly.

She hoped—she prayed—that the man in the Lincoln hadn't seen her turn, that he had lost her taillights among a handful of others.

Her heart sank. Yes, he had seen her! Now he turned after her. Seconds later she realized something worse. He was gaining on her very quickly.

She went up a hill, then down one, traveling much too fast.

Again, her eyes were on the rearview mirror. At first she saw only blessed blackness. Then there was the glare of headlights following from the other side of a crest. Then, as she hit a turn, the headlights were yellow and bright about a hundred feet behind her.

She heard herself muttering. A prayer to anyone who would listen: "Oh, no. . . . Oh, God, no. . . . Oh, God, help me . . ."

The other car was gaining.

It gained on her fast. Within seconds the pursuing vehicle was no more than sixty feet back, its headlights brighter, larger, and more yellow with every second.

She hit another turn.

Hairpin, this time. Much too sharp. And she was moving far too fast on an icy road.

She yanked her steering wheel sharply going into the curve and her tires betrayed her. They didn't hold the road. The van hydroplaned, fishtailed, and slid.

At the same time, the pursuing car pulled abreast of Rebecca's. All she was aware of was how close it was, tracking her down by cutting into the wrong lane. Then there was a loud crunching sound as her attacker turned his right front fender into her car to force it off the road.

The tactic worked. The Lincoln was a big heavy old beast, designed perfectly for forcing a smaller, lighter vehicle out of a rightful lane. Rebecca's tires whirled on nothing and her Dodge hit a patch of black ice. Its tires spun helplessly. Then, still forced by the crunching muscle of the Lincoln, Rebecca's car found the narrow snow-covered shoulder of the road.

And then it slid some more.

The van left the road, went down an embankment, ran over some short snow-coated shrubbery, and came to a jarring rest.

The Lincoln swerved to a halt. All Rebecca could think of was to flee.

Run, run, run as fast as she could.

All those miles, all that roadwork, and now—maybe if she were lucky—*maybe* it could save her life!

For a moment she was stunned. Then she looked up and screamed. The man had already jumped out of his car. He ran toward her.

She fumbled with the door handle. The man was twenty feet from her. Then, a second later, ten. She put her shoulder to the car door and shoved. It flew open. She put her hand on the baseball bat and clutched it.

The man charged her Caravan. He grabbed the other side of her door and pulled violently.

She screamed again. That face! That horrible brutish surreal too-white razor-shaded face!

He was practically snarling. She could smell his foul breath and feel the heat from his body. She could smell the sweat from under the leather jacket. He was big. Six-two. Six-three! And strong.

Inhumanly strong. That's what she remembered thinking.

"No! No! No! Help!" she screamed again.

But he had stopped her on the most deserted stretch of the road. There were no homes, no houses. Little chance of another car coming by.

Zero chance of the police.

My God! she thought. *He knows me so well that he knew I'd come here. He let me lead him to this spot to kill me!*

He pushed a gloved hand into her mouth to silence her. His other hand wrestled with her left arm.

Rebecca got lucky. Her right hand emerged from the darkness of her car, wielding the small bat.

She swung as hard as she could.

Her blow glanced off the top of her car door. But the rest of the blow found its mark, hitting her attacker across the side of the head. She followed with another shot. She got only a piece of him, but the piece was significant.

Impact. Loud!

Blood came from a gash in his forehead.

He staggered, cursing obscenely. But he released his grip.

She swung again with all her strength. The man was already bleeding hard. He raised his hands to block her third blow.

She felt the crack of the bat against his forearms. It was just enough to cause him to recoil. When she shoved the car door at him, and hit him solidly, she forced him back a little more. She had just enough room to turn.

He lunged for her. Huge arms. Big powerful hands in black gloves.

She felt his hand like a vise on the back of her thigh, but when she swung again with the bat, he braced his arms in front of his chest to protect himself. He lost his footing on the ice and she was able to run.

She knew better than to choose the road, where he could

follow and see her. She chose the woods, instead, seeking cover like a hunted animal.

A rabbit. Again, the defense of the rabbit.

The man yelled after her—she would never forget that voice, either—and cursed profanely again as she darted into the darkness.

She knew these woods. Even with several inches of snow on the ground, she knew exactly where they would come out on the other side.

She stumbled slightly as she ran. At first, at the edge of the woods, there was light that was reflected from the headlights of their two vehicles. The trunks and branches of the trees cast strange shadows and silhouettes among the trees. She moved from one shadow to another, going deeper.

Forty or fifty feet into the woods, she stopped and looked back. The man had stopped. He had something in his hands. And somehow, her assailant knew approximately where she was because he raised the thing in his hand and it definitely became a gun.

He pointed it in her direction and began to randomly spray the area. Three shots. She heard them whistle and clatter through the low frozen branches of the trees around her.

The nightmare was real.

She crouched low to the ground, feeling like wild game in hunting season. She nestled close to a fir tree for cover. She would always remember the feel and smell of the evergreen branches.

What did he want to do? Kill her, cook her, and eat her? She couldn't shake the vision of being devoured!

The man stood for a moment, then fired two more times, even closer to her. She heard one shot thump into the ground a few feet away from her. Another one thumped into the trunk of a nearby tree. Her heart kicked like a boot in her chest.

Rebecca wondered if the man knew where she was or was

just guessing. When he took three or four more steps into the woods, she realized that she couldn't wait to find out.

She turned and fled farther. At one point he must have thought he saw her because he fired another bullet.

But the snow protected her. It muffled her footsteps in flight. And the ice on the branches created a clatter that distracted him. Best of all, more snow was starting to fall, inhibiting his vision.

She fled farther, until she couldn't see the road. Then, going by instinct and her own sense of direction, she continued on.

She felt like crying, but was too terrified. Plus, she knew she couldn't. To stop meant to court death again.

She continued through the woods. Her eyes, frozen with tears, adjusted to the dim light. Given the terrifying circumstances, she found her way to the other side of the woods with relative ease. She guessed that she had been in the woods for half an hour.

She came out on Hillspoint Road. Hillspoint, she knew, led to McSherry Street, where she lived. She shivered from the cold, and from the sweat beneath her clothes. Her own perspiration was freezing to her, but she kept walking.

Twice, sets of automobile headlights appeared on the road, both times from behind. Twice, in response to the lights, she hid in shrubbery by the roadside. It took seventy more minutes to find her way home.

She entered the house without her keys.

Her children were with Bill down in the playroom. Her husband came upstairs. He froze when he saw her. Stunned at her presence. Her condition. Astonished at the sight of her.

"Becca?" He called her by her pet name. "What the—?" His brow knit into a deep frown.

He opened his arms to her.

"What *happened?*" he insisted.

Her emotions released. Tears came so fast and so vehemently that she was unable to coherently tell him what had happened.

"Becca, kid. Just calm yourself," he said tenderly. "Then tell me. What happened? Where's the van? Are you all right?" He held her. "An accident? Did you have an accident?"

She was shaking. She saw herself in the mirror. She looked a wreck. She *was* a wreck.

She still couldn't talk.

"Did someone hurt you?"

She couldn't answer.

"Do you need a doctor?" he asked.

No. She finally shook her head.

"The police?" he asked next.

She nodded.

"I want you to calm down first," he said, his voice still soft and understanding. "I'm not even leaving to go to the telephone with you in this state."

She took his hand and clutched it. Bill Moore had never seen any woman this traumatized, much less his wife. He knew full well that something terrible had happened to her.

"I was about to come out with the other car to look for you," he said. "Now what happened? Come on, honey. You need to tell me. *What happened?*"

Fortunately, Patrick and Karen stayed in the downstairs playroom. She was able, with trembling lips, with her husband's trusted arm around her, to begin to tell what had transpired. He led her through the story, growing angrier as she spoke.

Eventually, she collapsed again into her husband's arms and sobbed uncontrollably.

When she had told the entire story, Bill Moore picked up the telephone and called the Connecticut State Police.

ii

Two police cars—three cops, two in uniform—responded within twenty minutes. A young plainclothes sergeant named David Chandler was in charge.

Chandler was in his late twenties, big, strapping, and blond. He was alone in his car while the two uniformed men shared a patrol vehicle.

A neighbor watched Karen and Patrick as Sergeant Chandler drove the Moores back to the spot on Tremont Lane where Rebecca had left her van. The Dodge was still off the shoulder of the road in the snow of a shallow ravine. Someone had turned the ignition off, cut the headlights, and closed the door.

Bill Moore sat with his wife in the back of a detective's car. He watched as the two uniformed men carried a pair of heavy flashlights, scanned the woods, and looked for clues. The snow was steadier now, bringing peace to what had been a tableau of violence. Yet the snow also covered any clues.

Too much snow had fallen to find footprints near the car, or tire tracks or skid marks. Chandler thought he could see the point where Rebecca Moore had entered the woods to flee, but he couldn't be certain.

He walked back to the Moores' Dodge and looked at the ground. Then he came back to his car.

"Mrs. Moore, you said you hit the man with a baseball bat."

"Two or three times," she said. "A child's bat. My son's. I swung it hard."

For a moment, Sergeant Chandler had a congratulatory look in his eye. "Did it draw blood?" he asked.

"I saw blood," she said. "Right by the front window of my car."

"What did you do with the bat?"

"I ran . . . and when I ran into the woods, I dropped it."

Chandler nodded. He walked back to his car. The police radio crackled and the heat thundered out from under the dashboard.

"Just be calm," Bill Moore whispered to his wife. "No one's going to hurt you now."

Chandler was joined by the two uniformed men. They discussed something among themselves. One of the uniformed men grimaced. Then two of them went to the edge of the woods and looked in vain for footprints in the fresh snow.

Nothing.

Chandler pushed a booted toe through the freshly fallen stuff near Rebecca's vehicle. Like the officers at the edge of the woods, he found nothing.

Then he opened the driver's side door to the Dodge Caravan, leaned in and pulled out the baseball bat.

He walked back to where the Moores sat in his car.

"Is this the bat?" he asked.

She looked at it.

"Yes, it is."

"It was in your car."

"Then someone put it back."

"It's clean," he said, inspecting it. "Clean and dry." He paused, raising his eyes, and studied her for a moment. "No blood on it. But I can have it checked for prints as well as a serology exam."

She stared at it, also.

"The man was wearing gloves," she said. "I just remembered."

"Uh-huh." He looked at her again. "I'll have it checked for prints, anyhow," Chandler said.

"Did you find any blood? In the snow?"

"No. None on the car door, either."

Chandler trudged thoughtfully to his two uniformed men.

He said something to them, then came back to his own vehicle.

"I'd like to take you to the station to get a statement from you, Mrs. Moore," he said. "I'd also like to take your van into our garage for fingerprints. May we do that?"

Bill Moore put his hand on his wife's.

"My wife already told you that her assailant was wearing gloves, didn't she?" Bill Moore asked.

"Her attacker might have taken them off," Chandler said. "Plus there are paint scratches where another vehicle hit your front left fender."

"That's from when he ran me off the road," she said.

"Then I need to take some paint samples," Chandler said. "See, Mr. and Mrs. Moore, it's your call. But I can't do anything without your help. Can I take the van?"

"How long do you need it?" Bill Moore asked.

"Two days maximum."

Rebecca sighed. "I don't think I'll be up for driving much tomorrow, anyway," she said.

"You can take it," Rebecca's husband told the detective.

They went back to the supermarket parking lot and drove around, looking for the car that had run her off the road. Rebecca didn't see it. Nor did she see the man with the wraparound sunglasses who had tried to kill her—except in her mind where she saw him continually.

Then they went to the State Police headquarters just off Interstate 95 in Westport.

Another detective, a woman named Rhonda Larsen, joined the inquiry. Detective Larsen asked Rebecca to run through her story again. She obliged. Then she told it a third time when detectives from the Town of Fairfield joined them.

Rebecca then spent an hour looking at photographs, her husband watching her the whole time, offering her support.

"Anything?" Sergeant Chandler eventually asked.

Rebecca shook her head. The answer was the same after an hour. At one point, Chandler turned to Bill Moore.

"What sort of work are you in, sir?"

"I'm an architect," he said.

"You work locally? Commute to New York?"

"Both. I do free-lance assignments when they're subcontracted to me." A slight pause and he added truthfully, "I'm trying to open my own business."

Chandler nodded. "So you work out of your home? Or do you have an office somewhere?"

"Out of my home," he said. "Went to University of Virginia School of Architecture. My former roommate's got his own firm in Southern California. He's been trying to get me to go out West and join him."

"Don't want to relocate to California, huh?" Chandler asked.

"I've given it some thought. Both Rebecca and I have."

"You must like it here."

Bill glanced at Rebecca. "Up until this evening I did," Moore said. "Now . . . ?" He shook his head. "Never thought this type of thing would happen to us. Know what I mean?"

Chandler nodded, commiserating.

"I guess people come in here every day and say that."

"Right again," said the policeman.

Rebecca quietly continued through the photo albums, prom shots of violent felons.

"The whole country's turning into a jungle," Chandler added philosophically. "See, it used to be that crimes like this only happened in the cities. Now stuff like this is everywhere. Drugs. Guns. You even get violence on kids' TV shows." He shrugged. "You won't find California any safer. Maybe you'll find it worse."

"I just want to make a living," Moore said. "And I want my wife and family to be safe."

Sergeant Chandler nodded.

Bill Moore had the feeling that the policeman's questions hadn't been all that superficial. He had been probing for something. But whatever the cop had been looking for, Moore had apparently satisfied him. Chandler dropped the line of questioning and all three of them went back to the mug shots.

Still nothing. After another hour, the police took the Moores home.

Rebecca took a sedative to be able to sleep that night. But she found herself awake toward 3:00 A.M., aware of every nighttime creak of the house.

But Bill slept soundly beside her. She was grateful for her husband's presence. Mentally, she applied her own makeshift security check:

The locks were secure downstairs. So were the windows, every one of them locked tightly. The electronic burglar alarm, which was usually off at night, was turned on.

The town police said they would watch her block carefully for the next few nights. Once, at 3:30 A.M., she rose from her bed and looked out a window. She saw a police cruiser sitting right in front of the house, like a dark oblong phantom nestled in the falling snow and the muffled moonlight. The car's engine was running—she could see the exhaust—and the light was on within the vehicle. The policeman was probably reading, she figured.

She took the occasion to check Patrick and Karen, in their individual bedrooms. Both were safe, sleeping blissfully. Little angels. She kissed them both. Never had she thought that she wouldn't live to see them grow up. Never had she been more appreciative of being alive.

When she awakened at 4:00 A.M. and checked the front window again, the police cruiser was gone. But it was back again at a few minutes past five. Rebecca's senses were so on edge that, lying in bed, she could hear the police car's engine.

Then, from five to six-thirty, she managed to sleep. Her clock radio alarm beeped at its usual hour and, heavily fatigued, thinking back on the previous evening as if it had been some horrible nightmare, she rose to get her children off to school.

For the next few days, Bill was greatly indulgent with her, taking care to give her her way on all things, allay her fears, and tell her that he loved her.

The police returned the Dodge Caravan a day later. The crime lab had taken the paint sample and searched the vehicle for fingerprints. But nothing had turned up.

Similarly, the baseball bat that Rebecca recalled dropping in the snow revealed no prints other than her own—and those of her son. Nor did it even appear to have been in the snow. If it had been moved, it had been moved by a gloved hand. Nonetheless, the Fairfield police continued to keep their block under surveillance. State Police cars came by frequently, too, making a display of their presence.

Detective Chandler made every effort to attain some progress in the case. He sat with Rebecca Moore as she went over thousands of mug shots of violent felons provided by neighboring communities, from the Bronx to Massachusetts. Again, Rebecca found nothing. A police artist did a composite photo from Rebecca's description of her attacker. The computerized likeness of her assailant was an excellent one. It ran in the local newspapers. There were a few crank calls, but in the end, nothing emerged there, either.

Emotionally, Rebecca was a wreck.

Like most women coming out of a violent assault, her nerves were shattered. Little inexplicable noises in her home, a cranky radiator or a creaking floorboard, were enough to send her heart racing. Twice in the days after the attack members of her family appeared in her bedroom quietly and unexpectedly—once it was Bill, the other time it was Karen—and on both occasions Rebecca let out a shriek.

Her husband conferred with the family physician. There was a psychiatrist in Southport, the doctor suggested, named

Todd Miller. Dr. Miller had had considerable success helping stressed-out crime victims. The Moores made an appointment. Rebecca felt comfortable talking to Dr. Miller every Thursday morning.

Detective Chandler made a file of every newspaper article Rebecca had written for *WestPress* in her six years as a reporter. He created a list of people of whom she might have written unfavorably. He searched for someone she might have harmed. Some violent sorehead with a grievance. He came up with a dozen names. Ten men and two women.

"Any of these people?" he asked. "Would any of them feel strongly enough to have you attacked?"

Rebecca and her husband gave that angle a long consideration. They narrowed the list to three names, all men. Chandler diligently followed the leads until they disintegrated. There was no progress here, either.

Quietly, Chandler even made inquiries locally about Bill Moore. In Connecticut at least, he had been a model citizen for the last seven years. Chandler dropped that line: it was proving as fruitless as the others. Fact was, looking for a motive for someone trying to kill Rebecca was as elusive as finding bullets in the freshly fallen snow the day after the crime.

The bullets and the motives had one thing in common: they just weren't there.

And, of course, neither were the tire tracks. Nor was there blood from the man she had said she had hit. Or any footprints. Even the paint marks on the front of her van failed to help. The paint could have been from anywhere.

The whole thing seemed elusive. And eventually, it seemed suspicious. That was the only angle, in fact, which began to emerge for Chandler. The absence of everything.

Three weeks passed. Then a full month. April arrived, and with it a thaw from the worst winter of Rebecca's life.

Sergeant Chandler went back to Rebecca's husband as a suspect. The detective played around with theories again, some of them even involving Bill as the attacker or Bill as the instigator. But then he ditched them. That line of thought didn't work. Or at least Chandler couldn't make it work. Bill Moore seemed so supportive. He needed his wife. He wanted his wife. As much as could be seen, Bill Moore appeared to love his wife.

So where was a motive in this case? Where was financial profit? The Moores had a bundle of life insurance, but who the hell didn't in Fairfield County? Was sex a motive? Chandler couldn't make that one fly, either. Neither Bill nor Rebecca Moore was a known carouser or swapper in the neighborhood. True, Rebecca had seemed like an intended target. But increasingly, the assault looked like a random act.

It could have happened to any woman.

Or, following another theoretical line, had the assault happened at all?

Sergeant Chandler was at his desk one night seven weeks after the initial incident. He put his feet up and kicked back. For almost half an hour, he worked on a theory that he had been playing with but hadn't voiced.

Then he let his chair return to earth. He took out his file and looked through it again, examining Rebecca Moore's sworn statement from the day following the alleged incident. He examined her statement against the thorough lack of any supporting evidence.

Then he began to fine-tune his theory.

Two days later, he saw Bill Moore's car parked near Hazelwood's Appliances on Main Street in Fairfield.

Chandler parked his car and waited. Bill Moore came out of a paint store two doors down from Hazelwood's. He was just placing a hand on his own car door when he heard a familiar voice.

"Mr. Moore? How are you?"

Moore turned and recognized the policeman.

"I'm fine," he answered after a moment's hesitation.

"I saw your car, see?" Chandler said. "So I waited."

Bill Moore gave the policeman a nervous smile. "What's going on?" he asked. "Anything new on Becca's case?"

"Nothing new," the cop said, "but I need to talk to you."

Now it was Bill Moore's turn to break a sweat. "Can we talk here?" he asked.

"Is your wife with you right now?" Chandler asked.

"No. She's not."

"Then here would be perfect."

"Tell me what's going on," Moore asked again.

Sergeant Chandler walked Moore toward his police car. Bill Moore looked jittery, as if he were going to be arrested. But of course, he had long ago been eliminated as a suspect.

"In a case like this," Sergeant Chandler began carefully, "we can use computers, work out theories, speculate, make a hundred phone calls, and wear out a lot of shoe leather. But in the end, all we really have is what's in front of us. Do you know what I'm saying?"

"What you're saying is that you can only go on the facts you have. Anything else is worthless."

Chandler smiled. "That's pretty close," he said. "We work up all the evidence and draw our conclusions. Still with me?"

Moore was. Nervously, he was right with it.

"Taking your wife's case," the policeman continued. "What have we got? See, we have a damaged car, deep brown paint on the front left side. The paint, the bump, the scratches. These things could have come from anywhere. Then we had some skid marks in the snow where her car went off the road. And we found some footprints where your wife ran toward the woods. But nothing really in the woods themselves." There was a long pause. "We have photographs of that. But then again, the snow fell heavily between the time of the alleged attack and the time we went to the woods."

Chandler paused, hoping Moore might pick up the line of reasoning and address it. He didn't.

"Yeah? Keep going," Moore nudged.

"And against this, we found no fingerprints, no blood, no footprints, no witnesses."

"So what are you suggesting?" Bill Moore asked.

Chandler drew a long, disappointed sigh.

"How have you been getting on with your wife?" the detective inquired. "How were you two getting along at the time of the incident?"

Bill Moore bristled. He was instantly defensive. "We get along fine," he said.

The detective waited.

"We love each other," Moore continued point-blank.

And still the policeman waited.

"Look, where's this leading?" Moore asked. "What do you want me to say? Rebecca and I have had our bad days like any married couple. But what are you implying? That *I* attacked her?"

"Mr. Moore? Would she have been able to come to you if she had a serious problem?"

"What do you call this?" Moore asked. "This was a serious problem."

Chandler sighed again. "You're missing my point," he said. "I'm not saying this incident on Tremont Lane didn't happen," Chandler said. "But no one can prove that it *did* happen."

Bill Moore looked baffled.

"See, let's suppose your wife had an accident, Mr. Moore," Chandler said, in a suddenly kindly tone. "Suppose she'd scraped and dented your new van. Suppose she was afraid to tell you what had happened. So she makes it appear—how shall we say?—that something somewhat different transpired. Suppose she made it look like an attempted abduction. A possible carjacking or kidnapping."

Bill Moore responded with a stunned silence.

The detective was ready for Rebecca's husband to go ballistic over the suggestion that his wife had been lying. But Moore didn't react that way. And he almost looked relieved.

"Let me get this straight," Moore said. "You're saying—?"

"I'm only offering a theory, Mr. Moore. You're free to reject it, accept it, or think about it."

Bill Moore was already thinking about it.

"You think Rebecca might have filed a false police report? And you theorize that she may have done this because she may have damaged the car herself? And she was afraid to tell me the truth?"

Chandler shrugged. Then he nodded.

"Just between you and me and the four walls," the policeman said, "it's a theory that works with all the available evidence."

Bill Moore pondered it for what seemed like several minutes. The time lapse was actually only ten seconds. Then he replied with what appeared to be some additional increment of relief.

"If Rebecca had been in an accident, for God's sake," Bill Moore said, "all I would have cared about was her safety. I'm not going to yell and scream. We have car insurance just for something like this."

Sergeant Chandler looked at Bill Moore very carefully.

"Maybe you should *tell* her that," the policeman said softly.

"She should know it already," Moore answered.

"Maybe you should remind her," Chandler suggested.

Another moment passed. Moore watched a couple of leggy high school girls walk into a music store. Chandler watched Moore watch the girls.

"So," Moore finally said, thinking as he spoke, and choosing his words carefully, "you can't find any evidence of anyone trying to harm my wife. No tire tracks. No witnesses. No one who saw the Lincoln in the parking lot. No one who heard one car hit another. No spent bullets in the woods.'' He paused. ''Absolutely nothing. Is that it?''

''Nothing at all,'' Chandler affirmed. ''But, as I said, it's not surprising that there were no witnesses, considering the time and the place. The bullets allegedly fired would have been the best documentation that an incident took place. But we had another snowfall very soon thereafter, remember? And another few inches of fresh snow after that. Looking for bullets under those circumstances would be like looking for a needle in six haystacks.'' He paused and brought home his point. ''People still find arrowheads in these woods. The arrowheads have been lying around for a hundred-fifty years.''

Bill Moore nodded. Then he got to the point.

''So you think Rebecca made the whole story up?'' Moore asked.

''I can't come right out and say that,'' Chandler said. ''Nor do I want to suggest that to my chief of detectives.''

''But you *think* that?''

The young state policeman grimaced and opened his hands. ''I'm not going to press the point,'' he finally said. ''I only offered you a theory.''

''Is Rebecca in trouble?'' he asked. ''For filing a false report?''

''Well,'' Chandler said slowly. ''She can't prove the alleged incident *did* happen. And I can't prove that it didn't. So it would never see a courtroom under those circumstances.''

''What are you telling me? You want to suspend the investigation?''

The cop gave him a pained expression.

''I'm half telling you that,'' Chandler explained. ''We can keep the case open and leave it exactly where it is. But in practice it only gets more attention if a similar incident occurs or if we find new evidence.''

Bill Moore nodded. "I hear you," he said. He seemed to ponder the matter very seriously. "To tell you the truth," he said, "it wouldn't break my heart if the investigation went inactive. Maybe it would be best that way."

"I'm not sure what you mean," Sergeant Chandler said.

"There's always the chance that you're correct. That Rebecca had some—I don't know—mental problem. Like you said, no matter how hard you look, you can't find anything."

"She's seeing a doctor now?" Chandler asked. "A psychiatrist?"

"Dr. Miller over in Southport. One of the best in the area."

Chandler nodded. "Have a good talk about the situation with your wife, sir. If you need to get back to me, you know the number."

"I'll have a heart-to-heart tonight with Rebecca," Moore said. "And I'll call you tomorrow."

Sergeant Chandler said that would be fine.

iii

The Moores had their talk that night after their children had gone to bed. But it wasn't the talk that Sergeant Chandler had suggested.

Instead, Bill Moore asked his wife how she would feel about moving away from the area. It was an idea that they had entertained in the past. Now it loomed more logical than ever.

They were both sick of winters and the misery that usually accompanied them. They were tired of chipping cars out of ice, plowing driveways, and struggling across sleet-slicked roads to take Patrick and Karen to school.

"Maybe a change would be better for all of us," Bill Moore said.

"What prompts this?" Rebecca asked.

"We've lived here too long," he said. "The financing fell

through for my own business today. But I still have the opportunity with Jack McLaughlin.''

"In California," she mused. In the past, she had rejected the idea. Now it seemed much more tenable.

"Jack badly needs a part-timer in his office. He's been after me for years. Maybe now is finally the time." He paused. "And then there was the incident in February," he said.

"The man? In the car?" she said.

He nodded.

"You've been tense as a frightened cat ever since that day, Rebecca. I'd love to see you out of here. I don't think you'll ever feel safe in this area again."

She pondered it. "Los Angeles, huh? Earthquakes. Riots. Floods. Property taxes. Smog."

"Millions of people are comfortable there," Bill Moore said. "There are suburbs if you don't want to be in LA proper."

She thought about it.

On their honeymoon they had traveled the West Coast, driving from San Diego all the way up to the Napa Valley, three memorable weeks of sunshine, wine, great restaurants, beaches, and lovemaking. Now he was reminding her that every day could be like that.

Sort of. He took her hand. "I will try as best I can," he said, "to make this the best move of our lives together. That's a promise, Becca."

Half a minute passed. She examined her thoughts, her fears, and her hopes.

"I think," she said, "I could finally buy this idea."

"And," Bill Moore said, "Mr. Shaved Head would never have any chance to turn up again."

Her eyes found his. "You're trying to tell me that you're doing this for me?" she asked.

"It's for both of us. Or for that matter, all four of us. We're in our thirties. If we cash out here with the house, we'll have enough money. If we don't like California, we'll kiss it good-bye after a year or two.''

Another few moments of thought.

"I just bought the idea,'' she said.

He came to her and kissed her. He never mentioned Sergeant Chandler's final spin on the Tremont Lane incident.

In the weeks that followed, the Moores did some cosmetic fix-ups on their home, then put the house on the market. They set a reasonable price and hoped for a quick sale.

Bill flew to California and back to secure his position in his former college roommate's architecture firm. While he was away, Rebecca and the children stayed with friends. She didn't wish to be alone. And the more she considered the move, the more receptive she was to the idea. Once a week, she saw the psychiatrist to help her deal with the memories of the incident on Tremont. Even Dr. Miller thought that a major change of scene might help ease her residual fears. Miller also offered the name and address of another man in California, a Dr. Henry Einhorn, to whom she could speak if she felt she wanted to continue seeing a professional.

She graciously accepted the contact and put Dr. Einhorn's name in her address book.

The police investigation of her attempted abduction—or whatever the incident had been—receded from the forefront of Sergeant Chandler's caseload. The young detective thought about the incident repeatedly. It was like a tune that stays involuntary upon one's mind early in a day and of which one can't rid oneself.

There was something about the case, Chandler kept thinking, that wasn't quite right. But damned if he could figure what it was. Someday, he vowed, he'd take a walk in those woods again and see if he could get lucky and find an arrowhead.

Or a bullet.

But Rebecca Moore kept seeing the face of the man who

had attacked her. Somehow she knew that he had been there to kill her. And she sensed all along that the police were skeptical about her story.

But *she* knew that there had been a beastlike man. And she knew that he had been bent on killing her. What she didn't know was why. Or how it would change her life. In her mind, the incident kept replaying like a film projector stuck for eternity on the same reel. She searched for clues and for meaning. And hundreds of times a day, in her mind, she saw the horrible face of her assailant.

When Rebecca had been in her early twenties, she had more lovers than many other young women. More than was healthy, probably, not that she regretted any of them. And not that it had been only for sex.

She had been in love with each of the boys and young men who had joined her in bed. And in odd moments of fancy continuing well into her twenties and thirties, she had always told herself, for one reason or another, that she would never forget the face of a lover.

And so, in a similar way, it was now. She would never forget the face of a man who had tried to kill her.

And, in the same way that she had perhaps had too many lovers, it would occur to her over a long course of time, that there would be too many killers in her life as well.

But before packing up from Connecticut and moving across the continent, this too was something she would have no way of knowing.

2

"I think you might like this," Esther Lewisohn, the real estate lady, whispered in a mildly conspiratorial voice. She stood on the porch of a neglected seven-decade-old Queen Anne house in West Los Angeles.

Mrs. Lewisohn was a pleasantly pushy woman with a crown of platinum hair that gave her the final three inches of a five-foot-four stature. She specialized in private homes in West LA, Beverly Hills, and the better neighborhoods contiguous to both. She had done well for herself over the last twenty years—much better than she had done as a math teacher in the New York City public school system in the first two decades of her working life.

She fished through her purse, pushing aside two open soft packs of Marlboros and three in-progress packs of sugar-free gum. Then she found the right key.

"I think," she said, "this might be exactly what you're looking for."

With those words and with all the rosy promises contained therein, Esther smiled to her customers who had flown in from the East, Bill and Rebecca Moore. Then she held aloft the key that she had picked up from the lawyer's office half an hour earlier.

"Something told me," she said in a salty, chipper, I-can-sell-you-anything-I-damned-well-wish-to tone. "Some little inner voice that Essie always listens to, that's what told me. It said that *you* should see this house right away, Mr. and Mrs. Moore. Let's see if Essie is right."

Then she turned the key in the drop bolt lock to the front door at 2136 Topango Gardens. It was the sixth house the Moores had seen on that warm afternoon in early July. Real estate overkill was starting to set in for the day and Essie was smart enough to know it.

The drop bolt fought her. But then the rusty innards of the locking mechanism gave a little shudder. As Essie persistently jiggled the key with her arthritic sixty-two-year-old fingers, she could feel something like a small pulsation.

Then the key moved grudgingly clockwise and the tiny tumblers gave way within. The resistance expired, like little grasping fingers losing their grip.

"There!" Esther said. "We're going to be the first damned people to see this house since it came on the market yesterday. Judge it not for what it is. Judge it for what it can be."

Bill Moore grunted something noncommittal. His wife, Rebecca, was more optimistic.

Esther reached to the doorknob and turned it.

The front door of 2136 Topango Gardens gave a few inches, accompanied by a hesitant creak. Then the real estate broker pushed the door and it, like the lock, abandoned its fight.

"No lock can keep me and the Moores out of this house," Essie proclaimed. Bill and Rebecca Moore watched as daylight flooded onto the bare floorboards that had awaited beyond the front door. Bold sunlight, reflected off an untidy front lawn of brown grass, attacked the shrouded darkness within the building.

Two unsettled worlds colliding: a conflict in an unfathomable, misunderstood universe where time did not exist. Somewhere within the house, something stirred from a long dark

narcosis of sleep. A blast of tomby mustiness, a hostile cold
from an undisturbed basement, an anti-valentine from an-
other world, rose from God-knows-where to confront the in-
truders.

But no human could see it. Not yet.

"There," Essie said, opening the door on the faded dwelling in West Los Angeles. "Maybe *this* is a place you can call
home. But as I warned you, you *must* use your imagination.
This is a wonderful house. It has a *soul.* But it's been sadly
neglected." She paused. "Well, Mr. Moore, you're an architect. You can see that for yourself."

Essie recoiled from the mustiness of the place. An aroma of
stale agedness accosted them. It gripped them the way fog
grips a city, and then brushed past them. They thought they
could feel something cold as it wafted by.

Essie stepped forward.

Bill and Rebecca followed.

"The lady who lived here for many years passed away just
before Christmas of last year," Essie said, leading them in.
"Judith Dickinson was her name. Lovely woman."

Mrs. Lewisohn flicked a light switch, but the power was
down.

"This building has been tied up with the damned estate
lawyers since then," she said disgustedly. "I've been wanting
to put it on the market ever since Mrs. Dickinson died. But of
course I got no cooperation from Nickels The Lawyer."

"Who?" Bill Moore asked, glancing around the front hall
and moving behind Essie toward the living room.

"Nickels The Lawyer," Essie said. "His real name is Ted
Nickels. But 'Nickels The Lawyer' is what I call him." She
mouthed his name with growing venom, as if she had been
dealing with a Bensonhurst wiseguy: Vinnie "The Hammer"
or Patty "The Torch."

Nickels The Lawyer.

She paused for a moment. There was a resonant echo of the Grand Concourse in her pattern of speech.

"Lawyers," she said disgustedly. "I hate lawyers. My late husband was a lawyer. Nickels is a cheapskate. That's the problem. Tell me how I can show a house without electricity? How can my customers *see?*" Essie wrote herself a note. "How can I sell real estate in darkness?" she pleaded.

The Moores smiled, their only response to Essie's rhetorical flights.

"If the electricity's a problem we could come back," Rebecca Moore offered.

"Not a chance," Essie said. "I wouldn't waste your time. Ignore the damned electricity. It's bright outside. We'll open doors. We'll pull up shades. You'll be able to see perfectly. Let me show you the house."

Bill and Rebecca Moore already knew a few things. They knew, for example, what their eyes had told them on arrival.

For starters, this particular house was the eyesore of an otherwise genteel block. It was a rambling, wooden dissolute Queen Anne—seven-eighths dead, not from old age but from neglect—looking for a final shot at resuscitation. It was the most prominently downtrodden building in a neighborhood of gorgeously restored Spanish, Victorian, and Queen Anne homes situated among leafy trees and plush lawns.

Its entrance featured seventeen uneven flagstones traversing an untidy front lawn which was brown with dead grass. There should have been nineteen flagstones, but two near the sidewalk had either been stolen or had walked off by themselves. There was also a front porch that sagged painfully, the one upon which they had stood to enter. Upon it stood the skeleton of a torn-apart cane rocker.

And beside the front door there was a sign that said, rather wistfully, FOR SALE. The sign had been put there by the late Mrs. Dickinson. She had actually never wanted to sell the place, Essie explained as they walked through, but she had greatly enjoyed the company of people coming to the door to inquire.

The sign had also been there for a while, though only a fraction of the time as the house. Like the paint on the wood of the dwelling, the sign was faded, peeling, and fly-specked.

Mrs. Dickinson had lived with nine cats, the aroma of which kept the visiting time of callers at a minimum. Even Nickels, the cheapskate lawyer, had agreed to invest a few bucks to have the joint fumigated after Mrs. Dickinson's earthly departure.

On the ground floor there were some boarded front windows. And on both sides were their companion pieces: windows with glass so old and filthy that they looked tinted. Broken green shades hung unevenly on the inside of each. As the Moores discovered when Essie gave them their tour, the windows looked even dirtier from the inside.

Strangely enough, the house wasn't really a monstrosity. It only looked like one. But initially it didn't look promising, either. In fact, Bill Moore's first impression was one of menace. What made it worse was that as Bill Moore stood in the living room, and as Essie set down her notebook and her glasses on a small table—the sole remaining piece of furniture in the living room—he could have sworn he heard a voice.

Or a thought. Somewhere.

Who are these intruders?

But then the women came back from the kitchen.

"You know, Bill," Rebecca said, "like Mrs. Lewisohn said, if you use your imagination . . ."

"It will take a *lot* of imagination," Bill Moore said. "And a lot of money. And a lot of scraping and painting. Which doesn't rule it out."

"I know," Rebecca answered.

"I'm just being practical," he said.

"Of course. As always."

Essie gave him a smile. She loved it when married people bickered gently in front of her.

"Take a look at the backyard, honey," Rebecca said. "You can see it through the kitchen."

"Nice?" Bill asked.

"I could picture Karen and Patrick playing there," she said. "Once we get it cleaned up."

Her raised eyebrow, connoting interest by her for the first time, was met by a similar gesture from him.

Essie smiled.

"You young people just wait till you see the whole house," Essie continued, forging ahead. "Then you can talk and compare notes. Or we all can talk. Whatever you wish."

Bill nodded. As Essie turned away, Rebecca blew him a little kiss. He watched carefully. His wife was starting to like the place.

Essie led them upstairs. The steps groaned under their shoes.

Bill, with his architect's eye, inspected each step as they trod. Old wood, he noted. Probably the original stairs. Might have to be replaced, might need some support, he judged. But the staircase *felt* structurally sound. Interesting. And someone had used excellent wood when the house had first been built. Interesting again.

He was further intrigued when he came to the second floor landing. There had been a bathroom on the first floor. There was a second bathroom, plus a half on the second floor. The porcelain was aged in all three baths and would have to be torn out, and the half bathroom would have to be expanded. The walls were filthy. And the cats must have had the run of one of the four bedrooms, because he still caught a strong whiff of something unpleasant coming from somewhere.

But again, this was cosmetics.

Bill put his hand on the doorknob to the fourth bedroom and couldn't make it move. It was as if there were some force on the other side holding it. Bill Moore was startled for a moment, because the knob almost seemed to have a life of its own.

It pulled back against his hand. He was certain.

And again, Bill cocked his head. It was almost as if he could hear someone murmuring in a low disquieting voice.

Not that he could make out the words.

He stood very still. Yes, indeed! He had heard something!

Was he experiencing some strange current of sound? Was there a radio on somewhere? Perhaps in a neighbor's house. He was tuned into something that sounded like the low rumble of an electronic voice in a distant room.

He listened for another two seconds, his hand still upon the stubborn doorknob. Yes, again! He was certain that he was hearing a—

"Trouble with the door?" Essie asked, appearing merrily next to him. "It happens with the weather. We get a Santa Ana blowing this time of the year. Even with the dry wind, sooner or later the doors and drawers start sticking. It's part of the price Californians pay for all the sunshine."

Essie put a hand on the knob, pressed it downward and then, with decades of experience selling homes jerked the knob and twisted it. She gave the door a sharp uppercut shot with her knee.

The knob released.

"There," she snorted.

The door opened onto a corner bedroom, square on one side, rounded on the other. The chamber was badly dilapidated, but otherwise it was a splendid little room.

Rebecca followed her husband and poked her head in.

"This is so cozy," she said. "The kids will fight over it."

For a moment, a noxious odor overtook them, something acrid and very sour. They all noticed it, and Bill thought that this had been the source of the cat stench that he had noticed throughout the second floor. But before anyone could remark upon it, it was gone—as if opening the door upon a closed room had caused it to dissipate.

They all walked into the room. There was a grand turret on the side of the old house and this was the second floor room contained therein. Bill and Rebecca both reacted the same way: The strange construction made the room distinctive.

"Tell me again. How many children do you have?" Essie asked, ignoring the smell.

"Two," Bill said. "So far."

His wife blushed.

"We have a boy named Patrick who's seven, and a girl Karen, who's five."

"That's lovely," said Essie. "I have a daughter who lives in the East with her husband. Went to the University of Pennsylvania, then married a dentist. Stayed east. I only see her twice a year." She grinned. "But that's also when I get my dental checkup."

"That's too bad," Rebecca said. "I mean, that you don't see your daughter more often."

"She has her own life," Essie said with a shrug. "And she's happy. And the dental work is not bad."

"Grandchildren?" Rebecca asked.

"Two. I'd bore you with the pictures, but they're downstairs in my purse."

Bill walked around the empty room.

"You could make this a playroom," Essie said, noting Bill's interest and shifting back to commerce. "With four upstairs bedrooms, you could keep the master for yourselves, give the kids two on the side, and keep this as a playroom. Or a study for you, Mr. Moore."

"Either could be done," Bill said, the architect speaking again. "There's a wall here that could be taken out, too, and moved. There's a way this whole floor could be reconstructed very easily." He eyed the walls, putting a firm hand to one. "If we wanted to, that is," he added.

"Structurally, this is a very very sound house," Essie said. "Last big earthquake in January of 1994? Not a crack in the plaster anywhere."

"I'm impressed, Essie," Bill Moore said. "I have to admit. There are possibilities here."

Essie agreed. So did Rebecca.

She and Mrs. Moore left the room. Bill left last, turning to look behind him as he left. No voice anymore. He tried the doorknob and it was no longer resistant to his touch.

Odd.

He left the door open and followed the women.

Essie led them upstairs to the attic, a hot unfinished chamber with one small window and several exposed beams from the roof.

This could be converted. . . . Rebecca found herself thinking. *Bill could put in a skylight, enlarge the window. Give it a southern exposure, redo the floor . . .*

She was still thinking when Essie led them back down the attic steps.

They walked all the way back to the ground floor, Bill trailing the women. At one point on the steps leading down from the second floor, he thought he heard that murmur again—

. . . Damned ignorant fool. Why do they come here. Why don't they leave me be? . . .

—and was disturbed by it, stopping short again to listen. But he still couldn't place the direction from which it had come. And after two or three seconds, he continued down the stairs, convinced that whatever he heard—or thought he heard—was his imagination. And it made no difference, anyway. Someone somewhere had a radio or television on.

Fool!

Esther led them to the only part of the first floor that they hadn't seen, a section under the turret room of the second floor.

First they visited the dining room. The floor was a wreck.

Clawed and scratched. But the old boards were sound beneath the damage. Bill looked at them carefully. An architect's trained eye saw that the damage and the dirt were superficial. Beneath that was something solid. And then there was a den, adjacent to the living room. Mrs. Dickinson probably hadn't used that room too much. It didn't show much wear.

Then they arrived back in the living room. For some reason, Essie's notebook had fallen on the floor from the table. And she couldn't find her red-framed reading glasses.

"I *know* I put them down here," she was saying. "I'm absolutely *certain* of it. Or at least I think I did."

She gathered the notebook from the floor. It looked like it had tipped off the table and landed hard. She searched her pockets and her purse and still no glasses.

"Did either of you see my reading specs?" she asked.

Both of the Moores shrugged.

"Do either of you remember my wearing them? Usually I need them to read."

"Do you have another pair?" Bill asked.

She did. There was a second pair in her purse. Or maybe, Essie confessed, it had been her first pair.

"Sometimes I think I'd lose my head, too," she offered in a rare moment of candor, "if it weren't attached."

The Moores smiled.

"When you get to my age," Essie continued, "the memory plays tricks sometimes. I guess I never had the red-framed pair here at all."

In any case, they weren't there now. And there was more business to discuss.

"What's the neighborhood like?" Bill asked.

"It's lovely," Essie answered quickly, although to those selling houses, any house they were in was in a lovely neighborhood.

"It seems nice," Rebecca said. "From what we saw of it."

"It used to be somewhat shabby, I won't lie to you," Mrs.

Lewisohn explained. "But a lot of young professional people moved in the mid-1980s. Bought a lot of these old houses for a song, came in and fixed them up. So it's definitely a neighborhood that's up-and-coming."

"Even ten years later?" Bill pressed. "It's still 'up-and-coming'?"

"I don't think the values have peaked yet. I think they'll go up steadily," Esther Lewisohn said. "Take this house for an example. It's the blight of the block. As soon as someone buys it and fixes it, everything on the block improves, including this house. Someone wins twice by playing Mr. and Mrs. Fix-It."

Bill went to a window and peered out to the west. He saw nothing that would have made a liar out of his broker. The next home was Victorian, complete with turrets and curlicues and a splendid porch with—of all things—a restored antique glider. The property was perfectly kept. And in the neighbors' backyard, on deep green well-watered grass behind a wooden fence, was a child's bicycle.

"Who are the neighbors?" Rebecca asked.

There was a family named Cook who lived in that house to the west, Essie said. She didn't know much about them, other than that both parents worked.

The next house in the other direction belonged to a childless couple named Kauffman. When the Moores went to the easterly windows they saw another Queen Anne, also immaculately kept. And the owners weren't broke. There was a maroon Jaguar of recent vintage sitting in the driveway.

"Where are *your* children?" Essie asked. "Are they with you on this visit?"

"No. They're with their grandmother back East," Bill said. "Westport, Connecticut. They'll be joining us just as soon as we find a home."

"You mean you haven't already?" Essie intoned with a

smile and a raised eyebrow. "I can see what you're thinking."

"Tell me about the schools," Rebecca asked.

"The elementary schools in this district are excellent," she said. "People try to move into this neighborhood just so they can use the schools."

Rebecca nodded. Idly she wondered if any broker in the history of the world ever conceded that a school district was terrible and that residents tried to move out just to avoid the schools.

"Let's take a look outside," Bill suggested.

"Of course," Mrs. Lewisohn said.

Essie led them through the kitchen to a back door. They left the house and found themselves first on an old-fashioned stone patio and then upon an unkempt lawn that cried out for both a landscaper and a gardener. But again, it also cried out with potential.

The house was on a quarter of an acre, a generous plot for that area. Bill spent most of the tour looking at the foundations and the conditions of the woodwork on the side of the house. He was impressed with the sturdiness of the old dwelling. Whoever had put this place up had done the job solidly and professionally. Bill Moore wondered if the same builder— circa 1910, he guessed—had put up the whole block.

"Now I'll show you something unusual," Essie finally said. "I'm taking a chance here because this bothers some people. But it doesn't bother me and I hope it doesn't bother both of you."

She led them to the high brick wall that enclosed the rear garden. There was an old bench against it. "See if we can stand on the bench," Essie said. "See if it will hold us."

Bill did the testing, climbing on the bench and bouncing on it very slightly. He pronounced the bench safe.

"Now look over the wall and tell me what you see," Essie requested.

Bill offered a hand to his wife, who climbed up with him. Together, not knowing what to expect, they gazed at the adjoining acreage.

They saw nothing but lawn until they let their line of vision wander farther. And then their eyes settled upon an armada of tombstones and granite markers, some appearing quite grand and ornate from a distance. Bill and Rebecca were looking at the back side of a cemetery.

"We're adjacent to a *graveyard?*" Rebecca asked. "Is that what you mean?"

"San Angelo Cemetery," Essie said. "It doesn't bother you, does it?" She paused and answered her own question. "It shouldn't."

Rebecca didn't answer, suppressing a little shiver that she couldn't explain.

"The near territory is vacant," Bill observed. "It looks like all the burial plots are farther on."

"That's correct. What you see is the rear of the cemetery," Essie said without looking. "I'll tell you what that means for you."

"You don't have to," Bill said, warming to the circumstances. "It means no noise, no loud parties, and no new houses."

Esther Lewisohn smiled. She could not have phrased it any better herself.

"I think of it as a rather cozy situation," she said. "But it gets even better. There can be no new graves back there, even though you see empty space."

"Why is that?" Rebecca asked.

"By local statute," Essie said. "The zoning laws in this section of Los Angeles were changed shortly after World War II. Nothing new goes into San Angelo."

Quirky, the Moores decided, but it worked to their advantage.

Essie raised an eyebrow. "Now, if I'm not rushing you along," she said, "let's go back inside."

The Moores followed. Essie called a powwow in the living room.

"I want you young people to listen to me for a moment," Essie said next. "You'd be doing yourself a favor to look at this property very very carefully. The estate is very anxious to close the deal. The price is 355 but they're very very soft." She frowned slightly. "As I said, Mr. Nickels is handling the estate. Ted Nickels. *Not* one of my favorite people. The less he gets his three percent of, the more it pleases me, even if it comes off my commission, too."

Rebecca wandered off for a moment. She took a second look at the kitchen. She liked it. The room was big and spacious, with more glorious old wooden cabinets than she would know what to do with.

"Just how soft *is* the price," Rebecca heard her husband ask.

"Squishy soft," Esther said triumphantly.

"Okay, Essie. Just tell me. The tops I can go is maybe two hundred fifty thousand. Two sixty if we really push it. How 'squishy soft' is Ted Nickels?"

"I think if you came in for two seventy, he'd start to salivate," she said. "But being a lawyer"—here she grimaced again—"he'd be obliged to dicker. I'd tell him you were firm, but might—if I talked to you—let you go up a little."

"What's a little?"

"Two-eighty. I think for two-eighty you could take this. Then go to the bank and build an extra twenty thousand dollars into your mortgage loan to use for fix-up. And I think you'd be in business."

Outside there was a friendly sound of a breeze. Then something passed over the sun. There was a creeping shadow for a second, and then the brightness returned.

"Anything else about the property I should know about?" Bill asked. "Or the location?"

Essie pursed her lips. "I don't think so," she said.

"Two-eighty, huh?" Bill asked. He looked at his wife. "Becca and I will have to talk about it."

"Don't talk too long," Essie warned. "Century 21 is showing 2136 Topango this afternoon. I wouldn't want them to sell your future home out from under you."

"I won't be rushed into a decision, Essie," Bill said.

"I'm just warning you, dear," she said. "I wouldn't want you to be disappointed."

"Of course not," Rebecca said. She took her husband's hand and gave it a squeeze. After a moment, the squeeze was reciprocated.

That evening, just at dusk, Bill and Rebecca Moore set out in their car and toured their prospective neighborhood. They started to like it just a little more. It was a highly atmospheric section of Los Angeles, quiet and detached from the hubbub of downtown LA and its commercial center, or even Beverly Hills and Hollywood.

The area was an island of quiet and serenity. Immediately surrounding them were several blocks of old houses with tall leafy trees along the streets. At one point, Bill and Rebecca stopped their car, parked it, got out and did the strangest of all Los Angeles activities. They walked. They felt the cool breezes of evening caressing their faces. Here and there was a whiff of jasmine.

"You know," Bill said as they walked, "in its way, it's fascinating. If you focus on the houses, and phase out the cars, certain blocks haven't changed much since the 1920s."

She agreed. She had noticed the same thing.

"I like it," Rebecca said. "You know I like it."

"I like it, too," he said. "I wonder if it's snowing back East yet."

"In July, right?"

"It gets cold in New England," he said with a straight face.

They both laughed. They went back to their car. For a moment they both sat, entertaining similar thoughts.

"I wonder how badly we can lowball the estate," he said.

"I don't want to be greedy," she said.

"It's not a matter of greed. It's a matter of making a shrewd business deal. For us."

"I'll listen to you," Rebecca said. "You can handle it."

"We have to both agree on something first, don't we?"

"What's that?"

"Do we want the house?"

They searched each other's eyes.

"I think we've already made that decision," she said.

"Okay. Let's get really gross," he said. "Let's offer 255."

"You're disgusting," she said.

They both laughed. Then, "Well?" he asked.

"I'm your supportive wife," Rebecca said. "Go for it."

Bill phoned Esther Lewisohn the next morning.

The Moores entered a bid for $255,000 for the house at 2136 Topango Gardens. Mrs. Lewisohn gagged, choked, and for a few seconds tried to talk him into some higher numbers.

But Bill Moore was hearing none of it. He hung up the phone and congratulated himself on his keen way of doing business.

Essie called back an hour later to say that the offer had been declined. Ted Nickels would negotiate, she said, but he didn't want to be insulted.

"What's that mean?" Bill asked.

"It's Ted's pidgin legalese for, 'Make a better offer, you're getting close,' '' Essie said. "He's such a cheap son of a gun, you know. But he *will* be anxious to close the deal."

"Hardball him," Moore said. "Tell him you don't think I'll budge past two-sixty."

"He'll still try to move you up some," Essie warned.

"No matter what I offered, he'd try to move me."

"I'll call you back," she said.

Ted Nickels sat on the offer for two overnights. He said he'd talked to the inheritors of the estate. He could make a deal for $270,000, he had said. But only if the paperwork were handled quickly.

Bill and Rebecca Moore agreed. Essie called Ted Nickels back and told him that he had just sold a house.

The Moores' home in Connecticut sold two weeks later, right at the end of July. Rebecca made immediate plans for the move from East Coast to West.

She made sure that their belongings and furniture would be packed properly and she hired the movers with the best reputation for a coast-to-coast trip. Her mother came east again from Illinois, helped her, and stayed with her during times when her husband went to California to initiate work with McLaughlin & Company. While on the West Coast, Bill Moore also oversaw his mortgage application. It was approved by the first Friday in August.

Essie Lewisohn was more than helpful. She bullied Ted Nickels into letting the Moores have access to the property they were purchasing in advance of the closing date. Thus Rebecca and Bill—on a subsequent visit west—were able to enter the house, measure rooms more accurately, and make decisions on what furniture would go where and what they would need to buy.

One afternoon, Essie came over to see how they were doing. They were doing fine, as it turned out, though Rebecca was engaged in a battle with the fourth bedroom on the second floor, the one which had the reluctant doorknob.

"The turret room," as she now called it, in reference to the architectural quirk that gave the room its odd shape. And she could not get the smell to depart that room, although strangely enough, the odor seemed to come and go on its own.

Perhaps because of weather. Perhaps because of humidity.

What bothered her most was that the odor was vaguely reminiscent of a dead animal, as if some household pest had gotten lodged between a wall and was in a state of decomposition. Why, she wondered, didn't it just go away, once and for all, rather than recurring?

Rebecca was working with a spray disinfectant the afternoon Essie came by. And Bill was measuring the turret room, making plans to take out a plasterboard wall that had formed a small storage area in front of the real wall.

"By the way," Essie said in passing, glancing at the window. "That burial grounds behind you? I'll tell you something interesting."

"What's that?" Bill asked.

"I told you it was called San Angelo Cemetery. But that's only the proper name. The people in the neighborhood have their own name for it. It's had its own name for many years. Generations, I think."

"Don't spare me," Bill said. "What do they call it? I just bought this house. I suppose it's called 'Graveyard of the Walking Dead' or 'Land of the Chainsaw Zombies,' or something that will keep my children awake all night."

"Nothing of the sort," Essie said. "In fact, the name that's used is rather quaint, I think. Very reassuring."

Bill and Rebecca Moore waited.

"They call it, 'Cemetery of Angels,' " Essie said. "Isn't that nice?"

" 'Angels'? From 'San Angelo'?" Rebecca asked.

Essie pursed her lips and made a mystified expression. "I

have no idea how it acquired that name," she confessed. "But I think it sounds rather poetic, don't you?"

"Just what we need," Bill said, his sarcasm running to the surface. "A poetic graveyard nearby. In case a houseguest drops dead suddenly."

"Cute remark," Essie said. Then she bade them good-bye.

" 'Cemetery of Angels,' " Bill said, repeating the phrase and holding the thought.

Rebecca shrugged. It *was* poetic. She already felt a certain kinship with her backyard burial plot.

Bill Moore walked to a second story window and looked across the brick wall behind his new property. His eyes were upon the cemetery. "What do you think of that?" he asked his wife.

"Like Essie said," Rebecca answered, "poetic."

There was just one other disconcerting note. After the purchase of the property was complete, on a hot afternoon in late August, Bill Moore drove over to the house without his wife. He took with him some carpentry tools.

Bill was still intrigued with the "turret" room on the second floor. There was one wall in the room which was nothing more than a plasterboard partition that had formed a storage area. If the plasterboard were taken out, the room would be four feet wider. So why not rip it out?

Bill went into the turret room and set down his tools in the middle of the floor.

He walked from one wall to another, picturing how this chamber could become a playroom. He examined the wall that separated this from the open section on the other side.

Then he took a hammer. There was nothing supportive about the wall. It was nothing more than a weak room divider, installed perhaps about seventy years ago, he guessed, judging by the building materials.

He took his sledgehammer to it, took a swing, and punched

through it. A huge section gave way. A second swing knocked out even a larger piece.

He was starting to enjoy this now. Blasting away with the hammer, he followed with blow after blow, taking the wall down quickly.

Then he suddenly stopped.

Midway into his work, he was sure that he had heard a voice. A low murmuring again, much like he had heard in this room once before. And there was something androgynous about the voice. It was high-pitched and shrill. Almost musical.

Had he really heard it, he wondered. He froze and listened.

Nothing now. Not even a sound outside. Nothing at all.

Some places had strange acoustics, he knew, and some places trapped distant sounds in ways science could never explain.

He figured that this was just such a quirky place. In any case, several seconds after being certain that he heard something, he convinced himself that he couldn't possibly have.

He took down the rest of the wall and stepped back, savoring a sense of accomplishment. The first bit of renovation was already complete at 2136 Topango Gardens.

He gathered his tools and went downstairs, then outside to his waiting car. He heard nothing more. And within another few minutes, for the time being at least, he had forgotten all about it.

3

The Moores' household possessions came to California via a pair of moving vans.

The first van arrived on the day of the legal closing for the property, the twenty-fifth of August. The second moving van didn't navigate the highways of the American Midwest quite as speedily. It arrived the day before school started on the last Tuesday in August. It was only then that the living room furniture from the East came into the house—in addition to a new print sofa they had just purchased locally—and the Moores finally had a dining table and chairs. On the same day, the Moores purchased a new Toyota Camry to go with the Chevrolet that they had driven coast to coast. The Dodge Caravan, and the memories that went with it, they had sold.

Five-year-old Karen found two friends her own age right on the same block, three doors away to one side and five doors away to the other. Karen was the quieter, more shy and less assured of Rebecca's two children, and Rebecca was elated that her daughter had made friends so easily. Patrick, older and more gregarious, would never have had problems. So he easily found a friend, too, a boy one month older than he, who lived next door, the owner of the bike that his parents had seen in the neighboring yard. A certain geometry of personal relationships began to assert itself as the Moore family eased into their new neighborhood.

The angles and lines began to make sense for Bill Moore, too. He spent much of the first week away from his new home. He was constantly over in Brentwood with Jack McLaughlin at McLaughlin's architectural depot. Some nights when he came home, he seemed tired and distant. Moody. Almost surly. On other evenings, he was enthusiastic and full of vigor.

Some nights, as a husband, he was the same way—tired and distant. He treated his children similarly. Some nights there were bedtime stories that were playful and energetic and ran much too late. Other nights it seemed like Bill could have cared less.

In the midst of a second marriage, Rebecca was used to such inconsistencies from men in general and her husbands in particular. She would have loved it if life weren't like that, but life was. So she grudgingly conceded that his behavior would probably always be like that. Typically male, she conceded.

Perhaps it was all part of Bill's past. Or her past. Or, for that matter, the combination of the two.

Her first husband, the father of her two children, had been an artist named Thayer Sullivan. A brooding wanna-be genius from North Carolina, he had created massive and occasionally brilliant abstracts on canvases frequently (and intentionally) too big to be carried out of studios. He had been eight years older than she. As his work got better, as his creations became more striking, he became more and more depressed about his failure to be immediately recognized by the fickle world of art criticism. Subsequently, his work took a catastrophic artistic journey from light into darkness.

Where once there had been euphoria there was next a condemned and boxed-in feeling. Rebecca recognized Thayer's sense of spiritual exhaustion, but was unable to reach through it. One day, when they lived together in San Antonio, the police came to Rebecca's home. It was about six months after

Karen had been born. And the police were coming directly from the Alamo Motel and Motor Lodge, where, earlier that morning, Thayer Sullivan had hanged himself after entertaining a prostitute. His way of getting back at the world.

Rebecca had met Bill Moore less than a year later, late in 1991, when she was still trying to put her own life back together. Bill (never ''Billy'') had just pushed past thirty. In him, Rebecca saw—or thought she saw—a brilliant but previously unmanageable son of a well-to-do family.

In a private school in Richmond in his teens, Moore had learned to smoke pot, set off cherry bombs in trash cans, drive a car without a license, and play cards for money. At an Ivy League university, he learned more colorful bad habits: how to spend vast amounts of money, create a thriving dealership in soft drugs, acquire unwholesome friends, spout Marx and Mao just to annoy the campus Republicans, and hang around with off-campus high school girls. None of this, however, ever affected his grades. He landed in an architectural school of national renown and cruised through there, too, graduating with honors and two arrests for disorderly conduct.

After the intensity and self-absorption of her Thayer Sullivan, Rebecca looked upon Bill's mildly evil past with fondness and amusement, seeing in him the proper formula for a successful attack on the game of life. He amused her. He embodied the nerve and outrageousness that she had always wished for herself. Or, at least, between his good and bad moods he did. Eventually, Rebecca and Bill became lovers and within seven months of the time they had met, they presented themselves to a justice of the peace one night—almost on a whim—in Columbia, Maryland, and married.

Bill Moore promised his new wife he would clean up his raucous act and behave. She, in turn, became something of his keeper while he was her lifetime reclamation project. To her, as he lurched into his thirties, he gave every indication of reforming. He even finally became serious about his profession.

After all those years of schooling, after breaking the hearts of his parents and assorted girlfriends from good Northeastern families, he actually gave the outward manifestations of actively being interested in becoming an architect. Accordingly, they moved to Connecticut, pooled their money, and bought a small house.

Which didn't mean that their marriage didn't have its rough edges. The free-spiritedness of his past was held against him by potential employers, though he always seemed to find just enough free-lance work to pay bills. He was given to disappearances on "business" trips, ostensibly to ferret out assignments in other cities, of which he provided few details. He occasionally became moody, and they fought sometimes for a day or two at a time. And his mood swings could fluctuate wildly.

And yet, only one aspect of Bill's behavior *really* troubled her.

She sometimes wondered if her husband's moods were chemically affected. That is, had he messed his brain up somewhere along the line with some druggie concoction that he'd cooked up? She couldn't remember Bill being moody and inconsistent like this when she had first met him. But then again, that was when she was more than overanxious to find a new mate, and was willing to overlook much. Sometimes those years before Bill, that part of her life, seemed so distant as to be another lifetime.

Of course, a worse thought was upon her, too.

Was Bill still dabbling in chemicals? Not in the house, of course. He didn't or wouldn't do that. But off with Jack McLaughlin, his old druggie pal?

She hoped that this was just one of those bits of paranoia that had troubled her since—she cringed to even think of it—the incident in Fairfield.

Labor Day weekend came.

The Moores went off to one of the beaches south of Malibu

to spend the day. They had seen a few of their neighbors go by and had managed a few brief words of greeting and instruction. There was a young woman with gorgeous black hair who lived in one house and drove a yellow Mustang convertible. There were several men who donned suits every morning and set out for jobs that looked to be professional and in the straight world. There were several wives who appeared to have careers and an equal number of women who stayed home and managed their children and households.

But during the day, the neighborhood was quiet. Most residents seemed to be out. Rebecca, home by herself, getting their new house organized, was quite aware of this. A handful of the people in the neighborhood, however, kept irregular hours.

The neighborhood looked to be what Bill called "upper–middle-class California composite," meaning young to middle-aged adults (mostly) who seemed to be bent on successful careers, whatever they were. Though they had met the other parents on the street, no one had reached out to befriend them. This unsettled Rebecca more than Bill. But she wasn't yet ready to admit that it bothered her.

"It's okay," Rebecca said late one evening. "Let's get the house in order first. Our social life will follow."

"I second that thought," Bill said.

They sat before their fireplace in the living room. It was still warm in September and the windows were open to allow a breeze.

"Maybe we should have a party," Rebecca suggested.

Bill looked up from a newspaper. "Try that one again," he asked.

"Maybe we should have a party," she said. "It's just an idea I've been playing with."

"A party?" he asked.

"Yes. Something informal. Just drinks and hors d'oeuvres.

For everyone on the block. We'll get to know everyone at once.''

This was one of Bill's sullen nights. He said nothing. He only looked at her, turning over the idea in his head.

"It's just an idea I've been playing with," she repeated.

He surprised her. "Might be a good idea," he said. "We'll get to know everybody at once."

"That's what I just said."

"Mmm. It is, isn't it?"

Another minute passed.

"Should we do it?" she asked.

"Sure."

She smiled. She leaned over and kissed Bill on the side of the face. "Great idea *you* had," she said.

New friendships were all over the place, waiting to be made. The kids had made an interesting one, too. Or so they reported. They had an imaginary friend, as children often do.

Imaginary, as opposed to the real flesh-and-blood friends that they were making in school. Imaginary, as opposed to the many friends they had back in Connecticut.

He was a man, they said, and he came by every couple of nights to make sure they were safe.

"How's that again?" Rebecca had asked the first time she had heard of this.

"He lives in the turret room," Karen said.

Rebecca looked at her children. And unfortunately an image of the horrible man in the parking lot was before her.

"Oh, he *does,* does he?" she asked.

Both kids smirked.

This first came up, Rebecca would remember, about a week after Labor Day. She was in the living room with Patrick and Karen. It was just before bedtime.

"What are you guys talking about?" she asked.

"Ronny," Patrick said.

"Ronny Sinbilt," Karen giggled. The kids shared a magnificently childish laugh, as if they were the private partici-pants in an off-color joke that was too funny for words.

"Come on," Rebecca insisted. "Share it with me, guys."

"Ronny looks in on us to make sure we're safe," Karen said. "After you and Daddy go downstairs."

"Uh-huh," Rebecca said. "And how do you know that's what he's doing?"

"He told us," Karen said.

"We asked him who he was and that's what he said he was doing," Patrick answered.

Bill came into the living room from the kitchen, tuning curiously into the conversation.

"And you've both seen him?" Rebecca asked. "This same dude?"

The kids nodded in unison. Patrick said that he had seen him first. "But then I saw him real soon after that," Karen added.

Bill listened to this and looked from boy to girl and then back again. "Uh, huh. Right," he said.

"And he's a big guy? Like an adult?" Rebecca pressed.

The kids agreed that he was. A nice man with shaggy brown hair, dark pants, and a white shirt. There was disagreement about the rest of his description, however, but they did agree that he lived in the turret room.

"How do you know he lives there?"

"That's where he comes from," Patrick said.

"And that's where he goes to," Karen said.

"And doesn't the smell bother him?"

They shook their beautiful young heads. Rebecca always marveled at how gorgeous, fresh, and fair her two young ones were.

"Oh, no," Patrick said.

"I asked him that," Karen added, "and he says he *likes* that bad smell."

More laughter. Both kids. Ronny—or anyone—actually *liking* that sour acrid stench was a real thigh-slapper.

"And, uh," Rebecca asked, feeling her way along, "Ronny comes out of there every night?"

The children looked at each other.

"Not *every* night," her son said, hedging slightly. "Only sometimes."

"Well," Rebecca said, rising to the moment. "Let's go upstairs right now and see if we see him. I'd like to meet Ronny, too."

Again in unison, they answered. "Okay." They were enthusiastic about introducing Mom to their friend.

Bill bailed out of the event, giving Rebecca a bemused raised eyebrow and a bored-but-understanding smile. She walked upstairs hand in hand with her small brood.

No Ronny.

The kids brushed their teeth and put their pajamas on. Bill came upstairs and prepared a bedtime story for two. Something about a rabbit running through the woods and stopping for a carrot-and-lettuce pizza (hold the cheese, please!) on the way home. Rebecca took the moment to walk over to the turret room and glance in.

There was only a mild hint of the smell that had been bothering her. Otherwise, the room was empty, awaiting renovation and renewal.

And still no Ronny.

"Yoo-hoo," Rebecca finally called softly to the empty chamber. But no imaginary guy tonight.

Then both parents kissed their children good-night and went back downstairs.

"An imaginary friend?" Rebecca asked softly, not wanting to be heard upstairs. "With a *name?*" She shook her head.

"The only imaginary Ronny that I knew of in Southern California was the former president," Bill grumbled, hardly looking up from his reading.

"It *is* a little creepy, isn't it?" Rebecca said.

"What is?" Bill asked.

"An imaginary friend. With quite so much detail."

"Didn't you have one when you were a kid?" Bill asked.

"Have what?"

"An imaginary friend, with or without a lot of detail."

She thought about it. "Yeah. I did," Rebecca admitted. "She was a girl my age."

"Did she have a name?" Bill still wasn't looking up.

"Her name was Sally," Rebecca admitted.

"Then what bothers you about Ronny?" Bill asked.

"Aside from the fact that I find it a little strange that they both see the same guy?"

"McLaughlin and I work on the same architectural plans. Same principle: joint creation. Is that creepy?"

"No, but—"

"A joint creation of the mind," her husband said, finally raising his head. "Patrick and Karen working in tandem. Now what's *really* bugging you?"

She thought about it. She knew the answer. It took her a few moments before she had the nerve to give voice to it.

"What bothers me is the way they keyed in on the turret room," Rebecca finally admitted.

Bill looked fully at Rebecca. "What do you mean?"

"There's something about that room that bothers me. Always has."

Her husband was watching her. A look of concentration was on his face. Then she saw something unsettled in his eyes and she felt his gaze settling in on her. It almost scared her when her husband's moods changed so quickly and so extremely. Sometimes, since the incident in Connecticut, even the man she slept with scared her.

With slightly narrowed eyes, "Like what?" he asked.

"The smell in Ronny's room, for one thing," she finally

decided. She tried to make a joke of it, hoping that might drive away the whole problem.

"It's not 'Ronny's Room!' " he snapped. "It's the god-damned 'turret room,' soon to be the fucking 'second floor playroom.' Now, anything else?" he asked.

She searched. She didn't want to dredge up her feelings from the attack in Connecticut. She had done so well since the move in conquering all those old anxieties and fears.

"No," she said sullenly. "Nothing specific. Just a feeling."

He continued to gaze at her. Then his annoyance dissipated and he eased off. "The room will be a lot more comfortable, a lot more welcoming, once we renew it," he said. "You know, paint it. Get some stuff in for the kids. Even I admit that it's a little tiny bit creepy right now."

"You feel that, too?" she asked.

"I didn't say I felt *anything,*" he said, his annoyance growing. "I just said that maybe that room should be a priority. I don't want it to turn into something that's scaring the kids."

"It's now a priority," she said. She knew when to ease off and agree with her husband. She had learned in her years of marriage to him that this was sometimes the only way to avoid a major fight.

So she pondered the point and tried to make a joke of it. "I wish Ronny would do something about that smell while he's wandering through our upstairs," Rebecca added.

Bill went back to his reading. "Maybe you can get him to paint and reinforce the walls while you're at it, too."

"You're such a pragmatist," she said.

"The turret room is empty," Bill said, losing himself in his reading again. "So Patrick and Karen fill it with their imagination. I think that's fine as long as they're not scaring themselves. And obviously they're not." He paused. "They think this 'Ronny' asshole is funny. So let them think that."

Rebecca sighed again. There was a creak in the floorboards behind her husband.

"And by the way, architects *are* pragmatists by nature," he continued. "Theories don't hold buildings up. Nails, wood, and the proper use of physics do. *Comprenez?*"

"Bill, you really are one of the great bullshit artists of all time," she said. "Or should I phrase it, *'artiste de merde de taureau'?*"

"Call it anything you like, Becca," he half replied without looking up. "And thanks for the accolade. You made it sound real elegant."

"You're welcome," she said. Then she waited for a full minute. "Want to do some sex after the kids are asleep?"

A curled eyebrow in response from her husband, two eyes glancing up. "How about tomorrow?" he asked. "I have a lot of reading to do for Jack McLaughlin tonight."

"You animal," she teased, maybe with a little too much sarcasm. "I don't know how I resist you."

But Bill let the comment pass, continuing with his reading.

Twice miffed, she tuned her husband out the rest of the evening. And she felt a pang of loneliness, on the other side of the continent from her best friends and passively ignored by her husband.

And this "Ronny" nonsense didn't help, either.

In fact, the uneasiness about "Ronny" carried over for several more days. Twice a week, Rebecca phoned her widowed mother in Illinois. Somehow, in their next conversation, Rebecca drifted toward what was bothering her: the imaginary friend both her children saw.

This Ronny.

"Isn't it obvious?" Rebecca's mother answered. "Patrick and Karen left friends behind in the East. So they're imagining new ones until they're secure with their new playmates at school."

Rebecca thought about it. And her instincts were at work

again, the same extra sense that had once told her in a Connecticut parking lot that her life was in danger. Here she didn't feel danger. She just felt . . . well, creepy. Silly, she told herself, but sometimes in the house she had that old sense of being watched again.

"It still unnerves me a little," she admitted to her mother.

"Don't let it, dear. Your nerves are still tingling from that horrible incident in Connecticut. And Ronny will be replaced by real friends in a matter of days."

"I guess," she said with a sigh.

Sometimes mothers are right, even on the long-distance horn. Like clockwork, within the next few days, Patrick and Karen started talking more about new acquaintances at school. No more mention of Ronny. And Rebecca didn't ask about him. Somehow she associated him with trouble, though she didn't quite know why.

But indeed, he *had* vanished. And to celebrate, Rebecca convinced Bill that they should throw their party on the first Saturday in October.

Silently, he brooded about the date for several minutes. Then he gave his blessing.

"Yeah. That'll work," he said. "It'll give us time to fix the place up a little. It won't look so bare when we have people in."

She smiled and kissed her husband on the cheek. She went out the next day and picked out fifty invitations. Almost without notice, her sense of being observed vanished at the same time.

There was another positive note, too. Over the next two days, Bill stripped the walls in the turret room and prepared them with white primer. Rebecca held her breath as her husband worked. But the first step of renewing the room went without incident.

In other words, no Ronny.

* * *

Two afternoons later, a sunny Wednesday, Rebecca was stepping out of her car in front of 2136 Topango. She heard another vehicle on the road. She turned. She saw the dark-haired woman in the yellow Mustang convertible. The woman drove past her without acknowledgment. Rebecca had been about to raise her own hand to wave, but the convertible passed too quickly.

As she unloaded her own car, without being obvious, Rebecca watched the yellow car. A garage door rose automatically in the house three doors down and the car disappeared within.

Then, again with unseen hands, the garage door closed.

Rebecca turned her attention back to the contents of her car's trunk. Paint and rollers. Brushes and pans. The turret room was soon to undergo phase two of the Moores' full attack.

Rebecca made two trips into the house with her purchases. She came back outside to make sure she had locked the car. She thought she was alone when someone spoke to her.

"Hi!" The voice was friendly and female and came from behind her. Rebecca turned.

There was a young woman at the edge of her driveway. Rebecca had never seen her before.

"Hello," Rebecca answered.

The woman stood twenty feet away.

"Just move in? I'm one of your neighbors. I thought I'd stop and be a new friend."

Rebecca smiled.

She walked toward the woman. Her visitor was thin with short blond hair and fair skin. A pretty face with freckles. She wore blue jeans shorts and a pale pink T-shirt. A thin gold chain circled her neck and hung at the top of the shirt. At first Rebecca thought she was perhaps college age because she had a young figure with long tan legs. But then, immediately, Rebecca drew a second impression, one that told her that the visitor was maybe ten years older than that. Early thirties.

"I'm Melissa Ford," the visitor said. "I've been watching you."

"You *have?*"

Melissa smiled and set Rebecca at ease. "In a neighborly way," she continued. "I live two doors down."

She pointed at the house two doors away where the yellow convertible had just disappeared. 2141 Topango.

"I'm Rebecca Moore," Rebecca said. "I'm happy to meet you."

"I was out walking. I thought I'd stop and say hello," Melissa Ford said.

"Thanks. I thought I just saw your, uh—"

"Roommate. That's June. She just drove by, right?"

"Right."

"And you went to wave and June didn't see you."

"You were watching *carefully,*" Rebecca said.

"June's antisocial," Melissa said. "She does rude stuff like that all the time. She didn't wave to me, either."

"Then I won't take offense."

"There was none intended." Melissa glanced toward 2141 and then back to Rebecca.

"I've seen you going in and out," Melissa said. "You've got two nice-looking children and either a husband or a boyfriend or some sort of full-time stud. I don't care which."

"It's a traditional setup," Rebecca said. "He's my husband. And you?"

"I have a roommate," Melissa said. "Nontraditional, maybe you'd call it. I don't know."

"Do you work in the neighborhood or—?"

"I *was* on the adjunct faculty at UCLA," Melissa Ford said. "American Civilization; my concentration was on California in the early twentieth century."

"Was?"

"Modern life," she said. "I was terminated."

"Oh." An awkward pause. Rebecca wasn't sure what to say. "Well, it sounds like a fascinating field. I'm sure you'll find something else."

"I'm working on it." She winked as if to suggest something even better was already lined up. "I like California, so I've made a commitment to stay. I came here in the mid-eighties. Drove out all by my lonesome in a Volvo station wagon and a degree in AmCiv from Sarah Lawrence. Decided I liked it—California, not Sarah Lawrence—so I stayed. I studied and got a gig at UCLA."

"Sounds fascinating," Rebecca said. "I'm impressed."

Rebecca locked her car and turned to her friend. "Want to come in for a minute? I've got coffee. Ice tea. Soda. Anything you want."

Melissa seemed surprised. Rebecca could see it in her eyes. "I'd really like that. Thanks."

Rebecca led the way into the house. The small talk continued. Melissa was starting to sound like the type who told her entire life story within the first five minutes of one's first meeting her. Rebecca didn't mind at all. The conversation drifted back to the adjunct faculty position at UCLA by the time they reached the kitchen.

"Teaching beats answering telephones in an office, which is what a lot of AmCiv graduates end up doing," Melissa said. "Have you met Dr. Lerner yet?"

"No. Who's that?"

Melissa eased into a stainless steel and plastic chair at the kitchen table. She moved her head to indicate a house four doors down Topango Gardens on the north side of the street.

"Maurice Lerner," Melissa said as Rebecca unpacked the bag of groceries. "He's a shrink. Faculty at UCLA. He's a fully tenured professor in the psych department, if you want to be impressed. Or *psycho* department, maybe I should call it, since it's UCLA. Anyway, Maurice is a brain. He's written a dozen scholarly books.'' She rolled her eyes, beautiful brown ones. ''Puts little old me to shame.''

''I really don't know anyone in the neighborhood yet,'' Rebecca said. ''I mean, I've met a lot of people. But I don't really *know* people. Understand what I mean?''

''I hear you. But now you know me.''

''Thanks. I do.''

''And within a few weeks you'll meet everyone else. I promise you that you'll like it here. How's that? My personal verbal guarantee, worth the paper it's printed on.'' Melissa smiled.

''Thank you. That's very encouraging.''

''You're not from California,'' Melissa said. ''I can tell. My guess is you're from the East. You've got that reticence that Westerners sometimes mistake for latent or not-so-latent hostility.''

Rebecca frowned. ''You're really right-on, aren't you?'' she asked.

Melissa smiled very prettily. ''No use hiding what we think. Is there?''

''I'm from Maryland originally. My husband's from Virginia. Most recently we lived in Connecticut.''

''Congratulations. Three of the original thirteen states, each contiguous to the Atlantic. How often do you hear the word, 'contiguous'? Why'd you come here?''

The incident in Fairfield flashed before Rebecca's mind. She rejected it.

''My husband's an architect.''

''Aah. Nice. So he's going to join a firm?''

''He wants to open his own firm. But he has a contact here. In Brentwood.''

''Nice area. Money, you know,'' Melissa said approvingly. ''Can't live well in this town without oodles of money.''

"The contact's a friend from graduate school. The friend has too much work for his own firm so he subcontracts."

"Nice arrangement. An architect is a smart thing to be around here. If we ever have The Big One, someone's going to have to put up a lot of new buildings."

" 'The Big One'?"

"The big quake. A whammo 8.8 job. The one everyone thinks is inevitable."

Rebecca shuddered. Nothing more sobering than thinking of her house leveled to the ground within weeks after the mortgage approval.

Melissa laughed. Rebecca finished unpacking a brown bag.

"Sometimes when I refer to 'The Big One' to women from the East, they think I'm talking about an orgasm," she said.

Rebecca laughed.

"I wish I were," Melissa said, raising her degree of candor to the next level. "As a single woman, you never know what you're going to have next."

"Have a boyfriend?" Rebecca asked.

"Would I be concerned about my next orgasm if I did?"

Rebecca laughed again. There was something about Melissa, a frankness and irreverence, that was infectious. Rebecca felt good just laughing with her.

"How does ice tea sound?" Rebecca asked.

"I never knew it made a sound."

"I mean—"

Then Melissa started to laugh and Rebecca joined in a second later.

"I'm sorry," Melissa said. "I couldn't resist." Still laughing. "Ice tea would be terrific," she said.

Rebecca set to making some. Fresh brewed, plus ice, plus some mint, lemon, and sugar. Melissa watched her and admired the finished product when it was served.

Rebecca sat down at the kitchen table, joined her friend, and sipped.

"This is delicious," Melissa said.

"Thank you." Rebecca sipped, too. The brew *was* good. "Did you say you were from California?" Rebecca asked a few moments later.

Melissa smiled. "Do I look it?"

She did. The blond hair. The tan legs. The shorts. Or at least she looked as if she had been there for a while. Rebecca didn't know what to say.

"Think hard," Melissa said, sitting with perfect posture and leaning back in a chair. She folded her hands behind her head.

Then Rebecca remembered. "Oh, of course! You just told me. You drove out in—"

"—in a non–air-conditioned seven-year-old orange Volvo with a leaky fucking radiator in August of 1985," Melissa said, expanding. "No wonder I stayed. Who the hell would drive back after that?"

Rebecca smiled. She was starting to like Melissa. In her eyes was a certain sense of mischief.

"I don't care if I do or do not look like I'm from here," Melissa continued. "I take it as a compliment either way." She paused. "I'm from Milwaukee. Jeffrey Dahmer's hometown. Hack-and-Sack on Lake Michigan."

Again, Rebecca grinned. "What does your roommate do?" she asked.

"June? She goes the god-awful model-and-actress routine," Melissa said with a trace of boredom. "She gets her share of work. But mostly she struggles, wards off lecherous males trying to hit on her, and gets in fights with people."

"Sounds like you don't get along."

"Actually we do. But we each know exactly what's wrong with the other."

Rebecca nodded knowingly. It almost sounded like a marriage.

"June used to be one of my AmCiv students," Melissa

said. Her eyes traveled the kitchen. "You know," she said, changing the subject, "this house has a wonderful feel to it. I've never been in here before."

"Think so?"

"I sure do. Don't you? You bought it?"

"I just. . . . Heck, I've just been transplanted. Everything takes some getting used to."

"Sure," Melissa said with another sisterly smile. "Of course it does." She finished her tea and a few more minutes passed in idle but friendly conversation.

"Look," Melissa finally said, "I'm going to run along. If you ever want to talk, I'm usually around."

"I'd call first."

"It's F-O-R-D," she said. "Same as June's Mustang. Count me as a friend now."

"Thanks," Rebecca said.

"Look, I'll tell you what. Let's make it more precise. Tell me what's a good time for you and I'll give you an informal tour of the area. An insider's tour, since I've been here for a while."

"I'd like that," Rebecca said.

"So would I. How about 11:00 A.M.?" Melissa suggested.

"Perfect." She paused.

"Know what? I'll meet you here. Right where I met you today. How's that sound?"

"It sounds wonderful, Melissa. And my friends call me Becca."

Melissa reached over and offered a handshake. Rebecca reciprocated. Melissa's right hand was cool. It also bore four rings, previously unnoticed. And her wrist was seriously bangled with a set of pastel bracelets.

"Be good, honey," Melissa Ford said. "Eleven A.M. tomorrow."

Rebecca stood and walked her friend to the door. As she

left, Melissa gave her a tiny wave and a thousand-kilowatt smile.

Rebecca watched her go for a moment, then went back to unloading the paint from its bags. Even the turret room didn't seem so annoying anymore. Rebecca had a great feeling at having so easily made a new friend.

4

Dr. Henry Einhorn's place of business was in an office-and-apartment complex in Century City, a high-rise white building overlooking the former back lot of a movie studio. And like every other doctor's office that Rebecca had ever visited, Dr. Einhorn's office was on the ground floor. Rebecca visited Einhorn that same afternoon.

Rebecca rang the doorbell. She was met by a young man who introduced himself as Delbert Morninglori, the doctor's assistant. "You can call me Del," the young man said. "As in Del Shannon. Do you remember Del Shannon?"

"Only courtesy of oldies radio stations," Rebecca said to him.

"Well, that's good enough." Del, as he called himself, whistled a few bars of "Runaway" and invited her into the office.

Del was politely mannered, soft-spoken and had a gold earring the size of a quarter. He wore a black T-shirt, a beige buckskin vest, and harem pants. He seemed to have put together his ensemble out of an *International Male* catalog.

Nonetheless, Del was charming. He led Rebecca into a large apartment, which didn't seem much like an office. And with reason. This was also Dr. Einhorn's home.

"Up until just recently this was Dr. Einhorn's home *exclu-*

sively,'' Del Morninglori continued. ''Then the doctor outgrew his office across the hall. The neighboring apartment became available so Dr. Einhorn obtained it and we broke through the wall.''

Morninglori indicated an area where the junction had been made. They were now in an area that seemed to be half a study, half a waiting room.

''Did he?'' Rebecca asked. She took a seat in a comfortable armchair.

''Yes, he did,'' Delbert said, taking the question literally. ''So now, for better or worse, work and home can be the same.''

''Convenient,'' Rebecca said. She began to wonder if Delbert was live-in help.

Delbert grinned. ''I know what you're thinking,'' Delbert said. ''And shame on you.''

''What am I thinking?'' Rebecca asked.

''You're wondering if I live here, too. I don't,'' he said. ''I have my own place around the corner. Right down the street from Beverly Hills High School. You know: Nine Oh Two One Oh? It's only about a one-minute drive to get here.''

''Convenient,'' said Rebecca.

''And do you know what else is convenient?'' Delbert asked.

''What?''

Delbert indicated a red hanging lamp near a pair of sliding doors that led to a porch. The lamp was on a ceiling mount and suspended from three feet of chain.

''At the first hint of an aftershock or a new quake,'' Delbert said, ''that lamp starts swinging wildly. Gives us all warning. It's sort of a pendulum, quake monitor, and lighting system all in one.'' He paused. ''If I were naughty, I'd hang on it.''

''Convenient,'' Rebecca said again.

''But I'm not naughty,'' Delbert professed.

''Uh-huh.''

"Oh, it's much better than having a cat," Delbert expounded. "If you look real carefully, you'll see that the lamp hangs crooked. It wasn't like that before the quake of January one-seven ninety-four. Know what that means? The crookedness? That means that the foundation of the building is still a little bent from the quake."

Rebecca looked at the lamp. By God, the suspended cord *was* crooked, she noted. But, if the laws of gravity applied to this place, the cord couldn't have been crooked, which meant that Delbert was right, the building was.

Bent. In her mind, she repeated the young man's terminology. She was in a building of which the foundation was, well, *bent.*

She sighed. La-La Land struck sometimes when she least suspected it would.

Delbert disappeared for a moment, then reappeared with a clipboard. There was a printed form on it. The usual medical insurance crap.

Rebecca filled out the form while the further ramifications of visiting a quake-crooked building started to weave their way into her mind. Then Delbert disappeared with the completed paperwork and quickly appeared again with voices— one male, one female—in the background.

"Here's the doctor now," Delbert said merrily.

Rebecca looked up.

Through a slightly ajar door, she could see into the doctor's office. The office had an exit directly to the outer hallway and the doctor was dismissing his previous patient, also a female.

Moments later, Henry Einhorn, M.D., emerged from his office. He was a package of surprises. A small package.

Einhorn was a tiny man with a dark complexion and intensely handsome features, the chiseled cheekbones and the brooding face of an early screen star. It occurred to her quickly that Dr. Einhorn might have come by these attributes through the skilled hands of a surgeon rather than through a favorable gene pool. Then it occurred to her almost as quickly that Henry Einhorn might have had a wonderful career on screen were it not for his other most salient attribute.

The doc was no more than five feet two inches tall.

Rebecca had had a girlfriend in high school that insisted that men under five-three were actually tall dwarfs. The comment came back to her over the course of years and Rebecca had to suppress a grin as Dr. Einhorn came to her to offer a hand.

"Hi," he said. "I'm Dr. Henry Einhorn. And I'm very pleased to meet you."

"Rebecca Moore," she said.

She took his hand and stood, feeling as if she were riding an elevator as she did so. She was shorter than he one second, and four inches taller the next.

Life in Southern California, she thought to herself. Up and down in the matter of seconds. Everyone's in show biz, everyone's a star.

And some days everyone was nuts. Even her, she speculated, which brought her back to the reason she was here. Or was she the only one who was sane?

"Very nice to meet you, Rebecca," Dr. Einhorn said. "Come on into my office. Let's get to know each other."

He led Rebecca into his inner chamber and closed the door.

The elfin psychiatrist was dressed simply, but immaculately. Dark slacks and a hundred-dollar shirt with an open neck. West Coast upscale casual. Nothing tacky like his assistant in the harem pants. And yet she was waiting for him to say, "Hi, I'm Hank, and I'll be your psychoanalyst today."

But he didn't.

Instead, he avoided his desk and sat down in a chair across from her. And he talked to her sympathetically and intelligently. Fears of quackery disappeared very quickly.

Henry Einhorn and Rebecca exchanged small talk for several seconds, then Einhorn drifted toward the business end of his conversation.

"I'll make things more comfortable by doing much of the early talking," he said to her. "I'm a clinical psychiatrist. I know you were seeing Dr. Miller in Connecticut, but he has more of a family practice, so to speak. My specialty is PTSD. Post Trauma Stress Disorder, which is why you were referred to me. I've been written up in all the journals. If you want to see any of the articles, ask Del on the way out."

Rebecca nodded. She remembered the explanation Dr. Miller had given her.

"Post Trauma Stress Disorder," he repeated. "I know you're college educated and you know what PTSD is all about. But let's run through it in a sentence or two."

The doctor's hand drifted to his desk. There were some M&M's in a dish. He treated himself to a couple, carefully picking out only the green ones.

"In lay terms," he explained, "PTSD is a catchall term for the psychological bruises which afflict crime victims. I don't have to convince you, because you know: victims of violent assault suffer in many different ways. First there's the assault, itself. There's maybe the financial or physical harm. But then, second, there are also the mental damages, and don't ever let anyone suggest that the psychological part isn't the worst. The head problems. The insecurities. The self-doubt. The feeling that you're continually in jeopardy. The constant feeling of being on edge: jumping out of your skin if a family member appears quietly in the same room with you."

His gaze was gently upon her.

"Am I making sense?" he asked.

Rebecca nodded. "You are."

"Am I connecting, Rebecca? Am I describing the way you feel?"

She nodded again.

"Good. That's why you were seeing Dr. Miller in Connecticut and presumably that's why we are here today talking," he said. "If I'm on the mark, you can take some comfort. It means your reactions are those of an intelligent woman who is reacting to a horrible deed in a normal way. Okay?"

He winked.

"Okay," she concurred. Dr. Einhorn may have been unorthodox. But he was sounding less kooky and more sympathetic by the minute.

"Rebecca, I'm not in business to treat people for years, assure them there's nothing wrong with them, and then insist that they should keep coming. I want to make myself obsolete. I want to lead you to an understanding of yourself, then throw you out of here and fix someone else while you get on with a happy life."

Dr. Einhorn called each case—each patient's head—a "fix." To him, that's what it was. His line of work: fixing heads.

"I'd also like you to be aware of what I call The Dachau Principle," he continued. "It affects you, I would think."

It sounded somber. She held her breath and waited. "Go ahead," she finally said.

"It's very simple. In the years since World War II many former concentration camp victims have been treated for severe psychological disorders. Call it Post Trauma Stress Disorder in its most extreme example. Many psychotherapists treated these people while holding to the theory that the patients themselves were mentally ill. My theory is they were disturbed, not ill. Their extreme reactions were the reactions of normal sane people who had been subjected to unspeakable inhumanity. Do you see my point?"

"I think so."

"I'll make it directly, anyway," Dr. Einhorn said. "Psychological disturbance following extreme trauma—particularly life-threatening trauma—is to me a normal and logical reaction by a mentally healthy individual. My approach, therefore, is not to treat you as someone who is ill, but rather to guide you through your thought processes. *I* want to lead *you* into an understanding of them. That way you can understand yourself and control your own mind. It really is that simple.'' He paused. ''Sometimes,'' he concluded.

''Look,'' Rebecca said, ''I don't have a problem with any of that. It's just that I'm not at all sure that I even need to be here.''

''Bravo! Excellent,'' he said. ''Congratulations.''

Dr. Einhorn smiled easily and made an expansive gesture with his hands. ''Then we're halfway home,'' he said.

She looked at him. ''Halfway where?'' she asked.

''Halfway to where we want to be. You suspect you might not need to be here. As soon as I feel the same way, you won't need to be.''

She blinked slightly. Einhorn had a way of putting her at ease. ''You make it sound very easy,'' Rebecca said.

''As I said, sometimes it is, Rebecca. Human beings are very resilient. The mind responds to its stimuli. Threat is answered by fear. Knowledge begs rational comprehension as its response. I have no reason to think you won't respond that way, too.'' He poached another few M&M's. This time, yellow only.

She gathered herself emotionally. ''Thank you,'' she said.

''What you're also telling me,'' he said, ''is that someone near you prompted you to come to me. A husband. A lover. A family member.''

''My husband,'' she answered.

''Nothing wrong with that. He's obviously concerned about you.''

She surprised herself with her response. ''That, or he thinks I'm more disturbed than I am.''

''Cynicism can be counterproductive, Rebecca. You should be aware of that.''

Again, she nodded. Was she imagining it, or, by remote

control, or by an unseen cue, had the lights lowered in his office. Yes, indeed, she concluded. They had.

"I'd like you to talk to me a little bit," he said. "You took the trouble to come by. That suggests something right there."

She nodded. "My doctor back East in addition to my husband," she said. "They both thought it might be a good idea if I 'talked' to someone here in California."

"But do *you* think that's a good idea?" Einhorn asked.

She thought about it. Then she nodded. "Sometimes," she said. "Sometimes I get very scared. Thinking back."

She looked at the doctor's folder and for a moment wondered how much he knew about her background. "I think back on the incident in Connecticut," she said. "You know what I'm talking about?"

"Of course I do. Dr. Miller forwarded everything," Einhorn said. "I've read the complete transcript."

She nodded.

"Someone tried to kill me," she said. "I don't know why. I don't know who. I don't know where that man is today. Sometimes I think that . . ." she paused. "I think that I'll open a door and he'll be standing there."

She had another sentence but didn't complete it.

"Why would he be there again, Rebecca? That horrible incident was on the other side of the United States."

She shrugged. "I don't know," she said.

"But you think there might be a reason?"

"I don't know why he attacked me in the first place," she said.

"No one was ever arrested?" he asked.

"No. No arrests. Whoever did it is still out there."

"And you think it was you he wanted to attack? You *specifically?* You don't think it was random?"

"No." She explained why. Einhorn nodded.

"Do you think you might have done something in the past?" the doctor asked. "Something to provoke this?"

"She threw up her hands. "I—? Who knows? What could I have done?" she asked. "And to whom?"

"But you don't dismiss that possibility?"

"Should I?"

He admonished her with a laugh.

"Rebecca, you're a bright lady," he said. "And I see that you've worked as a reporter. But if you don't mind, in my office, I ask the questions. Okay?"

She smiled. Even when she was on the receiving end of a mild rebuke, she found talking to him was much easier than she had anticipated. "Okay," she agreed.

Then he asked her the question she herself had posed. "Should you?" he asked. "Should you dismiss the possibility that you might have done something to bring this upon yourself? Take some time, Rebecca. Really examine that question. Look at your past. See where it takes you."

She let her mind go with it. Her thoughts almost seemed to float. Distantly in the other room, she heard Del Morninglori arguing loudly on the phone with someone about a bill for bottled water.

"No," she said after several seconds, answering the doctor. "We shouldn't dismiss that. I can't imagine what it could have been, but we shouldn't dismiss it."

"Then it's something you want to talk about?"

She nodded.

"Today?"

"Maybe not today," she said.

"Then why don't we talk about it in the future?" he suggested. "All right?"

Rebecca nodded.

"As I said, this can be very easy," he continued. "As easy as sharing our thoughts and seeing what we can discover." He paused. "I should tell you, I have a purpose for prowling around in your past. And I'll tell you what it is."

"Go ahead," she said.

"Sometimes when there's something too awful, too hei-nous, in our memories, we don't want to accept it," Dr. Ein-horn said. "So we block it. It's a little memory trick that we play on ourselves. But the key to knowing what's going on in our heads right now is knowing what's locked up in there from the past. Am I connecting?"

"You are connecting."

"But we can't know if we continue to block. Right?"

"Right."

"That's our 'thought for the day,' " the doctor said. His gaze was intently upon her. Then he smiled.

She reciprocated.

"Keep close track of your own short-term memory, also, Rebecca," he suggested. "Little things. Misplacing objects. Forgetting errands. Short-term remembrance problems some-times betray a lack of concentration on events as they tran-spire."

"I forget stuff all the time. Isn't that normal? Don't most people?"

"Sure," he allowed. "But how much forgetting we do can be symptomatic of two things: First, how much untidiness there is inside our heads. And second, how much we might—again—be willing to block something big. Something big and bad."

Her eyes found his shoes. Expensive. Brown leather. Pale green socks. She wondered if he was a charlatan, after all. Could anyone serious wear pale green socks?

"Rebecca?" he asked.

Her eyes rose. "I'm listening," she said. "I'll keep track. Short-term memory, right?"

"As seen as the key to long-term." He closed his notebook. "I give lollipops at the end of each session. Do you want grape or orange?"

She stared at him.

"Just kidding," he said. "I don't do the lollipop trip. But our time's up. I hope you come back."

Again she found herself nodding, and liking the tiny Doctor Einhorn. When their session was over, she had no difficulty making an appointment with Delbert for a follow-up in two weeks.

On her way out, the old phrase came to her about the inmates running the asylum. But the next thought that followed that one was to wonder whether, on occasion, it was such a bad thing if the inmates *did* take over from time to time.

After all, in leaving, she felt refreshed. In truth, she felt pretty good. She was already looking forward to her tour through the area with Melissa the next day.

5

Rebecca heard the soft knocking at the stroke of eleven the next day. At first her heart skipped, thinking it was something within the house, or worse, something emanating from the turret room upstairs.

Then, upon half a second's reflection, she realized that the rapping was at the front door. It was Melissa. Right on time. The funny thing was, the knocking had a strangely settling effect on Rebecca. That she had mistaken it for something within the house told her that other sounds within the building could be misleading, too.

But she didn't dwell on the point. Instead, she answered the door.

"Hi," she said, greeting her friend.

"I'm not too early?" Melissa asked. "I was thinking of giving you a few extra minutes."

"You're fine," Rebecca said. "My car or yours?"

"Is yours okay?"

"Mine is fine," Rebecca said.

Rebecca backed her Toyota out of the garage and they were off.

Melissa was an excellent guide. She had made a study of the area in an informal way, but knew it as an academic might.

She knew the little ins and outs, the anecdotes, the little pieces of history.

"There's only one *real* place to start," she announced. And she guided her driver up to the Hollywood sign. They spent several minutes in sunshine overlooking the city—a layer of thin gray smog lay below a bright sky—then continued.

It was the type of drive-around that Rebecca had been meaning to do by herself, but hadn't had the chance. So the opportunity was as welcome as the guidance.

Melissa brought Rebecca down Vine Street straight into Hollywood Boulevard. Then they turned west and drove out to Beverly Hills, Bel Air, and Brentwood. Melissa showed her favored places to eat, shop, and drink or flirt, if the mood so inclined her.

"The whole area never ceases to fascinate me," Melissa said, settling back into the passenger's seat in the front of the car. She guided Rebecca through Beverly Hills toward Sunset and the Westwood area around UCLA. "In LA everyone is a bit of a tourist. Just passing through, just looking for the California-American dream like everyone else. Know what I mean?"

"I know exactly," Rebecca said.

"It's fascinating. A person can go as far here as she's able to invent or reinvent herself. That's what the city's all about."

"Entertainment, you mean?"

"Not just that, although that's a big part of it," she said. They drove on Beverly Drive, through the Hills. Rebecca watched the sharply conflicting architecture float past her window. English Tudor next to Adobe Modern next to Mission Revival. *Ah, Tinseltown,* she thought to herself. She was starting to love it. Its very brashness was its glory, its inconsistencies were its charm.

"The first settlers out here were fruit farmers and oil wildcatters," Melissa said, apropos of nothing. "While Northern California was having a gold rush, Los Angeles was still a dusty outpost of fruit farmers and oil prospectors. It wasn't until Cecil B. DeMille came out here from New York before World War I that the movie industry took hold.'' She paused. ''The first movie pioneers were met by signs that read, NO DOGS, NO ACTORS. Did you know that?''

Rebecca laughed. ''No. I guess they didn't take that sentiment too seriously.''

''The old-line people out here were very conservative. Blue noses,'' Melissa said reflectively. ''They'd be spinning in their graves to think that La Pueblo de la Reine de los Angelos, became synonymous with sin, vice, and hedonistic living. But the movie industry wasn't built by people who listened to rules and restrictions.''

They came to a stoplight. Melissa's eyes settled on the busy intersection of Sunset Boulevard with Beverly Glen. ''Take a turn here,'' she said.

''Where are we going?''

''I'm taking you to meet Marilyn Monroe.''

''*What?*''

''Just drive, honey.''

''Yes, ma'am,'' Rebecca said with mock formality. Melissa eased back in her seat. She had slid her shoes off and was sitting with one bare leg propped up against the dashboard.

''In the grand scheme of things, do you realize how recent that was?'' she asked.

''Well, it was a couple of generations ago,'' Rebecca answered.

''Sure. Seventy years. But do you see how quickly Los Angeles reinvented itself? By the mid-1920s, when talking pictures came in, Los Angeles had almost overnight become a different city. The entertainment capital of the world. From a town of oil and oranges it became the entertainment capital of the world. A whole empire built of celluloid and fantasy.''

''From listening to you, Melissa,'' Rebecca said, ''I sometimes can't tell whether you love it or hate it.''

"Both," she answered. "But I'm here to stay, I'll tell you that. In LA for the next eternity. Earthquakes permitting."

They both laughed again.

Melissa guided her driver to the Westwood stretch of Wilshire Boulevard. They parked the car and set out on foot. Minutes later, Melissa led the way into Westwood Memorial Cemetery, a small burial ground nestled onto a block behind a massive office building.

"I *love* cemeteries," Melissa said by way of introduction.

Rebecca curled a lip.

"You don't like them?"

"I find them a little spooky. That's all," Rebecca answered.

"Oh, lighten up," Melissa said. "You're thinking of graveyards as the musty old crypts and Dracula movies. Cemeteries are peaceful. Calm little islands of tranquillity, like the one right in our neighborhood. They're *liberating,* that's what they are," she chirped as she walked. "And above that, as a scholar of American Civilization, I will tell you that they are nothing less than fascinating. Cemeteries are mirrors to our past and mirrors to ourselves at the same time."

Rebecca watched where they were walking. She fell respectfully silent. Melissa seemed to know her way around here all too well. She led Rebecca to a wall crypt which contained the remains of Marilyn Monroe, a surprisingly modest resting place, marked with a simple sign and a generous assortment of fresh flowers.

Recent donors. Anonymous fans who had outlived their idol for a third of a century already, and counting. Then Melissa gave Rebecca a little nod and drew her in another direction within the same burial yard. Less than a minute's walk and they stood before the final resting place of Natalie Wood.

Another modest marker. And another armload of fresh flowers. Rebecca studied the scene and tried to figure whether there was a subtext to what she was being shown. What was her friend trying to tell her?

She turned her head slightly and discovered that Melissa was watching her intently. And she was smiling.

"What?" Rebecca asked.

Melissa had a look of mischief across her face.

"I'm going to change your mind," she said.

"About what?"

"Cemeteries."

"Oh, Melissa . . ."

"Don't 'Oh, Melissa' me," she said insistently. "Who's giving the tour here?"

"You are."

"Then trust me. I'm going to change the way you look at life and death. Or at least the way you look at Los Angeles."

"I'm not sure I asked for this service," she said.

"You get it anyway, honey," she said. "Come on."

Merrily, Melissa led Rebecca back out to the car. The sunlight glistened upon her and Rebecca wished she could look as young and pert at her age. And then she recalled that they were probably the same age, give or take.

They got back into the car. Melissa settled back again, a leg up to the dashboard. She glanced ahead. "Take the turn on Beverly Glen. A left. Then we're going for a bit of a drive."

"Where are we going?"

"Glendale."

"Melissa!"

"Trust me, dear lady. You will not be disappointed."

"It's a good thing I trust you."

"I'm watching over you, my dear. It's a good thing you met me."

"Yeah, right."

"You think I jest?"

"I think you might."

They came to a traffic light. She needed to make a left turn against traffic. Rebecca waited for the green arrow, thought for a moment, and glanced at her friend. Then she reached to Melissa's nicely tanned arm and placed a hand on it.

Then she pinched Melissa's arm.

"Ow! What's that?"

"You're *too* interested in these damned graveyards," Rebecca said. "I'm making sure you're real."

"You're not crazy or something, are you?" Melissa asked.

"Some people think I might be. I'll tell you about it sometime."

Melissa raised an arched eyebrow. "You could tell me now, except your fucking light just turned green."

An impatient car horn sounded behind them. Probably a transplanted New Yorker. Rebecca hit her accelerator nice and hard. Her tires left a nice East Coast–style screech on the asphalt as she sharply made her turn.

Both women laughed merrily. They were on their way to Glendale, out to the flatland of suburban sprawl at the foot of the San Fernando Valley.

In truth, Rebecca was having fun driving around with her new girlfriend. Patrick and Karen were at school and her husband was at work. Rebecca and Melissa could play a scaled-down Thelma and Louise for the afternoon.

"What's in Glendale?" she asked.

"Forest Lawn," Melissa answered.

"Oh, come on . . ."

Melissa shrugged aned giggled. "You've already made the turn," she said. "You might as well listen to your guide."

Rebecca sighed, then joined her friend in laughter.

The drive took twenty minutes.

Then they entered the gates of what was more a vast park than a graveyard. Forest Lawn Memorial Park was three hundred meticulously landscaped acres of statues, sculptures, and various art treasures, including a replica of Da Vinci's *Last Supper*, done entirely in stained glass. In the chapel, the Hall

of the Crucifixion-Resurrection, Rebecca stared at the world's largest oil painting of the Crucifixion. It gave her shivers. Rebecca was silent. Melissa gave her a nudge when it was time to go.

She led her outside. "This place was the model for the setting of *The Loved One*," Melissa said. "Evelyn Waugh. Ever read it?"

"No," Rebecca was embarrassed to admit.

"You should."

Then there were the dead. Or merely the departed. Near the Freedom Mausoleum were markers for Walt Disney and Errol Flynn. But Melissa led Rebecca inside. In silence, within the cool mausoleum, Rebecca had never before been in the presence of so many celebrities. So what if they were dead? Crypts were everywhere: Nat King Cole, Gracie Allen, Clara Bow, and Alan Ladd.

After a few minutes, Melissa led her guest back out into the sunlight, then to the Great Mausoleum a five-minute walk away. There, among numerous others, Rebecca found herself communing with the departed spirits of Carole Lombard, Clark Gable, and Jean Harlow.

Then they were back outside.

"Over in the Hollywood Hills there's a sister park to this one," Melissa said. "Forest Lawn, Hollywood. They've got Stan Laurel, Liberace, and Freddie Prinze over there." She spoke as if she were comparing sports teams: The Dodgers had Mark Piazza, but the Angels had J.T. Snow.

"What do you do? Keep track?" Rebecca asked.

"American Civ, my dear," Melissa said again. "What tells us more about our culture than our final resting places? These are the spots where our spirits will rest indefinitely."

"Don't you mean, 'eternally'?"

"Who knows?" Melissa shrugged.

"I'm not sure if I believe that spirit stuff," Rebecca said.

"I mean, when you're gone, you're gone. I wish it weren't that way, but I think it is."

They arrived back at the car. Melissa gave her a facetious wink. "As you get older," Melissa said, "you might change your mind. I did."

"What are you talking about?" Rebecca asked. "Ghosts? Spirits? Reincarnation?"

"That's a subject for another day," Melissa said. "Right now, however, if you want to do some more world-class tomb crawling I'll take you over to Hollywood Memorial Cemetery. It's at the intersection of Gower, Santa Monica, and Van Ness. Douglas Fairbanks and Rudolph Valentino are in there. Want to go look?"

Rebecca sighed. "Quickly," she said. "On the way home."

"It's a deal, honey."

They found the Toyota and started back.

"Want to know my favorite Tinseltown burial story?" Melissa asked a few minutes later. They were on the expressway southbound toward Hollywood from Burbank, moving with moderate traffic.

"I'd be afraid to guess what it is," Rebecca answered. "And I have a feeling that I'm going to hear it anyway."

"Hollywood Memorial," Melissa said. "One of the more venomous producers ever to screen a film in this town is buried there. Harry Cohn." She paused. "He's in a burial plot for two."

Rebecca glanced at Melissa. "Give me that again."

"Harry Cohn picked out his own gravesite," Melissa said. "He was the head of Columbia Pictures at the time. An absolute tyrant. So he picked out a site that was across the street from the studio. Legend has it that he could keep an eye on the studio after he died. And he bought himself two plots, figuring he was bigger in Hollywood than anyone else. So he should have two. And everyone else has one."

Melissa was correct, Rebecca was starting to conclude. Death could be fascinating.

"So tell me," Rebecca asked, "was Harry *able* to keep an eye on the studio?"

"After Cohn died, the studio moved," Melissa said. "And it was beset with any number of failures and scandals. So who knows? It was apparently beyond Harry's sight. And power."

Thirty minutes later, Melissa showed Rebecca Cohn's tomb, right by a little man-made lake. In Hollywood Memorial Cemetery, a pantheon of stars had found a final refuge—sort of—from their fans. Douglas Fairbanks had the most elaborate memorial in the sixty-five-acre yard. But Rudolph Valentino, in crypt 1205, still drew visitors, although the famous "lady in black" who used to bring flowers on the anniversary of his death had long since slipped into her own tomb. Rebecca noted Tyrone Power, Peter Lorre, and Cecil B. DeMille. In an eerie touch, Paramount Pictures—which DeMille had established in the 1920s—still existed over the garden wall from his tomb.

There was a Jewish cemetery across the street, Beth Olam.

"I'll take you to see Bugsy Siegel," Melissa offered. "He was shot down in his home in B.H. almost fifty years ago, but we can still visit him in Beth Olam."

"I think, honestly," Rebecca said, "I've had enough of tombs. How about lunch, instead?"

It was two-thirty and Melissa agreed. She knew a great place in Hollywood where fresh light sandwiches came on croissants. It was a fitting end to an unusual morning and early afternoon.

Rebecca treated Melissa to lunch and then took off to pick up Karen and Patrick from their after school programs. It was a day that had been as unusual as it had been fascinating.

* * *

Bill called her at six that evening and told her to go ahead with dinner. Some late work was going to keep him at the office for a few extra hours. Bill sounded good over the phone and seemed relieved that the extra work was coming together.

Rebecca gave the kids their meal. They spent half an hour reading after dinner, then disappeared to play a game with each other in Karen's room.

Rebecca straightened the downstairs of the house. She kept dinner warm for Bill in the kitchen.

At eight, Rebecca walked upstairs to help conclude the game.

"Time to get ready for bed, guys," she said. "Let's wrap it up."

Her maternal concern was met by the predictable groans.

Rebecca went back downstairs. The kids came down at quarter past the hour, giggling to each other. It was time for a downstairs story from a book, perhaps, but both Karen and Patrick seemed more concerned with some conspiratorial point between them.

"What's going on, guys?" Rebecca asked.

Karen looked at Patrick. "You ask," she whispered.

Rebecca looked at both of her children. Yes, indeed. There was a conspiracy. And a question. Something they wanted to know from Mom.

"Okay, guys," Rebecca inquired. "Ask me what?"

There was a pause.

"Patrick?" she asked. "You're the older. Let's hear it."

The kids giggled.

"Is Ronny good or bad?" he asked.

"What?"

"Is Ronny good or bad?"

"Ronny who?"

"Ronny Sinbilt," Karen said.

A wave of anxiety washed through Rebecca. Not Ronny. Not again. She thought she was rid of this.

"Why are we talking about Ronny again?" Rebecca asked.

"Because he's back," Patrick said.

"Back *when?*"

"Back now," Patrick said. There was a solemnity to his voice. As if he knew he wasn't supposed to see Ronny, but did, anyway.

"What do you mean, 'now'?" Rebecca asked. "Today?"

"Tonight," Patrick said.

"He's upstairs right now," Karen said.

What Rebecca felt, against her better judgment, was fear. Plain and simple.

"Listen guys," she said, stifling a little tremor. "Will you do your mommy a big favor?"

She waited. They waited.

"Okay?" Rebecca asked. "A big favor. It bothers Mommy when you talk about Ronny. It bothers me because Daddy and I are the only ones in the house besides you. This is our home and no one else is here."

"But—"

"Patrick!" Rebecca snapped, barely able to subdue her anger. "Ronny is your imaginary friend, right? So you have to remember that something that is in your imagination is *not* real."

She had never quite seen a reaction like this from her son. He looked to his younger sister for help, but kept quiet. He looked as if he knew his mother were wrong, but didn't want to disagree.

Rebecca drew a breath, tried to dissipate the tension building within her, and told herself, reminded herself, that she was never ever to lose her temper with her children at times like this.

"Ronny's real, Mommy," Patrick said.

"He's upstairs now," Karen said.

A second passed. "No he's not," Rebecca answered.

The kids didn't disagree. Instead, they kept quiet.

Rebecca thought about it. Then she tried another tack.

"Okay," she said, mounting up her courage, "he's up-stairs, right?" she asked.

Karen nodded. Then Patrick did, too.

"Where upstairs?"

"In his room," Karen said.

"The 'turret room'?"

Patrick nodded.

"How do you know?"

"We saw him go in there."

"Did he talk to you tonight?"

They shook their heads. Rebecca glanced upstairs. The second floor was completely quiet. The landing at the top of the stairs was shadowy.

Rebecca tightened up her courage just a little more. "Okay," she said softly. "Show me."

Patrick took one of her hands. Karen took the other. Her children led her to the stairs. They walked up the steps together, as if they were upon a great expedition.

Rebecca felt her heart thumping hard in her chest. At the top of the steps, she hesitated slightly. She pulled back her hands and wiped her sweating palms on her skirt.

"Okay," she said. "Your mother can walk the rest of the way." She looked at the dark doorway to the turret room. The door was half-open. There was some light from within, proba-bly from outside. The house was quiet. She wished to hell that Bill were home.

She walked to the room and stopped, trying not to appear too frightened as she looked past the door. She was reminded of being a child, imagining a monster in the closet and being too scared to go over and open the closet door. She tried to remind herself how foolish those childhood fears had been. And yet she was beset with the same fears now in a modern adult form.

"What's the matter, Mommy?" Patrick asked. "Don't you want to go in?"

She looked at her children. Four imploring eyes. And for a second she nearly screamed because in her mind—for a snap of time that had no measurement in real time—she was terrified by the image of the sunglassed man from the parking lot standing behind the door of the turret room.

"Of course I'll go in," she said. She reached into the room quickly. There was a chill. Or so she thought. Or so she imagined. She flicked on the overhead light. Then, with a foot, she shoved the door forward.

The door flew wide open. The light from the bare overhead bulb filled the turret room.

Nothing. No Ronny. Just painting equipment sitting in the middle of the floor.

"Your friend is gone," Rebecca said.

The kids looked around the room. They appeared disappointed.

"And now it's bedtime," she said.

The kids grumbled. Rebecca felt a huge wave of relief wash over her.

"Come on," she said. She turned the light off and stepped back. For good measure she pulled the door shut and closed it firmly. So Ronny could stay the hell put, she heard herself thinking.

"He'll come back," Karen said.

"Karen!" she snapped. "That's enough. All right? And I don't want to hear about this again!"

The little girl looked crestfallen. She liked her new friend.

"Come on, guys," she said, practicing being chipper. "It's bedtime, bedtime, bedtime. Let's brush those fangs."

She heard a low rumble of an engine. At first she thought it was an airplane. Then, to considerable relief, she realized it was Bill.

Good, she thought. He could help her read a story. And she

wouldn't feel so alone in the house. Thank God he had come home when he had.

The kids brushed their teeth and pulled down their covers. Bill came in and announced that he'd had a good day with Jack McLaughlin. McLaughlin had a considerable amount of new business and plenty would be coming his way. She kissed her husband and forgave him when he seemed preoccupied.

"Can you do a bedtime story for Patrick? I'll do one for Karen," she suggested.

He paused over a cold beer from the refrigerator. "Yeah," he said. His tone was preoccupied and without conviction. "Yeah. Sure."

Rebecca hated that tone from her husband. But they walked up the stairs together to put the kids to bed.

"I can't tell you how much it upset me," Rebecca said to her husband half an hour after their children were asleep. "This whole thing with Ronny. It's starting to get to me."

"No one's there, Becca," he said. "Don't be ridiculous. There is no one in this house except us, the family who pays the mortgage."

"Then why does it bother me?"

Her husband looked carefully at her. "I don't know," he said. "Maybe it's a little too much following, you know, what happened in Connecticut."

She thought about it for several seconds. "Maybe," she said with a sigh of exhaustion. Then she shook her head. "I'm tired of jumping at shadows. I'm tired of feeling funny in my own home."

He put an arm around her, almost in the tender way that he used to. "Why don't you talk it out with the new doctor?" he said. "What's his name?"

"Einhorn. Henry Einhorn."

"Have you mentioned it to him yet?"

"No."

"Can it do any harm?"

More thought. Then a conclusion. "No," she said. "It probably cannot do any harm."

There was a creak upstairs. Her eyes rose to find the spot. The kids moving around? Or something else? The noise seemed to have come from a midpoint in the hall, not far from the door to the turret room. And why—she found herself wondering with a sense of dread—did those creaks *always* seem to come right after a mention of the presence in the house?

"I'll mention it to Dr. Einhorn," she said. "You're right. It can't hurt."

When the Moores went upstairs to go to bed later that night, Rebecca froze. The door to the turret room was open again. She closed it and tried to tell herself that Patrick or Karen had tiptoed over to peek into the room again.

That would have explained the open door. And it would have explained the creak in the floorboard that she had heard earlier. Trouble was, that's not what she believed in her heart. With a mother's instinct, she didn't think either of her children had wakened from their sleep.

Rebecca went into the master bedroom and changed into her nightgown. Bill got into bed first and was asleep in a few minutes. That left Rebecca, the only one awake in the house.

She sat down on the edge of the bed and left a light on. Her eyes were glued upon the open door to the hall. The house was very quiet. It was so quiet that she was aware of a low noise at regular intervals.

It started to rattle her. What the hell was it? What was she hearing now. Her heart began to race.

Then she realized. What she was hearing was her husband inhaling and exhaling right next to her.

Still, she got up from bed and went to the door. She looked out on the wide quiet hall. Her gaze instinctively found the door to the turret room.

She was relieved. The door was still shut.

She left an extra light on in the hall and went to bed. She had difficulty relaxing enough to sleep, but sleep did claim her by midnight. The next morning, she was equally soothed to see that the door to the turret room had remained undisturbed through the night.

Nonetheless, she maintained her resolve to "reclaim" the room.

She worked out a budget for furniture and went to IKEA the next day. She ordered a daybed for the room, plus some play furniture. The store had some great posters, a toy chest, and various games with blocks and climbing. Rebecca got everything she needed for less than two hundred dollars. The store said delivery would take six days.

That was fine.

First the paint, she told herself, then the furniture. That would be the last she ever heard of Ronny.

By God, this was her home, she vowed. She would be damned if she would be run out of it by a figment of her own children's imaginations!

6

The Moores' housewarming party took place the following Friday.

The first guests to arrive were the Sorensons, who walked from down the block. Melissa Ford, the UCLA lecturer, was next. She arrived with a woman named Claire who was about ten years younger and wore the shortest skirt of any woman that evening. Melissa said Claire was a graduate student. Bill shot his wife a curious glance when neither was looking, as if to wonder exactly what sort of couple Melissa and Claire made. As for Melissa's roommate, June, June didn't show, as usual.

Another dozen and a half people drifted in over the next forty minutes. They all seemed to know each other, yet ranged in ages from Mr. and Mrs. Jansen, who were retired and in their sixties, to Roger Davis and Terry Hopkins, an unmarried pair of strivers, both of whom had jobs with banks. He was an MBA from Wharton and she had a similar academic license to steal from Stanford. Rather than making a family, they were setting to make some money and seemed to be doing a good job at it so far. Bill, ever with a nose to possible financial and business contacts, struck up immediate friendship with the Davis-Hopkinses while every once in a while eyeing young Claire and her gams.

Claire, in fact, served as a magnet for any stray straight men—there were three—for the evening. Eventually, she retreated to Melissa's side.

The crowd was mildly eclectic, but remorselessly white and upper-middle-class. Then again, who else but the upper-middles could afford to put down money for a house on that block of Topango? Most of the Moores' guests had steady mainstream jobs, but one, Tony Arsdale, was a television director and Marty Gross and his Russian-born wife Nadia both worked for Columbia Pictures, he in marketing and she in development. Nadia also had the second shortest skirt in the place that evening, a fashion statement Rebecca noted immediately upon introduction.

Then there was a single woman named Francine Yerber, who was a photographer. Francine was a diminutive woman with sharp features, big front teeth, and short dark hair. She looked like a small caricature of a female Jerry Lewis, and she walked with a very pronounced limp.

Francine's home, Rebecca learned from talking to her, was also her studio. When Bill pressed her about the type of photography she did, she demurred and made it all sound very esoteric. It took Melissa to happen by and spell things out more clearly.

"Francine's got a Pulitzer, but is too modest to tell you," Melissa said.

"Is that correct?" Rebecca asked.

Francine rolled her eyes. It was correct, she admitted.

"When I was a kid I used to go around and risk my life getting pictures," Francine said. "Some of them appeared in newspapers. Some of the ones in newspapers won some awards."

By when she was a kid, she meant, in her twenties, and by risking her life, she meant that during the fall of Saigon in 1975, she was there, snapping shutters from rooftops, stopping only long enough to duck bullets.

"Were you afraid of the Vietcong?" she asked.

"Oh, no," she said blithely. "Actually, that's where my sympathies were. The Vietcong officers knew me and let me take all the photographs I wanted. It was the American marines who were shooting at me."

"You're joking," Bill said.

"Why would I joke about that?" Francine asked. There was anger and contention in her tone.

Bill walked away to talk to the bankers while it sank in upon Rebecca that Francine wasn't kidding.

"Francine is the resident pink lady on our block," Melissa said, giving her a hug. Francine grinned.

"Well, no matter how you got it, the Pulitzer is impressive," Rebecca said.

"I have two of them," Francine said.

The other came in 1987 and had to do with conditions within migrant camps. That one led to an assault by some security people and an attack with ax handles. Francine still had a ten-million-dollar suit in California Supreme Court against one of the state's largest avocado packagers. It also explained the limp.

"If Francine wins and collects the full amount," a man named Jim Doleman interjected, "it will raise the cost of the average avocado two cents per fruit for the next two years."

This set off a wave of laughter, even though Doleman, a CPA, wasn't kidding.

"I do a lot of female nudes right now," Francine continued. "It's a lot more pleasant. I'm trying to get Melissa to pose for me."

"I haven't given in yet," Melissa said with a laugh, overhearing. "And probably won't."

Rebecca excused herself to meet other guests.

There was a bearded man, stout and fiftyish. He was the other person attached to a university, aside from Melissa and her girlfriend.

Rebecca went to him.

"Hi," she said. "I'm Rebecca Moore. I'm your new neighbor."

The man's face creased into a smile above a trim gray beard. "Maurice Lerner," he said. "I'm in the house four doors down, opposite side of the street."

Ah, Rebecca thought. The psychiatrist whom Melissa had mentioned. An author and fully tenured professor in the UCLA psych department.

"Is there a Mrs?" Rebecca asked.

"Not anymore. My wife passed away four years ago."

"Oh, I'm sorry."

"Don't be," he said. "She hasn't left the neighborhood."

It took Rebecca a second, but then his allusion registered.

"The cemetery?" she asked.

"Cemetery of Angels," he said evenly. "And my angel is there already."

"What are you talking about?" Rebecca asked. "I thought there were no new burials there since World War Two."

Dr. Lerner blinked once. "Officially, no. There aren't," he said. "But I didn't want my wife to be distant. So I just went in there one night with her urn. She was cremated, you see. I just buried her in the field behind the tombstones." He paused. "I'm probably not the only one to do something like that. Security is non-existent in that yard. Just an old Chicano man during the day. I suspect my Deborah is very happy where I put her."

He said this in a completely even, primarily cheerful voice. It carried not the slightest trace of sarcasm, not the subtlest hint of the saccharine. He just said it as fact.

"May I get you a drink?" Rebecca asked.

"A cold beer would suit me fine. Anything but Coors."

"We have plenty," she answered. "Olympia and Samuel Adams."

"Either would be fine," Dr. Lerner said. "And I wouldn't have come if you didn't have beer."

The widower, it turned out, was also a practicing M.D. and a lecturer in hypnotherapy. He was joined that evening by a Doctor Lim, a friend in the same field, with whom Dr. Lerner had a tennis match every Sunday.

One of the bankers came over and engaged the doctors in conversation. It was just about then that Rebecca heard a heavy noise from overhead.

Something like a chair scraping. Or a very heavy footstep.

Shit, she thought to herself. Her pulse rate quickened. That room again. Ronny's room.

She looked around for Bill and didn't see him. Her heartbeat eased. It had to be her husband upstairs, she told herself. She wondered what he had gone upstairs for and, for that matter, what he was doing in the turret room, which remained empty.

Consciously, she turned her attention back to her duties as the new hostess in the neighborhood.

A half a dozen of the invitees brought their children. Two of the boys who came over were teenagers and quickly departed with their parents' blessing, skateboards and all. Rebecca and Bill were glad to have met them, but equally gl   to get them out of the house. They went back over to Jim Doleman's house to shoot some hoops at a basket above the garage door.

But Karen and Patrick came out as big winners. They were, in fact, in their glory. There were two boys about Patrick's age and a girl about Karen's. Rebecca watched from a distance and was tickled to death when the kids hit it off so well. She began to think that there was some justice in the world and that sometimes things worked out with a perfect geometry.

There was one African-American family, Ronald Johnson and his wife, who called herself Mandy. Ron Johnson was a Princeton graduate and no one's fool. He was barely a day over thirty and was already a vice president in charge of something with one of the film studios. He was a gracious, well-spoken man, with the build of an Ivy League athlete, and underneath he had a tone of toughness that Rebecca measured to be tough as steel. His wife was equally charming. She'd gone to Bryn Mawr and majored in Twentieth century French literature.

"If I ever have a question about *Céline*," Rebecca said, "now I know whom to call."

Mandy Johnson laughed.

"In this town," her husband added, "mention *Céline* and everyone thinks you're talking about Celine Dion."

Melissa and Claire exploded with laughter. One of the bankers heard the joke, smiled uneasily, and obviously had missed it. Terry Hopkins struck up a conversation with Claire, and Rebecca took the opportunity to straighten the hors d'o-euvres table and put out some fresh ice for the booze and soft drinks.

She scanned the room, checking on everyone, trying not to catch anyone's eye in particular. Not right then.

Then she heard another noise from upstairs.

She looked up. Directly over her head.

Same thing. It sounded like a chair scraping. Or sudden set of distressed footfalls.

What the hell . . . ? she found herself thinking.

She realized she was again looking up at the same spot in the ceiling, the spot just under the floor to the turret room.

Damn! she thought. *Who the hell* is *up there?*

Bill, showing off the house? She wondered. She hoped. Was he up there making his usual boasts and promises about what he was going to do with the upper floors?

She was sure it was Bill. Then, a moment later, her eye wandered across the room and caught her husband sitting on the sofa engaged in a tight conversation with Marty Gross's wife. Nadia's skirt had somehow, as she was sitting on the sofa, worked its way three-quarters of the way up her thighs, and if Rebecca weren't so even-minded, she might have been annoyed.

Hell, she thought. She *was* annoyed. She smoldered at Nadia, who was flirting shamelessly. Rebecca decided to ignore it. But she also made a mental note not to extend full friendship to wives in the neighborhood who made a point of flashing legs and anything else of interest to other women's husbands. What the hell was Nadia trying to prove, anyway? Then again, she reasoned, she could probably ignore it if Nadia's own husband could. Then she wondered just where flirtation ended with Nadia and where back porch seduction began.

Then, idly, Rebecca wondered how much of that was going on in the neighborhood. Was spouse-swapping "in" or "out" on this block? She suppressed a smile. So far, she hadn't seen anyone who would even tempt her.

Then Rebecca had a second distraction. She noticed that Karen was across the room, too, holding court with Katie Ross. That made Rebecca curious. She went to the den and saw Patrick sitting at the television with one of his new friends.

Hello? she thought. So no family member was upstairs? Rebecca walked slowly back to the spot where she had heard the noise. She stood still and cocked her head.

And then she heard the mystery sound a third time.

"Shit!" she muttered to herself. "Time to investigate."

"Becca?" A woman's voice asked. The voice was near to her.

Rebecca turned. It was Melissa standing only two feet away. Something funny in her eyes, a sense of the perverse, maybe, that Rebecca had not noticed before.

"Hi," Rebecca answered. She kept moving.

"What's going on?" Melissa asked.

"What do you mean?"

"You look like something's bothering you. Maybe just a little, but I can see it's on your mind."

"One of my more aggressive guests seems to be upstairs," Rebecca said with perturbation.

Melissa glanced around. "How do you know? Who's missing?"

"Melissa, damn it, I don't even know everyone who's here, much less who's disappeared. All I know is I heard something three times and no one comes downstairs."

"That's LA for you." Melissa smirked and raised a mischievous eyebrow. "Your guests have found a spare bedroom. Must be something in the air."

"Then they're doing it on the floor, because that room is not furnished yet."

"As I said, 'That's LA for you.' "

"I am *not* amused," Rebecca said.

"Apparently."

"Follow me while I lead the strays back to the corral."

"Sure thing." Melissa giggled conspiratorially and followed.

"Ask me whatever you were going to ask me," Rebecca said. "Just come with me."

"Sure enough," Melissa said. They went through the living room, where Rebecca noted that the hors d'oeuvres were running low. Time to replenish the plates when she came back downstairs, she told herself. Maybe she could enlist Melissa's help.

"Thursday would be good for me," she said.

"Good for what?"

"To continue your tour. Remember? Hot spots and cemeteries."

"Oh, God. That's right."

They climbed the stairs together.

"If you're not interested anymore—"

"I'm interested. I'd just forgotten."

"Then how about Thursday?" she said. "I can pick you up at ten in the morning and we'll travel till four. I know a place we can have lunch."

"As long as it's inexpensive."

"Honey, it'll be out-and-out cheap."

"My kind of place."

The hall was dark as they arrived at the top of the steps. The light was off. Rebecca was sure that she had turned it on. So who the hell was walking around in the dark?

"No one's up here," Melissa said. "It's dark, honey."

Rebecca stood in place at the top of the steps. "I heard something."

"Like what?"

"A chair scraping. Or footsteps."

"Whoever it was must have come downstairs."

"We would have passed them."

"So who walks around in the dark? Which California wacko?"

"I'm not sure I want to know."

Rebecca made her first move. She turned the light on. A nice warm glow bathed the landing and central hall.

"Is there a back staircase?"

"Not that I know of."

"It's your house, honey."

"I mean, no."

"Where were the footsteps?" Melissa asked.

Rebecca nodded toward the turret room, the kids' future playroom.

Ronny's room.

"Then let's have a look."

The two women walked together, Rebecca more apprehensive than her friend. The door to the room was open. It loomed large in front of her and a funny sort of light glowed within it. She saw a movement but within another moment knew it was her own shadow.

She reached the room and stepped in. That sour odor accosted her again. Then she quickly flicked on the light.

The overhead bulb illuminated the room. Harsh. A bare bulb.

Rebecca's eyes covered the whole chamber in a flash. No one there.

Nothing.

Or so it appeared.

Melissa read the look of concern on her friend's face.

Then Rebecca saw the closet door move, and the worried look turned to fear.

The door moved just slightly. Just a little. As if someone— something inside—had nudged it.

Just a whisper.

"Oh, shit," Rebecca said.

"What?"

"The closet door." Rebecca's voice was barely above a whisper. She raised an unsteady hand and pointed. "It just moved."

Melissa looked at it and looked back to her hostess. "Bull-shit," she said.

"Melissa, I *saw* it."

"What are you telling me? Someone's hiding in the closet?"

Rebecca made a gesture. "I don't know. Maybe."

"Don't you know, it's a California tradition."

"What is?"

"You get invited as a couple to a new neighbor's house. Then you sneak upstairs and go to a closet and copulate. It's known as the 'California closet fuck,' and after you've lived here for a few months, you and Bill can come over to my place and do it."

Rebecca stared at her.

Melissa continued. "The *polite* thing to do, honey, is ignore them until both of them—or at least the woman, assuming there's only one woman—has her orgasm.''

''*What?*''

''What I'm saying to you, Becca, is that I'm *joking,* okay? And this is a lot of bullshit,'' Melissa said. ''There's no one in that closet.''

''I'm going to go get Bill.''

''And have him laughing at you all night, right?'' Melissa said. ''Yeah, sure. Make a nutcase of yourself. You're going to go get no one.''

''Melissa—!''

''Watch me,'' Melissa said.

Melissa crossed the room. Slowly. As if she were creeping up on the door. As if she were going to throw it open and expose fornicating lovers.

Or something.

And Rebecca continued to have bad feelings. Nasty vibrations. Something terrible beyond that threshold.

''Melissa, be careful!''

Melissa made a good girl scout–type gesture. She stood outside the closet door. Her hand went slowly to the knob. Then her hand was firmly upon it.

Rebecca felt her heart pounding. Her hands rose toward her face as if she couldn't bear to look.

Then Melissa yanked.

The door flew open. For a nanosecond, Rebecca thought she saw a flickering image, like a film reel gone berserk. Then that transformed into something dark. But then that was gone, too, and all she had left was a shadow. Melissa's shadow: the sole occupant of the closet.

''You got one great imagination, girl,'' said Melissa.

Rebecca exuded a massive sigh of relief. She calmed herself.

''I *know* I heard something,'' she said softly.

''Yeah,'' her friend answered. Melissa remained in the

closet. With a foot, she poked at the walls and corners within it.

"No secret passages, Becca," Melissa said. "No false floor and"—she reached a long gangly arm upward toward the ceiling of the closet—"no escape hatch out the top like an elevator."

Melissa stepped out of the closet. She glanced to the window, which was partially open. A little breeze stirred.

"There's your culprit right there," Melissa said. "Mom Nature. Don't you know not to fuck with Mom Nature?"

"I know I heard something."

"A scraping and a bang. Something like that?"

"Yes. Three times."

Melissa pushed the closet door shut. It scraped the floor as it moved. It banged when it closed. Then the door latch gave way and the door opened again.

"Presumably, with the help of the breeze, it could have repeated that motion into the next millennium," Melissa said. She looked at her friend. "Still not happy?"

Rebecca sighed. She *was* relieved. A little. "Only ninety-eight percent," she confessed.

"Okay. Come on. Let's not screw up the party. We'll do a room-to-room search," Melissa said, "until you're satisfied."

"It's a deal."

They walked together from room to room. But each chamber was dark and quiet. Karen's room, Patrick's room. The master bedroom. No one. Nothing. Peace on earth.

"Let's go downstairs," Melissa finally said.

They crossed the hallway. Rebecca had an urge to tell Melissa about the incident in Connecticut, the horrible abduction in Fairfield. Rebecca felt she could trust her new friend. And she felt that it would allow Melissa to understand her better.

Instead, however, she kept quiet.

They walked down the steps together, Rebecca going first.

The party was still going well. Bill had taken care to replenish the food table and Karen had joined Patrick in the den. They were playing some video game called Mist and entertaining their new friends.

Melissa went over to Claire and sat down next to her. Jim Doleman had been chatting Claire up, but somehow felt awkward as soon as Melissa arrived. A moment later he excused himself.

Rebecca found her husband.

Bill put an arm around her and she felt like the perfect hostess. No incidents, no awkward moments; she had survived the investigation of the turret room and she felt as if she had made two dozen new friends. *Hey,* she told herself, *not bad.*

"What's going on?" Bill asked.

"Nothing's going on."

"I watched you go upstairs. You looked like there was a problem."

"I thought I heard someone."

"Someone where?"

"Upstairs."

He looked concerned and glanced toward the steps. Things like this could always set him off. The old paranoia of an amateur college druggie, always waiting for the narcs to come in.

"And?" he asked. A certain jitteriness pervaded his tone. "Was there anyone?"

"No. Of course not."

"Why didn't you let *me* look."

"I didn't want to bother you."

"Next time," he said, "bother me. I don't like the idea of someone wandering around upstairs." He looked back toward the steps. And she could see that he was actually annoyed.

She sighed again. If she had interrupted him with Nadia, he would have accused her of causing a jealous scene. In some situations with Bill, she couldn't win.

"Honey, there wasn't anyone there," she explained. "It was just a door scraping in the turret room."

"Next time, let *me* find out," he said.

"Bill, what's wrong with you today?"

"Must have been our buddy 'Ronny Sinbilt,' " he said after a moment's pause.

"Something about that isn't funny," Rebecca said.

He thought back to her abduction, and how jittery she'd been since. She was just starting to calm down.

"Sorry," he said. "I didn't mean that." He grimaced and released her. It was as much of an apology as Rebecca ever got from him.

Melissa and Rebecca walked away.

"Who's 'Ronny Whatever'?" Melissa asked.

"Some imaginary playmate that our kids see. Or think they see."

"Where? Here?" Melissa asked, curious as a brace of cats.

For the first time, Rebecca was annoyed.

"There's no one up there," Rebecca said. "No one when you just looked, and no one when Karen and Patrick think they see someone. Okay?"

Melissa thought about it.

"Maybe you have a ghost," she said. "Maybe even a pair of ghosts. That happens sometimes when—"

"Jesus Christ! This is my home! I have to live here! I don't think this is funny," Rebecca snapped.

Melissa was very calm and answered evenly. "I didn't mean it to be funny. LA is one of the most fertile ghost haunts in the United States. Why, did you know—?"

"I don't believe in such things," Rebecca said tersely. "And I would appreciate your not putting such thoughts in the air. In fact, I have to tell you this. Some of this death and cemetery stuff that you've been going on and on about is *giving me the creeps!* All right? I've pretty much had my fill of it!"

"It's not meant to scare you," Melissa explained. "It should reassure you."

Rebecca sighed. "Melissa," she said, boldly and authoritatively. "I like you. You're my best friend here. But sometimes you have to respect the fact that you and I might be on different wavelengths. Okay? I really don't feel comfortable with all this death and dying and graveyard stuff."

Melissa knew that a raw nerve had been touched. She was anxious to get away from it. She backed off.

"Oh. Sorry," Melissa said with a shrug.

"I know I live adjacent to a graveyard and I'm okay with that," Rebecca said, calming. "But we don't have to bring the graveyard into my home. Do we?"

Melissa looked almost crestfallen. But then she perked.

"No, we don't. Of course, honey. Not if you're uncomfortable with it. Again, I'm real sorry. Okay?"

Rebecca sighed again. "Okay." She relaxed.

"My apology is accepted?" Melissa asked.

"Of course it is."

"You want to be reassured? I'll reassure you," Melissa said. "We just looked around upstairs. That upstairs is M.T. Period. Nothing there. *Niente. Nada.* No spirits. No ghosts."

"Thanks. That's much better. Right." She looked at her friend. "I'm sorry I jumped down your throat. I've been edgy."

"Hey, honey," Melissa said, "it's not a problem."

Aside from that incident, the party was a success. Essie Lewisohn even turned up, handing out her business card to anyone who would take one. She also buttonholed Bill and Rebecca individually, asking if her long-lost red reading glasses had ever turned up. They hadn't. Essie sighed. The red ones had been her favorite pair, she said.

The party broke up about 10:00 P.M. Karen and Patrick went straight to bed. Bill helped Rebecca with the cleanup. Then he surprised his wife.

"I'm horny as a bull moose," he said near 11:00 P.M. They were still downstairs, listening to some music in the living room.

She set down the magazine she was reading and looked accusingly at him.

"Probably from looking at Claire all night," she said with more than a dash of irritation.

"I'm looking at you right now, Becca," he said.

When she walked past him a moment later, his hand settled on her wrist. She let him have his way. She drew the new blinds in the den and felt a little of the old excitement that she used to like when her lover wanted her. She let Bill undress her and they christened the new month-old sofa by making love upon it.

7

Alone in an airy apartment in a quiet neighborhood of Pasadena, Detective Edmund Van Allen sank into a comfortable chair in front of a television.

He hoisted his feet onto the coffee table in his living room, pushed his shoes off, and let them drop. They hit the carpeted floor with a couple of hearty bachelor's quarters clunks.

With one hand he squeezed open the cap on a brown bottle of his favorite elixir, Henry Weinhard beer. His other hand played with his favorite adult toy, the remote control of the TV set. Beer and television, he thought to himself. Those were the staples of a newly single man's existence. Well, he told himself, it could be much, much worse. After all those years on the LAPD he had seen many men stagger through middle age with far more undesirable baggage than his own.

It was quarter past eleven on a Tuesday evening in mid-October and Van Allen was waiting for the sports. Specifically, he wanted to see how the Lakers had performed that night.

Or, more precisely, as he readied himself for another small installment of negative sports news, he wanted to learn exactly how they had probably lost again. Never mind that it was still the exhibition season. A win was a win and a loss was a loss.

He sighed. As he waited for sports, he was able to indulge in one of the few other small pleasures he felt was left to a single white man of Northern European heritage: A big artery-clogging roast beef sandwich with Russian dressing. It was a behemoth of a sandwich, half a pound in weight and about five inches tall. Big, soft, chewy bread, with dressing running down the side. This was the type of guy-food concoction that his recently departed wife Margaret had always hated.

She hadn't just hated the sandwich, she'd hated the idea that he would eat such a thing. Ten years into their marriage, back in the mid-eighties, something had snapped inside lovely Margaret's brain and she had become a vegetarian.

Something had snapped. Well, that was Ed Van Allen's spin on the development. Why else would an otherwise sane human being become a convert to moose food? Of course, she had called it "eating smart," with all the sanctimoniousness that the phrase could carry.

Worse, Margaret had not just become a passive lettuce-eater. Oh, hell, no. She had become a proselytizing one, always seeking converts to the bloodless world of groats and sprouts and curd.

The daily menu had been the first fissure in their marriage. Other firefights followed, as inevitably as the rise and fall of Pacific tides.

The television news faded from the television screen and disappeared in favor of a commercial from a Mitsubishi dealer in Long Beach who said he would sell any customer a car without running a credit check.

Ed Van Allen sighed again. He could remember a more orderly time in the Southland when you at least had to have a job and the inclination to repay in order to get a car loan. Times *had* changed. He could also remember when most people in Los Angeles spoke English.

His thoughts drifted again. Sometimes he wondered if Margaret would ever come back. Or if she would get tired of this

New Age horseshit she was into and even *want* to come back. Sometimes, as other insecurities and uncertainties bedeviled him, Van Allen longed for a time ten years earlier when he was forty-two years old and had just made detective second grade. He still lived with a doting wife in a comfortable house ten blocks from his current apartment. His children were still young and Magic Johnson controlled both the floorboards at the Forum and the rest of the NBA.

Van Allen settled back. Tonight, at least, the beer was cold and the sandwich was excellent. There was even a nice clump of macaroni salad on the side, along with a kosher pickle the size of a peewee football. Sometimes, in some small ways such as these, life could be good. Every once in a while, he liked to let his cholesterol count go to hell.

Of course, paradise can never last. Sports finally came on the damned tube.

The Lakers had lost 92-86 to the Nets in New Jersey. The parvenu *Nets* for God's sake! In swampy, faraway Piscataway! Was there no decency left in the world? The Kings were locked out, the Dodgers and the Angels were on strike, and who cared about the Clippers? The Mighty Ducks were out at Disneyland where they belonged, and the Raiders and the Ram Chops were trying to see who could pull out of the area first.

Sometimes, in some small ways such as these, life stank.

Then there were the larger issues in his life.

Ed Van Allen had served more than a quarter century in the Los Angeles Police Department. He had come on the job a few weeks before the Tate-LoBianco slayings and was still suffering through the carnival of the Nicole Simpson–Ron Goldman slayings. (To keep his priorities in order, Van Allen always remembered cases by the names of the victim, never the accused, even a celebrity accused after the fact.) Over the course of twenty-five years, he had seen too much and forgotten almost none of it. And nothing in that quarter century had done anything to convince him of the ultimate goodness of mankind.

Quite the contrary.

And recently, this line of thought had joined a growing list of things bothering him. If he really pressed the point, he feared that deep down he really knew the reason for his disquietude.

Lately, also without quite knowing why, a general edginess had set upon him. He attributed it to an unpleasant anniversary. It had been on the first of the preceding October that he and his wife, after several unpleasant years, had terminated the marriage that had occupied the better part of two decades.

Their children were grown. His daughter Celia was currently selling pottery and cohabiting with a twice-divorced bisexual man twelve years older than she in Eugene, Oregon. The last time Van Allen had seen Celia, she looked as if she were dressed like a nun.

His son Jason was doing better. Jason was currently caught up in the state university system. The boy was at the University of California at Santa Clara. There he manifested healthy male traits: he chased coeds and played baseball. To his father's pleasure, he actually was doing quite well with both.

So it wasn't exactly as if a family unit had been put asunder. But at an age when the prospects of a pipe and slippers and some simple uncomplaining female companionship had seemed like a welcome vision at the end of each day, Margaret had started talking about her independence.

Her life. Her freedom. Her resentments . . .

For years he groaned every time the subject arose. Who in God's name had put these ideas in her head. What magazines had she gotten hold of? What militant feminist tract had she taken to heart?

Eventually, all of this culminated in her desire for a divorce.

"Maybe I'll even go back to school," she had once said to him at the lawyer's office.

"To learn what?"

"There you go. Belittling me," she said. "Suggesting that I'm dumb."

"I didn't suggest anything," he had answered. "Did anyone hear me make a suggestion? I *asked* what you wanted to study."

She had turned toward her lawyer.

"This is the type of thing I'm talking about," she told her mouthpiece. "This is what I've been putting up with all these years. Any new idea, he rejects."

"*What* new idea?" he had demanded. "I don't hate new ideas. What are we talking about? Education for women? Divorce? These are new ideas?"

"See?" Margaret asked again. "He can't deal with the modern woman in the contemporary world."

"*What?*" Van Allen had pleaded.

Her lawyer, a guy named Rob Swain, nodded indulgently and assured her that he couldn't have agreed more. She must have suffered horribly over eighteen years of holy matrimony, Swain suggested silkily. Mental torture. A prison without walls, he said.

If ever Van Allen had wanted to brutalize a civilian, this was it.

Swain knew just how to kindle, then fan, the emotional fire. And, of course, the counselor's eyes told Van Allen another story, that the hired mouthpiece hadn't a clue, either, when it came to women but was willing to noisily defend Margaret, nonetheless. Two months later, on one memorable evening, Van Allen also spotted them together at a Pasadena restaurant.

Van Allen wondered whether she was making a dent in the legal fees that night. But that was another story.

"I'm out-of-date, perhaps," Van Allen told himself when the divorce was final. "But at least I'm a man loyal to his own generation. There is nothing dishonorable about holding fast to certain standards of decency. Or morality. Redwoods are out-of-date, too,'' he further concluded, ''but they, too, can stand tall in all weather.''

It was an apt metaphor, for Ed Van Allen, particularly for an LA cop, was a bit of a tree-hugger. He had gone through university himself, holding a degree in criminology from San Francisco State. He had been in the foggy city by the bay as a kid of twenty-four during the heyday of Haight-Ashbury and the Summer of Love in 1968. Coming from a working-class family (his father had been a fireman in Palo Alto), he had sympathized with bedrock, conservative American values.

Yet the sixties counterculture had pulled him, too. The San Francisco Bands. Big Brother and the Holding Company. The Jefferson Airplane. And above all, the Grateful Dead. In the study in his Pasadena home, carefully mounted on his wall, was a rack containing his tapes of Dead concerts. He figured that for many years he had been one of the few cops regularly in attendance at Dead concerts not working as an undercover narc, just as today, he was one of the few LA cops to live in Pasadena, instead of the Simi Valley. He had long since stopped going to the concerts—too many conflicts of duty when he saw Feds and local crew cuts swooping down on kids with two joints while the real pushers were selling genuinely dangerous stuff in capsules twenty feet away. These days, just as his thoughts had turned inward overall, so had his appreciation of Garcia, Weir, and whoever else was still alive in the band. He would appreciate his tapes at home, or hook the band up to his headphones or car cassette player. But no more concerts in person. Too bad.

He nursed his beer and his thoughts returned to the present. Today, in his darkest moments, when he had time to reflect upon the end of his marriage, he wondered if someone (or for that matter *who*) had intentionally fed some feminist claptrap to Margaret. If so, it had gone into her as neatly as a refill into a Pez dispenser. Then again, in Van Allen's better moments, he saw a fantasy vision of himself remarried to some thirty-year-old fox whom he might see rollerblading on the promenade at Santa Monica.

Most moments, however, fell into the vast gray area in between.

He finished his sandwich. The late news concluded on the television.

David Letterman came on. Van Allen channel surfed up to Jay Leno, then took a tour around the dial. Some beach volleyball would have fit his mood. Hard-bodied babes in bathing suits. The sun. The shore. Yeah! How could any straight guy reject that?

Which reminded him: a trip to the shore was imminent.

Detective Ed Van Allen made a point every week of driving out to Santa Monica or Long Beach or Huntington Beach or even Malibu—anywhere convenient where the eastern tides of the Pacific touched the California sands.

The ocean renewed him. Always had. Always would.

Just being about to gaze upon it, to reflect upon its vastness, its capacity to always be the same yet never exactly be the same.

Sometimes he would sit for hours on a favorite bench in Santa Monica, a stone's heave from the old pier, and look out toward Asia, often accompanied by music on a Sony Walkman. Sometimes he did it when he finished a case. Sometimes it gave him a chance to reflect during a case. But always, *always,* once a week at minimum, he went to the ocean.

It knocked the cobwebs out of his head. Better yet, it revivified his soul. He knew he made a strange picture as a cop, a mellowed-out guy in his early fifties, packing a nine-millimeter automatic and headphones. But he could have cared less. After walking the earth for more than a half century, at least he knew who he was.

He continued to channel surf.

He had just cleared a case that evening, a bunch of Guatemalan car thieves. Illegals, naturally. After five weeks of work, Van Allen and two undercovers had managed to book half a dozen of them. They were enjoying free food, free legal advice, and free medical care as Van Allen sat channel surfing. There was even a *pro bono* (or pro-bonehead, as Van Allen liked to call them) ACLU lawyer studying whether the Guatemalans deserved political asylum.

Van Allen's thumb stopped on the button of the channel zapper. Now here was something. ESPN had real live rodeo, taped earlier in Montana.

Van Allen grinned. Bad-assed rednecks wrestling with longhorned dairy cows—or so it looked even if that weren't quite the case. A few minutes later, he turned the television off.

There were a pair of sliding glass doors in the living room of Van Allen's apartment, doors which led out to a small private balcony. The balcony overlooked a public park.

Van Allen walked to the doors and slid them open. He did this to allow himself to step out into the night air and enjoy the stars. But he did this for a second reason, too. And he might just as well admit it to himself.

Deep down, he had plenty of suspicions as to the origins of the creepy feeling that was now unbanishable within him:

There was the anniversary of his divorce. Then, with the wife and kids all gone, there was the gnawing loneliness he felt coming home to an empty apartment each night. Then there were the signposts of retirement which faced him. And there were daily reminders now that, although he had passed his personal half century in age, the years were finally starting to catch up with him.

Physically.

His muscles weren't as taut as they used to be. His favorite jeans were a bit too snug. So were some of his shirt collars. To his undying chagrin, he had recently caught himself massaging the gently sagging flesh under his chin in the hopes of tightening it.

Mentally.

He sometimes wondered if he were more forgetful than he used to be. To counter this, he had started writing more notes whenever he came to a new case.

Spiritually.

Hell, he hadn't been to church for years, other than Easter, Christmas, and funerals. But then again, he told himself, it didn't take too much more than that to be a good Protestant. But he also wondered if he might be missing something. He'd been in Southern California for almost all his life and still had a good appreciation of an entertainment industry anecdote.

It was said that W.C. Fields, an outspoken atheist in his lifetime, had begun reading the Bible on his deathbed. When asked why, Fields had explained: "I'm looking for the loopholes." In a less caustic way, Van Allen wondered if he felt much the same way.

He grimaced. So what was he? An aging half-hippie with a badge, contemplating the final third of his life?

Maybe. It was an interesting interpretation, he told himself. But none of this really nailed the target.

What really tortured him was this deep down, unyielding inexpressible sense of *imminence*. Ed Van Allen's instincts were skills he had spent a lifetime developing. His feelings, if the truth were known, were something that he felt bordered on the psychic, though he never would have described it exactly that way.

He was sitting on a big-time premonition, and not a very nice one. Never mind his age, and never mind everything else that had ever happened to him. He had a feeling that his life would soon be divided between everything that had gone before and everything that would follow this impending event.

What the hell was going to happen? he wondered. Phrased

differently, what could possibly transpire that already hadn't happened in his twenty-five years as a cop?

His death?

Is *that* what this was a premonition of? Is *that* what was behind this feeling that had virtually haunted him for the past few weeks while he'd been chasing car thieves through Altadena?

He sensed that he was soon going to die?

Was *that* it?

In the warm reassuring sunshine of recent daytimes, he scoffed at the notion. At night, sometimes wakeful with a sweat on his brow, the notion wasn't quite so funny. At age fifty-two, he had outlived more friends and peers than he cared to count.

He could hardly have described the feeling to even his most intimate friends, this gnawing in his gut, this little blue pilot flame on the other side of his subconscious. But if he had been asked for a metaphor, he would have likened it to standing on the other side of some bizarre door that was just about to open.

He had no idea what was on the other side of the door. He only knew that he was on the bright side, the side with the sunshine. The other side seethed with darkness.

There was no rational logic to what he felt. No signs in the sky. No demonstrable event to which he could point.

But what intuitive man's feelings were ever stopped by the lack of a logical argument?

He felt. He sensed. *He knew!*

So impatiently, he waited.

And, before all hell broke loose, he longed to go see the ocean again.

8

Rebecca walked into the turret room and drew a breath.

She stood perfectly still and listened. She heard nothing. She saw nothing. She felt nothing.

She stood still again and, with a twinge of anxiety, inhaled deeply through her nose. The odor in the room? It, too, was gone.

There, she told herself, this was an ordinary room like any other. Nothing wrong with it. Everything had been in her imagination. She moved to the window and opened it halfway, looking toward San Angelo Cemetery for a fleeting second.

She put a screen in the window and adjusted it. The screen didn't fit perfectly, but it would have to do. That was the thing about old houses, she reminded herself. Nothing fit anything perfectly anymore.

But the fragrance of a coral tree wafted in with the fresh air. The screen would serve just fine, she concluded. And she was starting to feel pretty good, pretty comfortable, about the task before her: painting the room a bright yellow.

She turned and surveyed the room. Yes, she had conquered her trepidations. Never mind the funny vibrations that Bill had given her. She was pleased with herself.

She went to her bedroom and retrieved a radio. She brought

it back and plugged it in. Reception proved difficult in the turret room. But she would have herself a party as she painted. KROQ all the way. Some good hard head-pounding rock would keep her jagged-up. She had attacked more than one apartment or house with brushes, rollers, and gallons of paint in her life: blasting rock music was an essential ingredient to the experience.

She fussed with the radio.

"Damn," she muttered to herself.

Reception in this room *just stank!* She tapped the radio slightly. She tried to reposition it. The receiver wasn't the newest one in the world. Maybe it just wasn't strong enough to pick up the signals. Not with that big old tree outside.

Then, on the other hand, she had never heard of a tree interfering with radio reception. So maybe there was something in the walls. A sheet of aluminum or some old wiring. Who knew in California? Or in any old house? Anything was possible. She made a note to ask Bill to have a look sometime.

Well, nothing would stop her today, she decided. She went to the den, located her battery powered cassette player and walked it back to the room. There would be no interference with tapes.

Guilty pleasures came along with her. A handful of tapes: Paul Simon. Billy Joel. Heart. Some new stuff that her husband hated: Concrete Blonde. Pearl Jam. R.E.M.

Yeah, she told herself. R.E.M. was the ticket today. She got some music going. *Monster.* Nice and boisterous. The music made her feel good. Bill would have loathed music like this. She put aside more R.E.M. to play next. *Automatic For The People.* Then she set about her task.

She swept the empty room. Then she put down drop cloths. She moved the brushes and rollers into the center of the room and positioned the tape player on the other side from where she would start work.

She surveyed the walls. They were white and smooth from

the stripping Bill had done and the primer he had applied. The walls were ready for her.

She shook a gallon can of paint. With a screwdriver she pried the first can open. She picked up a wooden stick that reminded her of a giant tongue depressor and she stirred.

She poured the thick yellow paint into a tin, tied back her hair, and donned a painter's cap. She selected the largest, flattest, least complicated wall and moved the tin to it. She began to paint.

The music filled the room. The paint went on smoothly and evenly. "Losing My Religion." Well, she had lost hers long ago, so who cared about the thought? She sang along with Michael Stipe. The tape eventually auto-reversed and she gave it a second play.

She finished the first wall in fifty minutes, including the trim. Rebecca was filled with a sense of accomplishment. She began the wall with the window and knocked off half of it quickly, carefully edged her way around the window, and went to the other side. She finished.

She stepped back and was on a roll. She began painting the third wall, another flat rectangular one with no uneven areas. And she realized she was out of paint.

She stepped back again and examined her work. She pondered whether to take a break. No, she decided, she would open the second can and keep going. It was barely past 11:00 A.M. What a sense of accomplishment she would have if she finished the whole damned room before lunch!

She clicked off the cassette player for a moment and switched tapes. She pried open the second gallon of yellow paint and poured a third of it into the tin.

The paint gurgled. Rebecca stopped. What *else* had she just heard? A noise somewhere in the house? Somewhere just beyond the door.

Then, for half a moment, Rebecca caught a whiff of that

smell that had bothered her. She smelled it—or thought she had—and then it was gone.

She looked toward the door and a feeling was upon her. A feeling that told her she was not alone. It was that instinct again. That sense of being watched. Her first indication way back in Connecticut that there was trouble.

She felt it again. She wasn't sure whether she was imagining it or whether it was the real thing.

Suddenly, she was very cautious.

She called. "Hello?"

No answer.

"Anyone there?" her voice again. Still no response.

She was hoping that Bill had come home unexpectedly. Or that Melissa had let herself in.

She went to the door. There was a creak somewhere in the hallway. She looked. Nothing. The floor creaked again, right before her eyes. She was looking right at the very spot that had creaked and she could not see anything.

A shudder was upon her. She was abruptly very scared. Reason told her not to be, but instincts told her that something was there. Something she couldn't see.

"No," she said softly. "This isn't happening. And I'm not scared."

She decided to prove it to herself. She would go back to work, ignore everything, and prove to herself what a brave woman she was.

Fear was in her mind, she told herself, and she was the mistress of her own mind. She would exorcise her own private demons and that would be the end of them.

She started the second tape cassette. More R.E.M. She filled the room with it, poured fresh yellow paint in the tin, and went to work on the third wall.

Now this was really weird. The music that she thought she heard so subliminally was still audible. It was still faint and in the background of her mind. But she could *hear* it beneath the sound of R.E.M.

Angrily, she turned. She reached to the cassette player.

"Damn!" she said. She had turned so quickly that two big drops of paint hit the player.

But she ignored the paint and turned the player off. And she *still* heard that subliminal tune. Only now it had taken a very recognizable form. There was a pattern to the music, though it resembled no song that she had ever before known.

"Jesus," she mumbled to herself. "What instrument is that? What am I hearing?"

Then she realized that there was no instrument at all. It was a human voice. A man's voice humming some damnable melody. And it was inside her head.

Then, as mysteriously as it had appeared, it was gone. She couldn't hear it anymore. There was a stark stillness in the room and suddenly a loud bang.

Right before Rebecca's eyes, the screen collapsed from where it had held the window open. The screen flew into the room as if thrown. It skidded toward her and Rebecca moved her feet fast to avoid it, though it stopped before it hit her. The bang, however, had come from the window sash, which crashed down in the absence of the screen.

It had slammed shut. Hard! Real hard.

Rebecca stepped back from the window and stared at it. Her heart kicked furiously. What she had seen was something that could not have happened. The window couldn't just slam shut like that. The screen had been secure. She knew because she had wedged the screen into the window herself.

And yet, it had come down so fast that, had she not seen it herself, she would have sworn a strong man had shoved it.

Bravely, she approached the window. She placed a cautious hand on the top of the lower panes. She ran her fingers across it. Nothing unusual.

She listened. Yes, she could hear the music again, that damnable tune. Sounded like a man humming somewhere.

Somewhere.

"Yeah, Dr. Einhorn," she said aloud. "It's all in my head. It's all because someone tried to kill me in Fairfield, Connecticut."

Then it stopped again.

There was another old house creak in the floorboards. She turned. Nothing. This was the creepiest damned room she had ever encountered in her life.

The odor was back. It worsened. It smelled like . . .

Like what?

Dead something.

Dead what?

A dead man, Rebecca?

"What?" she asked aloud, as if someone had addressed her. But no one had. No one she could find.

She turned back to the window. She raised it again letting in some fresh air. A whole blast of it. She held the window open in the spot where it had been earlier. How on earth could it have fallen by itself? The sash was *stubborn!* There was no way it could have collapsed the way it had.

But, of course, it *had* happened. Right before her eyes.

She fixed the screen in the window again, doing it in such a way that her hands were never at risk if the sash dropped again.

She stepped back. Still, the music. She could hear the humming. God damn it! Where was it coming from?

She looked at the window. Bright day outside. Autumn in Southern California. A shadow—a cloud—passed over the sun.

"Maybe the kids won't even be happy in this room," she started to tell herself. "Maybe this room should be used as . . ."

. . . as what?

A reading room. Or a sewing room. Something that Bill and she could use. Hell, she found herself thinking next. Bill could have the damned room. Pointless to put the kids at risk.

Risk?

She asked herself. What in hell was she thinking about? What sort of risk? Deep down, what was she thinking about this room? What was in it that she couldn't see? What was she feeling? What was the source of her moods involving this part of the house?

Another bang! A loud one! Deafening! Right behind her!

"Oh, shit!" a voice filled the room. A woman's voice. Her own. A scream in her throat. The door had slammed. Or someone had slammed it!

She was terrified.

She turned and went to the door, half–scared to death of what might be on the other side.

"Bill?" she called. *"Bill!"* she screamed.

No answer.

She put her hand on the doorknob and tried to turn it. It wouldn't give. Wouldn't turn. Not in the slightest.

"Oh, shit! *Oh, shit!"* she yelled. The knob. That damned stubborn doorknob again. It wouldn't budge.

She yelled and pounded on it and yanked at the door.

"Open this! Open the door! Who's there? Bill, if that's you, this isn't funny!"

She pulled the knob again but it was the same way it had been when she had first come through the house with Essie Lewisohn. It wouldn't give.

The knob was as firm and steady as if a strong male hand were holding it on the other side.

Then her worst fears came true. She released the knob. She watched it.

The knob turned and settled very slightly—as if there *had* been a hand on the other side, a hand that had subsequently released it. She stepped back from it.

She stood in the partly painted room and tried to get her breath. She tried to summon a calm line of thought. She tried to think.

What to do? How could she escape?

Go to the window and jump? She would surely break a leg or an ankle in the fall. She was two flights up and these were high floors. The ground below was uneven.

Rebecca made a decision.

She walked back to the door and placed her hand again on the knob. She turned it slowly, her heart pounding in her chest.

She leaned to the door. She found words forming in her throat. In her eyes were something close to tears.

"Whoever you are," she said softly and emotionally, "please let me out of here. I've done nothing to you. I mean you no harm. But you're terrifying me . . ." She paused. She thought herself a fool, speaking like that in the empty house.

But she wondered next, *was* it so empty?

"Whoever you are," she said again, "I've done nothing to you. I am not your enemy."

For a split second, in her mind, flashed an image of the horrible man from the shopping mall, the werewolf-visaged killer in the wraparound sunglasses.

Then that image dissipated and she stepped back. In a funny sort of way, she felt some sort of wave of relaxation overtake her, or overtake the room. Like the drop in barometric pressure before a storm.

"Please . . ." she whispered again. "Do you just want me to admit that I know you're there?" she asked. "You just want me to acknowledge you? Is that all?"

She reached to the doorknob again. She placed her hand on it and tried one more time to leave the turret room.

The knob held firmly, as if the strong hand was still on the other side. Then, it eased. Rebecca could feel some pressure relent from the other side of the door.

Go ahead, something told her. Try the knob again.

She did. And it turned without hesitation.

Then the door began to move. She pulled it inward until it was wide open. She felt a breeze rush past her—ventilation from the window—and she stood on the landing in the hallway, looking in every direction.

"Bill?" she called softly. "Karen? Patrick?"

But she knew there would be no response from a family member. No one was home.

She walked slowly through the second floor hallway of her home, convinced that someone was there, equally knowing that no one could be. To reassure herself, she looked in each room.

The master bedroom where she and Bill slept was exactly the way she had left it. A glance into Karen's room and Patrick's room revealed the same. No movement. No sign of anyone since the kids had left for school. She stood at the top of the stairs, listened and thought.

She sighed. Dr. Einhorn and his stress. Dr. Einhorn told her things like this would happen. She had to firmly reject fantasy and tenaciously hold reality. "Yes, Dr. Einhorn," she whispered aloud, "I am listening to your good advice."

She walked back to the turret room, entered it, and stopped short. Now she really *was* losing her mind! The pan and roller were not where she remembered leaving them. They were closer to the door. And the cassette player, which she remembered turning off, was on. It was playing softly.

And the tapes had been switched! Paul Simon singing softly about a girl with diamonds on the soles of her shoes.

Rebecca raised her eyes and blinked. At first a surge of fear—or shock—was upon her. Then things settled as she convinced herself that her memory was playing tricks on her again.

Especially short term, Dr. Einhorn had warned her.

And *especially short term* was exactly what this would

have to be called. How else could it be explained that the painting was complete on the third wall? Or that she had put the wrong tape into the cassette player?

She stared at the room. Damn it, she was *certain* that she had left the third wall unfinished. She was *certain* that she had been interrupted with less than half of it complete.

But there it was. All done.

By a helping hand? A helping *invisible* hand?

No, no, no, Rebecca told herself. Such things didn't exist. Short-term memory loss, coupled with the distraction of the door blowing shut. She must have painted the third wall herself.

Must have.

She let the cassette play. Paul Simon settled her, a mellow soothing voice that reminded her of being twenty years old and in love.

She drew a breath and set to work again. The wall that contained the door was easy. She had it done in another thirty minutes. Then she poured out some white paint, took a three-inch brush in hand, and deftly did the trim and woodwork around the window and doorframe.

Then she stepped back. The door was done.

"That's one small step for Becca, one giant leap for Becca's sanity," she said to herself. And a whiff of beautifully scented autumn air blew in the window from the coral tree.

A thought arrived with the scent. It was as if someone had thrown her an invisible bouquet.

So, "Thank you," she said aloud.

There was a tap on the wall. One short tap. She felt goose bumps again and did everything she could to ignore it.

She turned her attention to the cleanup. Secretly, or maybe not so secretly, she just wanted to be out of that room.

She sealed the cans of paint and left them in the hallway, in case she needed to touch up later. She took the rollers and brushes to the basement and washed them.

Then she went back upstairs, picked up the drop cloth, and admired her work.

No smell. No noise. No humming. The screen stayed in the window and, she told herself, she was as sane as anyone else on the block.

In the evening, after the children had gone to sleep, she sat in bed with her husband. Music played softly on a bedside radio. He was reading. She was thinking. It was past eleven.

"Why do I feel so strange in there?" she asked.

"What?"

"Bill?" She turned to him. "Please put down your book for a minute and listen to me."

"Hmmm?"

She repeated. It took an extra second for her message to sink in. Gently, she reached to the book he was reading and lifted it from his hands.

"It's important," she said.

"Okay," he said. "I can take a hint."

She told him about the events of the day, what had transpired in the turret room.

"I want to know," she said. "First off, why do I feel so damned strange in that room? It's as if there's something wrong with the room itself."

He gazed at her. For a moment she thought she saw something in his eyes that she didn't like. Then it was gone.

"There's nothing wrong with that room. And there is nothing wrong with this house, either, if that's what you're going to suggest next."

"Then why do I feel so strange in that room?" she demanded.

"Your imagination."

"I don't think it is," she said.

"Rebecca," he reminded her. "Rational thought, okay? Isn't that what Dr. Miller and Dr. Einhorn have been asking you to limit yourself to?"

"Why did the screen blow out of the window?"

"It couldn't have been lodged in the window properly."

"I put it in myself. *Carefully.*"

"After the fact, you think you put it in carefully," he corrected her. "The truth is you probably just kind of balanced it in. Admit it."

"Why did the window close?"

"Why do you think?" he asked with an air of hostility. "Gravity. These are old windows with lead counterweights within the frame. Very well constructed, by the way."

"Come on, Bill . . ."

"What do you mean, 'come on'? This is an old house. Things like that happen all the time."

"Why did the door slam shut?"

"A strong air current. You said yourself that you had just reopened the window."

"Why did the door stick?"

He sighed with disappointment. "It stuck for Essie, too," he reminded her in a fatigued voice. "Humidity. The wood expanded and then the door slammed hard. It is not in any way surprising that it could get wedged in the doorframe."

"I pulled and pulled and pulled. It wouldn't move."

"And the latch is old."

"Bill, it felt like there was a *hand* on the latch!"

"Want me to phone Dr. Einhorn right now?" It was a bluff and she knew it. But it meant that Bill was getting quarrelsome, impatient with her, and weary of this line of conversation. She was unsatisfied with the conversation, but knew it was time to back off.

"Look," he finally said, offering her a small compromise,

"I'll change the latch tomorrow. Will that make you feel better?"

"Thank you. It might."

"Want me to change the knob, too?"

"Yes. I wish you would." She folded her arms across her breasts.

She let a few seconds pass. He tried to pick up his book again. She wouldn't let him.

"Bill," she said. "If I had to testify in court, I'd swear that there was someone on the other side of the door."

"Refer back to the answer to your first question."

"Which was . . . ?"

"The question or the answer?"

"Either."

"Expanded answer. Here goes," he said with irritation. "Your hyperactive imagination. That's why you feel that. Come on, Becca. We've been through this too many times now. You're not doing yourself any favors by indulging your macabre imagination."

She snuggled close to him, wanting to feel safe, wishing he would put an arm around her. He didn't. She felt alone in the world. She felt like phoning her mother, but it was too late in the evening.

"You almost seem to want to drive me to Dr. Einhorn," she said. "You want me to think that I'm mentally imbalanced."

"Becca," he said with utmost patience, "tell me this: Why would I be taking you to a renowned doctor who can do nothing except help you? Answer me that if you think I'm your enemy."

"I didn't say you were my enemy," she said. "I—"

"You're treating me as if I'm your enemy," he said tersely. "And I really don't like it."

She leaned back into her pillow. She closed her eyes, and

shook her head, taking solace within herself. The only place she could find it.

"I know," she finally said in a small voice. "I know. I'm being silly. I'm being crazy."

"Let's stop using that word," he said. " 'Crazy.' I don't want to hear it again. All I want is my wife back, the well-balanced fun girl that I married. Okay?"

He placed a hand on one of hers. She almost cringed at the gesture. It was a hand of obligation, not affection. Not support. It was an effort to shut her up. He didn't believe a thing she was saying and had no interest in addressing her fears.

She thought about it and wasn't happy.

"Okay," she finally said. Bill kissed her on the side of the face. His arm went around her for a moment and gave her a brief hug. Then he withdrew it. The hug was similar to the hand. It lacked passion and conviction.

Her husband's answers had been paragons of rationality, which was perhaps why she had resented them. They were concise. They had made sense in terms of a rational, predictable world. But they still didn't settle her.

Somehow, what was bothering her was outside of the field of rationality. And that in itself proved troublesome for her to accept. And she was afraid to even mention that wall in the turret room that she didn't even remember painting.

Her gaze drifted to the window and beyond. It stayed there for several moments. Bill resumed reading. Now it was twenty past eleven by the bedside clock, an hour when they normally turned off the light.

But Rebecca felt she would not be able to sleep without certain answers. Her gaze traveled through the room and returned to her husband.

"Bill," she asked slowly, "will you do me a favor?"

"What?" he asked.

"Will you put that book down and talk to me. I'm your wife and I need your help."

He sighed. He turned to face her and said nothing.

"Now, tell me two things with complete honesty," she said. "I don't want you to spare my feelings and I don't want you to mince words. All right?"

He closed his book for the night. He put it on the bedside table on his side. He looked back to her.

"What two things?" he asked.

"Do you think I'm crazy?"

"I think you should continue to see Dr. Einhorn," he said.

"That doesn't answer my question."

"Honey, I—"

"Do you think I'm *crazy?* Am I losing my mind?"

His hand moved under the covers and settled upon her bare knee.

"I think you've had a hell of a case of emotional trauma," he said. "And because of that, I don't think you're seeing things too straight. Not all the time. Just some of the time," he said.

His voice was finally reassuring, at least a little bit. "And if you think about it, deep down," he said, "you probably *know* that's the case."

"Am I crazy or not?" she insisted.

"No. You're not crazy."

He finally folded an arm around her and kept it there. Finally, it felt good. Warm. Supportive. Comforting. "But you should continue to see the doctor," he said.

"All right. I know," she sighed. "I'm continuing."

A long moment passed. There was a noise in Patrick's room. It startled Rebecca for a moment. But then she realized that it sounded suspiciously like a basketball rolling softly across the floor, a little up-past-bedtime boy putting it away carefully so that his parents couldn't hear. She decided, in light of the moment, that she'd let it go for a few minutes.

"There's another question," she said.

"What's that? Sex tonight? What position? What room?"

"It's a serious question, Bill."

"Shoot me with it."

"Have you ever felt anything strange in the turret room?" she asked.

A funny sensation went through his arm, as if he stiffened slightly. She felt it. It caused her to look him in the eye.

"Well?" she asked when he didn't answer promptly. "*Have* you?"

"What sort of thing?" he asked.

"Stop fending off the question and answer," she demanded. "*Any*thing strange or unusual? A feeling or an occurrence? Come on, Bill, you know what 'anything' means!"

He was silent for a second, then looked at her and shrugged. "No," he said. "I haven't felt anything in that room. Nothing at all."

She turned away and looked back toward the window. She couldn't shake the impression that he was lying.

"Okay," she finally said. "Thank you."

Before turning out the lights for the night, she checked Patrick's room. The basketball had indeed taken a roll on its own, or so it appeared. She picked it up and put it into a toy box. Patrick, she told herself, had probably gone to sleep with the basketball on his bed.

Rebecca glanced at the turret room as she returned to the master bedroom. The door was firmly closed. Warily, she even checked it. And that was just the way she wanted it. She left a light on in the hall and returned to her bed.

Bill turned the light out after she was settled.

She was able to sleep, but not without some unease. There was a feeling that was nagging her, and it wasn't even from the events of the afternoon.

Just before drifting off, she realized what it was.

That funny tune was flitting around in her mind again, but even *that* wasn't it. Rather, after living with a man for so long, she knew when he was lying to her.

And "lie" was written all over his answer to her final question. Had he ever experienced anything strange in the turret room? What had it been, she wondered, that he hadn't told her?

Her thoughts went weird as a half sleep claimed her.

Well, she concluded, if she couldn't trust Bill anymore, at least she could trust her children. And Melissa. She could trust Melissa. Plus, there was always Dr. Einhorn, too. Another instinctive feeling: at least there was *someone* watching over her.

The next day she continued her assault on the turret room.

She went to a flea market and bought a twelve-by-twelve carpet remnant. Great purchase. Only twenty bucks. At a thrift shop, she found a couple of cabinets that could be used for toys and games. Then she went to IKEA again and found a chest of drawers that could be used for play clothing. Item by item she brought her purchases back to the house. Conveniently, Melissa arrived in the driveway and quickly became part of the day's operation, helping Rebecca carry furniture upstairs.

"Where you going next?" Melissa asked toward 1:00 P.M.

"I thought I'd buy some classy, expensive curtains for the window," Rebecca said. "Any suggestions?"

"Von's," Melissa suggested.

The two women laughed and were in the car again. Rebecca found exactly what she needed. Something cheap that didn't look cheap. Melissa helped her hang the curtains. They were a dark navy blue with some red and yellow pinstripes through them. They hung perfectly and looked just right. On the final foray of the day, they found some posters in a variety store. Sports, ballet, and wildlife. The posters would fill the walls and add some color for a net expenditure of twelve bucks.

Once again, perfect. Rebecca was on a roll.

Rebecca and Melissa moved the furniture into the room that afternoon. They put up the posters. Together, over sandwiches and Diet Cokes, they assembled the chest. Then they stood back and admired what they had done.

"Nice job, partner," Rebecca said, taking Melissa's hand in a congratulatory shake.

"You did everything," Melissa said. "The room is *you* now."

And not Ronny's room anymore. It's Patrick and Karen's playroom, and that's final. She thought this but didn't say it. She hoped Bill would be pleased when he returned home.

She congratulated herself further. She had done a good job here, she told herself. She was a great wife and mother. One of the all-time greats, she laughed.

Then, no, she told herself, that feeling was *not* upon her again. That gnawing in her gut. Here she had freshly scrubbed the turret room, painted it a nice sunny yellow, and she still thought she had just caught a whiff of that sour, bitter smell that had followed her from the first day.

She stood still. She cocked her head. "Melissa?" she asked.

Her friend was admiring the job they had done on the IKEA chest.

"What, honey?"

"Goddamn it!"

Melissa's brow furrowed into an anxious frown. Rebecca could hear that pesky music again.

"Do you hear anything? Or smell anything strange?"

Melissa listened. The tune seemed to cease.

"I hear Maurice Lerner's mutt barking a couple of doors down, if that's what you mean."

"That's not what I mean."

Melissa shook her head. She didn't hear anything else. Then she sniffed at the air.

"There's a scent to the new carpet. That usually disappears in a few days. And I can still smell fresh paint."

"That's not what I mean."

Eye to eye across the room, Rebecca looked at her friend. Then Melissa glanced away.

"There's nothing wrong here, honey," Melissa said. "Stop worrying about everything. This is a beautiful room. You'll learn to love it, okay."

"But do you smell anything?" Rebecca pressed.

Eye contact returned. Now there was something in Melissa's eyes that Rebecca didn't like. Something she saw. Or thought she saw. Why, Rebecca wanted to know, was the whole world against her.

"Nothing, Becca," Melissa said. "I hear nothing and smell nothing other than what I just told you."

"All right," Rebecca said softly. "Thank you."

Why, Rebecca wondered, was the whole world so anxious to lie to her?

But the smell was gone and so was that subliminal tune. So she drew a breath and accepted her small victories where she could find them.

After all, she had dressed the room over in her image. If that wasn't the first step of reclaiming it, she didn't know what was.

9

Detective Ed Van Allen was home having coffee when the telephone rang at a few minutes after 1:00 P.M.

Van Allen looked at the phone in his kitchen and did not pick up. He had worked a double shift the previous day closing a case against a Cambodian fencing operation. The day's work had culminated in a night court appearance and the associated paperwork. It had kept him on duty until 6:00 A.M. Van Allen wasn't due at his office until four that afternoon. So when the phone rang, he growled.

He considered letting his answering machine do the dirty work. But deep down, owing to a perverse dedication to his job, he felt that answering machines were cowardly. So on the fourth ring, he grabbed it.

"Van Allen," he mumbled into the handset. His voice was striking in its lack of enthusiasm.

His own voice also echoed in his ear. It was the first word he had spoken since waking and—to his own thinking—his pipes sounded rusty. Almost creaking and elderly.

So he cleared his throat immediately after speaking and said his name more forcefully a second time. Then he listened.

The call came not from any fellow policeman or from his headquarters asking him to come in. It wasn't even a fellow detective advising him that the gang of Guatemalan car thieves whom he'd just spent five weeks trying to arrest had already been released on their own recognizance. That call had come late the previous afternoon.

Rather, this call came from one Armando Martinez, the seventy-year-old caretaker at the San Angelo Cemetery.

"I was wondering. Can you stop in here on your rounds today?" Martinez asked.

"You okay, Armando?"

"I'm okay, fine," Martinez said. "No danger. But something here you should see."

"Where are you? At San Angelo?" Van Allen asked.

"Yes, sir."

"I could come by on my way to my office. Between three and four this afternoon."

Martinez gave Van Allen a respectful hesitation in response. The hesitation told Van Allen that sooner would be better than later.

"The thing is, Detective," Martinez said, "I want you to see before anybody comes by and changes things. See this just happened. Or must have just happened."

"*What* happened, Armando?"

"I don't know, Mr. Edmund, sir," the caretaker said. "Maybe you will tell me."

Van Allen rubbed his tired eyes. If it hadn't been this call from Martinez, it would have been something else. There was never a moment's peace in this world for a conscientious policeman, never a moment when a man could grab a morning coffee a few minutes after noon and enjoy it plus the sports section without interruption.

"I'll be there shortly," he answered. "Is that good enough?"

Martinez said that it was.

Van Allen found a piece of coffee cake from the previous day. He nuked it in his microwave for thirty seconds to soften it.

He finished his coffee and pastry. He stuck the cup and a plate into the dishwasher, where they would keep company with the utensils of the previous two days. He fed some soap into the washer, and turned it on. A quarter hour later, he was in his car heading west on the 134, then south on the 5 from his home in Pasadena.

As he drove, he thought of his daughter up in Oregon and his son over at Santa Clara. He wondered how they would carry on if he died suddenly. Then he wondered why he was entertaining that thought. He wondered with whom his former wife was sleeping.

Then that creepy anxious feeling came over him again and he wondered whether it was anything like the feeling that domestic animals like dogs and cats felt right before an earthquake.

Each time he drove beneath a highway overpass, damn it to hell, he got nervous. But he couldn't help it.

Van Allen had known Martinez for a decade and a half. The old Mexican—as he affectionately thought of him—was one of the people in any neighborhood to whom Van Allen had always made a point to pay attention.

Caretakers. Janitors. Doormen. Postmen. Cab drivers. Car jockeys.

Some cops thought of these folks as "the little people," as if they were a pack of leprechauns or dwarfs. Van Allen thought of them as "the important people." He termed them such because that's exactly what they were. The human brick and mortar of any city. Even in a sprawling suburbanized metropolis like Los Angeles, these were the citizens who always had their fingers on the pulse of what was happening.

They followed the same routines five days a week. So they were the first to notice anything unusual. Van Allen had built up a lifetime of contacts and trust among such people. He had learned always to listen to them and to serve them. On occasion, he had risked his life to protect them. In return, people

like Martinez called him first, sometimes even before they di-
aled an emergency number.

They heard things. They saw things. And if Van Allen
played his cards right, they would always talk to him.

To seek protection. Or to let him know what they had seen.
Or what they suspected. Many times over the course of Van
Allen's career, a casual word from such a source had landed
an astonished felon in prison practically before the dust had
settled from a crime.

This call from Martinez, from the caretaker's hut at the entrance to the cemetery, had all the earmarks of one of those
messages.

Van Allen arrived at San Angelo in thirty-five minutes. He
stopped outside the iron gates and parked his car. He gave a
polite toot of his horn.

A lean gray-haired man in an avocado green shirt and an
American Harvester cap came out of the caretaker's hut on the
other side of the gates. The man raised a hand to greet the policeman.

"Hello, Armando," Van Allen said.

Martinez nodded but didn't speak. Van Allen could inter-
pret facial expressions pretty well. He'd spent his adult life
reading them, trying to discern from little twitches, of little
flitting evasions of the eye, who was a homicidal maniac and
who was an innocent victim. He could also read the guarded
expressions of old men like Martinez, to whom something bizarre had befallen. And that's what Van Allen saw here.

Martinez unlocked the gates of San Angelo. Chains and a
padlock rattled against the old iron bars. Idly, as he waited,
Van Allen pictured himself spending his retirement in some
state nuthouse trying to decipher the madness in the eyes of
lunatics.

"Thanks for coming over," Martinez said. "I know LA's
going to hell. But this tops all."

"You don't normally have trouble in this place, do you, Armando?" Van Allen asked.

"Normally, no. You know me, Mr. Edmund, and you know this yard. Ah, but these days, no one's safe. Anything happens." There was a pause. "And this I no understand."

"Show me. Okay?"

"I show you."

Martinez closed the gates behind them. He pulled a chain across the bars and locked them from within. Then they walked side by side, among old headstones and graves.

"You okay? You're not hurt, are you?" Van Allen asked.

The old man looked at the detective. "When my yard is hurt, *I'm* hurt," he said. "Know what I mean?"

Van Allen knew.

As he walked with the caretaker toward the south end of the San Angelo Cemetery, he made casual conversation. But Van Allen had this faculty of carrying on a concise conversation with the forward section of his mind while other lines of thought were being processed in the rear.

Today, that sense of being blobby and aging was upon him again, particularly as he walked through the soft soil of San Angelo. His feet felt unsteady, as if an ankle might buckle at any moment. His unsteadiness angered him; it mocked the usual care that he had taken of himself over so many years. Then, to make things worse, that confounding sense of imminence and anxiety was upon him again, the feeling that had been disturbing him for several days. He wondered whether it was all sort of a basic insecurity that followed every good cop all the way to the grave.

Those words repeated on him, ringing heavily with their irony.

—followed every good cop all the way to the grave.

And there he was with Martinez, traipsing through San Angelo. The Cemetery of Angels. Sometimes life's irony was staring a man right in the face; other times, such as this one, it reared up and bit him on the ass.

Something knocked him back to the present. Martinez was going on and on about the cost of water, the difficulty of keeping San Angelo irrigated and green, and the lack of care by the city of Los Angeles for its old cemeteries in general.

This was a peaceful place in the sunlight, Van Allen found himself thinking next, a spot of rest with open breezes even on the most oppressively hot days across Southern California. In fact, San Angelo was a little jewel of a cemetery, primarily because a man like Martinez had set it as his life's work to keep the place protected. In the recesses of his mind, Van Allen found himself dredging up an old fact: Money from a trust established in the 1920s by Lillian Gish, combined with the shrewd sale of some contiguous real estate over the years, had left San Angelo solvent into the 1990s.

Van Allen felt his concentration flash back to the custodian, but to his shame he wasn't even sure when the topic had changed.

His thoughts drifted again, this time back to his attitude of two and a half decades ago, back when he'd been a trainee out of the LA Police Academy. He had grown up in a working-class neighborhood in Palo Alto, but had been drawn by the sunshine of Southern California. He wanted a job that would keep him there, preferably something that would allow him to help people. The fire department in LA hadn't been recruiting. The police department was. The choice had been that simple. Yet now, today, he sometimes thought he was as ill equipped to deal with the world of 1995 as would be, say, some of the people buried beneath his feet.

And now this.

For Ed Van Allen, not only did life get stranger, it also got worse. Sometimes, there were fewer and fewer explanations for anything. Up ahead about a hundred feet a massive gray marker lay on its side.

Martinez fell silent as they approached. Then the custodian glanced at the detective.

"Almost there," Martinez said. "But you can see it already."

Van Allen's eyes scanned ahead to see what the "it" was. And then he realized that the marker itself, the one that was lying on its side, was their initial destination.

They arrived at it a few seconds later. It was a death monument of solid gray stone. It was about twelve feet in height with a base four foot square. And it was a striking piece, even as it lay on its side.

Van Allen recognized the monument and remembered it from where it had stood. It was the most striking and impressive marker in the entire cemetery. It was the figure of an angel, wings extended majestically, while one arm was raised in a gesture—presumably of peace and salvation, or was it a warning?—and the other hand held the book of God's judgment. Van Allen had never paid much attention to exactly whose grave the marker had adorned. But he remembered it as the angelic centerpiece of the cemetery, a statue that had set the motif for the yard and the style for several lesser tombs over the years.

Cemetery of Angels. And this had been the most prominent of the celestial spirits.

The policeman felt an eerie quickening of his pulse. "This is what you wanted me to see?" Van Allen asked.

The old man nodded. Martinez stared down at the fallen cenotaph and let Detective Van Allen take the first steps of trying to make sense of what lay at his feet.

"Take a good look," Martinez said. "Study careful. Then follow me, there's more."

The inscription on the marker—the part of the inscription that Van Allen could see—was in big bold letters. It said simply, "Billy."

Just "Billy."

The name meant nothing to Van Allen. The detective ran through his mind to try to figure whether the name should have meant something—in terms of the city, in terms of Hollywood or in terms of his own career in law enforcement.

Billy, Billy, Billy, he repeated mentally.

He still came up empty. And the granite marker was lying downward in such a way that the dead individual's first name, last name, and earthly dates were almost impossible to read, although he thought he could see a death date in the 1930s.

"Whose marker is this?" he called to Martinez.

The old man shrugged. "Been there as long as I been here," he said. "Billy something. An old actor. I never knew no more than that."

The caretaker's answer annoyed Van Allen. The detective leaned against the overturned angel and knelt down for a better look. But he still couldn't get the angle to read the inscription and quickly became impatient.

He pushed the marker. It was much too heavy to budge. When Martinez was looking farther down the south lawn of the graveyard, Van Allen put his shoulder to the marker.

He pushed again, much harder this time. He dug his feet into the ground for traction, shoved as hard as he could and felt something softly pop.

"Oh! Damn!" he bellowed. The pop was in his right leg, just below the knee.

Martinez whirled and looked, just in time to see the policeman clutching his right knee.

"What happened?" the custodian demanded, coming over to him.

Now Van Allen was sitting on the marker, massaging his calf.

"I think I pulled something," he said, trying to make as little as possible of the sharp pain below his knee. He'd pulled something real well, and he knew it.

"What were you trying to do?"

"Move the stone a little. I wanted complete name and some dates." He grimaced and tried to mentally dismiss the pain. He still came up empty.

"Man, you pick the wrong marker. That piece got to weigh two thousand five hundred pounds."

"Yeah. I noticed."

Van Allen frowned. "So?" he asked, a little anger starting to creep into his tone. "So tell me what's going on? Whose stone is this? And who the hell overturned it? For that matter, *how* was it overturned?"

Martinez nodded. "Uprooted *and* overturned."

"Vandals?" Van Allen asked. "That's not so unusual in the grand scheme of things?"

"Notice anything unusual?" Martinez asked.

Subliminally, Van Allen had already noticed. Van Allen looked around and still couldn't find the grave that belonged to the marker.

"Okay. No grave. You got me. I know this marker was in the cemetery. Where's the grave? Where's the marker from?"

"That's the thing," the custodian said.

Martinez turned and pointed to a strangely configured gouge in the ground about sixty feet away.

Van Allen was still trying to apply some logic. "Way over there?" he asked. As soon as he had spoken, he understood the long distance that the stone seraph had traveled.

"You haven't even gotten to the worst of it," Martinez said. "Come over here to the grave."

Something told Van Allen that he actually would have lived a happier life if he could have left the cemetery right then. But he couldn't.

They walked to the hole in the earth, Martinez arriving first. The custodian looked downward and waited. When Van Allen was next to him, without speaking, the custodian indicated with his gaze that the detective should peer downward in the same spot.

When things came into focus, Van Allen grimaced. The ground was ripped aside as if from some underground explosion. The hole, the way it had been gouged, was unlike anything Van Allen had ever seen before. It didn't follow any pattern of hand shovels or of mechanical digging.

Rather, the ground looked as if it had been pushed aside by some infernal feral beast tunneling—or even clawing—*upward.* Something buried that was trying to escape the confines of the earth.

But again, that still wasn't the worst of it.

At the base of the hole, about five feet below the surface of the graveyard, lay the remnants of the front of an old coffin. The woodwork looked like pine. No frills. Probably from the 1920s or 1930s, he reasoned. But the burial box had been broken open.

Van Allen, who had a pretty strong stomach, and who thought that he had seen almost everything, had never seen this.

"And the whole thing happened during my lunch hour," Martinez said.

"*What?*" Van Allen asked.

Martinez repeated.

"I walked back here this morning, so I know this grave was intact," Martinez said. "I was tending to some flowers back here."

The custodian turned and indicated a blooming garden several feet away. "I closed up at twelve o'clock and everything's fine. I come back at one o'clock and I see this!"

There was nothing going on in the back of Van Allen's mind now. His entire concentration was necessary to process what Martinez was giving him.

"How the hell does anyone human do something like that?" Martinez asked with thorough perplexity in his tone. "Would you tell me? How is this possible?"

Van Allen stared down at the defiled grave. He would have

been happier if Armando Martinez had never asked him that question.

"Someone came in with some equipment, Armando," Van Allen suggested. "They worked very quickly and—"

"The gate was locked."

"Someone else must have a key."

"It's locked by combination. Only I know it."

"Someone somehow discovered it."

"There's no tire tracks to move that monument," Martinez continued. "You'd need a small truck. Ten strong men couldn't carry the marker that far."

He paused. The imponderable questions posed themselves. How could a vehicle or an armada of workmen get in or out? How could they have defiled a grave so quickly? Where had they gone? *Why* would anyone have done this as a prank, even with Halloween coming?

"And then, how do you explain this?" Martinez asked next. "How do you account for what someone did here?"

He pulled a flashlight from his pocket. He threw a bright beam down the narrow hole so that Van Allen could get a better look at what lurked—or what no longer lurked—below.

Martinez's hand was unsteady on the light. But for one horrible second, which would always remain frozen in Van Allen's memory, the light was right on the spot where the wood of the coffin had been broken. Above, a cloud helped by passing over the sun, taking away some of the brightness of the day.

There, down below the earth, was the satin pillow upon which the head of the deceased must have rested for years. The pillow looked stained where the head would have lain, as did the sheet below it where the corpse would have rested. But Van Allen couldn't see any remains.

"Now. Final funny thing, Detective," Martinez said. "You see about the wood on the coffin. About how it broke?"

Van Allen had already noticed. He stared at it over and over but was helpless to make any sense out of it.

"The wood looks like it was broken from within the coffin. Not from the outside," Van Allen said evenly. "Is that what you're suggesting, Armando?"

"That's what," the custodian said. "Apply some explanation to this, please."

"Very simple," Van Allen said, stepping away from it and replying with all the cynicism that he had accumulated over two decades on the job. "After being dead for many years, this particular corpse tired of being in the ground. The corpse smashed open his box, burrowed upward while you were away on your lunch break, threw over his granite marker weighing twenty-five hundred pounds, scaled the gates, and is currently loose in Los Angeles. There, presumably, no one will pay much notice as long as he doesn't cause any other trouble."

Martinez held the cop's gaze for several seconds, then finally blinked.

"My guess—he's in West Hollywood," Van Allen added. "Or maybe Laguna Beach."

"Very funny," the custodian said. "Now, please. What you really think?"

"Sorry, Armando," Van Allen said, feeling the sun come out on him again. "Aside from the facetious explanation I just offered you, I have no guess at all."

The custodian let Van Allen's answer sink in.

"We got to file police report?" he asked.

"Yes, we do," Van Allen answered.

The policeman took out his notebook and reminded himself that he did better these days when he took notes. In the breast pocket of his jacket was his prized pen, a sturdy green Mont Blanc fountain pen that his father had given him upon graduation from college. The pen had some heft to it. It had always felt good in his hand. Using it made him feel professional.

Normally he had kept it on his desk at home. But now that he had decided to make more written notes, he carried it. A blond woman named Nanci had once shown him the joys of a Mont Blanc, and he had never forgotten her.

Van Allen began to write. At least, he told himself, he was now on duty and could bill the city for his time.

After several seconds, he looked up from his notepad. "Better let me see your telephone," Van Allen said. "And if I were you, I'd keep your gates closed this afternoon."

"Gates," Van Allen heard the custodian mumble with irony. "Gates don't seem to matter none, anyway. People. Bodies. They go in or out whether I lock them gates or not. Some kind of city we live in, huh? Some kind of place where dead men walk away at lunch hour."

"Some kind of city, Armando," Van Allen agreed.

Van Allen was busy writing. So he let Martinez's comments pass. But he had heard the old man very clearly, and was distinctly ill at ease with the idea.

10

Two hours passed. Van Allen remained at San Angelo. A squad car with two uniformed cops came by to witness the disturbance. And because a tomb had been violated, an investigator from the Los Angeles County Board of Health had to be notified.

The investigator, a fat, bald man named Jack Ritter, appeared in a Windex blue Chevy Nova. Then Martinez summoned a pair of union grave diggers. Martinez spoke to them in Spanish. They were Salvadorans and the presence of so many police made them nervous.

The diggers were also more than skittish about their task, which was—after the proper photographs had been taken—to enlarge the hole in the ground that had come up from the grave.

Van Allen crouched nearby, massaging the back of his leg where the pulled muscle still throbbed. He watched with growing apprehension and a widening sense of disbelief. Both the grave diggers and the investigator from the Board of Health remarked about the narrowness of the hole coming up from the grave. The two cops, a male and a female, stood nearby and watched curiously, puffing cigarettes, the exhaust from which drifted inexorably toward the man from the Board of Health. Eventually, the man from the Health Department bummed a butt from one of the two cops.

"Just wide enough for a man's shoulders, right?" Van Allen finally said, looking at the hole and giving voice to what they were all thinking.

No one answered when Van Allen made this suggestion. Six sets of eyes were perfectly averted.

"Come on, you bastards," Van Allen said. "Get a grip on reality. Tombs don't fly open by themselves."

"What's your guess?" Ritter asked. "What *did* happen here?"

"I don't know. What are *you* suggesting?" Van Allen asked. "Spontaneous combustion within the coffin? Or some restless corpse that came up to join us?"

"So *you* give *me* an explanation," Ritter said.

The Salvadorans hadn't communicated a single word in English during their entire visit. But they appeared to be tuned in perfectly to this conversation.

"Ask me again in a few weeks," Van Allen said. "We'll find out."

Van Allen's line of reasoning did little to ease the grave diggers. Once they reached the coffin, the Salvadorans couldn't wait to leave the pit. They spoke to Martinez in agitated Spanish and climbed back up to ground level. Martinez was trying to calm them. It was clear that he was failing.

"The men refuse to dig any farther," Martinez told Van Allen. "They no want to touch the grave any further, either."

"None of us do," Van Allen said.

The uniformed cops smirked. The Salvadorans laid their shovels aside and walked away from the pit. At the same time, two more cemetery workers arrived in a black vehicle that seemed to be part hearse, part pickup truck. There were chains and a winch in the rear of the vehicle. The truck's occupants stepped out of the vehicle and waited for some sort of command. Van Allen knew the procedure. Martinez went and retrieved a motorized forklift at the same time.

When all his helpers were assembled, Van Allen felt a fatigue in his own spirit. There was nothing quite like a task that no one wanted to do. He sighed. Then, bad leg and all, the detective jumped down into the grave.

The men from the utility van dropped four chains into the pit. One of the workmen came down into the grave very briefly with Van Allen. He and the detective attached chains to each side of the coffin. The Salvadorans returned to the hole and cleared dirt from each side. Then someone turned on the winch. Its mechanism, like a rusty lock giving way, began to grind. The handles on the coffin, presumably untouched for decades, creaked. So did the chains from the truck.

Van Allen and the cemetery worker climbed out of the grave and stepped back. Van Allen nodded to the man in the truck.

The winch noisily continued its work.

Then, with a groan, the coffin came completely loose from the earth. Van Allen gave an order to halt the digging for a moment and the chains stopped pulling.

The detective leaned down and steadied the coffin. Then the winch continued and raised the casket completely from where it had rested. When the casket was up to ground level, the forklift took over and transported the pine vessel to the truck. With effort, the forklift set the coffin into the vehicle.

Van Allen continued to watch it. Then he turned.

"I want everyone who worked on this to come over here," he said. He summoned all seven men present.

"I don't know what we're dealing with here and my guess is that none of you do, either," he said. "But I'm going to make a request of all of you. You know how the media eats up something like this. You know what a circus this can turn into. I'm asking you. Nobody tells what he's seen here today. Do I have a promise from everyone on that?"

Assurance was quickly forthcoming from all present, except the grave diggers. Martinez had to translate. Then the Salvadorans nodded their agreement. They seemed anxious to go. Van Allen released them, nursing a bad feeling about their ability to keep quiet.

It was nearly dark. The driver turned on the lights of the transport truck.

Van Allen climbed into the truck and knelt by the coffin. He put his hand to the side of it and found that there was plenty of give in the lid. He gave it a slight push and found that it would lift.

He wasn't sure what he would find, but he knew that he wanted to know. He held his torch light on the coffin and lifted the lid until it was up about a foot.

He felt that he was defiling something sacred. And perhaps he was. But he had already been drawn into this vortex of sordidness. It was his job—here on earth, at least—to discover as much as he could about what had transpired, to learn exactly whatever crime had been committed.

He peered in. With a shudder, he saw his worst fears realized.

The coffin was empty. Whatever body had been in the coffin, it was gone now. He let the lid close again, setting it down gently and respectfully.

"God of my fathers," he muttered to himself.

He turned and hopped off the truck. He signaled to the driver. The empty casket was now evidence in a criminal proceeding. It was being taken to an annex of the medical examiner's office. It would be inventoried and held as evidence. It couldn't be reburied without an occupant.

The truck started to move.

Van Allen knew he would have to call his captain of detectives as soon as possible. Minimizing publicity would be an excellent idea. Who knew what kind of nuts would be drawn out of the sunshine of the Southwest to visit the cemetery once this story got out?

But other thoughts also rustled through his mind as he walked toward the telephone. He asked himself: What sort of comment was this on the human condition?

Grave robbery. Body snatching.

There was no other way to term this. What in God's name did someone want with the embalmed corpse of a man who had been dead for perhaps sixty years?

What was this all about? A coven of Devil worshipers? A dark prank for the upcoming Halloween? Some new sort of Satanic cult? Or just some frightening new clique of California screwballs, the raw material for New Age nightmares?

Naturally, Van Allen reasoned, something like this would have to spring up in Los Angeles. Just what his city needed was another black eye.

Why couldn't this have happened back East in New York or New Jersey, where secretly Van Allen felt all this wacko stuff came from? Or why couldn't it have been in San Francisco, where in its sick rainy-seasoned sordidness it could have fit in with the mood of the city? How about Boston? Wouldn't that have been a better setting for this?

But, no. It had happened in his city, on his watch.

To this, he again asked the question that in his line of work, he never finished asking. *Why?*

These people, the sick criminals who had stolen a body, didn't deserve to be in California. They deserved to be in a zoo. Or at best a state nuthouse.

And yet, and yet . . .

Van Allen got into his car and followed the coffin to the Health Department. There he managed to cool any potential controversy surrounding the inquest.

By phone, he spoke to his captain, who shared his desire to keep a lid on publicity. He filed his police report, couched it in vague terms in his logbook, and mentioned only that a grave had been ''disturbed, probably by vandals.''

Then he went home.

But like many crimes he had dealt with over the years, this one followed him. He couldn't get it off his mind. It was like a bad dream that kept coming back, an atonal tune from some mysterious place that kept playing in his head.

Toward midnight, he realized what was gnawing at him. What bothered him most about the case, aside from the very fact that it had happened.

Deep in his gut, he had the impression that he was dealing with something much larger—perhaps much more evil—than he had any way of imagining.

He felt as if he were on the brink of some bizarre and terrifying sort of new experience. An image came to him from somewhere. He pictured himself in front of an unopened door, frightened of its opening, yet picturing a disembodied hand settling on the doorknob on the opposite side . . .

. . . slowly turning the knob . . .

What the detective felt was dread.

Pure and simple. Dread.

Then he realized: This was *it!*

This was the event of which he had had a premonition, a sense of foreboding and impending catastrophe.

What he had feared most was now right in front of him, waiting for him to figure it out. Explain it. Find an explanation.

''Grave robbery. Christ!'' he growled.

At a few minutes before 1:00 A.M., Van Allen was seated again in his kitchen. On the wall there was a picture taken at Huntington Beach several years ago in happier times:

His wife, Margaret, and their son, Jason.

The picture was in a cheap frame from a Woolworth's. The frame had warped considerably from heat and cooking exhaust. But as Van Allen sat at his kitchen table over a beer, the picture and its metal backing came loose. It slipped out of the frame and crashed to the linoleum of the floor a few feet from where Van Allen sat.

His heart leaped. He nearly jumped out of his skin.

He found himself on his feet—his heart hitting three beats per second, and, from years of experience, he reached for his service weapon. There was even a cry of fear in his throat.

For several seconds he looked at the picture and the happier times that had hit the floor. Then, as his heart settled, he picked up the picture and cleaned it off. Fortunately, there was no damage.

He vowed that the next day he would take the photograph to a decent studio and have it framed properly.

He set the picture down carefully on a table in his dining room.

The worst part about that episode was not that it had happened at all.

Rather, he was so spooked, so fatigued, and so upset with the day's events, that his mind was even playing tricks on him.

Distantly, he thought he heard laughter. A man laughing at him. Another beer and he dismissed the laughter.

But then, as he was going to sleep that night, in the moments before he drifted off, he thought he experienced something even worse.

A touch to his shoulder. Then, a few moments later, there was a tug to his bedcovers.

He sprang up and turned on the light in the empty room, one hand on the lamp, the other again on his service pistol.

He went back to sleep with the light on.

Jesus! he thought to himself.

He was going nuts, he told himself!

He was damned glad that he didn't have to peer into defiled coffins every day of his life. Otherwise he would have lost his mind years earlier.

11

Rebecca was in a strange land. It was night and she was mid-way between wakefulness and sleep.

She rolled over in her bed. She tossed. The night outside her home was quiet. The last thing she had seen when she had looked out the window was stars, plus a yellow moon.

So why couldn't she sleep? She was safe in her home, wasn't she? Her husband was near her. But a husband and a home were physical protections within the tangible world. And what was approaching her was emanating from another plane of reality. The one inside her head. Or an unfathomable one that could travel through walls, doors, or even flesh.

It was a thought. A notion. A feeling.

A vision.

An image. A horrible one was coming together in her sub-conscious mind, and she didn't like it. She knew it was going to be unsettling. Frightening. She knew it even before the image took over her.

She rolled again in bed.

She could almost here herself thinking.

Oh, God. . . . Oh, God, please help me . . .

She experienced the sensation of tumbling and she knew she was drifting off into the scarier nether regions of sleep.

And then she was shocked. She felt an extreme comfort.

She was lying somewhere. She was all dressed up in a favorite dress lying on white satin sheets. Her eyes were closed
and she was very still. Gradually, in her dream, into view
came people around her and she suddenly realized that the
people around her were crying.

These were people she loved. Her family. Her parents. A
favorite grandmother who was already deceased.

Her friends.

And, to make it all the more bizarre, a few old movie stars.
Gable. Lombard. Monroe.

*Hey, what a great turnout of people whom you didn't even
know!*

But they were all really sad.

They were crying because their Becca was lying perfectly
still and lifeless in a coffin, hands folded across her chest. Her
husband dry-eyed stood by, looking as if he had expected
something like this.

She tried to cry out in her sleep. She wanted badly to escape
this vision.

But this dream held her in its grip. In the dream, she
couldn't move, and she couldn't move in her bed, either. And
she realized that she was looking at herself estranged from her
own body. She was at her own funeral, seeing it through the
eyes of others.

The murmuring voice from the turret room again: *Rebecca,
be calm. Rebecca, there is nothing to fear . . .*

The voice was silky, yet familiar. It was from something
deeper in her past than her own birth, if that was possible.

Then there was something else. She saw her head turn
quickly in her own coffin. Her eyes opened and went wide.
Bright as a couple of little beacons, windows on a tortured
soul.

In her coffin she sat up. *Hey, what a great trick. We should
all sit up in our coffins. Scares the bejesus out of the mourn-
ers!*

"Where are my children?" Rebecca asked. "Where are Patrick and Karen?"

She searched.

"Who will care for them?"

Rebecca, Rebecca, Rebecca . . . I am protecting them now. And I will protect them through eternity . . .

"Where are they?" she screamed. "Who's talking to me?"

From the coffin she looked in another direction. There she saw her children. Two small coffins next to hers.

Children's coffins. Open. Patrick and Karen. Dead as the ages. A terrible beauty in their deaths.

Rebecca turned sharply in her bed, arms flailing, crying out in her sleep.

Don't leave now, Rebecca. This is the future.

She yelled again.

"Who is talking to me?"

A strand of irritating irrational poetry strangled her.

> *A mother's eyes,*
> *Tears wet she'll weep,*
> *Her children murdered*
> *In their tombs they sleep . . .*

The rhyme was like an inscription on a seventeenth century tombstone.

On the wings of the verse, the coffin lids slammed shut, closed by unseen hands. The hands of a phantom.

Or a dark angel.

Or a devil.

They were at a cemetery. Her husband, not a tear in his eye, stood by. The children were lowered into the ground first.

Rebecca felt a very real scream bottled up in her throat, ready to break loose.

She felt herself sinking again. Sinking like the children's

coffins going into the ground. The earth coming up around her. Four tight dirt walls.

Then she realized. She was going into the ground with her children. Her own coffin lid slammed shut and she was within it. She was being lowered into the ground, a closed, dark box around her, walls of dirt forever.

Even though she was within it, she could see it.

The scream broke loose. A wail like a banshee.

She bolted upright in her dark bedroom at Topango Gardens. A man was shaking her and instinct told her that she should be scared of him.

Terrified! So she was.

That voice again, accompanied by that maddening subliminal tune from the turret room.

Ronny's room.

Becca, Becca, Becca. . . . Careful, Becca, he's trying to kill you . . .

She opened her eyes and flailed at the man who had his hands on her. He was a handsome man but in the darkness she couldn't see his face.

The words of the dream and the words of reality merged.

"Becca! Becca! Becca!"

And then she had the sense that it wasn't a man at all, but something from another world—the fiend with the sunglasses, these were *his hands*—and she flailed away at him.

He released, she hid her eyes. The lights went on in the bedroom like a thousand flashbulbs.

"Becca?" a more familiar voice said. Demanding. Firm. Tough love or unvarnished brutality?

"Becca! Wake up!"

Hands on her shoulders again, shaking her.

Bill's hands! Her husband's!

He pulled her upright and held her close to him.

"Becca! Open your eyes and look at me! Open your eyes. . . . Open. . . . Open!"

Her eyelids flickered. She obeyed. This time her eyes did open. *Welcome back to reality, Mrs. Moore.*

And a stupefied 3:00 A.M. consciousness in a lit bedroom flooded into her brain. The room lights hit her eyes like an express train. It hurt like hell. Her pupils felt as if they'd been fried. But at least the terror slowly began to dissipate, like smoke from the dying embers of an opium pipe.

"Becca?" Bill asked. His voice was softer now. Beckoning. As rich and welcoming as warm fudge.

The scream was long gone from her throat. All she could feel was relief. The familiar arms were on her, the familiar man in the bed beside her. Never had she appreciated him more. She felt closer to him than she had in years.

"Oh, God, honey," she said, falling into Bill's grip. "It was absolutely horrible. That was the worst dream of my life."

"Jesus, Becca . . ." he said. "What's going on here?"

He steadied her and continued to hold her. His eyes asked what it had all been about.

She shook her head. Then she put her hand to her face. She felt like crying. He knew it and held her firmly.

"Come on," he said. "Come on. Talk it out so that you understand how silly it was."

She tried to gather herself.

"Not yet," she said, her voice barely audible. A car was passing outside. "I can't yet."

She was aware of a creak on the floorboards.

It sounded like someone leaving the room. She glanced in the direction. Nothing.

Bill didn't bother to even look. Maybe he didn't even hear it. But she looked again and there was no one at the door. From somewhere another line of poetic doggerel.

Like bad words to invisible music.

At three A.M.,
a spirit now walks,

In your home and heart,
to your soul he talks.

She shuddered, a very tangible shake. Then, gradually, Rebecca unburdened herself to her husband.

"I dreamed that . . . I dreamed that I was dead. The children were dead, too. We were all being buried and—"

He looked at her coldly, as if in shock, the same way he had looked at her that horrible night in Connecticut after she'd staggered home a near-murder statistic.

Then an expression of sympathy and understanding swelled onto his face.

"Poor baby," he said. "What were you watching on TV last night? Or what were you reading?"

"Oh, God, Bill. I don't know."

"Yeah? Well, we can find out real quick."

He reached to the bedside. His hand went around three paperback books. He examined them as she leaned back on her pillow.

"Oh, this is great," he scoffed. "Shows you the sweet dreams you get from these guys." He read the authors' names aloud.

"Stephen King. Dean Koontz. Rick Hautala."

Her husband shook his head.

"Bill—"

"Figures," he said. "I wish you'd stop reading that stuff."

"I haven't even *looked* at those books," she said. "I put them there a few days ago and I haven't even looked at them."

"Well don't. Why don't you read the phone book instead? Or how about the California state budget." He paused. "No, I take that back. That would cause nightmares, too. Our tax dollars down the civic tubes."

She managed a weak smile.

"Bill. I was so scared," she said.

He looked at her with something that passed for understanding. And finally he said the type of thing she wanted to hear.

"Don't you know," he answered, enveloping her in a full embrace. "I'd never let anything happen to you or the children. Never. Someone would have to kill me first."

Immediately, there followed another creak. It was out in the hallway this time. Just out of view. It was so loud that they both looked in the direction of the noise.

Compared to their bedroom, the hallway was dark. And just as kids envision monsters under their beds or in their closets, Rebecca suddenly entertained the fantasy of something horrible—something unspeakably bloodcurdling from another strain of existence—suddenly oozing into view in the doorframe.

She had the same feeling as when she had first seen the man in the parking lot.

Her thoughts ran away with her. *He's going to rip into my flesh. He's going to exsanguinate me. He's going to—*

She could almost picture it. Her eyes were there. Set and trained. So much so that Bill looked also. Then his hand went to her chin. He turned her head so that she had to face him.

"What do you see?" he asked.

"Nothing," she whispered. "I don't *see* anything."

"That's because nothing's there," he said.

He spoke with the voice of a methodical, logical man. An architect, used to using precise formulae and numbers to support both theories and buildings.

She sighed. Tired and frightened. Her hands were sweating. Leaking like old faucets.

"Nothing's there and I'm going to prove it," he said.

He started to get up from bed.

"Bill!" She clutched him. "Bill, no! Don't go out there!"

"I want to put an end to this," he said. "And I'm going to."

"Bill, no! Stay in here!"

He was defiant. He pulled from her.

"If there's anything out there I'm going to kick its ass," he promised.

He turned. Her hands went to her face. Her husband went to the door, then stopped.

He looked around. He stepped into the hall. He took two paces toward the children's rooms. She heard him stop and continue.

Then the sound of his footsteps came back toward the bed-room door. For a split second, she wondered who would appear at the doorway.

Bill or—?

"Happy?" Bill asked as he reappeared. "There's nothing here."

She exhaled a long breath. She settled slightly.

"Now don't panic," he said. "I'll be back in sixty seconds."

He checked on the children in their bedrooms. Unlike their parents, he reported when he returned and climbed back into bed with her, they were sleeping soundly.

She sighed again, sitting upright against her pillow, the pillow against the wall.

She put a hand on her husband's hand. "Billy?" she asked.

"Jesus Christ, Becca!" he snapped at her angrily.

"What?"

"Don't call me that!"

"Don't call you *what?*"

"Billy."

"I didn't."

"You did. I hate that name! You never call me that! What the hell's going on here?"

She trembled very slightly and shook herself. He was right. Not only had he always been uncomfortable with the name, but she had never wanted to use it for him. Something about it sounded wrong. So where had it come from now? What *had* made her call him that? Not only did she hate her husband's outbursts of anger, but she feared them. She had always dreaded that there was something malevolent lurking beneath the surface of his psyche. And she hoped she would never learn what it was.

"I'm sorry," she said.

Bill rose and walked to the window. He looked out. He took several deep breaths to cool off. "You don't have to apologize," he finally said. "You're upset. I have to understand when you're upset."

"The dream was just so real. So terrifying," she said.

"I'm sure it was, Becca," he said. "But it was also only a dream. *Comprenez?*"

She nodded. "Sometimes I wonder," she said.

"About?"

"About this house," she said. "I never had dreams like this before. I never had feelings like this. It's like free-floating terror."

"Honey," he said. "I'm willing to work on this till death do us part. But remember? You know? The incident in Connecticut? The one we agreed not to talk about unless you wanted to?"

"Uh-huh."

"You're going to have post trauma stress. That's what the doctors told you, right?"

"Right."

"Both Miller and Einhorn warned you about this, right?"

"They warned me."

"You have to recognize the stress when you feel it," he said. "It's your job to help dispatch it. You have to control your own mind."

She lay back down in bed.

"From Dr. Einhorn's lips to yours," she said.

"Only because I love you," Bill said.

"Hold me?" she asked.

"Of course."

She settled back under the covers. And she settled into her husband's arms.

"Tell you what I'm going to do," he said. "I'm going to let you go to sleep. With the light on. After you're asleep, I'll turn it off."

"I'm getting like a child," she said. "Afraid of the dark."

"I can fix that, too," he said.

"How?"

"If anything attacks us while I'm still awake, I'll throw the Beverly Hills phone book at it."

"Thanks."

"Just answer me one thing," he said.

"Was there anything about the incident in Connecticut that you never told me?" he asked. "Anything you've subsequently remembered that I don't know?"

She shook her head.

"Anything at all?"

"No," she said. "Why?"

A moment passed. Then he hunched his shoulders. "I'm just trying to understand," he said. "Just trying to help."

She gave his hand a squeeze in appreciation.

A few moments later, despite his promise, Bill was sleeping soundly.

Rebecca killed the room light and managed eventually to sleep herself.

Rebecca, however, woke toward 5:00 A.M., the bluish suggestion of dawn creeping into the bedroom from the outside.

"And where does dawn come from?" she found herself musing in a semiconscious way.

And then she was aware of something else. Something that could not possibly have been there, but which she saw, anyway. She found her eyes focusing on unmoving scenes in the darkness, human forms that weren't there and other phantoms of her imagination. Several times she wanted to throw the light on to have a better look. But in sleeping, Bill's arm was across hers. And anyway, she was still too frightened to move.

Even when one of those figures came right next to where she was lying—a man's figure—and seemed to incline over the bed in a feathery ethereal way, bringing his face close to hers in the darkness, she kept telling herself that it was her imagination.

So she closed her eyes to dispatch the phantoms. And this method seemed to work, for the next thing she knew her clock radio was on, it was 6:15 A.M., daylight was outside and she had survived the night.

Best of all, it was time to get up.

12

Ed Van Allen sat in his office at the detective bureau and glanced at the empty desk across from his. Where was Alice, he wondered. Where was Alice, he frequently wondered.

Detective Alice Aldrich was as close to a partner as Van Allen had. She was one of the new generation of detectives, or at least that's how Van Allen thought of her. Female, obviously. Frizzy dark hair. A free spirit who had grown up in Van Nuys and had quizzed well as a recruit. Spent a couple of good years as an undercover narc in Long Beach. She was cute. Five-eight, dark-haired, a nice figure. Bright woman.

There was something about her that made drug dealers want to trust her. Made them want to brag to her in their clumsy attempts at seduction. She'd put handcuffs on so many big shots that she had outgrown Long Beach and applied to join the LAPD.

She had quizzed well again and the city had hired her. She did four years on a beat, then aced the detective's exam. She hated the concept of partners as much as Van Allen did, and, like Van Allen, liked the Lone Ranger route. So they chose to work together officially, which meant they were actually partners, which further meant that they didn't work together much at all, except to bounce ideas off each other.

Alice was New Age and bright. She liked to read, go to foreign movies by herself, and had taught herself Spanish. At one point she had had a male admirer named Fred who was living in. This went back a year or two. Then Van Allen didn't hear Fred's name mentioned for a few weeks. He inquired about him and Alice said simply that Fred was "gone." No further explanation.

Alice complemented Van Allen nicely. Alice Aldrich. "Double-A," he called her. The other two Double-A's he knew of—Andre Agassi, who had personally brought the dark ages of the in-your-face nineties upon tennis, and Arthur Anderson, his accountant—he didn't care for as much. In his younger days, however, his daughter had lured him to a concert in Westwood by a blues singer named Arthur Alexander, of whom Van Allen had liked the musical sound. Until the advent of Alice Aldrich, however, Arthur Alexander had been the only Double-A Van Allen had known of whom he generally approved.

She was the type of woman, he mused, well, the type he'd like as a wife if he ever remarried. This was about as dangerous a thought as a detective could have on working hours, so he spent a good deal of effort suppressing the notion.

And this morning, in her absence, staring at Double-A's silent desktop, Van Allen embarked upon an unpleasant journey across the top of his own desk.

There were further wrinkles in the car thief case. It developed that the Guatemalans, bless them, had some wise guy friends and now had pooled all their money. They were entering a not guilty plea and had asked for a hearing on whether the evidence obtained against them was illegally obtained. And, of course, they were also claiming racism.

Van Allen had spent the better part of two months trying to nail these thieves, no matter what color they were, no matter where they had been born. He had followed the proper investigative procedures to the letter, and now they were claiming racism and an illegal arrest. And some white middle-class lawyer, the type of guy whose new car became their booty, was helping them do it, all at public expense.

Van Allen ran his hand across his eyes. What a system! What a world! People claimed cops were cynical, and yet there he was every day trying to make sense—and sometimes even justice—out of such things.

Something else had surfaced, also, this one tied in with the West Hollywood Sheriff's Department. A stickup suspect who had been hitting convenience stores across Sunset Boulevard had been busted by the West Hollywood Sheriff's Department. Could Van Allen come over and take a look at the suspect? He sure fit the profile and the m.o. of a guy Van Allen had been chasing for similar strong-arm stickups in 1993.

The funny coincidence about him was that while the suspect had been away visiting his aunt in Minnesota, the stickups in LA had ceased. They had started again four days after his return to California, or at least that was the way West Hollywood Sheriffs had put together the chronology.

Then there was Van Allen's new pal, "Billy."

Or, more accurately, the tomb with the big stone angel on top of it and his missing remains. Martinez had checked the cemetery records that morning and informed Van Allen that the tomb had been of one silent film actor named Billy Carlton.

Carlton had enjoyed being known around town as "Billy." Just Billy, Martinez explained. So, beneath that striking cenotaph, he had hoped to rest exactly the same way.

As Billy.

Van Allen had no quarrel with that. If only the old actor's remains could have stayed put, he would have had no quarrel with the Cemetery of Angels at all.

Oh, hell, he thought to his own amusement, *Billy probably would have been happy to have stayed in the ground, too.*

Probably wasn't even Billy's choice to come back up and join us.

Van Allen was getting goofy, he knew. Too many Jerry Garcia tapes on his own time, he told himself with no attempt at seriousness whatsoever. But he was at work now and it was time to concentrate.

So his thoughts became more serious. Mercifully, the press hadn't caught on to the tomb desecration yet. In Van Allen's worst nightmares, he saw that overturned granite angel on the front page of every two-bit tabloid in the country.

Just what he needed. He prayed that those damned Salvadorans would keep their mouths shut.

Why couldn't the damned angel just flutter back into place? Maybe he should see a priest, he mused. A Jesuit with some real clout Upstairs. Father Karras, where are you? Nah, he quickly decided. Wouldn't do a damned thing. And furthermore, he, Van Allen, was an atheist, not a Catholic.

He wondered next whether God answered the prayers of atheists. If The Almighty answered Unitarians, Van Allen mused, why not complete nonbelievers, too?

He smirked.

And when he felt his thoughts rambling too far in that direction, he knew he was overtired and preoccupied. He went out to the 7-Eleven and got himself a good large cup of coffee. Nothing like a good Cuppa Joe to get a man thinking right again.

Van Allen returned to his office. He set aside completely the file on his pals, the Guatemalans. The case only pissed him off. Instead, he picked up a page that had just been faxed to him while he was out on his caffeine run. The page was from the American Academy of Motion Picture Arts and Sciences. The dudes who gave out the Oscars.

Ah, he thought. This was what he had been waiting for. The page was a listing from an index of men and women who had worked in American films since the first bit of celluloid had passed before a camera.

Van Allen read it with growing interest:

Carlton, Billy (1892–1931) (William Bryan Carlton, Jr.) Handsome American character actor of the silent era. Often the sympathetic second lead, frequently in Westerns or light romance. Late in career made a moderately successful transition to talkies. Filmography: *Rio Grande*, 1920, *Desperate Trails*, 1920, *Man to Man*, 1922, *Trilby*, 1923, *Son of the Sahara*, 1924, *Captain Blood*, 1924, *The Texas Trail*, 1926, *The General* (with Buster Keaton) 1927, *Resurrection*, 1927, *Ramona*, 1928, *Evangeline*, 1929, *The Spoilers*, 1930, *Trader Horn*, 1930, *See America Thirst* (with Harry Langdon) 1930.

The listing told Van Allen little. It was a curriculum vitae. It accurately reduced Billy Carlton's professional lifetime to a neat three inches in a film directory. But it told Van Allen nothing about the man. Where he'd come from. What he was like.

Van Allen's eyes settled upon Carlton's dates. The actor had died young. Age thirty-nine.

Thirty-nine? That was curious.

Had there been an accident? A murder? Had it been life-style? Had William Bryan Carlton, Jr.—sorry, Billy—drunk himself to death?

Van Allen wondered. His policeman's suspicions surfaced instinctively.

Suicide? Illness? A murder that looked like an accident? His detective's instincts kicked in quickly and shifted into overdrive.

There had been an outbreak of influenza in Southern California during the Depression, Van Allen recalled. It was also

not uncommon in that era for actors to die of things like tuber-
culosis or Bright's disease, ailments all but eradicated in modern time.

Then again, he found himself thinking anew, there were
subtle forms of murder back in those days, sly poisons that
could have evaded detection then, but wouldn't now.

Had someone snuffed Billy Carlton and gotten away with it
for all these years? Well if so, Van Allen grimaced, fat chance
of catching the killer now. The policeman looked back to the
actor's date of mortality.

1931. Sixty-four years had passed.

A lifetime in itself.

Billy Carlton's lifetime. It wasn't even *that* far outside the
realm of possibility that Billy Carlton could have still been
alive. There were many thousands of Americans over the age
of a hundred.

He wondered how he could find out more.

Where was Carlton's body? Who in God's name could
have wanted it, particularly after all these years? Why was it
risen from the earth, however it had risen?

Then he almost shook himself.

Hey! Reality check, my man! How could *any* event from
1931 have any bearing on the world of 1995? He was thinking
too much on this case. Go back to the basest motives of all, he
reminded himself.

Money. Sex. Power.

Long ago as a cop he had realized that almost all crimes
were somehow motivated by one of these three components of
the insatiable human wish list.

Money. Sex. Power.

But where could there be any sex in this case? Where could
there be any power?

So? What did that leave?

Money. Always follow the trail of money.

He turned the question over again in his head. To whom

could this actor's remains have had some contemporary value?

There was movement at his door. He did a double take. His spirits lifted.

"Hey," he said.

"Good morning," she answered. Alice Aldrich came in and sat down at her desk.

Van Allen smiled. Double-A was eating breakfast. A carrot. And presumably not just any carrot. An organic carrot. "What's new?" she asked between crunches.

"Know anything about grave robbery?" he asked offhandedly.

"How's that again?" she asked.

"Someone broke open a grave over at San Angelo."

"Yeah? Whose? Anyone I know?" Alice knew how to get right to the point.

"Not unless you lived a previous life," he said. Van Allen knew he was on dangerous ground with Alice with a sentence like that. So he continued quickly.

"An old-time film actor named Billy Carlton," he said. He waited. "Name mean anything to you?"

She shook her head. "No. But I know this guy who's a silent film freak. I can ask him. Should I?"

"If you think of it. I have a film encyclopedia listing for Carlton, but it doesn't give me much."

Van Allen handed her his fax. She took it and examined it, crunching the carrot as she read. When the carrot was finished, she pulled another one out of her purse.

Van Allen looked her up and down as she read it. Only on the LAPD, he thought to himself: Double-A was part Cagney-Lacey, part Angie Dickinson, part Bugs Bunny.

"What's this San Angelo?" she asked. "Like part of Hollywood Memorial?"

"No. It's a small separate burial lot in West LA."

"Yeah? How come I never heard of it?" She gave the fax back to him.

"Nothing new has been buried there since the war."

"What war?"

"The Second Big One."

"Oh. That one." She digested the point, as well as the remainder of the carrot. "My dad was like in that one? You know, the World War? Normandy?"

From being on the streets so much, from being an inveterate "kid" herself even in her mid-thirties, she had picked up speech mannerisms that could have driven Van Allen to distraction. Frequent sentences would end with upward intonations, making statements sound like questions.

Like, didn't so many young people talk like that?

"Cemetery of Angels," Van Allen said, sticking with the subject at hand. "That's what San Angelo is called."

"Hm. Quaint."

"Yeah. Isn't it?" he agreed.

"Why's it called that? From Los Angeles? You know: like 'City of Angels'?"

He shrugged. "I don't know."

"That makes two of us," she said. "And I don't know anything about any Billy Carlton, either." She paused and thought about it. "Jesus. Body snatching. That's gross. Someone actually busted open his grave?"

"Opened his coffin, Double-A," Van Allen said. "The body's gone."

She curled a lip and shook her head again. "Jesus," she said. "I mean, like we got some sick people out there."

"Tell me about it."

"Think this is some sort of Halloween thing?" she asked.

A moment passed. "I thought of that," he said. "And I don't think so."

"Why not?"

"Instinct."

"That's good enough for me," Alice Aldrich said.

"It doesn't *feel* like a Halloween stunt," he said, leaning back in his chair and elaborating. "The methodology was too elaborate, too complicated. If someone wanted a decayed corpse, there were plenty of others that were much more accessible. You should have seen this huge monument, this big granite angel, that got overturned and moved twenty yards just so this grave could be dug up."

"Yeah?" she asked. The carrots were gone.

"Yeah."

"Ed, this is real weird," she said.

"We share the same impression," he said to her. He liked when she called him Ed and wished they shared more of the same thoughts, particularly on a personal level.

He kept to work, however. He was about to ask her where he might find out more about grave robbery, the motives and the twisted psychology behind it. But already he knew the answer. The Central Library. So he fell silent.

Alice took a pair of files from her desk. When she spoke again, she told him that she was working a vice ring along Sunset that peddled cocaine and pimped thirteen-year-old boys. She was posing as a mom with a snow habit who had a son and who wanted to make some money.

"Good luck," he said. "If you need me to watch your back—"

"Thanks. I'll let you know," she said. "I got a SWAT backup, though. I think they want to blow these guys away if they have a chance."

Van Allen grimaced and worried about her. "Have fun," he said.

Double-A vanished. Every once in a while, he noted with fascination, Alice Aldrich reminded him of his ex-wife when she was fifteen years younger. So he watched her go, not without a trace of an unhealthy interest, and not without wishing that he were fifteen years younger himself.

Which he wasn't.

So instead, Van Allen busied himself with paperwork till four that afternoon. Then he drove out to Santa Monica for an hour of much needed R & R.

It was time to see the ocean, time to clear his head and get it together at the same time. There was little doubt in his mind now that he was on the brink of something extraordinary.

Fine, he told himself. He would be ready for the challenge. The next move was for the other side. In the meantime, he would do his homework as best possible the next day, crawling among books and records that were as musty as graves themselves.

It was happening again to Rebecca. Another bad dream. The fourth in five days. She lay in bed in the darkness of her bedroom at 1:00 A.M. the morning of October 21.

This dream was every bit as awful as the others. Something terrible was going to happen to the children. That was central to all of these dreams. But now it was even more specific. In her dream, Patrick and Karen went out to trick-or-treat at Halloween and they never came back.

She tossed in bed. She couldn't evict the nightmare vision that was in her mind.

At the fringe of her consciousness, more doggerel;

> *Let them come,*
> *your children to me*
> *And in death's arms,*
> *protected they'll be . . .*

Her eyes popped open, reentry into the real world. The dream's message still in her mind, that insane poetry dancing through her head.

"Damn!" she reasoned sleepily. She would lay down the

law with Bill. She wouldn't even allow the kids to go out on Halloween. Whatever was out there waiting to menace her kids, she would thwart them by not even putting Patrick and Karen at risk.

She would keep them home.

There! That was settled!

She closed her eyes. An image of the horrible killer with the werewolf face and the wraparound sunglasses was before her.

Her eyes flashed open. The bedroom was empty, much as her thoughts tried to fill it.

Momentarily, she was reassured.

She had gone to see Dr. Einhorn again. The diminutive doc had given her some magic little yellow pills that would help her sleep. So far, she hadn't taken any. She wondered if she should. She wasn't getting one damned night's rest at this rate.

She tried to sleep again. But again she felt that sinking, falling feeling that so often led her into a nightmare. And she didn't think she could stand one more nightmare.

Rebecca? Rebecca?

In the darkness, someone was whispering to her.

She opened her eyes. The voice had called to her so clearly, summoning her from the realm of bad dreams, that she thought it had been Bill's voice.

"Bill?" she asked, coming upon her elbows in bed.

But her husband was silent, other than an even heavy breathing. He was soundly asleep.

Rebecca?

Damn! She heard it again. What the heck was that? Something creepy at the lowest level of her waking consciousness. Something calling her.

Jesus Christ! Her eyes were open now. She was *awake!* And she was still hearing it! Jesus Christ! What in God's name—!

She rose from bed, as if she had received an invitation.

And now there was something else. That creepy piece of music was really in her head now. She caught parts of it that she had never caught before, as if its source had moved closer. There was a discernible theme, a melody that she could almost repeat. And it seemed so much more prominent. Instead of being at the edge of her consciousness, the music was right *there* in front of her, at the forefront of her mind. Instead of thinking she was hearing something distant on the radio, this was as if someone were banging away somewhere at an old ragtime piano.

She stood at the doorway to her bedroom. The hall beyond was dim. The only illumination was from the night-light that she had installed when the second floor troubles first began.

Rebecca?

The voice was unmistakable now. Except, where was it?

She stepped into the hallway.

Rebecca?

The voice seemed to beckon from the yellow room.

The turret room.

Ronny's room.

She walked toward it. The only other sound was the thundering of her heart. She moved as if in a dream, smoothly and evenly across the old floorboards. Occasionally one would creak.

She found herself a few feet in front of the closed doorway to the yellow room.

The only way to dispel fear was to face it. Sure. That's what Dr. Einhorn had said. The only way to accept reality was to confront it. That's what everyone told her. That was even what she told herself. But, easier said than done, right?

All right. She would conquer.

She moved to the door to the yellow room. She placed her hand on the knob and summoned up all the courage she owned. There was no resistance to the knob. She turned it slowly.

With a loud click, the latch gave. The door opened to Ronny's room.

In her head, she realized the music had stopped. Like a cricket's chirp when a human walks too close. No more banging at an old piano.

Rebecca pushed the door hard.

It flew open, going so wide that it clattered against a metal doorstop. She expected a flood of demons to burst forth. It didn't happen. And immediately, before even a small demon could spring forth from the darkness, Rebecca pushed her hand into the room and found the light switch.

She could still hear a voice.

Softer now: *Rebecca?*

She flicked the light switch. The room filled with a hundred watts from the overhead.

Nothing moved in the room. All the furniture was in place. And she thought she heard a male voice whisper.

Yes, Rebecca. . . . Thank you.

But there was no one she could see.

She stepped farther in.

"Thank you for what?" Rebecca asked aloud. "I know something's here? I know there's someone here," she said. Her voice had a slight echo against the old walls. She looked at the children's toys, the new curtains, and the crisp colorful posters depicting the world of ballet and the world of professional sports.

It all seemed so logical between 1:00 and 2:00 A.M. on another morning when sleep fought her: this chat with an empty chamber. "So tell me," she asked in more conciliatory tones. "Thank you for what?"

Silence answered. Dead silence.

Then, *Thank you for coming.* It wasn't a voice this time, it was a thought, a notion, that seemed to take shape inside her head.

"Coming where?" she asked. "Here?"

Yes.

"Why?"

No answer. Not the slightest. No voice. No tinkling music. No thought from outer space slipping into her head.

Nothing.

She waited.

Still nothing.

"Find the message." The words formed on her lips. Rebecca wasn't certain whether this was her thought or Ronny's.

Find the message.

She asked aloud. "What message?"

She scanned the room. Something crinkled behind her. Something made a noise. Like paper being crumpled.

The sound came from the posters on the wall. A breeze beneath them caused the posters to flutter.

Of course.

But, no! Impossible!

The window was shut, hence a breeze was impossible. *Then how could—?*

Suddenly Rebecca jumped as if her body had been hit with electricity. She stared at the sidewall of the room, upon which were the two posters that had made the crinkling sound. And she could see that beneath them, almost subliminally, there were big bold letters on the wall.

She was incredulous. Her heart raced. She had painted this wall herself, and—

But, no! This was the wall that had seemingly painted itself. This was the wall that she didn't recall applying the paint to, but which was covered when she returned to the room.

She stared. There was a message on the wall beneath the yellow paint, as if it were trying to come forth, even though she had painted it over.

Yet this too, by everything she believed, was impossible. Bill had put a heavy white primer on the walls. There was no way that any old marking should seep through.

Her heart continued to flutter. Rebecca went to the wall. She placed a hand against it. The wall felt the way it always had. The paint was dry, the wall firm and secure.

But there was a large *ER* protruding from beneath one side of a baseball poster. Rebecca stepped back and realized that there was a large *I* between the posters. And when she looked to her left she saw the letters *YO* to the left of the first poster.

Look for the message. She had found one.

Her heart continued to kick. The poster on the left was of Heather Watts of the New York City Ballet. The poster on the right featured Mike Piazza of the Los Angeles Dodgers.

A message. It was nearly two in the morning, but Rebecca was going to read a message from God-knew-where.

She pushed a chair to the wall, stood on it, and took down the posters. Baseball drifted to the floor first, followed closely by ballet.

Then Rebecca stepped back and stared at once at the message before her.

Big block letters. A big loud message. Unmistakable, or so she thought as she read:

YOU ARE IN DANGER

Rebecca recoiled from what was in front of her. She backed her way toward the door to the yellow room, but stopped short of leaving. There was something so riveting about the message on the wall that she couldn't take her eyes off it.

She found a club chair and let herself drop into it. And she stared and stared and stared at the subliminal lettering on the wall. The more she stared at it, the more apparent it became, the more clearly the message emerged.

It was like a beacon:

YOU ARE IN DANGER

Somewhere over the next few hours, however, she must have closed her eyes. Must have, because the next thing she knew it was morning and Patrick was gently shaking her sleeve to wake her.

Rebecca came quickly to consciousness, though her eyes burned with fatigue. She assured Patrick that she was fine, then sent him to get cleaned up for breakfast.

Rebecca stood and looked at the wall again. No more big bold letters. But the message, YOU ARE IN DANGER, was embedded somewhere else now.

It was in her mind, to stay.

''Nonsense. There's nothing there.''

With their children already departed for school, Bill Moore stood in the yellow room with his wife. She showed him again the space on the wall where the letters had appeared. The two posters still lay on the floor.

''Bill,'' she said softly, trying to keep her patience and her wits in order, ''I know what I saw.''

Moore, dressed for work, sipped coffee from a cup.

''No,'' he said. ''You know what you *think* you saw.''

''Bill . . .''

''Becca, you got up from a dream. You walked out here. You were half-asleep. Your dream continued.''

''I heard a *voice*,'' she protested. ''Someone, something, called to me. I came into this room looking for a message and the message was right *there!*''

In her frustration, she gesticulated wildly, indicating the place on the wall that was now blank. ''I know what I saw!''

''Becca,'' he said softly, ''let's face reality. You had a bad dream and got up. You came into this room and dreamed the rest.''

She sat on the kids' play chest.

''It wasn't a dream,'' she said.

He sipped his coffee. "The only other explanation is that you never woke up at all."

"Bill, Patrick will tell you. He found me in this room when he got up this morning. I was in that chair."

"I know," her husband said. "So maybe we add sleepwalking to your problems."

She reclined, her back against the wall as she sat on the chest. She stared at her husband.

"You don't believe me at all, do you?"

"I believe you're a very, very disturbed woman, Becca. And God knows I understand where it's coming from. But this has been going on for several months."

"I thought at least you'd be sympathetic. But you're not."

He stood next to her, looking down. She was starting to feel much hostility from him, a man who had taken a vow to love and cherish her.

"I *am* sympathetic," Bill said. "But I'd be more sympathetic if I thought you were actually trying to help yourself."

"And you don't think I'm trying to?"

"Frankly?" he asked. "No."

She felt like throwing something at him, then felt like crying. She did neither. She was scared and hurt. She wanted to call her mother and tell her everything, but didn't even have the courage to do that.

Bill went into the master bedroom. Not knowing what else to do, she followed.

Her husband finished his coffee and set the cup down on her dresser. The dirty cup would be hers to take downstairs and wash. She resented it.

"When do you see Dr. Einhorn again?" he asked.

"Two days from now."

"Tell him about it," Bill said. "See what he says. See if it's any different from the spin I put on it, okay?"

"If his reaction is any different, I'm sure you'll say he's mistaken," Rebecca said sourly.

Bill Moore started to pull his jacket on. He shot his wife a look in response.

"I'm going to pretend I didn't hear that," he finally said. "But now that you bring the subject up, it *has* crossed my mind that Einhorn could be some sort of typical Southern California quack," he said. "What do you think his relationship is with that three-hundred-pound fairy whom he uses as a receptionist, for example?"

"That's aside from the point."

"All right. Well, here's a more germane point: The pint-sized Freud doesn't seem to be helping you all that much."

"I've only been there *three* times," Rebecca insisted. She folded her arms in front of her and turned her gaze away from her husband. She did not need this right now.

"First in a series of three hundred?" The argumentative tone of his voice was accelerating rapidly.

"I think he's making you a little nuttier," he said. "Know that?"

"Thanks!" she shot back.

"Are you going to be a lifer with the shrinks? You know, the one problem with this LA area is that everything in the country with loose marbles seems to have rolled into the country's southwest corner. The other day, for example, I was at a traffic light. I look to my right and here, right next to me, on a motorized unicycle, are these two—"

Furious, upset, she cut him off. "Bill! Screw it! I don't want to hear about it!"

He held the thought, whatever it had been, however entertaining.

A few seconds passed. Both husband and wife cooled down.

"Okay, okay," he said, relenting. "I'm sorry. I'm tense about some stuff, myself. God knows whether Jack McLaughlin and I will ever get some of this architectural stuff off the ground."

"I thought it was going well," she said.

"It is, it is. It's just difficult, okay?"

She sat on the edge of the bed. He leaned over and gave her a short hug. It was a brief one, without passion, and was over almost before it began. It was as if, she felt, a stranger had given it to her. She almost found herself recoiling from his touch. The first time ever, but she was that angry and disappointed with him.

"Let's see what Herr Einhorn says," he said, relenting slightly. "I'll go along with what the doc wants us to do, within reason. But I do think you have to work at this harder. Not indulge your own imagination."

"Yeah," she said. Her tone was as absent as his touch. And he knew it. But he let it go.

"I'll probably be late tonight," he said. "Don't wait with dinner. Call me during the day if you have a problem."

"Sure," she said again. He gave her a quick kiss and left the room. She found herself staring at his coffee cup.

She listened as he went downstairs and out of the house. When she heard his car pull out of the drive, she picked up the cup and flung it madly through the bathroom door. It shattered, leaving a dark mark on the porcelain of the shower stall. And Rebecca began to cry as she knew she would now have to touch up the tiling, just to cover the tracks of her temper.

She did find one sympathetic party later that afternoon, however.

Melissa came by, a loyal new friend with a willing ear.

Conversation followed. Eventually, Rebecca described for Melissa the events of the previous evening.

"I want to see it," Melissa said. "Show me the wall where the writing was."

"Why?"

"Because I'm fascinated by this whole thing," she said. "I have to see the exact spot."

They walked upstairs together. Rebecca took Melissa to the

yellow room. The two women stood before the freshly painted wall. No message, or even any sign of one. And Rebecca's friend seemed almost merry about the event.

"It makes perfect sense," Melissa finally said, nodding as if in approval.

"What does?" Rebecca asked.

"If the writing had appeared and remained on the wall, you would be safe to think nothing of it," Melissa said. "It would have been old seepage brought to the surface by the chemistry of the fresh paint. But the fact that it appeared and then disappeared? Why, then it's obvious, isn't it? Isn't everything very clear to you by now? The dreams. The noises. The feelings in this room, honey? *A message?*"

Melissa smiled magnificently. She was incandescently pretty when she smiled like that.

"Come on, Becca," Melissa continued. "You're fighting back your own orgasm. Let things go. Believe what your eyes and ears and brains are telling you."

"And what *is* that?"

"You got a ghost, honey. You got a friendly spirit in this place and yon friendly spirit is here to help you. Go with it, baby. Communicate with it. But whatever you do, don't fight it off because they only come forth when they have a good reason. And ghosts get their feelings hurt real fast."

Melissa continued to consider the point, eyeing the spot on the wall where the message had reportedly come and gone.

"I told you once before," Melissa Ford said, "this is a very fertile area for spirits. Sometime, not now, I'll tell you some wonderful stories, okay. Just don't be scared. For there's no reason to be scared."

Rebecca pressed her hands to her face for a moment and expelled a long sigh of relief. At least *someone* believed her. At least she had someone to confide in.

Her relief was tempered somewhat by the thought that even if she was crazy, maybe Melissa was just as nuts. Who knew, for example, exactly where Melissa was coming from with all her graveyard and supernatural fascination.

Then Melissa broke that mood, too, when they wandered into the master bedroom. Looking into the bathroom, Melissa spotted the fresh mark in the shower stall where the airborne coffee cup had shattered.

"Looks like you had a particularly tough morning," Melissa said, a sly grin crossed her face. "Husband problems? Or should I mind my own business?"

Rebecca nodded. "Husband problems," Rebecca said.

"Who threw something? You or him?"

"*I* did." Rebecca broke a smile. "*After* he left for work."

"You're a strong girl," Melissa said.

They both began to laugh.

"Got some spare tiles?" Melissa finally asked. "I'll help you touch up."

Rebecca nodded. Touching up would only take a few minutes. But Rebecca and Melissa did it together. And Rebecca thanked fate that she had at least one trusted friend in this strange new place.

13

Ed Van Allen sat down at a table in the research annex of the Los Angeles public library and felt—not for the first time—like a first-class jerk. It was, however, the first time that he had ever filed call slips for this particular section of the library's holdings: the LoBrutto Paranormal Research Collection.

He waited, wondering among other things who the LoBrutto guy was who had donated all this bizarre stuff to the city's reading public.

And then Van Allen waited some more.

Several minutes after he first sat down, he watched a short, slight woman with tightly bunned gray hair approach his table.

Her name tag identified her. Her name was Mildred Canary, she was a ''Mrs.,'' and her title was assistant reference librarian. Best of all, she was cradling an assortment of books in her thin arms.

''Here we are, sir,'' she said breathlessly as she arrived. She set four books upon the table. All of the volumes were old. None had jackets. One was very slim and all were aging.

Mildred Canary arranged the books in front of him so that he could see the titles on their spines. ''Detective Van Allen. File request number 132. Am I correct?'' she asked.

"You are," he answered.

"These are your research requests," she continued, looking them over. "Or at least this is what's available."

Mildred spoke in a meticulously intense, quasi-hushed voice that she must have learned while picking up her master's degree in library science from Berkeley. Where else could she have learned to talk like that? Where else, Van Allen wondered, could every librarian in California have learned it? Her tones and her diction added distinction if not a decibel level to each syllable she softly barked.

"You asked for five books. Subject matter was grave robbery and body snatching? Was that it?"

And at the five key words—*grave robbery and body snatching*—Van Allen felt several heads jerk up around the room. Instantly thereafter several lines of vision dropped upon him. He could feel it. He could see it. One young blond girl directly across the worktables and carrels in front of him looked aghast at Van Allen, as if she suspected that he had ordered "How To" manuals on the subject. There was a sallow-faced man with glasses to Van Allen's left who seemed telepathically to share her thoughts.

"Yes. That was it. Thank you," Detective Van Allen said to Librarian Canary.

"There was a fifth title, too," Mildred said, forging onward. "But it appears to be unavailable. It has probably been stolen." She paused. "Imagine. Stealing a book on stealing bodies."

Nothing she said did anything to stop people from watching Van Allen. From a corner desk, another curious head rose.

"Maybe these four titles will answer my questions," Van Allen responded with utmost courtesy. He took the books. She gave him a weak smile that suggested that, personally, she too thought he was a very sick man.

Then she abandoned him to his subject matter. The detective prepared a fresh set of pages in his notebook. He took out his Mont Blanc fountain pen and readied the writing end to take notes.

Van Allen drew a breath and scanned the room as he prepared to examine his books. Two heads, including that of the blond girl, were still trained upon him. Both quickly returned to their own work when he offered them a toothy smile.

Arbitrarily, he took up the thin book first—it was on top and it was the closest. If anyone had warned him twenty-five years ago, he thought as he opened it, that in the autumn of 1995 he would find himself sitting in the public library perusing the known literature on hoisting human remains from tombs . . .

The first volume was one of ancient history.

Van Allen scanned through it. There were several sections on the Egyptians. The pyramids along the Nile. The so-called curses of the pharaohs. Van Allen flipped through a chapter dealing with the attempted grave robberies of the great pyramids. Trained as a cop, he quickly saw the sole motive of the robbers. Financial gain. They wanted to plunder whatever treasures had been buried with the pharaohs. Human nature at its most basic.

He thought of the actor Billy Carlton and was unable to connect with any profit motive that could have been assigned to the actor's corpse. He kept prowling through the death rites of the ancient Egyptians. He went off on a tangent and read a few paragraphs about the mysterious relics left in the tombs of the ancient kings.

Wrote the author:

The ancient artifacts, artwork, and writings are unquestionably still possessed by the spirit that created them. They remain capable of revealing to psychometric discovery the modern or enduring human and spiritual realities to which they are connected. But at present their meaning remains encoded. They await a wise man who will press the intellectual key into their lock, just as the hieroglyphics themselves awaited the arrival of the Frenchman Jean-François Champollion in 1815.

Van Allen browsed forward. It was not lost upon him or the author of this book, that Champollion, who had unlocked the mysteries of the Rosetta Stone, had died a premature death at age forty-two.

Van Allen abandoned the book. As far as he could tell, nothing in it bore much relevance to the world four thousand years after the construction of the pyramids.

The detective went on to the next volume. It was much more modern and began to suggest some relevance. Van Allen found an account of the robbery of Lincoln's tomb in 1888. Robbers took the president's body and attempted to hold it for ransom, only to be captured and imprisoned without ever collecting a nickel. There followed some similar cases over the course of the late nineteenth and early to mid twentieth centuries. Not the least of which was one with a definite Los Angeles angle. The body of the movie industry's greatest actor, Charlie Chaplin, had been pilfered from its resting place in Vevey, Switzerland, in the 1970s.

Van Allen's attention perked. Here was a case involving another actor, albeit a much more famous one. Van Allen read the entire account of the case. A diversionary note emerged:

. . . most Americans were unaware of the meaning of the Latin term "fellatio" until it was introduced repeatedly at Chaplin's divorce hearing from Lita Gray Chaplin in 1927 . . .

Van Allen winced and skipped back to the 70s, when the great actor's legendary appetites were as dead as the rest of him. A bunch of low-rent European thugs had figured that they could extort money from *Charlot's* survivors in return for his remains.

Van Allen grinned. He could have imaged the ghost of Chaplin snarling to authorities not to give the extortionists a farthing. In the end the fools had been captured by Swiss police and had landed some serious stretches in a Château Gray Bar for their efforts.

Deservedly, thought Van Allen. Then he examined the particulars of the case.

Once again, profit had been the motive. And once again, the dumb-assed robbers had found themselves sitting in jail, not a penny richer for their troubles.

Grave robbery. The literature on the subject was meager. In another book, Van Allen found a case from New York City in 1826. A Dr. William Senfelt had been sentenced to seven years in prison for hiring immigrants to steal fresh bodies from an unnamed "Negro burying grounds near the Battery." Dr. Senfelt had wanted the corpses for medical experiments and research on human anatomy, or so he had claimed in court. Senfelt served two years of his sentence and apparently never was heard from again, at least not in New York.

Van Allen sighed. He was grasping at straws. All he was finding were isolated cases with predictable motivation. Not that it wasn't strange stuff.

In another book, for example:

Disinterment. St. Louis, Missouri. 1898. A saloon-keeper of apparently sullen and quarrelsome temperament was murdered by one of his customers, the identity of whom remained unknown. Three days after the barkeep's burial, his ghost was reported wandering the streets of the city at night, turning over property and frightening horses.

A priest was called. A mass was given "to drive out the demon" that was believed to be in the corpse. When that didn't work, some upstanding citizens got together, dug up the corpse with shovels, and attacked it directly. A former Confederate Army medic, who was now a local butcher, was given the duty of cutting the heart out of the corpse. The doctor's knowledge of anatomy turned out to be somewhat sketchy as he couldn't locate the heart. So he rummaged around through various intestines until a "truly foule (sic) and odious smell came forthe (sic) from the remains," causing such a stench that the entire body ended up being tossed on a makeshift funeral pyre later that evening. The pyre, in turn, ignited the neyghboring (sic) house . . .

Van Allen stopped reading as the account of a grave robbery transformed into an account of a municipal fire. He flipped some pages. This stuff was stranger than some of the stuff that happened in his station house. Maybe contemporary man didn't have any sort of lock on weirdness, after all.

He found another lively section in the same book:

Grigory Rasputin, the Mad Monk who had been advisor to Czar Nicholas II, was cornered by Bolshevik conspirators in Petrograd on December 28, 1916. He was beaten, shot and stabbed. But, according to those who murdered him, his body was still flailing when it was dumped into a hole in the ice in the frozen River Neva. Three days later, his frozen body was disinterred from its icy grave and paraded around before cheering revolutionaries . . .

Van Allen sighed and went onward.

He waded through a short history of modern burial techniques, particularly one detailing the breathtaking casualness with which Europeans discarded the remains of the dead.

He found an article published by a French historian named

Maurice DeMaison who had written in the early nineteen hundreds. The article focused on the Parisian cemetery of Les Saints-Innocents which was established in the Middle Ages and closed in 1780. The cemetery was a sprawling sector of land, adjacent to a small church. Its management—if it could be called that—typified the practices of the day.

Remains did not linger at Les Innocents. The cemetery's fame derived from the qualities of its soil, which were said to reduce a body to bare bones within a day. When the process was complete, or maybe sooner, the remains were disinterred to make way for a fresh corpse. The bones were moved to a "charnel house" where disjointed skeletons were piled up for the public to come and admire.

In the seventeenth and eighteenth centuries,

wrote DeMaison,

"Les Innocents" was a successful place of commerce, where merchants set up shops and where strollers might pass the time, same as they might at Palais Royale. There were several successful charnel houses in Paris before the Revolution and two lasted well until the Second Empire, until closed by order of the Bishop of Paris . . .

Van Allen was getting tired. He turned in three of the books and went for coffee. He returned half an hour later and continued, though a certain veil of exhaustion was starting to descend upon him.

He found another curious section in the final book he examined, a meditation upon the ways Western culture had reexamined its relationship with its dead starting in the middle of the eighteenth century. Moldering tombs and dank crypts gave way to burials in churchyards and even—for those wealthy enough who wished to lie for eternity with the saints—within the stone foundations of churches. But by the late seventeen hundreds many churches had had experiences with noxious fumes and diseases emanating from under-the-church burial yards.

The book cited a case in Virginia where the pastor of a Charlottesville church and twenty-one parishioners fell fatally ill after a body, only nine months in the ground, was accidentally unearthed by grave diggers.

A feeling took hold that the noxious dead should be moved away from the living as far as reasonable, for public health reasons if no other. Subsequently, the concept was born of the modern cemetery, a tidy burial ground usually at the edge of the city limits. The word "graveyard," for example, didn't enter the English language until the 1820s. And for the first time in Western Christian history, the remains of the dead no longer huddled around churches.

Van Allen rubbed his eyes. He had had enough for one day. He flipped forward in the final book and his eyes gravitated to a section that someone had highlighted.

Nearby, the librarians were readying to close the annex. Meanwhile, he read quickly some ruminations from some writer—probably now long dead, Van Allen reasoned—from several decades earlier:

The effects of death are horrific, but immortality redeems them. Yet, we've turned the consolation of immortality into another source of horror. For us, the notion that death is not the end, that the dead are among us in spirit is terrifying. If the dead sprout choir robes and white wings, as they do in newspaper cartoons, all is well.

But what if their bodies or their spirits really could return? What if they can walk through walls, move things, affect the living?

If we deny afterlife, we get what solace we can from the prospect of a painless oblivion. Yet what if—like most cultures in the world—we suggest that a living death might exist?

Then the souls of the departed may haunt us, as will the prospect of a loss of Christian faith.

Van Allen closed the book and spent several moments in long, difficult thought. For some reason, he thought of an advertising tag line that he had seen several years earlier on a movie poster for *Pet Semetary.*

Sometimes dead is better, read the line.

"Sometimes?" he asked himself. "Why not 'always'?"

But then again, he attempted to reason, the tag line was nothing more than a mid-1980s marketing gimmick. A catchy phrase relying on the proper flow of words to sell a movie to a public that was anxious to be scared, then quickly reassured, over the course of a hundred ten minutes.

Van Allen, on the other hand, was working on a very real criminal case in which a corpse was missing from a tomb. What Van Allen had before him wasn't a book and wasn't a movie.

It was a very real situation.

Now, for the first time in this case, a deep shudder gripped him. He had always considered himself to be a man who was willing to entertain any new idea, no matter how preposterous.

He began to ask himself questions to which the answers bordered on the unthinkable.

Sometimes dead is better? Okay, he pondered, what if "dead" doesn't always mean dead in the way he had always accepted it. The possibility of heaven and hell aside, what if mortal death didn't *always* signal the end of one's earthly involvement?

Mildred Canary trundled past Van Allen's table. "Five minutes, sir," she said. "We're about to close."

Van Allen nodded, thanked her, and slid the fourth book back to her. But he remained sitting there. Thinking. If he had

had another hour in this place, he thought, he might have done some digging into spirituality.

He methodically replaced the lid on his Mont Blanc and set it down next to his notepad. He thought back, ransacking his own memory. What were his own experiences?

Point: When he had been a boy, he and his entire family had been at the dinner table one evening. They all heard a car on the road by their house. There had been a terrible sound of skidding automobile tires, then a large ugly thump, following quickly by the yelping scream of an animal. They had looked out the window and seen their neighbor's Dalmatian running away from the sound, running faster than they had ever before seen the old dog move. Then there were the sounds of voices. Animated. Distraught. Twelve-year-old Eddy Van Allen came out of his home with his parents. The body of the dog was lying bloody on the road, exactly where the car had hit it. There were no other Dalmatians in the neighborhood. What, then, had the entire Van Allen family witnessed fleeing the scene of the accident?

Point: When Van Allen had been a teenager, he had been up late one night studying for a high school exam. It had been about 2:00 A.M. Suddenly, he was aware of the very strong scent of perfume. Not just perfume, but the specific lilac perfume worn by a favorite aunt. Van Allen looked around, not knowing why his aunt, who lived in nearby Chula Vista, would be in their house. He even rose from his work and looked through the house. The scent of the lilac perfume remained strong. Next day, he learned that she had died the previous evening.

Point: Van Allen's older brother and sister-in-law had moved into a new home about five years earlier. The home was in the Sherman Oaks. For the first year, they were certain that they heard a baby crying somewhere in the house. But they couldn't find the source of the sound, and no neighboring house had small children. One day, Van Allen's brother ran into the man who had previously owned the place. The brother inquired about the noise. The previous owner looked stricken. "Don't ever ask my wife about this," the man explained softly. "Our first child died in that house. Crib death, sudden infant death syndrome. That's why we moved. Too many painful memories."

And final point: In his own memory, his estranged wife was still chiding him. "You never open your mind. You never accept anything new. You're the sworn enemy of new ideas, Ed."

All right, Margaret, he thought to himself, addressing her in her absence, *here's one that will tax even you, so try it on: The dead walk among us. They come crashing out of their tombs every once in a while and mingle in with us while we go to the store or get our cars washed. Let me know if you see Billy Carlton, would you? Should be able to recognize him easily. He might not look too healthy; he's been dead since 1931. And say "hi" for me and tell him I need him for questioning.*

Telepathically, no response from Margaret.

Van Allen looked around him. The girl in the red skirt was gone, as was the nervous man with the glasses. Van Allen was the last reader left in the reference room. He rose and left the library.

Van Allen walked out into a cool evening and found his car. In one way, he was convinced that he had wasted several hours of his time. What he had really been looking for—some sort of insight into the mind of a grave robber—had escaped him. Other than the profit motive or the motive of medical research.

He put the key into the ignition and prepared to drive. He would stop first at his office and then take the expressway home to Pasadena.

He watched traffic carefully. It was dark. But what he kept seeing was very bright indeed, even though it was in his mind.

It was the trail of debris from Billy Carlton's coffin, coming upward from the earth.

Then this vision flew apart and he saw another one: that of the huge seraphic tombstone being lifted in the air, as if by some titanic supernatural force bringing it to land sixty feet away in the cemetery.

The thought gave him chills. And he saw it in his mind, bright as day, picturing it—he figured—much in the way that it must have happened.

Then, as he drove, he realized that this was what was bothering him. The more he consciously tried to stay away from a certain thought, the more the thought repeated on him. And each time it came back, it did so with increasing urgency.

It wasn't just that the human remains were missing from Billy Carlton's tomb. And it wasn't that he had failed to find something about the minutes of some coven of self-styled witches or Devil worshipers who might have stolen it.

What continued to bother him was that every shred of evidence from the crime scene suggested that the remains had somehow been propelled upward from within the coffin. That analysis kept formulating itself somewhere inside him and kept taking shape, despite his best efforts to dismiss it.

How the hell was he to explain something like that?

Even if some sicko had used some sort of unusual tool to burrow down to the corpse, how could it have been dragged upward without the skeleton falling apart?

How could the movement of the marker be explained?

And why had the grave of Billy Carlton been disturbed? Other graves in the yard were far more accessible.

Then, of course, there were the further logistics of the desecration. How had someone come in and out of San Angelo unobserved? Through locked gates or over high walls? How, in daylight without being seen? How, with equipment, without leaving any tracks?

Van Allen stopped at his office and returned half a dozen

phone calls, none of them important. He called Martinez and angled around to find out if anything new or unusual had happened at the cemetery. Nothing had.

He drove home, thinking back to the information he had digested at the public library.

Sometimes dead is better! Now there was a thought that pursued him, remaining in his mind all day. He took it to the next level. ''Yeah? Better than what?'' he asked himself again.

He thought back to Champollion, the Frenchman who'd solved the mysteries of the Rosetta Stone. Equally, he thought of all the other mysteries that were waiting to be unraveled. If only a man had the right key to the lock.

He made himself dinner and turned on the Lakers. They were back East, getting hammered by the goddamn Knicks.

He thought a final time of Champollion and how the man had solved this great mystery of the ancients, only to die prematurely.

It was another uneasy thought, sudden premature death. It stayed with him overnight, woke him at 3:00 A.M. and then was tiptoeing across his subconscious the next morning when he woke at 6:15 A.M.

That reminded him of something else.

Since being called to the Cemetery of Angels three days earlier by Martinez, Van Allen had been unable to get one good night's sleep.

He faced the new day and made a decision. A profit motive of some sort *had* to have been the motive for the desecration of the grave at San Angelo. Anything else was too horrific even to consider.

14

In Fairfield, Connecticut, Sergeant David Chandler was at war with the front right corner of his desk. Thereupon was a small bin for correspondence marked, in a sardonic attempt at humor, with a skull and crossbones.

The bin contained old business. Unfinished but open cases. Police investigations that defied closure. Cases that Sergeant Chandler and others had put in weeks upon without results. On the fourth Friday in October, the last Friday before Halloween Saturday, Chandler attempted to make progress against this bin. It was late in the evening, a time when he might have been home with his young family. And he was trying to clear old business off his desk, or at least as much of it as possible.

Many of the cases were incidents which he had worked with the local town police—Fairfield, Bridgeport, Norwalk, and Westport, in particular. Included were numerous housebreakings and car thefts. There was a smaller number of assaults. A pair of bank robberies that were part of a series with the same m.o. up and down the East Coast. The Feds had become involved in that one and they hadn't been able to resolve it, either. But several different law enforcement agencies in the area were waiting for the robbers to strike again and make a mistake.

As he went through the files, he remained familiar enough with each case to know it without reviewing it. Many of these investigations were matters upon which he had spent hours of thought on his own time. It bothered him that these cases could not be closed. But, as he well knew by now, the world was imperfect.

Most of these dossiers, as he sorted through them, returned to the right-hand corner of his desk. A few, perhaps one in every six, he managed to put into a deeper section of his department's files, one for cases that were likely to remain static forever.

At a few minutes before eleven o'clock, he came across the last file to be reviewed. It was the Rebecca Moore case from the previous February, the alleged assault that had commenced in the supermarket parking lot.

Chandler had kept it on his desktop "just in case."

Just in case another such incident occurred.

Just in case he eventually found some new evidence in the incident.

Just in case he eventually swayed from the theory that Mrs. Moore had filed a false police report and no such incident as reported had ever occurred.

Chandler held the file in his hand for several seconds, wondering what to do with it. Of all the files on his desk, he reasoned, this was the one in which further activity was least likely. No parallel incident had occurred anywhere in the area. And the Moores had departed for California during the summer.

Chandler sighed. Here was a candidate for burial in the inactive zone. A prime candidate.

He took the folder containing all the paperwork on the Moore case to the main files of the State Police headquarters. He prepared to bury it.

Yet something stayed his hand. Something wouldn't quite let him put the case to rest. If asked, he probably would not have been able to explain why, other than the fact that something about the case had never added up properly.

Mrs. Moore had seemed like a reliable witness and an actual assault victim. Yet no evidence of any incident having occurred ever cropped up.

Sergeant Chandler didn't like cases that contradicted themselves. There was something, he felt, inherently evil about them. Even in the infinite capacity of human beings for deception, there was usually a skein of logic. But the logic had always escaped him in the Rebecca Moore case.

So Sergeant Chandler closed the drawer of the master file, the dossier still in his hand. He walked back to his desk. Thinking about the case anew caused it to prey on his mind all the more.

There had always been something about the case that had eluded him. Something he couldn't see.

Chandler returned the file to his desk and, without much pleasure, dropped it back into the corner bin with the skull and crossbones.

The Moore case just wouldn't go away, he told himself, even after eight months. It was just like he concluded, as his thoughts rambled farther, a bad dream.

Yes, indeed, he decided, as he rose from his desk and prepared to go home. The Moore case was exactly like a bad dream.

Another thought came to him from somewhere: *Whose bad dream?*

Chandler finished working on his skull and crossbones bin. He glanced at his watch. He had put in more time than he had planned this evening, but at least he felt as if he had accomplished something.

He rose from his desk. Time to go home. He was due back at work within another eight hours. As a cop, he sometimes felt he was on a treadmill, and the treadmill never stopped moving.

Sergeant David Chandler turned the light off on his desk and departed. It was 11:00 P.M. exactly in the East.

At the same moment, on the other side of the continent, the subjects in what Chandler called "The Moore Case" were settling into their home for the evening. It was 8:00 P.M. in California. Rebecca and Bill had just put the children to bed.

Rebecca came into the living room, carrying a cup of herbal tea. She sat down on the new sofa, sinking onto the big cushions. She set the cup and saucer down on the table beside her.

She heaved a slight sigh. Across the room, her husband was stretched out on the other sofa, his nose—and his attention— in an *Architectural Digest*.

She sighed again, this time to get his attention. His eyes shifted and, as they had some many thousands of other times in their marriage, found her.

"Yes?" he asked.

"What about a fire?" she asked. "We scrubbed out the fireplace and had the chimney inspected. Let's do the fire thing."

"To burn the house down?" he asked, making a joke of it. "I thought you liked the place. And we're finally getting it fixed up."

"No," she answered, taking a sip of tea, "I was thinking more of containing the blaze to the hearth. You know, the type of thing we used to do back East. A fire on a chilly fall evening."

"Oh," he said, pretending to have not understood. *"That* type of fire. Why didn't you say so?" The intentional misunderstanding, played out in dry comedic tones, was part of an unwritten give-and-take between them, one that had become less frequent in recent months.

And, in truth, even for Southern California, there had been a little nip in the air on that evening. Something that really had—in a comfortable way—reminded them of the East. A little domestic conflagration, confined to the hearth, had been in the back of his mind, too.

A moment or two later he rose.

Rebecca had gathered some branches and small logs behind the house. He kindled a fire quickly and lit it. The flames hungrily took to the wood.

No, a fire wasn't really necessary to warm the room. But, yes, it did bring a glow and comfort to the house. Bill went back to his reading, and Rebecca studied the flames.

Her thoughts divided among the events of the day. She had gone to two job interviews. One interview had panned into nothing: a weekly newspaper in Orange County had wanted someone to sell classified advertising, not write or report. The other interview had been an unbridled disaster, held in the office of a repulsive little immigrant who called himself Ben and whose accent could have come from any of two dozen small, hot countries. Ben ran a free "people-to-people" newspaper in West Hollywood and needed someone who could handle English properly.

But sadly, Ben had been unable to control himself, either his grammar or his impulses. He had laced many of his questions with sexual undertone. As in, "How nice would pretty lady like you be to Ben if Ben gave you a job?"

Rebecca had walked out of the interview three-quarters of the way through. She had told Bill only that neither appointment was successful. She spared him the details, and spared herself relating them as well. Now, as the fire's warmth enveloped the living room of her home, she was trying to dismiss the whole episode. She wondered if the incident would someday be funny. She doubted it. And it sure hadn't been amusing today.

And then there was that creepy tune. That phantom melody again. It had been in and out of her subconscious all day, an unwelcome coda to the day's events.

When would this damned music go away? She didn't like it, couldn't place it, and it had been weighing upon her subconscious far too long now. As she sipped her tea and stared into the fire, she realized: that tune, that song that she couldn't place, that damnable assemblage of weird notes on an unseen instrument, was what had been bothering her all day. Not the crappy interviews for jobs that she didn't want.

Her thoughts were so involved with the song that she thought nothing of a creak somewhere else in the house, then another one on the front stairs.

Where the hell had that melody originally come from, anyway? she wondered. How the devil had it snaked its way into her head? Why the *hell* couldn't she get it out of her head?

Rebecca finished her tea. The fire seemed to give her some comfort. Then something flashed inside her when she realized that a small figure had appeared at the living room doorway.

Thoughts passed through her head, one after another, with a speed that had no measurement in time:

A miniature human being in the doorway! *In their home!*

A small adult. A child.

Her daughter!

Rebecca calmed quickly. Bill looked up from what he was reading.

"Mommy?" Karen said.

"What's the matter, honey?"

"There's someone in my room. He won't leave."

"What?"

"It's Ronny."

Rebecca felt a sinking sensation, followed by a surge of tension. It was as if the barometric pressure had collapsed all around her. She felt like something held her in its grip.

Karen came to her.

"Mommy, he *won't leave!*" Karen said. She was frightened. "We told him to leave and this time he won't."

"Jesus!"

Rebecca jumped again when Patrick appeared behind Karen. "He's there now," the boy said sullenly. "He wants us to go with him."

A man's voice next. Bill's. "He *what?*"

"He wants us to go with him," Karen said, repeating her brother.

Bill was on his feet. Rebecca was on hers. Both parents moved to the door to the hallway and brushed past their children. Bill looked furious. He grabbed a hammer that was sitting in a toolbox near the stairs. He clutched it as he sprinted up the steps.

"I've had just about enough of this!" he snapped to Rebecca. "It's about time to put an end to it." He shouted back to the children. "Where is he? Where's 'Ronny'? What room?"

Bill took one step toward the yellow room when the answer came back. Both kids, in unison. Ronny was in Karen's room, they said.

Bill charged into the room, Rebecca right behind him. He stopped short. So did his wife.

The room was empty as a broken vow. And a tiny breeze from nowhere riffled past them as they stood near the doorway.

"This is such bullshit," Bill muttered furiously.

Rebecca eyed the vacant room and made no such statement.

Bill calmed slightly, his temper subsiding. Rebecca could see her husband's agitation and his efforts to keep calm.

"Go get the kids," Bill said. "This type of thing has got to stop."

Rebecca went downstairs and retrieved her son and daughter. She led them back upstairs. They stood in the hallway.

"Okay. Where did you see him?" their father asked.

Karen pointed to her room. "He came in," she said. "I thought he was there to tuck me in."

"He's done that before, has he?" Bill asked.

Reluctantly, the girl admitted that he had. She gave a nod. Rebecca felt a little cringe.

"But he wasn't there to tuck you in?" Karen's father asked.

"He said we were going to travel tonight," Karen said. "He said we were going to have a long trip."

Bill Moore eyed his daughter, anger fused with impatience, understanding trying to creep in but not being very successful.

He looked at Patrick.

"Patrick?" Rebecca asked. "Tell me what you saw."

"Same thing," he said shyly.

"So this Ronny was in two places at the same time?" Bill asked.

"No," Karen said. "He came to my room first."

"Then mine," Patrick said. Rebecca's spirits sank a little more. To the consternation of their parents, the children agreed on the chronology.

Bill stood with his hands on his hips, looking at one child, then the other.

"All right," he finally said. "It's time for us to have a little family understanding about 'Ronny,'" he announced. "Ronny doesn't exist. Okay? No matter how much you guys think you see Ronny, he's *not here.* He's part of your imagination, all right?"

The kids looked disappointed. And disbelieving.

"And he's *not* your friend," Bill continued with barely concealed anger. "If you think you see him again, you tell him that this is not his house. He has to leave. And he has to leave you alone."

Patrick and Karen looked particularly glum.

"And if I hear anything more about it, you'll both be grounded for Halloween tomorrow like your mother wanted. Is *that* clear?" Bill asked.

Both children nodded. Then they looked to their mother.

"Your father's right," she said. "If Ronny appears again, you have to tell him that this is not his house. He has to leave."

"I didn't hear an answer," Bill said.

Patrick and Karen both nodded. Grudgingly.

"You'll tell him?" Bill insisted.

"We'll tell him," Patrick said.

Sensing momentum, Bill continued. "If Ronny's here at all," he said, "he's a bad guy. And he deserves to be thrown out."

Patrick objected.

"He says he's here to protect us," the boy said.

"From who?" Bill snapped. Rebecca was astonished how angry her husband quickly became. "What's he say? Ronny's going to protect you from *who?* From *what?*"

Rebuked, Patrick only shrugged.

Bill eased slightly. "Now," he said, sensing triumph, "not only does Ronny not exist, but I'm going to make sure that there is no one in this house other than us." His eyes darted from one child to the other. His gaze stopped upon his wife for a moment, then went back to his children.

"I'm going to chase Ronny away for good!" Bill gloated. "Or maybe I'll catch him by the nose and burn him in the fireplace."

Karen smiled a little sadly. Rebecca stroked her daughter's hair and gave her a hug.

Secretly, Rebecca was pleased that Karen had come downstairs. The fire warmed the home in one way, the love of her daughter warmed it in another. And if they *could* dispel all this Ronny stuff, so much the better.

"Okay," Bill finally said. "Let's go."

The Moore family walked room to room. On their search, they found nothing more terrifying than a faucet in the rear upstairs bathroom that wouldn't stop dripping. They looked in all the closets. As he calmed, as he became convinced there was nothing there, Bill made a joke out of it by holding a chair.

"I'm going to bash anyone who comes out," he whispered to Karen. "You get to pick up the pieces of his head."

Rebecca made a pained expression at the image of gore. But Karen started to laugh. A nice cuddly girlish laugh.

Bill got down on his hands and knees and checked beneath the beds. He poked behind and under furniture with a yardstick. He put bright lights on all over the upstairs.

No Ronny. Rebecca gradually slipped into the mood of the whole escapade. She wondered if this might have been just what they all needed to clear the air, to eradicate *whatever* was in the house. As they went from room to room, with their makeshift weapons, the search and destroy mission took on the air of an impromptu family party. Bill even gave the yardstick to each of the children to let them take a whack at the intruder.

After the search: No man. No disembodied spirit. Nothing scary.

"Bedtime again," Bill finally said to his daughter and son.

The children were tired by that time and didn't resist the prospect of sleep. Their parents put them to bed in their respective rooms.

Rebecca checked on both of them ten minutes later. Both Patrick and Karen were sleeping peacefully. Set on dispatching Ronny in any way possible, Rebecca also left an extra light on in the hallway so that either child, if he or she opened an eye during the night, would clearly see only the friendly contents of their home—and not the shadows that can turn into ghouls.

Rebecca went back downstairs.

She sat for several minutes on the sofa, leaning against her husband's shoulder. She and Bill listened to music on the CD player. Bill read for a while. Rebecca studied the way the flames in the fireplace so methodically consumed the wood that Bill had fed to them. It looked like a metaphor for something, or an image, and several ideas tried to form themselves in Rebecca's head.

But none of them would completely take shape.

And when the images tried to shape themselves, that damned melody interfered again, subverting anything else within her mind.

The onset of insanity, Rebecca mused to herself. *I'm thirty-two years old, an excellent age for a happily married woman, and I'm going quite crazy.* Next bizarre thought, vaguely associated: *I wonder if Bill would like to come with me.*

She smiled. And Bill, noticing that something had amused her, gave her a hug.

"I think it's important that they go out to trick-or-treat with their friends tomorrow," Bill finally said.

"I'm still nervous about it."

He shrugged. "Go with them then," he said. "And I'll be here dealing with the little ghouls that come to the door."

"Maybe," she said. A moment passed. The fire hissed and shifted. Was it talking to her, she wondered. Then she was startled for a moment. Before her eyes, something in a strange smoky shape rose from the fire and almost—to her mind— took shape. But it dissipated up the chimney before she could say anything to her husband.

For several seconds she stared at the fire, wondering if another such shape would form. When none did, her nerves eased slightly.

She closed her eyes for a moment in an attempt at relaxation. She didn't share her complete thoughts with her husband. Nor did she say anything about the phantom music that had been in her head.

Then, suddenly, her spirits lifted. What she would remember about the evening was the underlying sense of happiness that she now felt, basking in the glow of her home and her family. The sentiments of comfort seemed stable and powerful enough to defeat the other thoughts within her, the ones that made her uncomfortable. It was one of the first times that she had really felt that way since moving west.

She had something wonderful, she told herself, that no one could rightfully take away from her. She felt as if she had turned some invisible corner and could now indeed exorcise the spirits that pursued her.

Those images of happiness, of comfort, and of well-being, would stay with her for a while. And they would further define themselves in her memory in the time that followed.

For next morning, when Rebecca went to wake her children, she discovered that her life—as she had known it— would never again be the same.

That damned melody was in her mind, stronger and more virulent than ever. And when she opened the door to Patrick's room she found his bed unmade and empty.

She stared at this for a moment and assumed that the kids were together. So she walked quickly to Karen's room. In the back of her mind, something was starting to tell her that trouble was at hand.

She threw open the door to Karen's room. Her bed, too, was unmade and slept in.

But no Karen.

She called out. "Patrick? Karen? If you're hiding, come on out. You fooled me."

No answer. Silence throughout the house. If this was a Halloween gag, she thought, she already hated it.

"Come on, kids," she shouted next, moving back to her son's room. "The joke is over. Come on out!"

She opened closets. She looked in both bathrooms. She dashed up to the attic and back down. Her search was a perverse reenactment of the one the previous night.

First no Ronny. Next, no Karen or Patrick.

She was angry, bordering on frantic.

"Kids? Come on!" she yelled. "I mean it! Both of you, right now, down to breakfast!"

Still nothing. She stood perfectly still, waiting, hoping for a sound. A horrible vision flashed before her. It was the face of the man who had abducted her many months ago.

She cringed. His face always repeated on her like bad acid at times when something unpleasant was happening. She waved the vision away.

"*Kids?*" she yelled again.

Then she heard footsteps. They came from downstairs. It was Bill, walking from the kitchen to the base of the steps.

"Becca? What's wrong? What's going on?"

Stunned, she moved to a position at the top of the steps, that damned tune kicking in her mind again. She looked downstairs to her husband. And in a very small voice, she told him what had happened, almost as if it were some sort of ordinary event.

"Bill?" she said. "They're gone! Something's happened! Both Patrick and Karen are *gone!*"

He stared at her for a long second, then raced up the steps. He ran through his house like a madman, ripping open closets and pulling away bedspreads.

Yet at the end of ten minutes, the bottom line was the same.

Patrick and Karen were gone. Both of them. Completely.

And there was no sign of Ronny, either.

15

Detective Sergeant Edmund Van Allen parked behind the blue-and-white sector car that was already at the curb before 2136 Topango Gardens. He stepped out of his car and drew a breath.

He knew this neighborhood well, having worked it since the early 1970s. He knew it well enough to have recognized the address when it came across the phone lines at headquarters.

Two one three six, Topango. This used to be a rundown house belonging to an old woman named Dickinson, he thought to himself. He knew the old lady had passed away and that the place had been sold. He did not yet know the new occupants, though he could have recited many other names on the block.

Van Allen also knew this neighborhood to be peaceful and professional, the type of place where he was rarely summoned for anything violent. Housebreakings weren't uncommon, nor was the occasional auto theft. But those weren't usually the types of cases that Van Allen drew.

He knew many of the people around here and liked them. They tended to be attorneys, film people, and other professionals. These were people who considered themselves to be the social superiors of ordinary policemen, he knew, even though many of them were only one generation away from a blue-collar father themselves. Van Allen didn't hold their prejudices against them, but he didn't entirely forgive them, either. In any event, he could meet new people and hold back his own judgment.

He walked to the front door of 2136 Topango.

His knee was troubling him again this morning. He cursed his stupidity at trying to dislodge that damned granite monument at San Angelo. What the hell had he been thinking to try to do that? The pain made him feel old, not quite as good a man as he used to be. Not as fast, not as flexible, not quite as complete. Aging, he concluded, sucked.

But he steered his thoughts in another direction and admired the neighborhood again. He had to give these new people credit for the way they had fixed up old Mrs. Dickinson's place.

Fresh paint. Repaired front windows. New flowers around the base of the porch. Even the front lawn was green again. It was as if the house had sprung back to life. The batty old hen would have been pleased. He made a mental note to congratulate these new people, whoever they were.

He knocked on the door and waited. He even could appreciate the way the porch had been reconstructed. The last time he had been here, an evening four years ago when Mrs. Dickinson had reported a prowler—real or imagined—the boards beneath Van Allen's feet had sagged palpably. Now they were firm and supportive. He wished his stomach muscles could have been replaced as effectively.

Several seconds passed.

Van Allen looked at the neighbors' houses and scanned across the street where a Mexican adobe was slam-bang adjacent to an English Tudor. Well, despite the architectural incongruities, he would have loved to have lived on a block like this with his family. But hell, anyway, he thought to himself as he pulled himself together and limped to the front door. He couldn't afford a neighborhood like this, and never would be able to by virtue of being honest. His kids had grown up and his wife had left him.

So what did it matter? Maybe he was better off out in Pasadena.

And why no answer to his rap at the door?

He knocked louder the second time, figuring that the occupants might have been busy with the uniformed men somewhere in the rear of the house. He wondered if Alice Aldrich would also make her way over to have a look. She often came by to support him when he had an important call.

Two children were reported missing. That qualified as important.

A hopeful thought fluttered through his head.

Maybe the missing kids had turned up alive and giggling in the time it had taken him to drive over. But somehow he had a bad feeling. Somehow he knew it wasn't going to be that simple.

Life rarely was. And he already had adverse premonitions about being here.

The creepy feeling suddenly irritated him. He lifted his hand to hit the door again and this time didn't feel quite so polite about it. Then, several seconds after his follow-up knock, the door came open.

"Yes?" asked a defensive male voice.

A man in his thirties with a haggard, tired face—the face of a graduate student who had been up all night—loomed into view and answered.

Van Allen caught a blast of suspicion right off the bat. He pulled his gold shield from the breast pocket of his worn jacket. "LAPD," he said. "I'm Detective Ed Van Allen."

"There are already some cops here," Bill Moore said.

"In uniform?"

"In uniform."

"That would be standard, sir," Van Allen began. "They

took the '911' call. The follow-up on the case, assuming you need one, is done through the detective bureau.''

He paused. When Moore made no motion to move, Van Allen saw fit to add, ''That's me, sir. Detective bureau.''

Bill Moore gave him a look that landed somewhere between subtle distrust and overt dislike. Then Moore cooled slightly, nodded, and seemed to do nothing more than assess this newest visitor, though not in a receptive way.

Then, ''Yeah, all right. Come on in,'' Moore said.

''Thank you.''

Moore led Van Allen into his home. Almost immediately, Van Allen didn't like Moore. Something suggested that Moore wasn't all that keen on a police presence in his house. But in Van Allen's experience, that wasn't all that unusual, particularly in times of stress.

Outwardly, however, Moore was capable of being polite. After a few more seconds, he turned and offered a hand.

''I'm William Moore,'' he said. ''Sorry if I seem upset. But I *am* upset. We called the police. Our children are missing. I had no idea how many police would be involved. Are there more coming?''

He sank back into a chair, a man on the edge of hysteria.

''Only if I call for them,'' Van Allen answered.

''There are already two cops here,'' Moore said. ''Did I say that?''

''You did,'' said Van Allen.

Then the detective explained again that the uniformed men had already put out a ''Missing Juveniles'' report on the police radio. From here on, Van Allen said, the case would be handled by the detective bureau. He had drawn the case as the chief investigator.

Moore looked Van Allen up and down.

''Oh,'' Bill Moore said coldly. ''Look, I'm sorry, but this whole thing is already an awful lot to bear.''

''I'm certain it is, sir.''

"Halloween was tonight," Moore said. "The kids were going to go out. Am I not making any sense? Jesus. My world is upside-down. I want my children back."

Van Allen found himself reaching for the old standby lines of comfort. "We'll do everything we can. The sooner we get started, the better."

Moore exhaled hard. "I'll go get my wife," he said.

Moore disappeared into another downstairs room. Van Allen stood alone in the living room, feeling like a fish out of water, looking at the thousands of dollars' worth of renovations that had been made to Mrs. Dickinson's decrepit old place.

He waited. One of the uniformed men came into view, gave him a nod, and went out to work the radio in the sector car.

A few moments later, Rebecca Moore came into the living room with her husband. Her eyes were red and moist. But she was composed. Van Allen offered her a hand and then found himself reaching for more of the stock lines of reassurance that he always used in cases of disappearance. As he spoke, his hands went on automatic pilot. He retrieved his fountain pen and a small notebook from his inside pocket. The first pages of the notebook were covered with his jottings from the Billy Carlton tomb desecration.

"I think we need to have a discussion," Van Allen said to the Moores. "Is there a good place to talk?"

"Right here's fine," Bill Moore said. He motioned toward a new sofa.

The Moores sat down.

Van Allen pulled forward a chair, which allowed him to keep his injured right leg straight. He caught the Moores watching him nurse his limp. For some strange reason, he felt awkward around these people. They were both nearly twenty years younger than he and things like that had started to eat at him recently. An obvious disability only worsened his uneasiness.

"I pulled a muscle the other day," Van Allen said, attempting to explain away his affliction. "Normally I don't have leg problems. Used to jog fifteen miles a week."

"Uh-huh," Bill said.

"Mr. Van Allen, what do you think has gone on here?" Rebecca asked.

"I have no way of knowing," Van Allen said, "until you've told me as much as you know. Then we'll do everything we can. That much I can promise you."

Rebecca sighed, trying to stifle the hurt. The upset. The terror, in addition to the unbearable sense of violation. Who could have been in her home? Who could have taken her children?

During the first minutes of the meeting, Van Allen sought to cover the most basic details. He took a description of the children and put it out immediately on the police radio. Rebecca also provided for him a recent photograph of Karen and Patrick together. Two more uniformed men turned up a few minutes later. Van Allen sent one of the men to police headquarters immediately so that a copy of the picture could be transmitted to all Los Angeles precincts, plus those in the surrounding suburbs.

"What are our chances?" she asked, her voice starting to falter. "To find our children . . . alive?"

"The sooner you give us everything we need to work with," Van Allen said again, "the better the chances."

She nodded. She looked around. "Is this all we get? Four street cops? And one detective?"

"No, not all," Van Allen assured her. "This is all you see right here. And a forensic unit will also be by to check for fingerprints or any other potential evidence. But there will be dozens of people working on a case like this, if necessary."

A male voice, her husband's, softly inquired, "What do you mean by, 'if necessary'?"

"We might locate your children in fifteen minutes," the

detective said. "From my lips to God's ear, right? And yet, the sun might set today without our making any progress. Men and women will be assigned as necessary and *if* necessary."

"You make it sound so routine," Rebecca said. "And half my family is missing."

Bill gave her hand a squeeze.

"The disappearance of a child gets the department's highest priority. We also don't have problems calling in the FBI."

Moore snapped to attention. "The FBI. Is *that* necessary?"

"Well, it could be," Van Allen answered, surprised. "I would think you would want them."

"I just don't have much faith in anything J. Edgar Hoover had anything to do with."

"Try to keep an open mind, Mr. Moore. It's not politics, it's crime detection. They have magnificent computers. Nationwide networks of information. Informants. Thousands of very dedicated people. We have similar facilities statewide and citywide, too. But I would think you would want as many available resources as possible on your side." He paused. "I know I would."

"Of course," Rebecca said.

"But our kids could be right in the neighborhood somewhere. They could have just wandered off."

"Any particular reason you suggest that?"

"No," Moore admitted after a slight pause. "I'm speaking hypothetically. Do you know what 'hypothetical' means, officer?"

"I'm familiar with the word, Mr. Moore," Van Allen answered.

"Do we have to start notifying the FBI right away?"

"Do you have a problem with that?"

"I told you. I don't like them. I'm hoping my kids turn up alive right away. I don't want to unleash some huge law enforcement apparatus before we have that chance. We'll have newspaper and television reporters all over our front lawn.

Hell, I would think local connections and possibilities would
have to be hit hard first.''

"They will be. I assure you.''

Van Allen knew he was off to a rocky start with William
Moore. He wondered if the young architect was on some sort
of hostility-inducing chemical.

Van Allen eyed Mr. and Mrs. Moore back and forth. "Now
I need to ask you some questions,'' he said, almost apologeti-
cally. "May I?''

Moore nodded. His approval was grudging and impatient.

"Please go ahead,'' Rebecca said. She tightly clasped her
husband's hand.

"What time did you see your children last?'' Van Allen
asked.

"They went to bed at eight o'clock,'' Rebecca said.
"Sometimes they stay awake a little. You know how kids
are.''

Van Allen nodded. He knew.

"Did you go upstairs with them?'' the detective asked.

Rebecca looked at her husband and let him answer.

"We both did,'' Bill said. "I walked up with Patrick. I put
him in bed. That would have been about quarter past eight.''

"And what about the girl. Karen?'' Van Allen asked. "She
was already asleep by then?''

"Both the kids were up a little late,'' Rebecca said.

"Any particular reason?'' Van Allen asked.

A pause fell in the room. Neither parent answered for a moment.

Van Allen caught the pause. "Something unusual happen
last night, Mr. and Mrs. Moore?'' the detective asked softly.

"Maybe a little too much Halloween,'' Bill Moore said.
"Kids get excited.''

Van Allen would have bet a month's paycheck the Moores
were lying. He could taste it. But for the moment, he let the
point go.

"Were they going to go out tonight?" Van Allen asked. "Trick-or-treating?"

"They were," Rebecca answered.

"With other kids?" Van Allen inquired.

"I was going to take them," said Rebecca. "They were going to go with me. You know. They're very young." Her hands were wrenching a paper tissue now.

The detective nodded. His eyes looked sad, but pensive. He looked down and made several notes.

"Okay, so you saw your son and daughter in bed and asleep last night. Before you retired, yourselves."

"That's correct," Rebecca answered.

"And nothing unusual happened during the night?"

Bill speaking: "No, sir."

"No signs of a break-in, obviously."

"None," Rebecca said.

"Any sign of a struggle? Any bloodstains?" Van Allen asked gently.

Rebecca bit her lower lip and shook her head.

"Good," Van Allen answered softly. "That's actually a positive sign. No struggle." He thought for a moment. "Is there a relative or friend in the neighborhood whom they like? Whom they could have sneaked off to visit?"

"We're new here, as you know," Rebecca said. "No real close friends."

"And no relatives," Bill Moore added.

Van Allen nodded.

"Have your children ever disappeared like this before?" the policeman asked. "Maybe playing a trick. Anything like that?"

The Moores responded with a pair of heads shaking. No, again.

"And nothing unpleasant happened that might have made them angry with you?" Van Allen pressed. "Anything at all, no matter how trivial, which might have caused them to run away?''

Again the Moores answered in the negative.

Van Allen thought for a moment, still making some notes on his pad. Finally he looked up.

''So we know they were in the house, both of them, at about 8:15 P.M.''

''We know they were here later than that,'' Rebecca said.

''Tell me how you know,'' Van Allen asked.

''I checked the kids myself,'' she said, calming somewhat. ''Just before Bill and I went to bed. That would have been . . .'' Her voice trailed off as she tried to think back to establish the precise time.

''We watched the late news on KABC,'' Bill reminded her. ''Bree Walker.''

''That's right,'' Rebecca said. ''Then I went to our bedroom. It takes me about fifteen minutes to get ready and I always check Karen and Patrick right before I retire. So that makes eleven-forty-five.''

''You both retired at the same time?'' Van Allen asked.

There was a moment of hesitation.

''No, I stayed up a bit last night,'' Moore said.

''Until when, sir?''

''I watched David Letterman.''

''The whole show?''

''All of it.''

''I missed it myself last night,'' the detective said. ''Frankly, I often prefer Jay Leno. Or maybe an old movie on cable. Of course, I watch the Lakers, but who doesn't? Who did Letterman have on?''

The only thing that Moore could remember was Elle McPherson. In so many words, he remembered that the hemline of her skirt—as she sat in the guest's chair—or at least the height of it.

Rebecca gave him a sour look. ''Figures that's what he'd

remember," she said. "Our kids are about to be kidnapped and he's leering at some model."

"If anyone had told me they were going to be kidnapped," Bill Moore snapped back, "don't you think I would have done something?"

Her look was not terribly forgiving. The detective's gaze hopped back and forth.

Moore reached for an architecture book and turned back to the policeman for support. "I was also reading a professional journal," he explained. "I lie on the couch at night—this one right here—and read till I'm ready to sleep. I'm a new partner with my graduate school roommate in his firm. His name is Jack McLaughlin. Has offices in Brentwood, right off San Vincente near Barrington. Jim subcontracts to me. But I'm still interested in starting my own firm."

Van Allen found himself nodding.

"You can read a professional journal and watch television at the same time?" Van Allen asked. "I'm impressed."

"Sometimes I like something going on in the background. It helps me concentrate."

"Like Elle McPherson," Rebecca chimed in.

As he listened, Van Allen eyed the sight lines that Moore would have had on the sofa. Line of vision to the TV set, line of vision to the stairs. Moore's account made sense so far.

"Background noise helps you concentrate, does it?" Van Allen pondered. "Most people say it hurts their concentration."

"I'm different," Moore said.

"I suppose so," Van Allen said, writing something again, the Mont Blanc gliding like a Mercedes Benz on paper. "So you were awake alone?"

"That's right."

The detective turned back to Rebecca. "Mrs. Moore? How long would it have taken you to fall asleep?" he asked.

"I get up at six-thirty every morning," she answered. "I'm asleep as soon as my head hits the pillow."

"So, Mr. Moore, you were the last one awake. So was it you who locked the doors to the house?"

"No, *I* locked them," Rebecca answered. "At about 10:00 P.M."

"And neither of you opened any door after that?"

"No."

"No."

"Neither of you needed to check a car? Put garbage out? Grab a bit of air?"

"No."

"No dog to walk? No cat to put out."

"We don't have any pets," Moore answered.

They both agreed that the doors had stayed locked. Van Allen pursed his lips and looked up.

"Forensics might come up with something when they arrive," the policeman said. "But neither door shows any sign of tampering. Nor does any window on the first floor. That might leave a second floor window, but all of those appeared to be locked, too. Nor is there any sign that a ladder was pushed to the house."

"What are you suggesting?"

"Nothing. I'm trying to understand. It's like one of those puzzles," Van Allen said. "What's wrong with this picture? Your children are not in this house. But how could they have left? The door locks, the windows, are not the type that can be sealed from the outside. We agree on that?"

"We agree," said Rebecca.

"So how could anyone have entered? Or exited?"

The detective was met by blank stares from the Moores. Van Allen knew something they were telling him—intentionally or not—couldn't have been true.

"Mind if I have a look around?" Van Allen finally asked.

"Help yourself," said Rebecca.

"Thank you."

Van Allen stood, then stopped. "Oh," he said. "I nearly forgot. Just to reassure you . . ."

He pulled out his wallet, opened it and found a picture of his son, Jason. "I just wanted you to know," Van Allen said. "I'm a husband and a father, too. Well, sadly I'm divorced, but I'm still someone's old man. Two kids actually. This is my boy."

He drew the old picture of his own son out of his wallet. He carefully pulled it out of the cellophane and held it by the edges.

Mrs. Moore took the picture, looked at it, and somewhere in the depths of her spirit found a smile.

"Nice handsome boy."

"He's a young man now," Van Allen said. "Plays baseball at Cal–Santa Clara. I should be so lucky to have four years in Santa Clara, right?"

"Right," said Rebecca.

Bill Moore took the photo and was less impressed. "Nice kid," he said, holding the photograph with a thumb and forefinger. Van Allen took the photo back, taking it again by the edges and pushing it into his wallet.

"I just wanted you to know. I'm going to be on this case until I close it." Van Allen gave them his business card. "I'll do everything I can. Call me anytime day or night for any reason."

"Thanks," Rebecca Moore said.

Bill Moore nodded.

Detective Alice Aldrich turned up a moment later. Double-A took over the Moores for further questioning, leaving Van Allen to prowl around the house and see what he could intuit.

* * *

Fifteen minutes later, Detective Van Allen stood in the center of the turret room on the second floor. He watched two men from the chief of detective's office dust for fingerprints. His eye drifted across the room and settled upon a pair of toys.

Double-A had temporarily finished speaking with the Moores. Both parents had then followed the police to the second story of their home. Rebecca stood close to Van Allen, her arms folded in front of her. Bill Moore put his arm around his wife as they stood nearby and watched the detectives work. Four yellow walls surrounded them.

"I can't believe this is happening," Rebecca said softly. "It's all so damned unreal. Like something out of a nightmare."

Van Allen glanced at her.

"Sometimes these things have logical explanations and happy endings," he answered. "Try to begin with that outlook, Mrs. Moore. It will make things easier."

Rebecca bit her lower lip and tried to muster some courage. When her gaze settled on a snapshot of Patrick on the chest of drawers, however, her composure folded. She started to dissolve into tears.

"I'd like to take my wife downstairs," Bill Moore said.

"Of course," Van Allen said. "I'll be down shortly. Do you mind leaving us here?"

Moore said he didn't. But before leaving, Bill looked at the three policemen poking through their children's playroom. "It doesn't look like we have much of a choice, does it?" he asked.

"No, sir. I'm not sure that you do."

His antagonisms bubbled over. "Just see that you don't break anything," he said. "And see that everything's in the room when you leave."

Van Allen looked at him with growing antagonism of his own. Where was Bill Moore's hostility coming from, he wondered. What was the man hiding? Or was he simply handling the stress in a peculiar way? His reaction was curious.

What was he suggesting? That the LAPD would steal stuff from a children's playroom?

Van Allen sighed. There had been enough bad publicity for the department to fill three lifetimes. This, he supposed, was another receipt. He chose to not take issue with Mr. Moore.

"If anything needs to be removed for fingerprints," Van Allen said, "we'll be sure to let you know."

Bill Moore shot him a withering look and escorted his wife downstairs. Van Allen watched them go. Detective Aldrich went downstairs with the parents of the missing children.

Ed Van Allen looked at the same photograph that had caused Rebecca to lose composure. He held it in his own fingers, carefully shielding it from prints. He took a good look at the children.

He sighed again. He had to admit, for all the reassurance that he had just given the Moores, this didn't look good.

Missing children never did. And the longer they were missing, the more liable to remain missing. Permanently.

But already there was a strange spin to the case.

Two children disappearing *together?* From their home? With no sign of forced entry? No enemies in sight? No ransom message? It was the old "What's wrong with this picture?" game. A lot of things were already wrong with the picture at 2136 Topango Gardens. Some things just didn't make sense.

This case already looked like one of those things. Just like his last significant investigation, Van Allen mused. Billy Carlton's tombstone. That didn't make sense, either.

And that reminded him: he was in the same damned neighborhood. Fact was, he wasn't even far away from San Angelo.

Van Allen's brow crunched into a frown. He began to wonder about something.

He set down the picture of Patrick Moore. He walked to the window in the children's playroom. He looked out, scouring the backyard with his eyes. It was a small but tidy patch, recently renewed as the Moores had suggested. His eye traveled to the rear of the yard. Then his gaze climbed the brick wall and traveled farther on.

His eye climbed the wall and wandered through the field beyond.

Then he froze, a little wave of suspicion overtaking him, followed by a creepy bumpy feeling across his skin.

His eye rambled through the field and realized that he was looking at the south lawn of San Angelo Cemetery. Moments later, in the distance, he was staring at the exhumed grave of Billy Carlton. A little farther on, Van Allen could see Carlton's granite marker lying on its side.

A great big gray fallen angel, dead as a desiccated haddock, lying on its side.

Waiting to be lifted.

Or resurrected.

And waiting just to give wing? Give flight?

Van Allen wondered.

"Jesus F. Christ," he found himself muttering aloud.

"Detective?" asked one of the lab men looking for fingerprints, glancing up.

"Nothing," Van Allen muttered. "Nothing."

But he stared at the cemetery for several more seconds, then turned away. He now had two cases with inexplicable circumstances right within sight of each other.

In his line of work, he had always believed, there was no such thing as coincidence. Yet here it was, staring him in the face.

Unless there *were* parallels.

And if there were, perhaps he was looking at the very beginning of an explanation.

16

Halloween evening arrived.

Children from the neighborhood came by the house at 2136 Topango Gardens. A police car remained posted near the house, and the word quickly spread through the neighborhood that both Patrick and Karen were missing.

On Sunday, this translated into a stream of well-wishers from the neighborhood. They came to wish the Moores luck and offer support. Prayers were said in the nearby churches. Privately, most people feared the worst for Patrick and Karen.

Monday arrived. So did the first full week of November. The Moore case had made the local news. An FBI team was assigned to the investigation. Agents from the local office in Los Angeles interviewed Rebecca and Bill Moore again, asking them the same questions over and over. Their answers and explanations did not waver.

Bill and Rebecca handled their grief and their concern differently. Rebecca was given to bouts of sleeplessness and sorrow, including long fits of crying. Melissa stood by her and tried to be of comfort. Rebecca also played with the idea of calling her mother back East to let her know what had happened. But she continued to veto the idea. If her mother had come to California to stay with her and help her maintain a vigil, it somehow would have only made things worse.

For his part, Bill became quick-tempered and sullen, even more than usual. The tension of his children's disappearance exacerbated his work situation. It made it almost impossible for him to concentrate on architecture, he told his wife.

Still, he tried to work. Or at least he said he did, spending hours away from the house. It was Rebecca who was trapped at home with her thoughts. Again, Melissa was with her constantly, proving to be as good a friend as Rebecca had ever made.

Detective Van Allen set the San Angelo desecration on the back corner of his desk. Then, with Alice Aldrich assisting, he became the principal city detective in the investigation of the Moore children's disappearance.

Search parties, which included dogs, failed to find a trace of Patrick or Karen. No ransom note arrived. No friend or relative had seen them. No teacher had any reason to think that they might have been upset.

When Ed Van Allen went to Santa Monica next, passing an hour studying the ocean, he was a deeply perplexed man. From all accounts, the children had disappeared *inside* the house at 2136 Topango.

Van Allen cringed. He knew the direction his thoughts were taking. The last time he had a case that matched that description, two small bodies had eventually been found encased in the concrete of the foundation, their throats cut.

He turned over the point in his head. He thought he had honed some pretty good instincts over the years, and the Moores didn't seem like the type to have done something to their children. Bill Moore was a little difficult to decipher, he decided, but Rebecca Moore's grief and concern were legitimate.

He sighed. Unfortunately, he would have to ask the Moores to take polygraph tests, he decided. Not an easy step, as it would surely antagonize the people he was most trying to help.

But the administration of lie detector tests to the victimized parents was an increasingly common step in cases with missing children. Van Allen considered a recent incident in South Carolina, where a mother had drowned her two children by strapping them into the family car and driving them into a lake. An early polygraph might have saved the police days of trouble in that case.

By Tuesday morning, there were no new leads in the case. Van Allen asked the FBI agents in charge if they would administer the lie detector exams. The FBI said they would make the request, but reminded Van Allen that at this juncture they could only *ask* the Moores to comply. They couldn't make the test mandatory.

Yet.

But the request was made. Rebecca said she would do it. Her husband said he would consider it. His response did not endear him to the LAPD. The test was scheduled for late in the week. Probably Friday morning.

Tuesday died. Wednesday morning arrived.

Rebecca and Bill Moore began to accustom themselves to the presence of reporters near their driveway or spilling over into their property. There always seemed to be at least one reporter camped out in front of 2136 Topango Gardens. Usually, there were half a dozen.

The story of Karen and Patrick Moore's disappearance was one of regional interest now. And one of the national tabloids had sent a reporter, working on the angle of the children disappearing within the confines of their eerie old home. Inquiring minds again wanted to know.

The Moores both hated the idea of the lie detector. They couldn't comprehend what, if anything, a polygraph of victimized parents would ever have to do with the return of their children. But Rebecca reasoned further that if the test were enough to eliminate her as a suspect—which was the only real reason why detective Van Allen would want to have it done—

and send police in the proper direction, it was worth her time.

It was only then, when she scheduled the test for the next Friday afternoon, that her darkest doubts about her husband surfaced. She wondered why he wouldn't just accede to the test and remove himself from any lingering suspicions.

But he wouldn't.

Her ruminations were shared by Detective Van Allen. But neither mentioned their individual suspicions to the other. And Bill Moore was too busy burying himself in his work even to issue a denial.

But then again, there was nothing to deny.

Yet.

Thursday morning came. Still nothing new in the case. Rebecca had clipped from the newspapers a pair of classified ads for employment, but had no stomach anymore for going to job interviews. She lived in a constant state of tension, waiting for the moment when her telephone would ring with a break in the case, or when Sergeant Van Allen would arrive at the door with news.

Good news or bad news. Emotionally, Rebecca didn't even want to entertain the thought of a tragic end to the case. But subconsciously, she was readying herself for one. Or, worse, what if the case were never resolved at all? How would she live with that, never knowing what had happened to her two children?

At night, the nightmares were gone, replaced by real fears and real sleeplessness. She felt abysmally helpless. She spent her time around the house, preoccupied by fear and anxiety, and trying to keep busy with small tasks.

Small tasks like putting shelf paper in a cupboard on the second floor. Like taking the first steps in stripping and refinishing the steps that led to the attic. Like doing something about that dreadful scent—the scent of death—that still materialized from time to time in the turret room.

Strangely enough, a small touch of the bizarre intruded. In cleaning a shelf in the kitchen, Rebecca came across a smashed pair of red-framed eyeglasses in the rear of a cabinet.

She was about to throw them out, thinking they were left from the previous tenant. And then she realized. The glasses were the pair that Essie Lewisohn had misplaced on the day the broker had first shown the house to the Moores.

Rebecca turned the glasses over curiously in her hand. Essie had thought she had left the specs on a table in the living room? How could they have jumped to the kitchen cabinet? And why hadn't she or Bill noticed them before? When she found them, they were clearly visible. Why hadn't they been visible previously?

Who could have moved them? And why, for that matter, were they broken? Rebecca didn't understand.

And yet this, in turn, paled in relation to the events of Thursday afternoon.

Rebecca had spent the early part of the afternoon on the second floor of her home. She was, of all things, tending to her children's rooms.

She was trying to think positively of the current situation. She wanted to have both rooms ready for them the instant they returned home. She refused to think in any other terms.

Patrick and Karen *would* return, she kept telling herself, and they would return soon.

She was in Patrick's room, reorganizing the clothes in his closet, when she heard a noise in the hall. Rebecca left Patrick's room to investigate.

The noise had sounded like footsteps and she thought her husband was home.

When she stepped into the hall and called his name, however, she knew that she was mistaken.

"Hello?" she called. "Is anyone there?"

She walked through the hall and went to the front window. The same little knot of reporters was there that had been there all morning. Whenever someone came or went from the house, the reporters were on their feet with cameras and note-pads. They were sitting tranquilly now, so Rebecca knew no one had come or gone.

She walked back toward her son's room.

But when she passed the turret room she stopped short. Once again the door was open. And she knew that she had firmly closed and latched it twenty minutes earlier.

She stared at it for several seconds. And then a wave of goose bumps crawled across the entire flesh of her body.

For the first time in several days, she could hear the piano music again. Bold music this time. Not quite as tinny or canned as previous times. And the tune sounded like a theme. Or a background from an old movie. The music was clearer than it had ever been before.

Melissa's cheerful voice came back.

"You've got a ghost. Maybe two."

Rebecca could feel the hair rise on the back of her neck. And from somewhere came a shiver. She even felt herself fighting off a sense of dread, one of which she couldn't identify the origin.

Then there was a male voice. It was more distinct than it had ever been before. It was slithery, but clear. And Rebecca thought that it had a vague echo of a middle-Atlantic state. Virginia perhaps. Or Maryland.

The voice called again.

Rebecca . . . ?

It beckoned. It summoned.

Rebecca turned toward the open doorway. She slowly approached it. She felt herself thinking that she didn't want to know who had opened it. She didn't want to see anyone. She didn't want to know who was in the room.

Nonsense, Rebecca, dear. Don't be scared.

And yet, another part of her screamed out that she wanted
to know. Another part of her was drawn to the room. And one
way or another, she knew she had to find out.

Doors didn't just open by themselves?

Did they?

A hand is needed to turn a knob, even if the hand is invisible. A thought shot through her head. Maybe we are all surrounded by invisible hands, turning the knobs and locks to our
lives without our knowing it.

She was ten feet from the entrance to the yellow room.
Then five. Never before in her life had a doorway loomed so
large.

Rebecca Moore drew a breath.

She looked past the door to what she could see of the empty
room. All she could make out was some of the furniture that
she had bought for her children. That and the windows and the
walls.

But deep down, she knew. Someone, something, some
presence, was in that room. It was in there *now*.

Waiting for her.

Next, she was in the doorframe. She pushed the door wide
open, the feeling of dread now giving way to something else:
a mixture of both fear and attraction, polar opposites tangling
with each other, like the needle on a compass spinning wildly
out of control.

The door went wide. There was sunlight in the room. She
stepped in, expecting to see someone.

But instead she saw no one.

Didn't see. But knew he was there.

"Ronny?" she asked.

No movement. But there was this unbanishable sense of a
presence. A presence that she somehow thought she recognized. Something familiar, as familiar as a kiss from a lover.
And her sense of being watched, that old sense that she had
always had, was as keen as it had ever been.

It was more than fear that motivated her now. She felt that there was a pair of eyes upon her, a pair that she couldn't see but which was fixed very closely upon her, like some feral beast lying in wait for a prey.

But where were they?

I'm very near, Rebecca. Very near.

Then an even more unsettling notion gripped her: if who-ever had unlatched the door wasn't in the room, he—or she, or *it*—was somewhere else in the house.

But this thought dissipated, too, giving way to an even stranger one. This one had words to it, almost like a voice speaking to her. And then she realized.

Close enough to touch you. Close enough to embrace you.

The voice was *speaking* to her. No way to ignore it any-more.

Come into the room, Rebecca, my love. Please come into my room and be comfortable.

This voice that she heard now, and this low murmur she had heard on other occasions, were one and the same.

She stepped farther into the room. No one. But her feelings were ambivalent now. Her fear seemed to drift away, like a bad headache that was suddenly lifted. And the turret room seemed to embrace her.

Her heart, fluttering as it had been, calmed itself and set-tled. She drew a breath again. She inhaled and exhaled, deeply both ways. She moved to the window and looked out. Now she felt as if she were in a trance.

Am I mad? she thought to herself. *Have I finally gone com-pletely crazy? Have I finally slipped off the edge of sanity?*

No, darling, no. You are quite fine. You have merely en-tered another plane, where I have waited for you.

"Where are you?" Rebecca asked. "Who's talking to me?"

I'm near enough to touch you.

She whirled, looking everywhere, seeing nothing. "Then touch me," she begged.

Rebecca jumped. Something like a breeze fluttered through her hair, gentle and caressing, soft as a kiss.

"Where are you?" she asked, her voice a whisper now.

Promise not to tell? It's our secret?

"Where are you?" she asked again. "I want to know."

Go to the window. Look outside.

Rebecca turned again. She looked through the window.

"I don't see anything," she said.

Nonsense. You see everything! Concentrate!

"But . . . ?"

A whisper: *Concentrate on what you see.*

She studied the landscape. The backyard was coming around to good shape, she noticed. The brick wall was looking better since her husband had worked on it. Above it and beyond it, the fallow territory of the cemetery lay beneath a calm sky.

Was that what she was meant to see?

Then she noticed something funny. There was a tiny shadow creeping rapidly across the rear of the cemetery, like the image of a cloud moving at a very high speed. It came directly toward 2136 Topango Gardens.

It seemed to accelerate. It was heading straight toward her! She knew . . .

"Oh, God . . . !" she said.

The shadow crossed the fence and came across the back lawn of 2136 Topango. It came directly toward her home and then it covered it. And when it did, she felt something strange, like an acute change in the atmospheric pressure in the room.

Then she had the sense again of a pair of eyes upon her, stronger than ever before. And she knew she was no longer alone in the yellow room. Nor had she ever been alone in that chamber.

Now, my love. Turn. . . . Now you may look upon me.

Turning, she jumped. Her heart kicked so hard that it felt as if it were going to explode in her chest.

There was a man standing in the room, midway between her and the doorway. He had arrived in complete silence, which made no sense because all of the upstairs floorboards would creak beneath a footfall.

All she could do was stare. But there was no fear. Her fear was gone. Nor did she feel any menace. Instead, there was only an odd echo of familiarity, of attraction. She was reacting more on intuition now than logic, but also had the sense of having entered another world.

He was a handsome man, about six feet one with tousled brown hair and gorgeous dark eyes. He was simply dressed in a plain white shirt open at the collar. His waist was trim and he wore dark slacks, and his eyes were settled upon her.

Ronny, she found herself thinking. *So now I have finally met Ronny.*

He was just the way her children had described him.

Somehow, perhaps intuitively again, Rebecca Moore knew she was looking at a ghost.

The visitor's lips moved. He spoke softly. "Rebecca . . . ?" he asked.

Logic against emotion. Her soul split in half. Her brain against her heart. It felt like another explosion building up inside her.

"Rebecca?" he asked again.

Now other words formed inside her. Her own words. Her own thoughts. Her response.

"What are you doing here?" was all she could say.

"I've come for you."

She shook her head.

"No!" she answered. She shook her head a second time, violently. "No, this can't be," she insisted. "What do you mean, you've 'come for me'? Are you telling me I'm dying? It can't be my time."

"That's not what I mean. You're alive."

She moved her eyes away. Her gaze traveled through the window and out across the brick wall, out to the distant gravestones, and it was her thought that somehow, somewhere, in a quirky universe, that some spirit had slipped up out of the earth and had begun to wander.

She looked back quickly, thinking that the man might be gone, and that she might have been hallucinating.

But he wasn't gone. And she wasn't hallucinating.

"Talk to me, Rebecca," he asked.

"Where are my children?" she asked.

His answer was a beautiful smile.

"Do you have my children?"

He didn't speak.

"Where *are* they?" she demanded. "Are they dead or alive?"

"They're safe, Rebecca," he said.

Emboldened, she stepped toward the ghost. But as she approached him, he receded. He seemed solid, not opaque, and if she hadn't intuitively realized that he was a ghost, she might never have known.

Then, before her eyes, he disappeared. She experienced something unlike anything she had ever felt in her life—something like a very strong breeze or wind, carefully channeled and rushing right into her. She seemed enveloped by it, sort of like a gust of leaves sweeping past her.

Yet this current actually felt as if it were sweeping through her, like a powerful positive emotion, though that was impossible in the world she had always known.

And yet again, when she turned in the turret room, the ghost was directly behind her, flickering slightly now, like an image in an old film.

"You're a ghost," she said.

"I'm a spirit," he answered.

"You're dead."

"You see me. Hence, I exist. I have life."

"Why are you here? What do you want?"

Silence from the visitor. Then, "Don't you know me?" he inquired.

She felt as if a bizarre window had opened onto another world. *Know* him? From where? Yet there was something about him she couldn't place, an aspect of familiarity that had an eerie edge to it.

"What do you want?" she asked again. "Please answer me."

"I mean you no harm, Rebecca," he said.

"I want Patrick and Karen," she answered.

"You'll have them."

"When?"

He shrugged.

"When?" she demanded. She took a long look at the intruder. "Where are they?" she asked.

He smiled.

"You have them don't you?" she accused.

The ghost didn't speak. But it communicated an answer. Rebecca knew the response was yes.

The next question was difficult for her to say. But she knew she had to pose it.

"If they're with you, are they dead or alive?" she asked.

No answer. Instead, the ghost misted before her eyes, fading from a very solid and tactile presence into nothing but empty air. He was gone in a matter of seconds. Yet Rebecca also knew the ghost was still there.

Somewhere.

She felt something like a gentle breeze flow past her. Then suddenly something was touching her bare hand as it hung at her side. She pulled back, not in fear but in surprise.

Then she realized. The touch was similar to a female child's, reaching for a mother's palm.

"Patrick? Karen?" she asked in the empty room. "Where are you guys? Your mom and dad miss you!"

Another touch, or what seemed like one, on the other side of her. She turned in that direction, too.

It had been a firmer touch. More assertive. A male child, she was sure. *Patrick's touch!*

She flailed at the empty air. More nothing. Or nothing that she could see. But what had been there? Two small invisible hands seeking to grasp hers?

Was she loony?

And if her children were now invisible, if they had been turned into spirits, did that mean they were irretrievably—?

Dead in the middle of her thought, Rebecca heard footsteps on the stairs leading down from the second floor. It sounded like a man with two children.

She fled the turret room and went to the landing at the top of the steps. She looked to the spot from where the sound had emanated. She could still hear it. But she couldn't see anything.

Then another thought came to her.

Go to the window, Rebecca. Look to San Angelo. You will find comfort among the angels.

She walked back to the turret room, moving cautiously, her entire concept of reality forever changed.

She moved to the center of the room and hesitated about going to the window. She was afraid of what she might see. In some ways, the sequence had a dreamlike quality. She felt she was gliding rather than stepping; she had the sense of seeing herself as if from above, rather than living the experience directly.

But she found herself in front of the lone window in the turret room. Her gaze traveled through the backyard of her home and to the rear of the cemetery beyond.

The moment that followed would forever seem frozen, a

lingering still photograph, an image more than an actual event.

But she couldn't mistake what it was.

The ghost she had seen in her home now walked in the rear of San Angelo. It was unmistakably the same figure. He was clothed the same way and was of the same stature.

Rebecca's eyes went wide, however. The ghost was not alone.

He walked hand in hand with two young children. Rebecca's.

Patrick and Karen. They strolled as if with a father figure and they walked back toward the burial area of the cemetery.

Rebecca held this view for several seconds, before she screamed.

She called out their names.

"Patrick! Karen!"

And their young heads turned in response. Their cherubic faces illuminated with smiles. Ronny released their hands and both daughter and son waved to her. But they voluntarily remained with Ronny. And they looked happy.

The children's words echoed, from the night of their disappearance.

"He wants us to come with him."

She called their names again. They waved and walked farther with Ronny, back toward the tombstones. She called their names a third time.

This time they didn't acknowledge. They were much farther away now, linked hand in hand with their guide. Rebecca watched them go. Like a bird or an airplane, disappearing on the horizon, they became harder and harder to see.

Like Ronny, they misted, flickered, and disappeared, long before they reached the burial ground.

Another snippet of words came back to her, the message

that had emerged on the wall from under the fresh coats of primer and yellow paint.

"YOU ARE IN DANGER."

She had taken it to mean that she, Rebecca, was in danger. Actually, she now decided, it had been meant for the children. They were the ones who had disappeared.

But she turned it over in her head again. Who *was* in danger? Karen and Patrick? Or herself?

And who was in danger now, if anyone?

Rebecca gazed out the window like a madwoman, staring at San Angelo, a constellation of thoughts swirling around her. She held the view of San Angelo until she heard someone from below speak her name.

"Mrs. Moore?"

A woman's voice. At first she thought it was Melissa's. But Melissa would have called her by her first name.

"Mrs. Moore?"

She looked downward until she found the source. It was one of the reporters, followed quickly by the whole knot of them, drawn by her screams out the rear window of her home.

A gaggle of bemused, curious—almost accusatory faces—stared upward at her. Cameras clicked. A hand-held television camera whirred softly, its lens fixed upon her.

"Did you see something, Mrs. Moore?" a male stranger with a notepad asked.

"Did you see your children?" the first woman asked.

"Get the hell off my property!" Rebecca snapped.

But the press didn't move. They studied her every move and recorded it, like visitors to a zoo, until she slammed the window and drew the curtain.

Then she stood in the turret room for several minutes, alone in the silence, isolated in the madness—the impossibility!—of what she had seen. Her reaction was not so much one of fear, but one of shock.

She was again aware of the shadows passing through the backyard, and the lengthening of them, which suggested that afternoon was turning to evening. When she next consulted her watch, she realized that she had lost track of time. But she knew she had walked into Patrick's room to work in his closet at four-thirty. But now it was five-fifteen.

Somewhere forty-five minutes had disappeared.

She couldn't account for the lapse. It did not feel as if she had been in the turret room for anything resembling that amount of time. The only thing she could think of was that when she had entered the realm of the ghost other standards of time—or voids in time—existed.

She left the room in a daze and walked downstairs. She put on a light and sat down in the living room. She turned on the television for companionship, but didn't listen to it. Instead, she waited for evening, eager for her husband to return home. She was trying to sort out what had happened.

When Bill returned, she said nothing immediately. She sat in the living room of their home, mute, barely acknowledging his presence.

She forced him to come to her and speak.

"Rebecca?" he finally asked. "Becca, what's going on. Talk to me."

She then turned on her husband, felt a shiver of terror overtake her so violently that she felt like she was being shaken by a huge unseen hand.

She screamed uncontrollably, and then her screams dissolved into sobs, sobs which she muffled on his shoulder until they had cascaded out of her and diminished into nothing.

Only then, as she gradually regained control of her emotions, was she able to describe the events of the afternoon to the man with whom she currently shared her life.

PART TWO

17

With the blessing of her husband and the Los Angeles police, Rebecca scheduled an emergency meeting with Dr. Henry Einhorn for Friday at lunchtime. Detective Van Allen had allowed her to put off the polygraph test from Friday till Saturday.

Melissa drove Rebecca to Century City and accompanied her friend to the psychiatrist's office. Del Morninglori greeted Rebecca at the door to Dr. Henry Einhorn's suite in Century City. Del was solicitous and indulgent. It was obvious that he knew all about her children's disappearance, but he asked no questions about it.

Rebecca's session with Dr. Einhorn began at half past noon. Melissa waited in the reception room. Einhorn expressed his sympathy over what had happened involving her children. Sitting across from her in a chair in a shaded room, the psychiatrist angled her into the interview.

"When you called this morning you suggested that there was some urgency to this meeting," Dr. Einhorn said. "I'm aware of the larger personal problems you're having. Was there something else also?"

Rebecca held a long pause. She took a sip from a nearby glass of water to steady herself.

"I saw a ghost," she said.

Einhorn's eyes were upon her, soft and brown, fixed and set like a terrier watching a duck.

Very slightly, he settled back in his chair.

"What sort of ghost?" he said.

"It was a man," she said. "I saw him in my home. He was there as plain or as real as you're here right now, Doctor."

"Did he scare you?"

"The situation scared me," she said.

"But the man himself, the vision, didn't?"

"I don't know," she said. "He had my children with him. I found that frightening." She paused. "May I call what I saw 'a ghost'?" she asked.

"If you want to."

"Do you believe in such things?" she asked.

"I don't discount the possibility of anything, Rebecca," he said.

"So you're not laughing at me?"

"Of course not. It's not my place to laugh. You tell me what you think you saw."

She felt reassured. "Then I'll call it a ghost," she said.

"Why are you so sure?" he asked. "What *is* a ghost? What do you think it was?"

"My friend, Melissa, whom you just met?" Rebecca answered. "She says a ghost is a disembodied spirit. I think that's a good definition."

Dr. Einhorn glanced toward the anteroom. "Why does Melissa know so much?"

"She's a little strange. I guess she's studied these things."

"Did she in any way *suggest* that you might be seeing a ghost?" the psychiatrist asked.

"I don't think so."

"Did you have any previous discussions on the subject?"

Rebecca thought back to the night of the party. Melissa, now that Rebecca thought of it, *had* suggested the possibility. Rebecca recalled the incident and detailed it for the doctor.

"But I know what I saw," Rebecca added quickly. "I saw a ghost."

"And does your friend's definition work for you?" Dr. Einhorn asked. " 'A disembodied spirit'?"

Rebecca said it did.

"Have you always believed in such things?"

"Not until I saw one."

"Tell me a little more about what happened."

Rebecca described in detail how she had been in the turret room—the troubled yellow turret room—and had sensed something coming to see her. The house and the room had been empty. And suddenly the specter was there.

"And you said that it had your children with it?"

"Yes. He did."

" 'He'? It was definitely a man?"

"Yes," she said.

"A lot of people would have found this terrifying," Dr. Einhorn said at length. "But you didn't?"

"It was much less terrifying than the incident in Connecticut. That was so much more physical."

"Physical how?"

"The threat. It was so clear, so immediate. The incident with the ghost was, I mean, well it freaked me out. But the man almost seemed, I don't know. Familiar, maybe."

Einhorn's eyes narrowed.

"Familiar how?" the psychiatrist asked.

"It's hard to say."

"Well," he suggested, "familiar, as if you had seen this man on television? Or in a movie? Or familiar in the sense of knowing him personally?"

Rebecca pondered the point for a moment. "Familiar," she said, "as if I knew him personally."

"Knew him well?" Einhorn asked.

She thought about it. The correct answer seemed to come to her from somewhere. So Rebecca nodded.

Einhorn smiled reassuringly. "Where could you know him from?" he asked.

Rebecca opened her hands in a gesture of not knowing. "I wish I could tell you," she said.

"Another life?" the doctor said. "Like Shirley MacLaine?"

"Is that a serious suggestion?"

"Not really." The diminutive doctor tried to steer her. "Maybe he reminds you of someone else whom you know?" he said.

"No, no," Rebecca answered softly, shaking her head. "It was him *personally*. Thinking back on it, you see, that's what I find so strange. That's why I wasn't scared."

"Then maybe it was someone whom you used to know. But who is deceased now."

Rebecca sighed. "That explanation would work, except I don't know who it would be," she said. She thought about it for several seconds. "Know what it's like? It's like trying to think of a name. Or a certain word. It's on the tip of your tongue. Or it feels like it's on the front of your mind. But you can't quite find it."

"And yet, your husband says you were hysterical last evening. Is he exaggerating?"

"That was in the evening," Rebecca answered. "I was . . . I was deeply upset about the experience. Of seeing my children with what I took to be a ghost." She paused. "But as for fear of the man, himself? No," she said. "I remember it with considerable calm."

"How tactile was the experience?" Einhorn asked.

"What do you mean?"

"Did you touch or embrace the man?"

"No."

"Did you touch your children?"

"No. But something touched me."

"Did you feel as if you wanted to?"

"Wanted to what?"

"Strike him? Embrace him? Anything of the physical nature?"

"Nothing like that occurred to me."

"Do you remember anything else? Smells? Senses of hot or cold?" he asked.

Rebecca shook her head again. Her hands were moist. She played with a paper tissue. "And I'll tell you what really bothers me. Both the kids used to report seeing a man in the house."

Einhorn's head shot up from his notes. "A prowler?"

"No. An imaginary friend. They called him 'Ronny.' "

"Ronny?" the doctor repeated.

"I think Ronny was the ghost," Rebecca said. "I think they were seeing the same thing I saw. And this Ronny? The night before the kids disappeared, he said that he was going to take them with him."

Einhorn was fascinated. "This is a conversation you had with your children?" he asked.

"My husband will even verify that part," she said. "He was included in the discussion."

"I see," Einhorn said, thinking. "Where does this 'Ronny' name come from?"

"I have no idea," she said.

"Please think hard on this: Did you or your husband ever suggest the presence of an invisible friend. A 'Ronny'?"

"No."

"Keep thinking. As hard as you've ever thought, Rebecca."

"No," she repeated.

"Do you know anyone who has ever had that name?"

"No."

"Friend? Relative? Enemy? An old boyfriend?" the doctor pressed.

"No one," she said. "No one whom I can consciously remember. And yet . . ."

"And yet, what?" Einhorn asked.

"And yet, it all seemed *so* familiar, when I look back on it. Even more now today while I'm trying to concentrate on it. His face, his mannerisms, his hands. The way he held his arms."

"How did he hold them?"

Rebecca made a gesture of the way she first saw the ghost, arms akimbo, before he held the hands of her children.

"It was so . . . I don't know," she said, the stress rising in her voice. "There was *something* that I'd seen somewhere before."

"You're probably right," Einhorn said, easing back slightly. "There probably was. The question for us now is finding what that something was. And where it came from."

He glanced at the clock and led Rebecca through another quarter hour's worth of discussion.

Then Dr. Einhorn fell silent for several minutes, organizing his notes. At one point he stood and walked behind his desk to a bookshelf. Rebecca watched him as he went to a reference book of some sort, looking something up. He pursed his lips when he found it, and then returned to his chair. He wrote for another minute. Then he went to the window, adjusted the shades to increase the light in the room, and gave Rebecca a smile.

"If it's time to analyze," Rebecca said, "can Melissa come into the room?" she asked.

"If those are your wishes," Einhorn said, "I have no objection."

"Those are my wishes."

Einhorn hit the buzzer and asked Del to bring Melissa in. Melissa sat down in an extra chair on Rebecca's side of the chamber.

"I'll going to tell you what I think," Dr. Einhorn finally

began. "With everything that's been going on in your life, your case borders on the unique. So I think we should treat it in a unique, and aggressive, manner. Okay?"

"Okay so far," she said.

"Let me sum up a few things first. You are still dealing with the trauma from last February," he began, "and now there's all the stress and anxiety surrounding this horrible disappearance of your children." He paused. "From the standpoint of the mind, it's as if your body is attacked by a virus, and then medical complications set in."

He adjusted the pad on his lap and continued.

"If you wanted to do a pop-psych analysis of the vision you saw," Einhorn explained, "I think the conclusions that would be drawn are clear. Ghosts come from the land of the dead. Your children were with a ghost, albeit a benevolent one. Some therapists would suggest that you entertained this vision because your inner self is attempting to adjust to the idea that your children are, God forbid, already dead. And you want to believe they are with a responsible adult figure who will protect them."

Rebecca cringed slightly. "I expect to see my children again alive," she said. "I'm not making any such concessions."

"No," he answered gently. "Not consciously, you're not."

She waited a moment. "Why a man and not a woman?" Rebecca asked.

"The paternal figure in this instance is perhaps more reassuring to you," Dr. Einhorn said. "Many women would find the idea of their children with a substitute *mother* to be more of an adversarial situation. I know this isn't politically correct, so don't take me to task for it: but many women find the idea of a male protector to be very comforting."

Rebecca sighed and nodded. Melissa smirked.

"You may consider everything I just said," Einhorn continued. "You can accept it or dismiss it. Whichever, because I have some further thoughts on the incident. You see, I might be proved wrong here, but I want to venture out onto a limb. I think there's something else going on here, too. Something even more significant. And I'm not sure that it doesn't lie at the heart of everything."

"You're losing me, Doctor," she said. "Something else of what sort?"

"Don't know," he said thoughtfully. "I don't know because I can't see inside your head. But I sure would like to. And there *are* ways." He paused. "Since there's a criminal case involved, this might even be easier to arrange."

There was a slight hesitation, then the doctor asked, "Rebecca, have you ever been hypnotized?"

She was astonished. "Is *that* what you're suggesting?"

"Yes, I am."

"You want to hypnotize me?"

Dr. Einhorn shook his head. "Not me personally. *I* wouldn't. Hypnotism is a specialty. It has to be done very carefully and by a psychiatrist who specializes in hypnotherapy. There are a handful of doctors in Los Angeles whose practices center around such things."

Rebecca looked at Melissa, then back to the doctor. "I don't know," she said. "I've got to think that my head is scrambled enough already."

"This might be your finest opportunity to unscramble it," Dr. Einhorn said. "A hypnotist can get at something that's lurking even deeper than your reaction to recent events. A hypnotherapist can get right down to what's beneath the surface." He paused again. "You'd be amazed at what we might find."

"I might be frightened at what we might find," Rebecca answered.

Dr. Einhorn laughed slightly, then frowned, tiny spidery

lines furrowing his small forehead. "Why do you say that?" he asked.

Rebecca threw up her hands. "I don't even know why I said that," she said.

He looked at her very soberly. "All the more reason, Rebecca," he said. "You'll get to know yourself much better, as long as you go into this in a positive frame of mind."

"May I interject a question?" Melissa asked.

"Of course," the doctor answered.

"What if there's something subconscious about the disappearance?" Melissa said. "I didn't mean that Rebecca did anything to her kids. I know she didn't. What I mean is—?"

"Might we explore that avenue?" Einhorn asked. "Might we prowl around for something that's useful in that direction? Is that what you're asking?"

"Yes," Melissa said.

"That would be fifty percent of our objective," Henry Einhorn said. "If there were a chance in a hundred that we could find something that way, something you might have seen subliminally, something that might give the police a clue, I would think you would leap at the opportunity."

Rebecca looked to Melissa who gave it a thumbs-up gesture. Then she looked back to the doctor.

"Who would the hypnotherapist be?"

"The best hypnotherapist in the city is at UCLA Medical in Westwood. Dr. Chang Lim. I'll call his office if you'll permit me."

Rebecca looked to Melissa for support. Melissa gave her an enthusiastic nod.

"As I said," Dr. Einhorn continued, "I'll call his office. But if I were you, I'd get in touch with him right away. If this can have a positive solution, the sooner the better."

Rebecca nodded again. "All right," she said. "I'll do it."

* * *

In a different part of Los Angeles, at exactly the same hour, Ed Van Allen stood at his desk and picked up the results of a fingerprint inquiry.

He had a clear thumb impression of both Mr. and Mrs. Moore, as well as a forefinger print for Bill Moore. Both had been taken from the photograph of Van Allen's son Jason that the detective had pulled from his wallet. Van Allen always carried an extra photo for exactly that purpose.

He had run the prints through the LAPD's detective bureau on Friday morning. The results had came back near 1:00 P.M. There was no linkage of the Moores' fingerprints prints to any known criminal activity in Southern California.

Double-A came by Van Allen's desk and saw him looking at the results.

"So?" Alice Aldrich asked. "Are the Moores like in a cult of devil worshipers?" she asked.

"You think they're clean, don't you?" he asked, raising his eyes. Double-A was wearing a light blue shirt and tan slacks today. To Van Allen's tired eyes, Alice carried a heavy fox quotient, an especially high one for a member of the detective bureau.

But Van Allen stuck to business.

"I still don't like something about them," Van Allen said. "There's something wrong somewhere. I don't know whether it's with him or with her. It's just like the way their story doesn't work. What they're telling me is that their son and daughter disappeared without leaving the house."

Double-A shot him a skeptical glance. She took the fingerprint report from him and glanced at it.

"Don't believe me, huh?" Van Allen asked.

"I'm like just not following your line of investigation, okay?"

Van Allen reached for some coffee. "Let me tell you," he said, "if they had a walk-in freezer in that house, I'd want to look in it."

The detective took the prints back from his occasional partner and left the room. He faxed the prints to the FBI crime laboratory in Quantico, Virginia. Instinct again. Something about their damned case didn't make sense. Something *heavy*. Little details askew he could live with.

Double-A disappeared to work a competing case, an in-your-face housebreaking in Los Feliz. A local TV producer's apartment had been cleaned out a week after he had done a thirty-minute special on burglary prevention.

That evening, Van Allen drove by 2136 Topango Gardens on his way home. Rebecca was in-house again with Melissa. Bill Moore was still at work at 5:30 P.M., and the detective was starting to entertain the notion that Mr. Moore was avoiding him.

If so, he wondered, why?

He would have liked to have slapped a full-time surveillance on Moore—instinct yet again—but instead had to settle for keeping Rebecca under occasional scrutiny.

This evening, as was the case on other evenings, it was Van Allen's responsibility to inform her that no new leads were apparent in the case. In fact, nothing much of anything had happened since the children had first been reported missing.

Left to his own devices, Van Allen would also have liked to go into 2136 Topango Gardens with a search warrant. The more he thought about it, the more he would have loved to attack with some sledgehammers and taken the house apart. The thing was, he thought to himself, the LAPD's damned German shepherds had already sniffed all over the place and been alerted to nothing.

Van Allen hung around the house for several minutes. By prearrangement, Alice Aldrich came by, dropped off by another female detective, and they rendezvoused there. They kept looking for any sign of digging—a new rose garden or a newly planted tree that might have been used to cover a pair of small graves—or some sort of renovation under the basement.

But nothing was apparent. And when Van Allen thought about such things within the house, an uneasy buzz settled upon him. It was almost as if some unseen voice was telling him he was off on the wrong track.

"Fine," he eventually mumbled to himself. "Then what's the *right* track?"

No answer came to that one.

He and Alice Aldrich ran a small gauntlet of reporters as they departed. Van Allen shrugged and told them there were no new developments in the case. Then they left together in Van Allen's car. They tossed around some possibilities.

"Of course," Van Allen growled to Double-A, "if those kids are buried in six feet of concrete, no damned dog with a sophisticated snout is going to find them, either."

Alice might have offered a pretty sharp comment in her own right, but the case perplexed her just as much.

They rode in silence for several seconds. A police radio crackled under the dashboard of his car, but he ignored it.

"Know what?" Van Allen finally said. "Got a couple of minutes? I got that other case right in this area."

"Which one?"

"Cemetery of Angels. The grave robbery." He glanced at his watch. It was late in the day. Five-fifty. Martinez should have been just closing the yard.

"I have time," Alice said.

San Angelo Cemetery was just a few minutes away, and Van Allen had been correct. As daylight died, the old caretaker was hanging around the gates, anxious to put a chain and padlock on them. Most of the light in the yard at this hour came from neighboring streetlamps.

Ed Van Allen wished he had a C-note for every time in his life he had had to use the phrase, "no new development." As in the case of the Moore disappearance, he had nothing new in the Billy Carlton tomb desecration, either.

Martinez stood by the front gates with chain and padlock in

hand, listening patiently as Van Allen told him all this. Then Alice chatted him up for a few moments, while something within the cemetery caught Van Allen's attention.

Standing way back in the yard, about fifty yards away, back near where Billy Carlton had lain for many decades, a man in a white shirt stood facing the entrance of the cemetery.

Van Allen was surprised to see him. His gaze settled upon him with intense curiosity. The detective squinted, because the figure was in shadow-laced light from a streetlamp. His image was almost flickering.

Then the figure near the Carlton grave raised a hand and waved toward the detective. A friendly wave, not one of beckoning.

Van Allen waved back. Then he took his eyes off the figure and turned to Martinez.

"Who the hell's that?" he asked. "You got a crew working?"

"What?" Martinez asked.

"Who's that?" Van Allen asked again, motioning with his head.

"Who's *who?*" Martinez asked again.

Van Allen turned his head and looked again where the figure was. He didn't see anyone. He scanned, and still found no one.

"There was someone there a second ago," Van Allen said. "A man waved to me."

The old Mexican grinned. "You finally loco," he said. "We the only people in the yard," Martinez said.

"Horseshit," said Van Allen. "You got at least one visitor back there whether you know it or not."

Martinez was not a happy man. He looked in the direction that Van Allen indicated. His grin turned to a scowl. Like Van Allen, he couldn't see anyone now.

"You got better eyes than me? So you find someone," the

caretaker challenged. Sometimes Martinez sounded like Chico Marx. Now was one of those times.

Van Allen glanced toward his partner. "Okay, you wait here," he said to Alice. His suspicion was piqued. Who the hell would play hide-and-seek among tombstones, he wanted to know. "If anyone comes hustling out of here, detain him."

Alice nodded. "Cool," she said.

Moments later, Van Allen found himself padding across the thick grassy carpet of the graveyard, walking directly toward Billy Carlton's tipped stone. His strained calf muscle was irritating him again. He approached the fallen angel itself. Its arm was still upraised but now, tipped over, it pointed into the soil of the graveyard.

The soil of the graveyard. The soul of the graveyard.

Those phrases turned themselves over in Van Allen's mind, permutations of words he couldn't control within his psyche. Damn it, he was feeling weird these days.

He passed the fallen granite marker.

Who the hell had tipped that damned thing, Van Allen mused as he walked within a few feet of it. Better yet, who the hell was going to pony up the dough to set it right again? Not the city. Not the penny-pinching trustees of the cemetery.

Something invisible tapped lightly at Van Allen's shoulder as he passed the granite angel. Van Allen brushed at the spot and couldn't find it, but he did see—or thought he saw—a dragonfly a few feet away when he glanced.

"Damned bugs," he muttered. Ever since the big quake of the previous January there were bugs and pests everywhere they shouldn't be.

He brushed again. There was no second tap.

There was no one near the grave, either. Or any other grave. Van Allen stood and let his eye wander all through the forlorn old stones in the back quadrant of the cemetery. He let his eyes adjust to the shadows and the dim light. He wandered a few feet to improve his line of view, trying to see if anyone could have crouched behind any stone.

Then he had an idea. He turned to Alice and signaled that she should join him and that Martinez should remain in place.

Alice jogged to him.

"I *know* I saw something, Double-A," he said.

"Uh-huh?"

"Oh, stop treating me like I'm a head case and help me out on this," he snapped. "There's been trouble in this cemetery and there were two children who disappeared just over that cemetery wall. Does that suggest anything to you?"

"Yeah. Despite the high socioeconomic level of the inhabitants, this is getting to be a dicey neighborhood."

"Very funny."

"You asked me for my thoughts? Those are them."

"Would you stop cracking wise, keep your hand on your weapon, and cover me."

"What are you doing?"

"I'm going to walk to the rear wall of the yard," he said. "I want to see if someone is hiding back there."

"Damned convenient if we shoot someone," she said. "We can bury him right here and no one other than the old Mex has to know."

Van Allen glowered at her. "Now who's the psychopath?" he asked. She smiled sweetly and his irritation took wing.

"You're sure you saw something, aren't you, Ed?" she asked, turning a little more serious.

He looked at her as if she had suggested that he was insane. "I'm sure," he said.

"Then I'll cover you."

"Thanks."

Van Allen spent more than a quarter hour wandering among the old stones. Night and darkness tightened its grip on the yard. His leg was murdering him, and he was not unaware of that fact that it was in this very graveyard that he had aggravated it. Out of the corner of his eye, he saw Martinez standing near the gates, arms folded across his chest, waiting for some sort of resolution of something.

Cemetery of Angels, Van Allen mused. He would welcome a little help from the angels right now. For starters, he could use a new set of legs. Bionic ones this time, please.

Then there was a surreal aspect to the inspection of San Angelo. Shadows seemed to move and flutter as he approached them. He wished that he had a flashlight, a big heavy one with a solid beam. But he didn't. And he didn't find anyone lurking in the yard, either.

In the end, he hunched his shoulders to Double-A, indicating that he was giving up. Martinez stood by the gates, arms still folded across his chest, anxious to go home.

"I couldn't find anyone," Van Allen announced.

"Told you," Martinez said.

"Yeah, well I know I saw something," the detective snapped with uncharacteristic anger. His gaze swept the shadows for a final time. "I don't know what the hell's going on. But I looked. If you get vandalized again tonight, don't blame me."

Van Allen and Double-A stood outside the gates. The chains clanked on them as Martinez closed the aging iron portals to the yard.

"Aah," the old man said as he set the lock, "those walls. Only eight feet high. People climb over all the time. In out, all night. Kids, they use the yard as a place to fuck."

"Yeah. Right," Van Allen grumbled. For a moment it disturbed him that teenagers were popping in and out of San Angelo, using it as a casual place of assignation, while his own sex life was on the back burner. Then he fought off the thought.

He *knew* he had seen something, damn it!

He walked with Alice to his car. Abruptly, Van Allen cocked his head.

"What's that?" he asked.

Alice looked at him. "What's what?" she answered.

"You hear some sort of music?" he asked. "Sounds like an old player piano?"

"No?" Alice answered, an eyebrow raised.

He cocked his head again and it was gone. But he had thought that he had heard some kind of old-fashioned music. Some noisy neighbor banging on an antique keyboard piano. Skewered notes dancing in his head.

Tauntingly. He described it for her.

"Oh, great," Alice said. "Now you're hearing bells?"

"Okay, I imagined it. It's gone now, anyway," Van Allen said. "So forget it."

"I already have," she answered. "Otherwise, I'd have to note that first you think the Moores killed their own kids, then you waved to a man who wasn't there, and now you hear music when none is playing. Eh?"

"That's kind of the way my day has gone," he said. "Maybe all three events are related. Have you thought of that, oh, wise young lady?"

"Hey, I had a crappy day, too," she said. "But I'm not imagining any part of mine, okay?"

"And I'm not, either," he thought to himself. But he didn't say anything. He figured at this point any syllable he uttered would only have made matters worse.

Double-A, after all, was probably concluding that he was getting old. And, damn her, Double-A with all her thirty-something sex kitten insight might have been right.

That night, in Van Allen's home, after watching the Lakers bite the dust to the Celtics, after tuning in to a bootleg recording of a Grateful Dead concert from Dallas in 1978, and after going to sleep for the night, a couple of other peculiar things happened, too.

First, Van Allen was sleeping soundly when something snapped him awake in the middle of the night. He found himself lying in bed, bathed in sweat, his sheet and blankets removed.

He blinked at his clock. It was 3:00 A.M.

The sheet and covers were, in fact, on the floor across from where he slept. It was as if a strong pair of hands had yanked them off his sleeping body and had given them a good hard throw.

Van Allen snapped the light on.

There was, of course, no one else in the apartment so no one could have pulled the sheet and blankets away in the manner he had imagined. It bothered him nonetheless. It bothered him that he must have been having a violently bad dream—he could just barely remember something and he thought there had been a touch of that piano music to it—and he must have kicked away his dreamtime bed equipment.

He gathered everything up again, thought about it for a moment, and took a careful tour of his own apartment, gun in hand.

No one there that he could see. No one there at all.

Then Van Allen went back to his bedroom. He turned the light off and went back to sleep.

He slipped easily into his rest.

That's when the second peculiar thing happened.

Quick as a flash, he dreamed he was revisiting the Cemetery of Angels. This time he was standing forthrightly in front of Billy Carlton's tomb.

It was as if he were confronting the grave itself, albeit another man's. And he knew it was Carlton's.

He knew because the angel was back in place. That big grand marker was upright, proud and back where it belonged, the winged one erect upon its granite block, wings extended, and its right arm raised toward Heaven.

And in his mind, Van Allen blinked once, and suddenly

there was a face inches in front of his own, almost hermaphro-
ditic with chalky skin, pink lips, and two eyes that were as
wide as the night, peering intently into Van Allen's own soul.

Asking him something? Or telling him something? The policeman couldn't determine which.

Then the eyes blinked.

The face was gone in a flash. And next there was another
vision, that of moonlight sweeping across a legion of tombstones behind Billy's resurrected angel.

Then that tableau faded also and Van Allen's mind went to
black. The next thing he knew it was morning and, as he woke
up, he was wondering if he would ever be able to summon up
the nerve to ask Double-A out for dinner as a prelude for getting her to sleep with him.

He rose and had coffee. He felt as if his brain was coming
apart at the seams. And once again, he wondered if that was
one of the only things he was correct about these days.

18

The technician's name was Maria Valdez and she had been a civilian employee of the LAPD for fifteen years. For the last seven of those years, she had administered polygraph examinations.

It was Saturday morning and time for the lie detector test. Melissa had brought Rebecca by car to Ed Van Allen's office. Once again, Bill had disappeared to work on a set of architectural plans at McLaughlin & Co.

Rebecca sat down in a sturdy chair by the desk in an examination room at police headquarters. Detective Van Allen sat on the edge of the desk as Mrs. Valdez carefully placed the proper cuff, sensors, and wires on Rebecca's right arm.

Already, Rebecca felt violated.

What had *she* done? She, her husband, and her children were victims, not perpetrators. Why was she being treated like a criminal? As the machinery of the polygraph examination was set in place, Rebecca felt her resentment rising to a dangerous level.

"It's very simple, Mrs. Moore," Ed Van Allen explained in a soothing voice. "The test is painless and easy. You and I talk: I ask you questions, you reply honestly and to the best of your ability. That's all this test is about."

"I don't even know why I'm taking it," Rebecca said.

Van Allen shrugged. "Sometimes it's more helpful than anyone might imagine," he answered.

"Such as a case where parents might actually have harmed their own children?" Rebecca said.

The detective gave her a grimace, mixed with a knowing smile. "I know that's not the case here," he said, a statement for which he might have flunked his own polygraph. "But if you have any doubts in this department, this is your chance to dispatch them."

"So you're only interviewing me because you think I'm a suspect," she accused.

"If that's your concern, you can eliminate it within a few minutes, Mrs. Moore. That's the value of this session for you."

Mrs. Valdez gave Van Allen a nod. Everything was ready. Rebecca saw a light illuminate on the machine, indicating that the power was up. Rebecca felt herself turning fully against this entire procedure.

"Can we start?" Van Allen asked.

"I wish you would."

Mrs. Valdez pushed another button and the examination was under way. Melissa waited in the next room.

Van Allen began with basic background questions, but even the most fundamental—name and address, for example—seemed intrusive to Rebecca. She felt as if she were on trial. And in a way she was.

Van Allen gradually moved toward the point.

"Have you ever been in trouble with the police, Mrs. Moore?" he asked.

"No," Rebecca answered.

"Has your husband?"

"I can't answer for him."

Van Allen glanced at the track of the needle on the graph paper. He kept talking.

"Do you take drugs?" the detective inquired.

"No."

"Maybe just recreationally?"

"No!" she snapped.

"Have you ever?"

"Years ago. In college."

"And not since?"

"Hardly ever."

"What about your husband?"

She paused before answering. "Same," she said. "Years ago. In college."

"When is the last time you took something?" he asked.

Rebecca gave him a withering look. "What does this have to do with my children?" she asked.

"You can decline to answer that one if you wish," he said.

"I don't even remember," she said.

"And your husband?"

She paused. "He used to dabble," she said. "Same as half the people in the United States Congress."

Van Allen smiled sympathetically. "So did I," he said. "But I haven't since I joined the police department. What I'm trying to establish is that you and your husband are completely drug-free now. Can I conclude that?"

"Yes," she said.

"Absolutely?" he pressed.

"Yes, damn it!" she snapped. "Absolutely!"

The detective's eyes settled on the needle. Mrs. Valdez watched it, too. The needle's line was flat on the graph paper. So far—according to polygraph wisdom—Rebecca Moore was as honest as the summer day was long.

"And do you know your husband's business?" he asked.

"He's an architect."

"That's all he does?"

"What are you suggesting?" she asked.

"Nothing. I'm trying to establish you and your husband as completely blameless in the disappearance of your children."

"Well, we are. Completely blameless!"

"You're sure?"

"I'm sure."

"Good," the detective said. He posed a few side inquiries. The test reached the ten-minute mark. "Only a few more questions," he said.

Rebecca gathered the final part of her strength and courage. "I'm ready," she said.

"Are you hiding anything, Mrs. Moore?" the detective asked.

"What do you mean?"

"Anything at all. Is there anything the police would like to know that you or your husband haven't told us?"

"No," she answered firmly.

"Do you know where your children are?"

Rebecca thought of the ghost. "No," she said.

"Do you *think* you know?"

"No!"

"Does your husband know?"

"No!"

Mrs. Valdez's eyes were fixed upon the needle. Van Allen kept talking.

"Is there anything about their disappearance that you haven't told us?" he asked.

"No," she said.

"Do you want them back?"

Her voice was almost breaking. "Yes, damn it. I love my children! Of course I want them back!" she answered.

Now Van Allen's eyes were intent on the needle. He was nodding.

"I only have one additional question, Mrs. Moore," he said. "It's an all-encompassing one: Have you told me the truth in all ways as far as you believe the truth to exist?"

Rebecca sighed. Her eyes seemed very tired. She brought her free left hand up to her face and rubbed her eyes with her forefinger and thumb. She looked at Detective Van Allen with something close to fury.

"I have," she said. "I've told you everything."

Van Allen nodded. "Thank you," he said. "That's all."

Mrs. Valdez turned off the machine, then helped Rebecca to remove the strap from her arm.

"I found that whole thing insulting," she said. "No wonder Bill didn't want to take it."

"A necessary evil," Van Allen said, attempting to explain it away.

"An evil, all right. But I don't know how necessary." She looked at the detective. Van Allen made no further effort to communicate. "Well," she finally asked, "did I pass or not?"

Van Allen shrugged. "The results have to be analyzed and interpreted," he said. "If we need to speak with you further, we will. Do you need a ride home?"

"A friend came with me," she said. "She'll drive me back." Her fury was at its peak. "Now, I've answered all of your questions," Rebecca said, "so you answer one for me. When are you going to find my children?"

Van Allen sighed and looked her intently in the eye.

"I like to think we're getting closer, Mrs. Moore," he said. "But I really can't tell you yet. I really can't."

"I'm free to go?" she asked.

"You're free to go," Van Allen said.

Rebecca looked angrily at both Van Allen and Mrs. Valdez. Then she turned and stormed from the room. She let the door slam behind her.

The detective watched her go, then glanced to the polygraph chart that the technician had already removed from its monitor.

Van Allen's eyes widened. Maria Valdez looked at the chart knowingly. Van Allen then studied the entire track of the polygraph needle past his thirty-six points of interrogation.

Then he looked up.

"So she's lying like a rug," Van Allen concluded. He looked at the results from beginning to end. "Know what, Maria?" he asked. "I think if we got her husband in here, he'd probably lie even worse."

Rebecca parked her car at one of the meters west of Drake Stadium. Even in November, the midday sun in Westwood was strong. On the UCLA campus it poured down brightly. Undergraduates in shorts and T-shirts strolled unhurriedly from one class to another along Bruin Walk.

In Drake Stadium, a sunwashed field with concrete grandstands on only one side, the running track was sprinkled with runners and joggers. Rebecca entered the stadium from an entrance that led to the top of the seating area. Down below, on the running track, circling the green infield, she saw a familiar figure—Dr. Chang Lim—completing a lap.

She walked down several dozen stone steps and stopped in the front row closest to the track field. She watched Dr. Lim. He was trim and lithe, remarkably fit and fast for a man in his mid-forties.

Lim ran three miles a day, always at noon, always at Drake Stadium, which was ten minutes from his office across the campus. His secretary had told Rebecca exactly where to find the doctor. Now Rebecca sat down in the front row of the seating area and waited.

Lim kicked into his final trip around the oval, completed it, and slowed to a walk. He picked up a towel that he had left by the side of the running track, mopped himself, and walked another lap to cool down. When he returned to the grandstand side, he walked directly in front of Rebecca. He picked up a one-liter bottle of Arrowhead water that he had wrapped in a white towel.

He opened the water and swigged.

From a distance of thirty feet, his eyes met Rebecca's. She gave him a slight wave of a hand.

"Hello, Doctor," she called to him.

He looked at her curiously, not yet recognizing her.

"Hello," he answered. He thought about it for a moment. "I know I know you. From where? Was it—?"

"You came over to my home a few weekends ago. With a colleague. Dr. Maurice Lerner."

A moment, then, "Ah. Yes. For certain. Now I remember."

The doctor closed the water and set it aside. He walked over to his visitor. There was a trace of Hong Kong left in the way he chose words. "My secretary say you called. She say I might see you here."

"I wanted to meet you privately," Rebecca said. "My husband doesn't even know I'm here."

"We can talk in confidence," the doctor allowed. Then there was a flash of further recognition upon his face. Recognition mixed with shock.

"So very sorry!" he said abruptly. "I put two with two together. You're the woman who's been on television! Your children are missing!"

"That's me," Rebecca Moore said without emotion. "That seems to be how I'm defined these days."

"So terribly sorry," Dr. Lim said. "Anything new? Anything hopeful?"

"I'm trying to be hopeful about everything," Rebecca answered.

"Of course."

"I'm also here on a referral from Dr. Einhorn."

"Yes. I know. He phone."

Rebecca moved to the point.

"I was hoping you might help me," Rebecca said.

The doctor, still toweling his face and shoulders, slowed in mid-swipe. "Of course. I'd be most anxious."

Rebecca drew a breath. Her hands fidgeted with each other.

When she saw the doctor looking at this, she stopped abruptly.

"I want to be hypnotized," she said. "But not for the reasons that Dr. Einhorn may have suggested."

Dr. Lim waited. "Then for what?" he asked.

"There's something going on in the house I live in," she began. "The house you visited. I've never believed in this sort of thing before. But I think that there's some sort of supernatural or paranormal disturbance going on. And I think it's somehow involved with the disappearance of Patrick and Karen."

Initially, Dr. Lim looked skeptically at Rebecca. Then he eased. But, "Ghosts? Spirits, you mean?" he asked.

"Yes. That's what I think."

"I cannot do, Mrs. Moore."

She felt a sinking, disappointed mood take her. Then the disappointment turned sharply to resentment. When the hell, she wondered, was someone *really* going to help her.

"Why not?" she asked.

"I'm not a ghost hunter," he answered gently. "I don't investigate paranormal, supernatural. I'm a clinical psychiatrist."

"And you're a hypnotist," said Rebecca.

"Yes. And so? I use hypnotism, among many other forms of therapy."

"About a week ago I was in our home," Rebecca continued, "I was in one of the upstairs rooms, and I saw a man. I talked to him and he talked to me. But I'm sure he was a dead man. From some other point in time." She paused. "He knew me, Doctor, and I knew him. I'm sure of it. This *happened.*"

Lim studied her. A group of female runners passed them on the track. Lim watched the girls for a moment, then looked back to Rebecca.

"And so?" he asked.

"And so I want to know who I saw," she said. "I want to

know who I saw because I think it's important. I think understanding this might bring my children back.''

"Why do you think this?''

"I don't know why,'' she answered. "Something tells me, okay?''

Dr. Lim shrugged. "And Dr. Einhorn? He thinks this would benefit? Hypnotism here?''

"Dr. Einhorn recommended me to you and you to me,'' Rebecca said sharply. "He must think *something!* And I don't see how it matters what we talk about if it helps me locate my children.''

"Ah, it doesn't matter any. But this man you saw . . . ?'' Dr. Lim began thoughtfully.

As Rebecca waited for him to complete his thought, she began to be aware of something in his manner that she found disturbing. There was something that gave her a creepy feeling. She tried to dismiss it.

"This man . . . ?'' he said again. "Was he—?''

"He was a ghost,'' Rebecca said. "Maybe you don't believe in such things, but I didn't either a week ago.'' She sighed. "Now, please. No one is accomplishing anything. Can you at least *try* to help me?''

Dr. Lim had grown very still. Listening. Watching Rebecca.

"What you're saying is that you *think* you saw a ghost,'' he said. The sunlight washed over him so brightly that his brow formed big black shadows out of the sockets of his eyes.

"Doctor, I know what I saw.''

"You know what your mind told you that you saw,'' the doctor said softly, as if to get in the last word. "What was actually there was perhaps another thing.''

"Whatever,'' she conceded. *"Will you help me?''*

Dr. Lim sat down on the bench next to Rebecca and thought about what he had heard. She envied him. Her anxiety had her wound up tight enough to burst. And the more she pressured him, the more he seemed to relax.

"I have this right?" Dr. Lim said. "You want hypnotism so that you might be able to identify this man you have seen. This spirit?"

"Yes," she said.

"You feel drawn to the ghost 'man'?"

"Yes, I do."

He pursed his lips with interest. *"Why* drawn?"

She shook her head to indicate that she didn't know. Or at least that she couldn't explain it.

"And, if I may please ask, maybe you are trying to see this image, this specter, again? You think this may have bearing on whereabouts of your children?"

Rebecca nodded. "That's correct."

Dr. Lim grimaced. "Then, therefore, you surely suggest now that you could contact the dead through hypnotism? True?"

"Maybe," she said. "Look, please don't try to put words in my mouth or assign some tricky psychological motivation. I want my children back. I want to know what happened to them. I—"

He placed a reassuring hand on hers, cutting her off in mid-squawk. He shook his head and smiled.

"Never done before in my long experience."

"Never done what?"

"Hunt ghosts."

"I'm trying to find my children," she said again. "I'm trying to understand where they went. When I saw this spirit, my children were with him."

"Your children were *with?*" he asked, newly astonished.

"Yes."

"Then, to discuss, would not that mean that your children are—?"

"Dead? I don't know. But there might be a chance in a

thousand that this will help. So I'm begging you to help me try it.''

The doctor examined his own hands for a moment. To Rebecca, he suddenly looked as if he were miles away.

Lim had spent his adult life trying to disassociate himself with the grab bag of West Coast wackos and charlatans who practiced within his profession. Similarly, he had turned down tens of thousands of dollars worth of fees from people who wished to stage gimmicks or Las Vegas-style hypnotism shows with pinwheels and swinging medallions. Now Rebecca, whom he had met innocently through a mutual friend, sat before him on a nearly perfect November day and asked him about opening a window on the spirit world by a voyage through the unconscious mind.

But the doctor's eyes came back up and found Rebecca. He reached for his bottle of water and took another long drink, still weighing his response.

Then he looked back to her. As his understanding increased, so did the intensity of his assault on Western grammar.

''Must understand,'' he cautioned softly, ''that what you ask me to do carries peril. First, initial session of hypnotherapy might not even 'take.' Sometimes the mind reject hypnotism even if you outward feel eagerness to undergo a trance.''

Rebecca Moore nodded.

''Might be two or three sessions necessary to attain proper relaxation. Good mood. Then there are the dangers. Subliminal suggestion, please consider.''

''You mean, you giving me a 'posthypnotic suggestion'?'' she asked. ''Is that what you're warning me about?''

The doctor smiled slightly and shook his head. The mysterious Orient: ''Yes, but no,'' he answered.

She experienced that sinking feeling again. ''Yes, but, no.'' An answer that simultaneously meant everything and nothing.

''Exactly the opposite,'' he explained. ''We would go into

this trying to find what already in your head. In consciousness. Far from try to put something in, we try to prevent that, I think you agree. It counterproductive to your goals if you underwent hypnotherapy and suggested answers to yourself."

"I'm sorry, Doctor," she said. "You're losing me."

"We theorize: there are distinct levels of the mind's subconscious state," Dr. Lim explained. "Think of it in terms of different states—or depths—of sleep. The hypnotism act is enormously, *enormously*, suggestive in and of self. The last thing we want: something coming up out of deeper stages of consciousness and planting itself in one of the closer stages and project itself as a new 'truth.' As it were."

Rebecca remained confused.

"Are you saying that this wouldn't work?" she asked.

"No. I warning you about perils. I think we could get past this."

"All right," Rebecca said. "Any other warnings?"

"Only that we might fail."

"Where would these sessions take place?" Rebecca asked. "If you would do them. Your office at UCLA?"

Dr. Lim considered the point. "Maybe at office," he began slowly, "considering what we try to accomplish. But we would do best surrounding you with environment that would get you to the place you want."

"Such as?"

"I could come to your home," he said. "We could, I suppose, conduct our sessions—or at least first one—in the room where you witnessed the 'ghost.' "

Rebecca felt a chill. Excitement tingling with fear.

"Right in that *room?*"

"Yes. Why not, please?"

"Does this mean that you'll do it?" she asked.

Another long hesitation. Then, "I'm willing to make an attempt," Dr. Lim said. "But no media involvement. I don't want carnival atmosphere. And I can only attempt as long as there's no problem with the police. I assume: there are detectives working on children's disappearance?''

"Many detectives," said Rebecca.

"One particular detective in charge? Probably?"

"A detective named Ed Van Allen," she said. She paused. "He means well. He's sort of a pain in the—"

She caught herself. But Dr. Lim laughed crisply.

"—ass!" he proclaimed. "You too much of a lady to say, but I can."

Then Rebecca found herself liking the doctor and laughing with him. She was suddenly at ease.

"Detective Van Allen is a damned pain in the ass," she said emphatically. And they both laughed again. Rebecca also stopped short of saying that she felt that Van Allen had placed her on the top of a list of suspects.

"I have contacts within LAPD," Dr. Lim said, thawing out with a measure of helpfulness. "I could probably get proper authorization from above if it not forthcoming from the cops closest to the case."

Rebecca sighed with relief. "That would be wonderful," she said.

"How do you have police contacts?" Rebecca asked.

"I have worked major cases before. Los Angeles. San Diego. Long Beach."

"When could we begin?" Rebecca pressed.

Dr. Lim considered the point. "If I get the proper authorization this afternoon from the police," he said, "what about Monday? At my office. Westwood."

Rebecca nodded steadily in agreement. She felt a great burden lift from her, combined with a new anxiety over what might transpire under hypnosis. But she faced it bravely.

"I'll be ready for you," Rebecca Moore said. "You know where I live."

Dr. Lim nodded. An impish smile crossed his face.

"Ghost, huh?" he asked again, almost rhetorically this time. "I looking forward. I want to see."

Naturally, Melissa had her own spin on the situation.

"I'm not kidding about LA being a fantastic spot for ghosts and hauntings," she said on the drive from Westwood back to Topango Gardens. Melissa had borrowed roommate June's yellow Mustang for the trip. She and Rebecca drove with the top down.

"Ever driven past the Hollywood Roosevelt Hotel? Right on Hollywood Boulevard?" Melissa asked.

Rebecca wasn't much in the mood for this conversation, but allowed it, anyway. "I know where it is," she answered.

"Suite 1200," Melissa said. "Marilyn Monroe's ghost still haunts a mirror in the suite she used to use. Montgomery Clift, who stayed there while he was filming *From Here to Eternity*, apparently still paces the halls and plays a trumpet at odd hours. Isn't that great?" Melissa grinned. "And there's a problem up on the roof of the Hollywood Roosevelt, too," Melissa continued. She weaved in and out of traffic on Sunset as they drove through Beverly Hills. "An out-of-work actor named Harry Lee jumped to his death there in the 1930s. He still tries to push people over the side."

"Yeah," said Rebecca. She was more focused on Dr. Lim at this moment than Harry Lee. "Nice."

"The Comedy Store is haunted, too," Melissa said. "You know that big place on Sunset? It used to be Ciro's. Know what goes on down in the basement? You can still hear the murmuring of people who were murdered by gangsters during Prohibition. The place was a speakeasy back then."

A battered pickup truck with three workmen passed their Mustang. All three workmen turned to check out Melissa and Rebecca. One of them blew Melissa a kiss. In return Melissa tossed the man a chirpless bird.

"And, let's see," Melissa continued, unfazed. "The Alexandra Hotel has a ghost, too. A woman in her thirties in a high-necked black dress and a bustle. She wanders the hallways looking for her lover. She's quite harmless, really. Oh, and then there's Culver Studios. Know about that one?"

"No," said Rebecca.

"Ever heard of Thomas Ince? He was one of the pioneers of the film industry. He died while celebrating his forty-third birthday on William Randolph Hearst's yacht. This was about 1923, 1924, maybe. Anyway, according to the rumor mill of the day, Hearst caught his mistress, Marion Davies, kissing Charlie Chaplin on the boat. Hearst fired a gun at Chaplin, missed, and killed Ince. Ince founded Culver Studios. His ghost has been reported by carpenters and technicians for years."

Melissa grinned and shrugged, watching traffic as she drove. "Of course, those are just the famous stories. There's a load of private homes that are haunted. Elke Sommer had a house with a ghost that drove her out. Ever read about that? And then there are all the places that are kind of anonymous. Nothing special about the houses; they just happen to have ghosts."

Rebecca received it all with silence.

Melissa turned north from Sunset, taking the final leg of the drive back to Topango. "Is this conversation bothering you?" she finally asked.

"I could do without it," Rebecca said finally. "I like to think of Patrick and Karen as still alive, if you don't mind."

"Oh. Sorry, honey. Then I'll change the subject," Melissa said. She stopped at a traffic light at Highland and pondered what might next be appropriate. "You know our neighbor, Francine Yerber?" she asked. "The photographer?"

"Of course I know her," Rebecca said.

"Francine still wants to photograph me naked. Some picture book she's working on. *Nude California,* or something.

You know. Ordinary people, not models, caught informally jaybird naked in their backyards. Think I should do it?''

''Consider yourself flattered, Melissa,'' Rebecca answered, an edge to her tone.

''I do,'' she said. The car started again. ''So I might do it, after all.'' She giggled. ''I don't like the idea of some strange guys I don't know masturbating over me. But on the other hand, maybe it'll attract me a lover. I wonder if I should lose five pounds first. Who knows?''

''Who knows about anything anymore?'' Rebecca answered. ''Who knows anything?''

They were within two blocks of Topango Gardens now. They passed the gates to San Angelo Cemetery. There was an old man out front who looked like a caretaker. He smiled to the women as they drove by, then looked away.

And in passing the yard, Melissa felt some funny sensation that she had never sensed before. This whole thing, she realized anew, was getting creepier with each passing day.

19

Detective Van Allen returned home that Saturday evening, angry and frustrated. He went to his den and set down on his desk the files of the Billy Carlton case and the files of the Moore case.

He wandered to his kitchen and made himself a pair of sandwiches from the various contents of his refrigerator. He took the food back to his den along with a bottle of beer. He sat down. With a remote control, he turned on the small television that sat in his bookcase.

No Lakers this evening. Just the damned Clippers who, to make matters worse, were currently playing better basketball than the Lakers.

He groaned. The Clippers. Who were these guys dressed up as NBA players? He couldn't be fooled. These were the old San Diego Conquistadors in disguise. This Massenburg and this Seeley combined couldn't carry Magic's jockstrap. Van Exel wasn't half the player that James Worthy was in his prime. Where were Clippers who could equal the artistry of A.C. Green and Byron Scott?

Where was anyone who was a solid star these days? Well, maybe Shaq was a solid pro player. And that Sir Charles with Phoenix was okay until he opened his mouth.

Van Allen leaned back at his desk and kept a highly critical eye upon the TV screen. Somehow the NBA of the 1990s seemed to be leaving him behind. He kept waiting for Deion Sanders to sign with the Knicks. And it spoke volumes about the state of the game that the most noteworthy player in Los Angeles for the last couple of seasons had a name like Vlade Divac.

Vlade.

What Vlade needed, Van Allen decided, was a good nickname. Vlade the Lad. Vlade the Impaler. Vlade the Blade.

The detective took a long gulp of his beer. He devoured his sandwiches. Food tasted so much better when a man only got it once, late in the day.

Ah, it was silly time, Van Allen knew. He had been maxed out on work and his mind was freewheeling in strange directions.

The TV still entertained him. Names rebounded out of the roundball past. Jerry West. Gail Goodrich. Elgin Baylor.

Kareem!

He smiled. Why not trace those Lakers from Showtime all the way back to the Lakers of thousand-lakes country? The MinneNowhere Lakers. Hey, where are you today, Slater Martin? George Mikan?

A line of doggerel came to him:

Mais où sont les neiges d'antan?

Fine. Good line, straight out of a piece of high school French that he had learned by rote.

Where are the snows of yesteryear?

And, for that matter, where are the Fort Wayne Pistons of yesteryear, also?

"And where are the actors of yesteryear, Eddie-boy?" whispered something within his subconscious. *"Have you thought about that, Eddie-boy?"*

Whoa! Where had *that* thought surfaced from? Christ, he was tired! His mind was starting to play devious tricks.

"Eddie-boy" was a childhood nickname used by his father. His dad had been dead for nineteen years.

He blew out a long breath to break the mood that was overtaking him. At his desk, his gaze settled upon the green Mont Blanc fountain pen, a gift from his father those many years ago. Was that what had put thoughts of his dad in his head?

He couldn't stand watching the Clippers any more. He turned off the television and wondered why his mind was wandering in such bizarre directions. He had a funny feeling. Was it only overwork? Sometimes lately it seemed like there were an invisible pair of hands in his head, pressing. It was as if something had held his head at a certain angle so that he would only see certain things. Or pointed his thoughts toward the past.

He felt helpless to see certain things that he wanted to see.

Must be overwork, he told himself. It had to be! These past two weeks there were too damned many questions leading nowhere. He looked at the files that sat on his desk like small flat manila folder gauntlets. Here he had two impenetrable cases within a stone's throw of each other—one at the cemetery and the other at Topango Gardens—and he couldn't make sense of either.

"Well, one thing's for certain," he concluded, muttering aloud. "The cemetery might contain some angels. But Mr. and Mrs. Moore aren't so angelic."

Rebecca Moore had flunked key parts of her lie detector test. Bill Moore, that fine and sensitive human being who passed for her husband, still refused to take one. Van Allen had driven by McLaughlin & Company that very afternoon, just to nose around Lieutenant Colombo–style, just to see up-close-and-personal what Moore did when he wasn't home. Moore had practically broken a heavyweight sweat on the spot, as soon as Van Allen and Double-A trundled through the front door. There was even a loud silence upon their arrival

and a scurrying to cover "confidential" papers in various offices.

Then there was another thing Van Allen had noticed that
day. For an architect, McLaughlin didn't look like any Mr.
Clean, himself, although Van Allen would have admitted that
it was sometimes tough to tell with these forty-something
counterculture types. In Southern California, he mused further, a lot of things weren't the way they looked. He knew of
at least one law firm, for example, that operated out of Santa
Monica and Long Beach and which consisted entirely of surf-
ers. The firm had a few conference rooms and a lot of laptop
computers. When the partners weren't chasing ambulances
and torts, they were catching waves.

The Moores, Van Allen pondered, sitting at his desk and
trying to make sense of the material in front of him. What
about the Moores?

To Van Allen's line of reason, both were dirty.

He wondered who was the dirtier of the two: Bill or Rebecca. To make things complete, the FBI had informed him
late that afternoon that they had a file on Bill Moore. And the
Connecticut State Police had some tidbits, too. Both the Feds
and the headquarters for the state gendarmeries in Hartford
were sending material to Van Allen by overnight courier. He
couldn't wait to look at it. From the very beginning there was
something he didn't like about the Moores, but he didn't know
what it had been.

The material the next morning, he told himself, would con-
firm his suspicions. He was of the growing opinion that if he
could get loose with a shovel and an ax somewhere under that
house, he would find a couple of small bodies, and from there
it would be only a matter of hours before he could hang a double infanticide on Mom and Pop.

He cringed. What a horrible crime, to remove from the
world the small souls you've brought in. How in particular
could a woman be part of something like that? Van Allen

glanced at the framed photographs of his own son and daughter on his desk and felt a new revulsion for his chief suspects.

He finished his food. He went to his kitchen and found a second bottle of brew and came back to his desk. He sat down again and continued his line of thought.

He figured he was only a day away from asking for a court order to force a lie detector upon Bill Moore. And when he did that, which would signal to both of the Moores that they were key suspects in the case, he would also slap twenty-four-hour-a-day surveillance on both of them. The detective would make damned well certain that the Moores were not about to disappear before their children were accounted for.

Nine o'clock came.

Van Allen kept his nose buried in the material he had on his desk. He drew the files toward him, opening them both and lining the contents up side by side. He set to the task of reconciling his perceptions of the cases with what was established as fact.

Two perplexing cases. He asked himself: What did he know?

Fact: The Moores were not telling him the full truth about what had happened in their house. So what were they hiding?

Fact: There was no evidence to suggest that either child had ever left the house at 2136 Topango Gardens. So where were the bodies buried?

Fact: No ransom note had ever been received. No relative had ever been contacted. No indication existed suggesting that the children might have run away. What did that say about the possibility that a kidnapping or a runaway had ever occurred?

Then Van Allen looked studiously at the Billy Carlton file and tried to make a transition.

Fact: Carlton had died at a young age and under suspicious circumstances. Had a murder been committed many years ago?

Fact: There was no apparent motivation for desecrating Billy Carlton's tomb. No ransom request had been received by anyone concerning Carlton's remains. So why did the body snatching parallel the kidnapping?

Fact: The two crimes had occurred within a few days of each other within a few hundred yards of each other. Didn't this sort of put a charley horse in the long arm of coincidence?

Van Allen analyzed and tried to draw parallels. Parallels, he knew, solved crimes. Parallels always betrayed a perpetrator's way of accomplishing things. Find the methods, then match the perp to the methods.

So what were the parallels? Better, what was the most jarring parallel?

Both incidents, he concluded, revolved around impossibility. A grave just didn't blow open as it had. And children just didn't disappear into thin—or even smoggy—air.

Both cases. They just couldn't have happened as advertised. There was something else going on in each case, something unseen that Van Allen had not yet been able to factor in.

He wrestled with it. He asked aloud a key question.

"Why the hell would Rebecca Moore kill her own children? Or consent to having them killed?"

Were they in the way of her career? Or her relationship with her husband? Or compromising a relationship with a lover?

He agonized over it. "Fuck," he finally concluded, unable to get anywhere.

A full hour passed. Then a second hour. On the corner of Van Allen's desk was a Timex digital watch. It chirped twice to tell him that it was eleven o'clock. But Van Allen kept digging. Yes, there was new material coming tomorrow from both Connecticut and Quantico. But he scoured the material he already had, trying to see what he had missed, if anything.

A few minutes before midnight, he was jarred by a sound from the next room. His head shot upright from his reading. The front door to his apartment had opened!

His children had keys. So did the building superintendent. But it was almost midnight! Who would walk in at such an hour, except in an emergency?

"Hello?" he called.

No answer.

His policeman's instincts took charge. His hand went to the automatic pistol that was on his belt. His palm stayed upon it, waiting to draw it if necessary.

Van Allen stood from his desk and shouted again. "Hello? Who is it?"

Again no answer.

He moved to the door of his den and looked. He took one step forward.

The front door was half-open, as if knocked loose by the wind. Yet there wasn't any wind and he had latched it securely. He had even put a drop bolt in place.

He looked. He could see the entire room. There was no visitor that he could see. But he had a creepy feeling. His scalp tightened and he waited.

Then an event occurred that he would remember for his entire life. Before him, there were slow footsteps. Like a man walking in heavy boots on the wooden floor of Van Allen's living room. At first Van Allen thought he was imagining it, and then to his shock he knew he wasn't.

There were footsteps and they were resolutely approaching him. Footsteps of an invisible intruder.

Van Allen held his ground. A good soldier: he didn't retreat. But he felt himself break a sweat all over his body. His heart was ricocheting and he felt as if his chest would burst.

And the footsteps continued toward him while, very faintly,

he caught an echo of that piano music, like a distant roll on an old upright player.

The footsteps were within ten feet of him. Then five. Then they stopped. Van Allen cringed. He felt something strange, as if something like a warm blast of air was trying to press past him. He inclined against the invisible force. It didn't hurt. And it almost soothed him as it pushed past.

Again, he held his ground. He was aware of sweating profusely, but he managed to stand perfectly still.

A moment passed. Then he was jarred by a tremendous crashing sound that had come from the room behind him—his den, from which he had just exited.

He jerked around his head at the sound.

Initially, he wondered what had suddenly fallen over. He went back to the door and stared into the room. He felt a quickly rising rush of fear within him as he stared at what had to be another impossibility, something that could not possibly have happened.

The entire top of his desk had been swept completely clean.

Everything on it—telephone, papers, books, framed portraits of his son and daughter, coffee cup and lamp—had been propelled from the top of the desk with some abrupt violent force. The various items had flown around the room and were in disarray. The lamp and one of the picture frames were broken on the floor. The wood beneath them was deeply scarred from the impact.

Van Allen knew a few things about crime scenes and didn't have to examine what was before him to draw a perplexing conclusion. The items from the desk had been knocked away with a force almost exceeding anything a strong man could do. The big quake of January 1994 hadn't messed up his desktop so violently!

Instinctively, Van Allen's hand started to raise his service weapon. But then he released it. Deep down he knew it would be useless to even draw it.

His wide eyes scanned the room. There was no other human there, and he knew it. But something had hit that desktop like an invisible meteorite, or an angry superhuman arm, sweeping everything away. And Van Allen knew that, too.

He recoiled from the room, stepping aside from the doorway. He hoped his deference would allow whatever presence was there to be on its way.

"You've made your point," he whispered softly. "You've made your point."

He felt like a madman mouthing those words.

But he had no choice, because to see was to believe.

So for several seconds he stood there, barely moving, hand upon his toy of a weapon. Nothing else in the room moved. He lost track of time. The longest minute of his life came and went.

Van Allen then felt a deep, gripping chill, something akin to particles of ice flowing through his veins. It nearly paralyzed him to have to come to the conclusions that were forced upon him.

And it was only then, as he assessed what had transpired, that he knew that the moment he had augured had arrived. The moment which would define his life before and after, the incident after which his life would never be the same.

But he bravely stood his ground.

Then something invisible and powerful, cold as an iceberg and strong as the devil, rushed into him, through him, and past him. This time Van Allen had the sense of standing firm against a strong wind. Yet several random images tore through him at the same time and for an instant he thought—he was sure, then it was gone—that he had been transported to the Cemetery of Angels.

In his mind, he could see Carlton's tomb, set right again.

But then the invisible thing was gone. And Van Allen felt as if a great burden had been lifted.

His gaze found the cluttered floor of his den again and mentally he decided which he would pick up first.

The words formed. *My son and my daughter,* he thought, looking at the shattered picture frames.

Then to his considerable relief, he heard a pair of footsteps behind him. Then there was a comforting sound from the next room.

It was the front door to his apartment. This time, the damned door was closing.

Van Allen went back to his desk and slumped in his chair. He looked at the mess around the room and felt his mouth, dry and parched. He wondered if he had imagined everything that had transpired and if he had blacked out and caused the disarray himself.

But tonight he knew to the contrary.

He knew, because he trusted his own senses and his own observations as a witness. He thought back to the recent nights of bad dreams, of imagined intrusions in his apartment, and of the time he felt that the covers had been ripped off his bed as he had slept.

And he spent the night there in his chair, not even rising to gather the two scattered files. Instead, he stared around the room and tried to put this new reality in place.

At dawn, dopey, shattered with fatigue, his eyes burning, he thought he had it. He thought he had the philosophical twine that would bind the Moore case and the Carlton case together.

An invisible assailant, as he had witnessed it, had been the perp in both jobs. Consoled by this iconoclastic notion, he then leaned forward onto his desktop, folded his aching arms, and slept.

He awoke four hours later to a nasty jangling telephone and Alice Aldrich's worried voice on the other end of the line. He assured her that he was fine and would be on his way to the office shortly.

Shortly: which meant as soon as he could unscramble his

brain. His frontal lobe felt like an egg sizzling in a frying pan.

And his eyes still roared with tiredness and his brain now refused to assimilate the impulses of the previous evening. Instead, he told himself, the two cases had driven him to the edge of a nervous breakdown and he must have *imagined* the footsteps and the phantom visitor of the night before.

The mess on the floor, he further told himself, was the result of one clear swipe of his own arm, not one from another dimension.

He told these lies to himself again as he shaved, washed, and changed clothes. He looked in the mirror and was convinced that there were entire streaks of graying hair in his head that hadn't existed twenty-four hours earlier. And a whole new road map of lines surrounded his eyes, as well.

Age, age, age, he told himself. Age and dementia were creeping in on little crow's feet.

And when he got to work and when Double-A asked him what was new, he lied again.

"Nothing," Ed Van Allen said.

Then she left him alone. And he played with his own thoughts as he waited for yet two more visitors, the professional couriers who would bring him police reports from Connecticut and Virginia, reports which would anchor him back in reality and—he hoped to God!—offer him a more prosaic explanation of what was transpiring. The explanation that now rumbled beneath the surface of his consciousness was one with which he was distinctly ill at ease. So he fought it with all his might.

Haunted, for a rational man, was a tough concept to swallow.

20

The muscular, starkly featured man in the dark brown suit and open collar who stepped from US AIR 324 from Las Vegas at Los Angeles International that Sunday afternoon was a man with a mission. And this time, he would need to complete it. Having blown in excess of twenty thousand dollars in the Nevada gambling halls—unkind blackjack tables and commensurably compliant ladies of the house—within the last forty-eight hours, he was a man who needed to get back to his work.

At the airport, he took a shuttle bus to one of the better car rental bureaus. He produced a credit card in the name of Peter O'Neill and obtained a perfectly anonymous car, a white Chevrolet Cavalier, for three days. There was a young Vietnamese woman behind the counter. She found the man so unattractive and imposing that she was frightened of him.

But her fear was unfounded, in this instance at least. He spoke to her courteously, accepted the car she assigned him, and thanked her. Then he drove into the City of Los Angeles.

At one of the anonymous large hotels that catered to conventions, the man kept the identity of O'Neill tucked away in his wallet. Instead, he produced a second set of licenses and credit cards and registered under the name of Harold McDuffie. He engaged the registration clerk for a few moments in

conversation about the insurance business, a topic that assured
that the clerk's attention would glaze over. Then he placed
three hundred dollars in cash on deposit, enough to guarantee
two nights' stay. This clerk was male. But he didn't like the
visitor, either. There was something sinister about him,
though the clerk couldn't place what it was.

"I wonder if you would check if there's mail for me," the
new arrival said after signing the guest slip.

The clerk disappeared for a moment and returned with one
piece of mail for a Mr. McDuffie. It was a small four-by-six
manila envelope, sealed tightly with heavy tape. Had anyone
bothered to notice, the envelope bore a local postmark. It had
arrived three days earlier and had been awaiting this guest.

The man accepted his key and went to his room. He had
only one suitcase. He carried it himself. He was pleased with
the room as it was near a third floor elevator as well as the fire
stairs. Coming and going unnoticed from the hotel would be
easy.

He unpacked within a few minutes. He had two extra shirts
and one extra sports jacket. There were a few extra pairs of
underwear and a heavy pair of black sneakers, best for moving
around at night. There was also a heavy wool shirt of a dark
navy color, a black turtleneck, and dark indigo jeans. The man
had left his other clothing at an airport locker in Las Vegas.
He would pick up his things on his way back East.

There was a small knapsack in the suitcase. It contained the
man's working equipment. He donned a pair of gloves and sat
down on the edge of the bed in his hotel room. He opened the
knapsack and removed the contents, making a final check
over his professional equipment.

There wasn't much. A screwdriver. An up-to-date California license plate, recently stolen from a parking lot in
Northridge. And a six-foot strand of rope, recently removed
from a home not far from the Hollywood Bowl. There was

also a local street map of Los Angeles. The map had some markings on it in ink.

The man set the map aside for a moment and picked up the rope. He tested it. Very strong. He pulled it hard. It had no give to it. It would make a dandy garrote.

He rose from the bed and took the rope into the bathroom. He worked with it for a moment and made a noose out of it. He was more than adept at constructing a perfect hangman's knot.

He tied one end of the rope to the crossbar that held the shower curtain. He braced the bar with a powerful arm and felt the strength of the noose on the other extremity of the rope.

He was pleased. This was an excellent instrument of execution.

The man returned to the sleeping area and placed the rope back in the knapsack. He sat down again on the edge of the bed and mentally went through his plan.

He would need to complete his assignment within the next day. He would wait for a single telephone call that would give him the proper time. At that hour, he would switch license plates on the rental car so that no one would be able to place him in the area of his crime.

He opened the map and read the directions written on it, showing the easiest route to 2136 Topango Gardens. Attached to the map was a photograph of the recently refurbished Queen Anne house at that address.

He memorized the route. He had been in Los Angeles before, so the directions were not mysterious. He would have no trouble following them.

Why not take a quick drive by the area today? Case it. But don't get too close. One never knew how the bungling police could inadvertently tangle up the best-laid plans of execution.

The man took the elevator down to the hotel garage. No one

was there. Everything was going perfectly so far, as smooth as undisturbed ice in February.

He stepped into his car and started it. When he drove out of the garage, the attendant didn't even look up.

Then he was out into the late afternoon. The sun came out a few moments later as the man drove west on a busy Wilshire Boulevard.

When he got to the intersection with La Cienega, the sun was intense.

So he reached into the breast pocket of his jacket and pulled out his sunglasses.

They were a wraparound kind. He liked to think that they gave him a particular air of menace.

Not that he needed it. He liked to think that the air of menace that he carried within him was about as heavy as any living human was capable of.

Less than three miles away, Rebecca Moore sat in her bedroom and had no thoughts whatsoever of the man who had once tried to murder her. Instead, she listened to the quiet of the house around her. No mysterious music creeping into her home or her heart from places unknown. No creaking of floorboards or inexplicable ticking in the walls.

Nor was there the sound that she really longed to hear. The sound of her children's voices. The sound of her family.

Outside the day was sunny, but still. She rose from where she sat on the bed and went to a window. She pushed aside the curtain and glanced out.

Two weeks had expired since Karen and Patrick had vanished. Nothing new had happened in the last ten days, and Rebecca could see the results of this at the end of her driveway. For the first time, there was not a single reporter keeping a vigil outside 2136 Topango.

She felt very lonely. She went to the telephone and called

Melissa. But her friend was not home. Melissa had caught on to some private tutoring gigs in American Civilization during the last week and Rebecca had seen less of her. Not that she didn't call in or come by at least once a day. She was that type of friend.

Rebecca pulled her hand away from the window. The curtain silently glided back into place. She turned and walked to the bedroom door. She stood in it for several seconds.

Then she raised her eyes and looked to the turret room. Where was Ronny now? *Who* was Ronny? She looked forward now to her session on Monday with Dr. Lim. Maybe that would yield some answers.

Meanwhile, further questions besieged her. Why did the ghost appear only when he desired? She wondered if the spirit could be summoned. Was there something she could do to provoke him into coming?

And who the devil was he, anyway?

It was nearly 5:00 P.M. Kicking around this old house waiting for something to happen was surely driving her crazy. How could she hold on to her own sanity much longer? Why did Bill have to spend so much time at his office? And why was she starting to feel herself turning against her husband?

Resentment? Distrust? A different way of handling the tensions of Karen and Patrick's disappearance?

She didn't know. There were so damned many things she didn't know.

She must have been standing there for several minutes, she realized, when she became aware that her eyes hadn't moved. They were set upon the half-open door to the turret room.

She was aware of movement. A change in the lighting. A shadow crossing the floor. She couldn't see into the room because the door was blocking her vision. But she knew something had moved.

Something surged inside her. She walked stealthily across

the hallway and approached the room. She arrived at the door
and listened.

Music? That old-time piano tinkling?

No.

A voice? A heartbeat? A child's cry?

No. Not that, either.

In fact, nothing. Dire silence.

She pushed the door open. The hinges uttered a little tortured wail, but the door gave way easily.

Rebecca braced herself, waiting to see at least one human
figure standing before her. But again, there was none. And
now she realized what she had seen affecting the light in the
room. It was the sunlight through the wavering branches of
the large tree outside the window. That or a cloud passing
over the sun.

Or so it appeared.

She stepped into the room.

"Anyone here?" she asked softly. "Can anyone hear
me?"

She would have given ten years of her life to have heard
Karen or Patrick answer. She walked to the center of the
room, then turned in every direction. She knew exactly what
she was doing. She was trying to lure the ghost into com-
municating.

"Come on," she said aloud, her words echoing in the quiet
house. "Someone? Talk to me. Make yourself known."

Silence answered, a painful ironic silence because now silence was exactly what she did not want. There was too much
silence in her life now. The silence from a husband who
seemed to ignore her. The silence from the FBI and LAPD,
who seemed to accuse her but never resolved her case.

"I want to see you," she said aloud. "Whatever spirit is in
this room. Whatever soul haunts this house. Please. . . . Come
forth. *Make yourself known . . .*"

A creak responded in the attic above her. A creak that made her heart soar but which led nowhere.

She stared upward, toward the ceiling. "Ronny?" she asked. "Come on. Please."

She cocked her head. She listened more intently than ever.

Oh, how she *wanted* to hear that damned piano music now. Damn, how she would have liked to have felt that strange sense of something invisible sweeping by her.

She looked at the wall. The bold letters beneath the paint: *You are in danger.* In her mind, it was still there, its origins still mysterious as ever.

Had it been meant for the children? Or for her? she wondered. She thought of how her husband had tried to convince her that *she* had imagined it. Then a thought came to her from somewhere: she was only midway through this ordeal. And perhaps the biggest part was yet to be played.

"Ronny?" she asked aloud. "Did you just give me that notion? Did you send me a thought?"

There was another creak over her head. A response? Or a tick in the old floorboards.

She felt a shiver.

Then another image was upon her. That of herself as a mad-woman, wandering from room to room in a rattling old house, complaining of voices and spirits only known to her. She had seen crazy ladies in the streets. They wore tattered, once-expensive winter coats during the summer heat. Their glasses were crooked, their lipstick askew, and they talked to people unseen, rambling on and on over real or imagined grievances from decades past, asking for spare change from anyone whose eye they caught.

Was this her future, she wondered. Would she lose her children and would the loss send her tumbling downhill into just such madness?

"*No.*"

She almost jumped. "What?" she answered.

Again the house was still. But that answer had been as clear
as a bell. She had heard a voice.

Out loud? Or in her mind?

She wasn't sure.

But it had been a male voice. Human. Or ghostly human.
Whatever. She had heard it! She knew she had. Or was this,
too, part of the incipient lunacy?

"Talk to me!" she demanded, her voice loud and vibrating
through the turret room and the still hallway beyond. "Where
are you? Say something again!"

"You will be safe."

"Who are you? If you're the spirit who has my children, I
want to see you again! I want to see *them!"*

But the silence that answered was so complete that Rebecca
already wondered whether she had imagined the entire exchange.

"I *demand* to see you!" she said next. But her demand was
not met.

She waited several seconds for more to be forthcoming, but
none was.

She moved to the window, watching the day turn into evening. Her eyes traveled across the backyard of her home. Her
gaze hit the wall and lifted over into the cemetery.

She saw the same vision that nuisance of a detective had
had when he had stood in the same place. She felt herself in
his shoes, retracing his visual path.

She felt another thought forming inside her, but couldn't
grasp it yet. It was as if she were mentally trying to sort out an
accumulation of letters on a page, letters that made no sense
until rearranged into the proper order.

"Yes. That's correct."

"What's correct?" she demanded.

The voice was like a murmur now, a whisper from every
direction.

She continued to look out the window. Her line of vision

danced among the old tombstones in the cemetery. The old stone markers stood like little sentries, a small army of guards.

Guarding *what?* What was going on in her head?

"Keep looking . . . !"

"For what?" she answered.

"Rebecca. Look!"

"At what?"

Her eyes settled upon something strange in the cemetery. Something big and gray and misshapen that appeared to be lying on its side.

A heavy breathy whisper came to her this time, as from an invisible pair of lips not far from her ear. Lips that could kiss or caress or share a secret.

"Yes! Go!"

"What?"

"Go!" the husky voice demanded. And within the very room where she stood there was an angry thump. Like the weight of a man who had jumped into the air with heavy boots and had come down hard on the wooden floor.

"Go! Now!"

By this time she didn't know whether she had imagined the conversation and the demand. But she did know she would obey. And she knew what she had to do.

She ran from the room and down the stairs. She left her house through the front door and was again relieved to see no one with a notebook or microphone.

She went to the street and jogged to the end of the block. She turned and continued toward San Angelo.

The gates to the cemetery were still open when she passed through them. She saw no attendant or caretaker. She looked past the armada of tombstones and grave markers and could see the roof of 2136 Topango Gardens beyond the rear wall of the cemetery. She hurried forward, as if there were some element of time involved in this timeless place.

She walked in the direction of her house, which also took

her toward the overturned marker she had seen from the turret room.

The angel! The grandest angel in the Cemetery of Angels. Fallen.

She wondered:

Fallen from the sky?

Fallen from where he had stood in this yard?

Or fallen because his own universe was out of order?

The huge granite marker almost took on an aura before her eyes as she approached it. From the distance, she had been unable to make out its detail. Now its detail was almost hyper-real.

She moved to within a few feet of it and stopped. She was afraid to go any closer. There was something almost sacred about it.

A heavenly figure that had crashed to the soil. A graceful pair of wings that no longer gave flight. And that hand: over-size but ethereal. Sensitive but ever-protective.

A poor man's Michelangelo.

She was almost afraid to look at the face. She expected it to be that of her otherworldly visitor. Or she thought the eyes might blink. But she summoned the courage and looked. She saw a still stone face that she did not recognize.

Only the face of an angel. A solitary angel.

She looked at the base of the marker and read the name.

Billy.

She knelt down and ran her hand across it.

She liked the touch. It was tactile and bold. And strangely, while she had expected the stone to be cold, it wasn't. It was as warm as flesh. The sun had been directly upon it. But was that the reason?

"Billy," she said aloud. Then she repeated it as she stood. The name had an eerie familiarity, a gentle, comfortable ring on her lips. It was the name her husband had never wanted, the name she had never wanted to call him.

Why?

At the back of her neck she felt something cold. Hands touching her lightly. Hands causing her again to shiver. In fear, but almost as in passion. For some reason, she recalled how her husband-to-be, when they were first lovers, used to kiss that spot on the back of her neck.

He hadn't kissed it for years.

No, wait a minute, she told herself. Bill Moore had never kissed her there.

Never kissed her like that?

Then who had? She couldn't place it. But she knew there had been someone.

Her brow knit in confusion.

Then her eyes rose. Her gaze went directly over the wall to her own home. It settled on the upstairs window in which she had stood a few minutes earlier. The turret room.

What in God's name was going on, she wondered. What had prompted her to run over here and look at her home from the base of this fallen tomb?

So many questions, and she didn't have a single answer.

Her heart nearly jumped out of her chest when a nearby male voice addressed her.

"Miss?"

She whirled. A gnarled older man stood near her, studying her, obviously surprised by her presence.

"Yes?"

"The cemetery is about to close," he said. "I no can let you stay."

He was the caretaker, she could see quickly. An old Mexican with a kindly face. He was the man she had seen from the Mustang when driving by with Melissa the previous day.

"What happened here?" she asked, indicating the fallen tombstone.

The old man shrugged. "Tomb got tipped over," he said.

"How?"

He shrugged again. "Who knows?"

"Where's the grave?" she asked.

He pointed. A hole in the ground more than fifty feet away. She didn't understand.

"How did it get way over here?"

"I don't know," he said. "Maybe it flew."

He meant it as a joke. She didn't take it as one.

She looked at the distance and couldn't picture what could have happened. "So it just traveled through the air and landed here?" she asked.

He didn't have an answer. "Don't know," he said. "And I don't know how it going to get back. This is a private cemetery. Gonna cost two thousand dollars to get the marker put back. I just learned. We don't have the money for it."

"So it will just lie here?" Rebecca asked.

"I guess. Till somebody pays."

"The tomb only says Billy," Rebecca said. "Whose grave was this?"

"An actor in the 1920s," Martinez said. "Billy Carlton. You ever heard of?"

She thought about it. It had an odd ring. Almost familiar, but not quite. "No," she finally said. "I don't remember him. Sorry."

"I wouldn't expect you to," he said.

Several moments passed. The old man stood close to her, breathing heavily through his mouth and watching her. She was still trying to figure out the odd circumstances of Billy Carlton's granite angel when the old Mexican spoke again.

"I'm sorry, lady," he said. "I got to close the gates now. You come back tomorrow if you like."

It took a moment for his words to sink in. She was still unsuccessfully trying to fathom what was before her.

"Of course," she finally said.

Rebecca took a final look at the angel's face. Then she turned away from Billy Carlton's marker. The caretaker followed her to the gate. As she started home she could hear the chains and padlock going around the iron bars.

She walked back to 2136 Topango Gardens, hoping that she might run into Melissa on her way home. But no Melissa appeared.

The only car she recognized, in fact, was the one sitting in her own driveway when she returned. It was her husband's. And she found herself disappointed when she saw it, not that she hadn't expected it. It was just that, very strangely, her husband's presence now seemed like an intrusion of some sort.

And once again, she couldn't even decipher her own feelings. Even if she had tried to explain that sensation to a friend like Melissa, she would not have been able to do so.

21

Ed Van Allen looked at the file upon his desk in his office and felt his blood begin to boil. It wasn't just that his initial instincts in the Moore case were being confirmed. It was that they were being confirmed so flagrantly. Stuff like this made him look and feel like a damned fool.

Sometimes he wondered. Maybe he was one.

He uttered a low curse and thumbed through the FBI record on William Moore. And, Van Allen noted quickly, the fingerprints and social security number had confirmed what was in front of him. Rebecca's husband was the same Bill Moore as in these files.

Moore's résumé read like a criminal counterpoint to the film career of Billy Carlton. After all, the credits were stacked up much the same way:

Aug. 15, 1976, Richmond, Virginia, Penal Code 34-12, possession of controlled substance; charges dismissed; Oct. 21, 1979, Manassas, Virginia, Penal Code 34-02, attempted sale of controlled substance; pleaded guilty to possession of marijuana, sentenced to $500 fine plus community service, latter never completed; June 2, 1984, Maryland Anti-Drug Trafficking Ordinance 15T-6, arrested for possession of one pound raw

cannabis, charges dismissed on technicality surrounding
illegal search and seizure (local authorities declined to
prosecute), pleaded guilty to related firearm possession
(unloaded handgun under passenger's seat of car)
sentenced to one year probation, probation completed;
New York (King's County) May 16, 1990, arrested
possession of cocaine, pleaded guilty to DWI, sentenced
to fine of $1000, loss of motor vehicle operator's
privileges in New York State for two years. Fine paid.

Bill Moore was no one's choirboy. What emerged was a
portrait of a longtime chronic substance abuser and sometime
dealer, a man whose architectural endeavors might have some
financing that did not necessarily have to do with the construction or design of buildings. To Van Allen, the subtext
that emerged was the profile of a man who could easily harm
his own stepchildren.

Van Allen leaned back from his desk. How exactly this
played into the current crime, Van Allen didn't know. But he
sure had a new angle. He wondered whether to go after Moore
first or his wife. One thing was for certain—he would eventually need to play them off against each other. That's how
cases like this worked.

The only question, as he mused further, was how much
Moore may have lurked beneath this and how much his wife
might have been a victim, at least in part. But then Van Allen
thought back to sections of the lie detector test, the parts
where she had denied knowing anything that she hadn't revealed to the police. Van Allen thought he had the answer
there, too.

Alice Aldrich walked in and out of the room, looking over
Van Allen's shoulder, but saying nothing. The phone on his
desk rang. Van Allen picked it up and found himself talking to
a Sergeant David Chandler of the Connecticut State Police.
Chandler was returning Van Allen's earlier call.

Van Allen sat very still and listened.

Chandler spun yet another intriguing tale about the Moores, this one from the previous February. Chandler waded through all the details, concluding with a few cryptic words about the indeterminate open status of the investigation.

"I'm not sure I'm following you," Van Allen finally responded.

"This is all very unofficial," Chandler said. "But as far as we know, the alleged abduction from last spring remains unsolved. There never really was a close to the case. Probably won't be."

"No evidence?" Van Allen asked.

"No one ever saw the perpetrator. No other crimes or abductions in the area or, as far as I know, even in the state. God knows, I looked hard."

"So what was the bottom line?" Van Allen asked.

"We thought Mrs. Moore might have been making up the whole story," Chandler said. "Why, I don't know. I couldn't even guess. But when I put this to Mr. Moore, he did nothing to dissuade me from that theory."

"*Moore* agreed with that theory?" Van Allen asked.

"Yes. In some ways, he encouraged it."

Van Allen's brows knit in confusion. He searched for the angle. He could only apply the patterns of criminal behavior that he had learned through years of experience: whenever a suspect—and Bill Moore was now a suspect—wanted something, its benefits had to be carefully analyzed.

So why would Bill Moore have encouraged the investigating officers to disbelieve his wife's story?

"Didn't you say there were shots fired?" Van Allen asked. "Into some woods or something?"

"Rebecca Moore *said* there were shots fired. Again, no witnesses."

"You didn't find any spent rounds?"

"There was snow on the ground."

"Anyone look after the snow melted?"

There was an embarrassed pause on the Connecticut end of the line.

"No. No one looked," Chandler answered. "That was long after the fact."

"The rounds could still be out there," Van Allen said.

"So could a lot of things," Chandler answered.

"And you've had other cases and long ago you concluded that maybe the whole Rebecca Moore story was a fabrication," Van Allen suggested. "Am I correct?"

Another embarrassed pause, then, "I guess I'd have to say you're correct, Detective," Sergeant Chandler said. "Unofficially correct, of course."

Van Allen let a moment pass. His mind was alive now with images of floating-then-overturned grave markers, drug dealers turned architectural consultants, and now sloppy police work in a case where a shooter might or might not have ever shot.

"Why don't you have a look now?" Van Allen asked.

"Now?"

Van Allen sighed. "I mean, we're dealing with a major investigation on this end," he began. "Would that be some sort of major problem, to go have one more look for a spent round?"

A pause, then, "I guess I could take a look," Chandler said.

Van Allen thanked the young sergeant across the country. He put down the phone and stared straight ahead. He wondered where exactly any of the details in this case would start to intersect.

He again flipped open the file containing his notes. It was time to start turning the screws upon one of the Moore parents. He made a decision. Rebecca was probably the weaker of the two. He would put her feet to the flames first and he would do so right in her home.

After all, he told himself, the bodies were there somewhere, too.

Dr. Chang Lim's wife, Sonya, who was also his nurse, met Rebecca at the door to Dr. Lim's office in Westwood. It was Monday morning at eleven.

Sonya was a stout Swedish woman with an accent. She guided Rebecca into the doctor's interview chamber almost immediately after her arrival.

Dr. Lim received Rebecca cordially. He was wearing an open-necked print shirt, beige slacks, and green sneakers. No socks. He talked to her for a few minutes on the theory and philosophy of hypnotism. He noted that the success of the therapy was largely in proportion to how great the patient's desire to reveal the inner aspects of his or her consciousness.

"I need you relax, Rebecca," Dr. Lim stressed, Hong Kong still flavoring his English. "I need you to relax and trust me. And I tell you also this: if we fail today, that does not preclude our success on another day. We keep working."

"I understand," Rebecca said.

"Still want to give it a try?" Dr. Lim asked. He gave her a wink and a smile. Both sparkled.

"I'm ready," she said.

Dr. Lim directed Rebecca to lie on a nearby couch. He asked her to relax. He asked her to clasp her hands together and to close her eyes. Sonya Lim remained in the room, adjusting the lighting.

"You be inclined to open them again from time to time," the doctor said, "and if that makes you feel more secure, that's fine okay. But you want to enter the state of mind we need, so you need to keep them shut. Primarily."

"That's all right," Rebecca said again.

"What I'm going to try is have you clear your conscious mind, Rebecca," he continued. "You do that by having concentration initially on something so small that it will be akin to clearing your mind completely. In this case, the 'thing' will be an attempt to fall asleep. That, and how tired you feel.''

Rebecca nodded slightly. She nestled her back into the sofa and felt the room lights dim around her.

"Once your conscious mind recede, I will bring up your unconscious," Lim said. "Then we take a trip. Through your memory. Your past. We'll take it as far back as possible." He paused. "You be willing to go there with me, Mrs. Rebecca Moore?''

"I'm willing.''

"Then we begin.''

She held her eyelids tightly shut, then allowed them to relax slightly. She felt a rush of comfort coming over her, like a big warm frothy wave.

"Just think of sleep now. Think: you are getting very tired and falling asleep," Dr. Lim suggested. "You are very tired, your eyes are heavy, your body is limp, Rebecca. And your head is heavy.''

He paused, working on the cadences and rhythms of his approach.

"You want to sleep," he continued. "You want very badly to sleep. Your body is very heavy and you are falling, falling, falling asleep.''

Rebecca's eyelids flickered. She wanted badly to follow the doctor and slip into the state of unconsciousness to which he was leading her.

Her eyelids flickered a second time and the last thing she remembered was Sonya Lim tiptoeing out of the room in clogs.

The sight was so absurd that it almost broke her concentration and made her laugh.

But instead, she plunged through the boundaries that Dr. Lim had set for her, and she drifted into a light trance.

"Think of this, Rebecca. A tunnel," she heard him say. "Think of a long, familiar, friendly tunnel."

She obeyed.

There was an image before her of her life running in reverse, from the present day quickly back through that horrible incident in Connecticut and then, rapidly accelerating, through college and into her high school years.

The inconsistency of Dr. Lim's voice and grammar superimposed upon events of her past didn't bother her. She felt as though she were passing rapidly through a tunnel, soaring through darkness.

She was a girl again, with her mother and father in the old family home.

... *Still sailing backward* ...

Scenes from her life were like billboards passing into her view as she voyaged on a speeding subway train. She was on an express tearing through all the stations.

Image after image shot by.

She arrived at her own birth. Then went into a deeper and more troubling blackness.

She struggled with something and didn't know what it was. It was some sort of barrier. Physical. Psychological. Some sort of impediment to the exploration of her past.

"Hey! What the hell *is* this?" she asked herself. She felt the vibrations of her own voice in a high whisper, speaking aloud.

Her own birth. She grimaced.

A previous death. She felt herself flail on the psychiatrists couch. She uttered a short low scream of horror.

"I'm dead. But I'm alive," she blurted.

"*Now*, Rebecca!" Dr. Lim's voice soothed. "Yes. Very good, go! Keep traveling. Keep voyaging backward. See if you again can come across visions in the tunnel."

Absurd, that idea, she caught herself thinking. There is no life before birth. The blackness was enough to attest to that.

I am in uncharted territory, she thought to herself. *I've been here but I haven't been here.*

"*Come back to me,*" a beckoning male voice said. It was warm and friendly. Familiar.

She heard herself whisper aloud to the doctor. "Where are you taking me?" she asked.

Lim's voice, inquiring. "Have you passed your own birth?"

Rebecca, answering. "Yes. I'm in darkness."

"And you're still traveling?"

"I am. The darkness is moving."

It was like looking out of an airplane on a pitch-black night. Nothing visible, but a clear sense of forward motion.

Lim again. "Excellent. That means there's a place to go to. There's something there."

"How will I find it?"

"It will find you, Rebecca. Be available. Wait for it. Let yourself sail into the light."

Her hands clasped each other tightly. She was in darkness. The darkness swirled now. She almost had a sensation of plunging. Then that, too, stopped.

"I'm coming to lightness," she said.

"Keep going," Dr. Lim said. "Face the brightness. Welcome it. It's another world."

"It's what? It's *what?*" she asked.

"Don't question," he urged softly. "Voyage."

Rebecca had the image of sailing up over a horizon and bursting upon a brilliantly lit landscape. She felt like a bird, soaring euphorically, gliding upon a sunlit reality.

Then she felt herself coming to earth. And with reality, her spirit became very heavy. An unbearable sadness was upon her. Some great tragedy was pulling her downward, reaching up to her soul and retrieving it in its grasp, and guiding her down into the sorrows of the world.

She fought it.

She cried out. "No! Stop it! No! Please."

"Go to it, Rebecca," the doctor said. "Go to it so that we understand."

"No. It's horrible!" she spoke aloud in a normal voice. Her own words echoed in her ears. "I don't want to go!"

She felt the doctor's hands upon hers, calming and reassuring as his voice continued to narrate her voyage.

"You have to, Rebecca Moore," he said. "You have to see it and accept it to know where you are today."

Crying out, resisting it, she answered, "I don't want to! I can't! *I can't!*"

"You have to," he answered. "You've gone all this way. Don't turn around."

"I won't!"

"You have to meet your own ghosts," he said. "You have to locate your own children."

The children! Patrick and Karen. Where in God's name were *they* in this?

She turned back toward the imagined light. On the couch, her body contorted. It was as if her feet had hit the ground with a thump.

She was on the ground. Looking around. People around her slowly came into focus.

She blinked. She was in a black dress and she stood among many people near a grave. There was a casket in place waiting to be lowered.

"Oh, God," she murmured. "Oh, God, no . . ." She started to cry. Dr. Lim's hand reassured her again.

She felt as if her children should be at her side, but they weren't. She was alone.

Her eyes came up.

Of course! The tragedy! Now she knew what it was. The actor, Billy Carlton, was being buried. A doleful Protestant minister was completing the ceremony, but his voice, his words, were only a dull hum under the wind.

"This place," she whispered aloud in the doctor's office. "I recognize this cemetery."

Then a few words did catch Rebecca's ear. They were the thoughts of the friends of Billy Carlton, assembled at San Angelo Cemetery at the moment of his interment.

"Murdered . . ." one said.

"Poisoned," said another.

". . . never convict anyone . . . though we all know who did it . . ."

Rebecca found herself looking around, searching the faces of friends. They were all looking at her. She watched the casket being lowered and felt a sense of grief far more intense than she might ever have imagined.

She felt as if love itself was being lowered into the ground. And when the coffin disappeared from view, the minister turned in her direction.

"Mrs. Carlton?" he asked.

He gave a slight nod to a rose she held in her hand.

"Mrs. Carlton?" he asked again.

It was only then that Rebecca understood what was being asked of her. So she, as the widow of the deceased, approached the grave. In silence she threw the rose after the coffin. She watched it disappear downward into the ground, followed quickly by other roses from the aggregation of Billy Carlton's friends.

Her last image was that of the roses tumbling downward to where they would join Billy. Then Rebecca turned.

A friend's arm comforted her. And then, as Dr. Lim summoned her, she began her return trip to the consciousness of the present day, arriving back after forty minutes of hypnosis, blinking her way back into a reality which may have been no more or less real than several others.

* * *

"More people should seek out their past lives under hypnosis," Dr. Lim said a quarter hour later as the session of hypnotherapy ended. "I think a lot of people would be surprised."

"I'm sure," Rebecca said.

"Souls have to come from somewhere," he added. "Why shouldn't they have their own recycling process?" he asked. "Why shouldn't the spiritual have the same qualities of creation and destruction as the physical?" He paused. "Eastern thoughts. Sorry. You are free to share or dismiss. But then, you have traveled, so maybe now you believe."

Dr. Lim raised an eyebrow and shrugged.

Slightly shaken, Rebecca spent only a few more minutes in conversation. Then she wrote out a check and hurriedly departed.

22

One hour after leaving Dr. Chang Lim's office, Rebecca Moore stood in the upstairs landing of her home and waited. She waited for the visit that she knew, if she willed it, would now come.

She walked first into Patrick's room, then continued to Karen's. She moved in a slow stroll, feeling the emptiness of the house around her.

She tried to picture her children and where they might be. In the custody of the ghost? What did that mean? Were they living? Dead? She wasn't sure. She only knew that she wanted to join them.

Join them and a man she had once loved.

Somehow. Some way.

In some manner their lives had been intertwined once before, hers and the actor known as Billy Carlton. And somehow now he had come back.

To take her? To protect her?

She didn't know.

Unless, of course, she had somehow gone insane. And none of this was happening.

She went into the turret room and tried to feel Billy Carlton's presence.

"I'm ready for you," she whispered. "I want to see you."

She waited and the ghost of the actor did not come. Several
minutes passed. She listened for the piano music, the tune that
she had dreaded just a short time ago. She couldn't find it. She
tried to will it to come forth. Now, its absence pained her, like
a lost love.

She wanted to hear a creak in the ceiling or in a nearby
floorboard. No dice there, either. She badly wanted a visita-
tion, and none was forthcoming.

She went to the window that looked toward the cemetery.
She opened it slightly. A breeze wafted through as it so often
did.

Her gaze stayed with the cemetery.

Then her senses gave a little start. There was a shadow
moving from Billy Carlton's fallen marker. And it was moving directly toward her house.

Rebecca smiled like a madwoman. She glanced upward. In
the sunny sky above Southern California she saw no cloud.
And still the shadow moved.

She turned. She walked calmly from the turret room and
across the upstairs landing. She went to the master bedroom of
her home.

She loosened her blouse and sank into a chaise lounge in
the master bedroom. She looked at the doorway. For several
seconds the open door framed nothing. She waited for the
ghost and it did not appear.

She clutched her hands together and brought them to her
chin. She wanted to know—wished, maybe?—if this spirit,
this man, would follow her into the bedroom she shared with
her husband.

Still, nothing appeared in the doorframe. She wondered
now, had he vanished? She craned her head slightly and gazed
beyond the door. There was a creak in the hallway and her
heart gave another tremor. She felt a cold draft and then that
telltale dropping of the atmospheric pressure. She was sure
that he would appear.

She was certain.

She looked. Nothing.

She listened. Nothing more.

She spoke. "Billy?" her voice was barely a whisper.

No answer. Then—

"I'm here, darling!"

Simultaneous to his words, there was a touch. Unseen, the ghost had appeared beside her. His fingers settled on her shoulder and gave her a shock; not an electrical shock, but a surge of physical excitement.

And his fingers. They touched her as if they were able to pass through the fabric of her blouse.

She recoiled, but his hand followed her. He laughed gently, a rich warm laughter. A stage actor's trained voice in merriment. And then he was behind her and both hands were upon her shoulders.

"Please . . ." she said. But she had no idea what she was asking for.

Please don't? Please be gentle? Please go ahead?

She didn't know.

"I would never harm you," he said.

She wanted to relax into his clasp, but didn't have the courage to do so. She started to relax, then caught herself. Somewhere inside her, some distant warning bell sounded. Something about women who yield to advances from intruding males in the bedrooms they share with their lawful spouses.

She pulled herself away. Then she felt a pair of strong arms upon her shoulders. Billy's hands secured her. She felt a passion rise within her, a physical drive for lovemaking, unlike anything she had felt for years.

She felt his body behind her. No longer was he a flitting figure at the edge of her consciousness. No more was he a shadow in the most remote corners of her mind. Now he held

her as strongly as any man had ever held her. And then his
arms closed around her.

He kissed her at the back of her neck and again she recognized his touch from long ago. His hands went to work on the
buttons of her blouse. And she felt the urgency continue to
rise within her.

A reunion.

Yes, Rebecca felt herself thinking, it seemed like a reunion.
And she knew that it was.

She wondered if he was going to take her to the grave with
him, to rejoin her children. And she barely cared.

She turned to face him and looked into eyes that she felt had
been watching her for a lifetime. Or perhaps they had only
been upon her since she had moved to this place. There would
be a lot of time, she reasoned, to learn which.

He was no longer cold but now was very warm, as warm as
her feelings and, for that matter, as warm as any man who had
ever held her.

She closed her eyes, let him kiss her, and let his hands continue to help her out of her clothes.

She woke up two hours later on her bed, the covers pulled
across her naked body. For a moment she did not know what
had awakened her, then she realized: it was the sound of an
automobile engine.

The identity of the engine was unmistakable. It was her
husband's car. Then the thoughts came flooding back to her.
The ghost, first in the hallway, then in her bedroom.

Then in her.

If it had really happened. She took stock of herself, and how
her body felt, and concluded that it had.

Another moment passed. For an instant she was happy. She
felt loved and felt that somehow she was that much closer to a

permanent reunion with a man who loved her and with her children.

Would they all be buried together in San Angelo, she wondered idly? Would they lie together for eternity—Rebecca, Billy Carlton, and her two children?

The thought didn't disturb her in the slightest. The specter of death was no more fearsome than an old swinging gate in a country churchyard, to be passed through with great ease. An easy trip from one place to another.

She lay in bed for another moment, thinking. The late afternoon sunshine was flowing in the bedroom window like honey. It was a brief pure moment, sweet as fresh cream.

Then it vanished. She heard her husband enter the house downstairs and call her name. Her heart felt heavy as a weight. Bill Moore was the intruder, she felt. An intruder in her heart and an intruder in her body for too many years now.

"Becca?" he called.

She didn't answer.

She scrambled for her clothes, pulled them on and straightened the bed, all in the same movements.

He was at the foot of the steps.

"Becca!" he called a second time. The normal ring to his voice. Surly, impatient.

"Up here," she called back.

She heard him trudge up the steps. Why was the creaking footfall of the ghost now so welcome, and the step of her husband so repellent?

She thought she knew the answer.

Moore came into the bedroom and cast her a glance. No affection. No nothing. Not even—thank God!—suspicion.

"Napping?" he asked, as if to suggest that she shouldn't have been.

"Yeah," she said. "I felt real worn-out."

"Any word from the police?" he asked.

"No. Is there ever?" she answered, trying to act as normal as possible.

"Of course not."

As was his habit, he emptied his pockets onto the dresser, loosened his dress shirt, and disappeared into the bathroom. She watched him with a new sense, a new awareness, that had been brought on by the events of the afternoon.

She felt like a longtime adulteress and, like those new to the activity, wondered if the word was written right there on her face.

She even looked in the mirror to see if she looked the same as she had an hour ago.

She did. Or at least she thought she did.

But nothing else was clear or reasonable or unencumbered. There was no straight explanation for anything. And she had the feeling that there never would be again.

23

Sergeant David Chandler pulled his patrol car to the perimeter of the road and edged the right-side tires onto the dirt shoulder of Tremont Lane. The Connecticut state trooper turned on the emergency flashers and stopped the car. He cut the ignition and stepped out. He left the car open, but took the keys with him.

He stood at the roadside and tried to make sense of the jumble of trees and woods before him. Back in February and March, when he had first been working on the Moore case, Chandler had come back here several times with Rebecca to reenact the alleged crime. Back then, of course, there had been snow on the ground. For months in early 1995 there had been a white shroud over all the evidence. Today, seven months since he had last given the area a look, there was just the normal blanket of dead leaves and underbrush on the floor of the woods.

Chandler placed himself where Rebecca claimed she had fled among the cover of trees. He let his line of vision carry among the scrub and underbrush in the presumed path where she had fled.

He saw nothing other than the hopelessness of finding any evidence after all this time.

But something told him to take a walk. At least, when Detective Van Allen called back from Los Angeles, Chandler could honestly say that he had toured the crime scene again and, in good faith, had found nothing. And at worst, it wasn't a bad day for a walk among the trees.

He took his first few steps. He felt dead leaves and twigs crunch beneath his shoes as he stepped into the woods. Rebecca had run—if she had run at all—in a scattershot zigzag path among the trees. That's how she had described it. So David Chandler once again tried to put himself in her position and—for perhaps the tenth time—tried to figure from where her assailant might have fired after her.

Finding a spent bullet in this mess was one pop in a million. Well, he pondered further, the state lottery was even higher odds and he took chances there, too. So why not here?

And yet, the task was no more daunting now than it had been months earlier. If the rounds that had been fired at Rebecca Moore had traveled straight, they could have carried hundreds of yards into the woods. Equally, they could have hit the ground within seventy or eighty feet and dug themselves little graves in the topsoil.

Or they could have hit branches and ricocheted wildly, flying in any direction before spending their velocity and settling. People sometimes still found arrowheads in these woods, Chandler thought to himself again, untouched for two hundred years. Sites around Civil War battlefields, where millions of people have walked for a century and a quarter, still yielded the occasional uncovered bullet. So how was he to find specific rounds ten months after the fact, rounds from a crime that he personally doubted even happened?

He sighed.

His head was lowered and the toe of his shoe pushed through the brush and decomposing leaves at the base of trees. He spent the better part of an hour wandering. In another few weeks, he mused as he explored, another settling of snow would be upon this same ground.

"Five more minutes," he said aloud. "That's all I'm giving it."

A couple of those minutes passed. Chandler looked back toward where he had come from, trying to position himself again, and something surprised him. He saw a man walking near his car.

The man stopped and looked at the police cruiser, as if to wonder what the vehicle was doing there. It was unusual to see a man on foot in that location. This was the suburbs; most people drove everywhere.

Then the man stopped. Chandler was alert very quickly, watching the stranger. But the man seemed to offer no threat. The pedestrian turned and quickly saw the policeman.

The man raised a hand and called. "Hello?"

Chandler waved back. Not that Chandler needed help, but the man seemed to divert himself from his stroll. He walked fifty feet into the woods until he came to the state police detective.

He was about forty, Chandler guessed, with a face that was almost handsome. Brown hair, neatly cut. Just a shirt on and a pair of slacks. The cut of both struck Chandler as a little old-fashioned, but never did the policeman consider himself an arbiter of fashion.

"Everything okay, officer?" the man asked.

"I'm fine," Chandler said.

"Anything I can help you with?"

Chandler smiled grudgingly. "Not unless you're a magician."

"A magician?" The stranger laughed. "I'm afraid I'm not," he said. The stranger watched the policeman. Chandler's eyes examined the man carefully. There was something not quite right about him, but Chandler couldn't place what it was.

"It's a little chilly today, isn't it?" Chandler asked, noting the thinness of the man's shirt. "Aren't you cold?"

"I like the air. The chill doesn't bother me. Invigorating. Can I help you with anything?"

"No, thanks," Chandler said.

"You must be doing something out here," the man said.

Chandler hesitated, then answered. "I'm trying to find a spent bullet. From an incident that took place several months ago."

"Oh?" The stranger was thoughtful. "The time that woman was assaulted? Is that it?"

Chandler's suspicion rose. "Yeah. How'd you know that?"

The man shrugged. "I remember the incident. Horrible thing."

"You live around here?" Chandler inquired.

The man shook his head. "Just visiting."

"Who do you visit?"

The man suddenly laughed. It was a funny sort of laugh. "Am I suddenly a suspect?" he asked.

"Not at all. But I interviewed everyone in the neighborhood. No one was much help."

"I didn't see anything," the man said. "I just remember hearing about it." The man offered a hand. "I know people just up over the hill," the man said.

"You have a name?" Chandler asked.

After a pause, the stranger said, "Paul Hammond."

The cop knew a lot of the names in town. But he didn't know this one. "And you live up there?" Chandler asked, motioning with his head.

"Yup."

Chandler shook the man's hand. The man's hand was chilly, as if he had been out in the cold too long. But Sergeant Chandler had long since stopped worrying about the health of adults. He had enough on his plate already.

"*Where* up over the hill?" Chandler pressed. "I thought I knew everyone up there."

"You don't know me."

"Guess not. You stay with people up there?"

"Near the church," the man said.

The response made no sense to Chandler. But frequently there were small homes tucked away on quarter acre residential parcels zoned in the 1920s. It was strange, but, within context, believable. And he was, after all, a state cop, not a town gendarme.

But, "Funny I've never seen you before," Chandler said, still angling.

"Real funny," the man said, watching the policeman. "You sure you're looking in the right area?"

"I'm not sure at all," Chandler said. "The evidence is several months old. The trail is cold. Who knows what's out here?"

"Who knows?" the man echoed.

"One place to look is as good as the other," Chandler said. "After all this time, chances are real slim."

"Is that a fact?" the man said.

"That's a fact," Chandler answered. He glanced at the stranger and then glanced away. The visitor was starting to irritate him. If this had been a normal crime scene and a normal search, which it wasn't, Chandler would never have tolerated the presence.

"So did the man spray bullets all over the area?" the man asked. "Or in one spot?"

"The victim was fleeing," Chandler said. "She knows two shots came near her at first. If I recall, she said she ducked down near a fir tree. After that . . . ? Who knows?" He looked around. "And you know how many goddamned fir trees there are out here?"

Chandler's self-appointed helper nodded. His eyes swept the area along with Chandler's. There were evergreens of all sizes, standing like little sentries among the bare-branched birches, oaks, dogwoods, and maples in the woods. And yet,

his expression appeared serious. Chandler glanced away from
him for another moment, then looked back and—in the space
of a couple of heartbeats—the man had quietly moved thirty
feet from where Chandler had last seen him.

Hammond was nosing around a clump of small pine trees.
Then, as Chandler watched him, he was inclined forward.
Then he knelt. He was looking at something toward the base
of a fir tree.

Chandler felt himself fascinated, watching the man. There
was still something about him that wasn't quite right, but
Chandler remained unable to place it. He didn't move quite
correctly, the policeman decided. Chandler wondered if he
had had some terrible accident when he was younger. And
then, strangely, the man seemed to know that Chandler was
watching, or at least he assumed he was, for he spoke without
even looking up.

"Maybe this?" the visitor asked softly.

Chandler walked toward him, pushing his way noisily
through brittle branches, some of which cracked as he pushed
them. The man never moved, but looked upward to the policeman as Chandler arrived.

For a second, the eyes of each of the two men locked into
each other's. And Chandler sensed something with which he
was deeply uneasy. A fathomless look in the other man's
eyes. A wateriness, a liquid nature, an unusual depth. And
there was also even a sadness and a sorrow which he had
never encountered before.

Chandler wondered if this Hammond was some sort of psychic. That, or a mental patient who had walked away from the
local sanitarium that was normally reserved for suburban al-
coholics to do a convenient dry-out.

Then Hammond interrupted Chandler's free-floating
thoughts. "Don't look at me. Look at the tree," the stranger
said softly. "Look at these scars."

The stranger turned his own head and gazed toward what he

wanted the Connecticut state trooper to examine. Chandler pulled his eyes away from the man and looked.

About eighteen inches up from the ground was a gash in the flesh of the tree. The bark had been ripped away, as if by high impact. There was a tear in the trunk of the tree as well. Chandler knelt.

"Jesus," the cop said as he examined it.

There it was. Plain as the sun in the sky. Exactly what Chandler had been searching for.

Maybe.

What looked like a nine-millimeter slug was lodged hard in the trunk of the fir tree. The logistics of it looked just right. The injury to the tree looked as if it had had several months to recover. But not enough time had passed for the tree to fully absorb the steel bullet.

Rebecca's words echoed from nine months earlier:

First one shot, then another quick one, right where I was hiding at the base of an evergreen. I ran and he fired wildly after me.

Was this the spot? Chandler ran his hand higher up the tree and found nothing. No second scar in the bark. When he looked lower, however, he found another bullet.

"I'll be damned," he said.

Chandler's helper stood. He stepped away so as not to block the light that filtered through the branches above. "Be thankful you're not," he said.

After a second, Chandler asked, "Not what?"

"Damned," the man said.

Chandler glanced at his companion, but ignored the remark. "Yeah," he muttered.

Instead of talking, he went straight to work. He pulled a utility knife out of his pocket. He dug aggressively into the trunk of the tree and pried loose the upper bullet. He let it fall into his palm. He hefted it.

"That what you were looking for?" the man asked.

"I can't believe this," Chandler said. "It could be."

Carefully, Chandler tucked the bullet in a secure shirt pocket and clipped the pocket shut. Methodically, he used the blade of the knife to go after the second round. Within seconds, he had pulled it from the body of the evergreen. It seemed to match the first bullet, but a lab would have to tell him for sure.

"You got some kind of magic touch after all, mister," Chandler said. He glanced at his benefactor for only a second, long enough for the stranger to give him a cryptic shrug.

"Glad to help. I got lucky, that's all," the man said. "And now I got to be on my way."

"Sure," Chandler answered, distracted by his discovery. "And, hey. Thanks, Mr. . . . What was your name again?"

"Hammond," he said. "Remember me as Paul Hammond."

"Sure," Chandler said again.

The stranger looked down and something caught his eyes. "Hmm," he said. "Look at this. We got spirits from all over the place here today."

Chandler watched as the stranger leaned over and ran a finger through some leaves. He flicked away a bit of dirt and his fingers settled upon something that looked like a jagged stone pointing upward through the soil.

Hammond drew it up from the ground and brushed more dirt away from it.

"You have kids?" Hammond asked.

"Two boys," said Chandler.

"This is an arrowhead," the stranger said. "Still find them occasionally in these areas. Take it home."

The stranger winked and smiled. Then he dropped the arrowhead into the astonished detective's hand.

The man turned to leave. For a few seconds, Chandler was aware of the man moving through the woods, back toward the road, pushing quietly through chilled branches as he moved.

Then, as Chandler marked the evidence, he was aware of being alone again. And the feeling of being left alone was very similar to the feeling of a door closing, of a change in the atmosphere around him. It felt strange again.

But Chandler stayed with his work. He had a piece of yellow tape in his pocket and tied it around the base of the fir tree so that he could return to the exact location. Then he turned and stood.

He wanted to thank the stranger again, afraid that he had been abrupt in not thanking him sufficiently the first time. Chandler looked for him, expecting him only to be at the edge of the woods by now. But the visitor was nowhere in sight.

Chandler walked back to the road. He didn't see the man there, either.

For a moment, the state policeman stood once again on the spot where Rebecca had fled into the woods. And now he was quite perplexed.

"Hammond" had appeared as if by magic and then disappeared with remarkable speed. He wondered whether this was some sort of weird setup: Chandler gets asked by an out-of-state cop to revisit a crime scene, then a helper just *happens* to be on hand to guide him.

It made him suspicious.

Chandler looked up and down the road in both directions. No one.

After another moment's thought, he got back into his car.

His curiosity piqued, Chandler drove back to State Street, the main thoroughfare between Westport and Fairfield. He again failed to find the man. Then he turned his car and drove all the way back up Tremont Lane. He passed the spot where he had stopped to retrieve the bullets. He continued all the way up to the Congregationalist church on the crest of the hill.

He didn't come across a single person walking. And near the church, as he had expected, he found no small plots as the stranger had suggested. There were only full one- and two-acre lots, plus the church property which included the parish house and the small old cemetery.

And no one anywhere was named Hammond.

Chandler drove back to the State Police headquarters, thinking things over. The two spent rounds were both nine-millimeter as he had judged. A forensics expert guessed that they might have been in the tree for more than a few weeks, but less than a year.

All of which made a strong but circumstantial case that an attack on Rebecca Moore really had transpired.

It was enough to make Chandler lean back in his chair and try to rethink the entire case.

He cursed the fact that he had given up on the case rather than pursuing it. And he blamed himself for allowing the case to drop.

What kind of amateur cop was he, anyway, he demanded of himself.

And where did this stranger get off, flitting in and out of a case like that?

Then Chandler picked up the telephone and called the number in Los Angeles that Ed Van Allen had left.

A woman named Alice answered in lieu of Detective Van Allen. Chandler wasn't comfortable leaving vital information with partners, so he left only the request that his call be returned.

"I have something in one of Detective Van Allen's cases," Chandler said. "It might be something and it might not be. Have him call me when he can."

Double-A said she would.

Chandler put down the telephone.

The two bullets were back on his desk. He stared and stared and stared at them, wondering what they were trying to tell him. Also on his desk was the arrowhead, which Chandler found almost equally perplexing. And even more difficult to figure, for that matter, was what higher message the stranger might have brought, as well. For some reason, David Chandler felt a queasiness and a shiver when he replayed to himself the events of the morning.

It was a feeling that would not go away.

On the other side of the country, Ed Van Allen stepped out of his car in front of 2136 Topango Gardens. He was prepared to do what he had refrained from doing all along. Confront his two chief suspects, one at a time.

The flock of reporters in front of the house had dispersed several days earlier. He brought along Alice Aldrich in order to have a policewoman present when he confronted Rebecca Moore. And he had called ahead to make sure that the suspect was home.

"No, nothing new, Mrs. Moore," Van Allen said when Rebecca inquired upon his arrival. "We'd just like to ask you a few more questions."

Rebecca eyed him and his partner at the door, then allowed them in.

"I wonder if we could chat upstairs," Van Allen suggested. He wished to be closer to where the children had last lived. Better vibrations, he felt, and possibly better to wrench a confession from his suspect.

"I'm really not sure what this is about," Rebecca said. "If you don't have anything new, what are we talking about today?"

"I have a new thesis," the detective began. "And I'd like to try it on you. May I?"

Rebecca shrugged. She led them into the yellow room, the turret room, by default.

Ronny's room.

Rebecca sat down on a folding chair while Alice stood near a window and Van Allen positioned himself at the room's epi-

362 *Noel Hynd*

center. For a moment, he thought he heard piano music from somewhere. Then he was sure he didn't.

"Mrs. Moore," Ed Van Allen finally began, "I think it is about time that you began to tell me the truth."

Rebecca's mouth went open in astonishment. "I *have* told you the truth," she said.

"The complete truth," he suggested.

"I don't know what you mean," she countered.

"Mrs. Moore, you've told me *part* of the truth," Van Allen said. "But you haven't told me *all* of the truth. Another way to say it, Mrs. Moore," he said, "is that you've lied to me from the very beginning."

"I haven't," she said.

"You flunked your polygraph," Van Allen said. "And we're going to get a court order to force your husband to take one. But why don't you make it easier for both of you? Why don't you start telling us what we need to know before we talk to him."

Alice leaned against the windowsill and watched the proceedings. When a tree rustled behind her, she turned, glancing at it with disinterest. For a moment her eye drifted to San Angelo. Then she turned and looked back to the room.

"I've told you the truth," Rebecca said.

"You flunked the polygraph on three questions in particular, Mrs. Moore," Van Allen continued. "I asked you if you were hiding anything. I asked you if you knew where your children were. And I asked if there was anything significant that you hadn't told us."

He paused, his own anger and resentment building.

"Know what, Mrs. Moore?" he then went on. "You concealed something when you answered each of those questions."

Rebecca was incredulous, failing to understand.

"And I want to know what the proper answers are right

now, Mrs. Moore, because I'm asking you those same questions again.''

She went to the window, moving closer to Alice, wringing her hands. Once again, her children were missing and she was being treated like a criminal.

"I don't know," Rebecca said.

"Yes, you do, Rebecca," Alice said gently, playing the former role in the good-cop–bad-cop routine. "And you're going to have to tell us."

"I'm waiting, Mrs. Moore," Van Allen said.

From somewhere a very cold draft struck him. He found it uncomfortable and unpleasant. He shifted his position in the yellow room and was okay for a moment. Then the draft found him again. It felt like an extreme chill.

"I know there was an incident with the police in Connecticut, Mrs. Moore," Van Allen said. "And I know there was a question whether the incident as you reported it ever occurred."

She turned, furiously. "I was nearly *killed,*" she said.

"I also know your husband had an arrest record in New York, Maryland, and Virginia, Mrs. Moore," Van Allen said. "You could have told us about that, too."

"An arrest *what?*"

"Don't play games with us, Rebecca," Alice said. "It will only make things worse."

"You can't get away with anything and I'm still waiting," Van Allen repeated.

Rebecca shook her head, grappling with her emotions. Her eyes went to the space on the wall where the message had appeared under the yellow paint. YOU ARE IN DANGER. Surrounded by these cops, to Rebecca the cryptic message took on another spin. The message seemed constantly opening up like a kaleidoscope with new meanings, new vistas, every time she thought of it.

Then the cold blast touched her, also. But on her it had a

different effect. It almost served to settle her, to embolden her reaction.

"Tell us what you know, Rebecca," Alice said. "It will make everything easier. You have to tell us."

Rebecca turned and looked at the two detectives. And she now knew what had made the polygraph needle jump.

"You won't believe me," Rebecca said.

"I've been a cop in this city for two decades, Mrs. Moore," Van Allen said. "I'll believe anything." He paused. "So try me."

"There's a supernatural being in this house," Rebecca said. "And he took my children."

There was a leaden moment in the room when everything seemed to stand still.

A long, long pause, as Van Allen fought off a sinking sensation. Then, "How's that again?" Van Allen asked.

"A ghost," Rebecca said. "There's a ghost who abducted my children."

Completely deadpan. "A ghost of what, Mrs. Van Allen?"

"I think it's the spirit of someone I knew. Maybe in another life. I don't know. Somehow I know this man and he has my children."

"Are you saying that your children are dead, Rebecca?" Double-A asked.

"I don't know what I'm saying about that. All I know is that this house is haunted. There's a spirit. It often appears in this room. The children saw it several times before they disappeared."

"And you've seen it?"

"Yes."

"And why do you think the ghost has the children?"

"It's the only explanation," she said. "And he told me."

"He told you."

"He told me."

"When?"

"A few nights ago."

"Can I talk to him, too?" Van Allen asked, his cynical skepticism highly evident.

"Maybe. I suspect he's here right now. Watching us."

"Make him materialize," Van Allen said, his tone almost mocking.

Rebecca waited for a moment, hoping the ghost would make itself known. It didn't.

"I can't bring him forth," Rebecca said. "It's not something I can control. It's up to him."

"You'd better arrange it with him damned fast, Mrs. Moore, because without speaking to this ghost—"

"Ronny."

"He has a name?"

"He spelled it out. On the children's blackboard. Look."

She led them to Patrick's room. She walked them to a small blackboard and picked it up.

"A few nights before the children disappeared, they told me that he had put his name on this board. But he did it with scrambled letters. Then they had rearranged them. They found the letters that spelled 'Ronny,' so that's what they called him."

Van Allen looked at the alphabetical jumble and the circled letters linked together that had been unscrambled to spell the spirit's name.

Alice Aldrich and Van Allen exchanged a glance as she spoke. When she looked up from the blackboard, she caught the glance.

Van Allen blew out a long dispirited breath.

"So what you're telling me, Mrs. Moore," he said, "is that a ghost named Ronny came into this house and abducted your children. That's all you're going to tell me?"

"I'm afraid it is," she said.

"And that's what you call this ghost, huh?" Van Allen asked. "Ronny, huh? Like the former president."

"The kids call him Ronny. I think his name is Billy."

Van Allen felt a twinge at the name. "Why do you think that?"

Rebecca shrugged. "I just do."

"Billy. Like your husband, huh?"

Rebecca shook her head. "Bill *hates* the name Billy. He never wants to be called that, I never wanted to call him that. Bill and Billy are two separate things."

Rebecca was nodding merrily, as if she were on lithium. Van Allen looked at her and then looked at his partner.

"See that you don't leave the area, Mrs. Moore," he said tersely. "And tell your husband we'll be speaking to him tomorrow."

He cast her a withering look and signaled to Double-A that it was time to leave. He had had quite enough of this charade. He was ready to come back to this house with a steam shovel if it was necessary to uncover the bodies of Karen and Patrick Moore.

The two detectives got into their car.

Alice buckled into her seat belt. Van Allen didn't.

He glanced at his partner and then looked angrily at the house at 2136 Topango Gardens.

"Jesus Christ," he said sullenly, sliding the car key into the ignition. "These people just moved here from the East. And already they're homicidal maniacs." He shook his head. "Only in California."

24

Edmund Van Allen angrily returned home at eleven o'clock on what would become the strangest night of his life. How could he sustain anymore the illusion that Rebecca Moore had not done something to her own children? How could he have been so resistant to the evidence from the start?

Why hadn't he slapped a lie detector on both of the Moores in the first moments of the investigation? How could he have ignored for so long the basic facts: the children had never left that house. They were buried somewhere within. That left the Moores as the sole comprehensible culprits.

And how, faced with his accusations, could Rebecca Moore even *hope* that he, as a rational policeman, could believe any of that supernatural mumbo-jumbo.

He sat at the desk in his den and put on another Grateful Dead tape. Galveston, August 1980. He listened as Jerry Garcia's bumblebee-style guitar riffs calmed him slightly.

Ripple.

Yeah, Jerry, Van Allen mused, calming a little more. An unseen hand making ripples in the water. Fine in a philosophical sense. Okay in a poetic sense. But Van Allen still rejected the supernatural in the case of Rebecca Moore.

Ripple.

Yeah. There was also a pretty lousy wine by the same

name, if he recalled properly. A cheap drunk for people who hadn't sunk to getting bombed on hair tonic.

Van Allen opened up the green Mont Blanc pen that lay across his desk set. The cherished heirloom from his father. The tactile security of the pen eased him somewhat, too.

He went to his refrigerator and found a bottle of beer. A nice cold green bottle to match the color of the pen. He took a swig or two, then put the beer on his desk. He left the den for a moment to get some notepaper. He came back and sat down. At his desk, he finished some notes on the Moore case. Then he closed the file.

He reached for the beer. The bottle was empty.

He froze. *Oh, yeah?* What the hell is that all about? He knew the bottle had been full when he had pulled it from the refrigerator. He had taken only a couple of swigs.

But had he *drained* it?

It didn't make sense. He stared at the bottle. A creepy feeling overtook him. But his rational self battled back. He must have been so distracted from work that he didn't even remember finishing the brew.

He set the bottle aside. He looked back to the file before him.

He listened as the tape ended. He sat for several seconds with his hands folded across his chest, wondering if by any chance he had missed something in the Moore case. He decided he hadn't.

He closed the file. Yes, he told himself again, he had made his decision. The next day he would proceed with arrests.

He showered and changed for bed. He took a final walk out to his desk and stopped short when he entered his den. Somehow, the beer bottle had taken leave of the desktop and had shattered on the floor.

Another creepy feeling was upon him, but again he rejected it. He examined the desktop. He breathed slightly easier. Somehow, a stack of books had slid to the left and must have knocked the bottle off the work area. Why it had landed so hard that it would break several feet from the desk was another question. But that was also a question that he didn't feel like exploring at that hour. And as for the sound of the breakage, well, he had been in the shower, blasting himself with warm water.

He cleaned up the glass and turned off the light in the room. He discarded the glass in the kitchen wastebasket and turned off the lights throughout his apartment, except for the bedroom.

Midnight arrived and passed. But he was in bed before 1:00 A.M.

The first part of the night came easily. It was restful and calm. But as the dark hours of the morning progressed, other forces began to claim the detective's sleeping hours.

Something was taking command of his head. Van Allen began to dream. The sequences of the reverie made no sense, but they were rife with phantasmagoric images: A parrot with a human head was talking to him.

Deviation. Absurdity of life, a voice told him.

Another image: Both his parents stood on the edge of a cliff, looking over a vast horizon. They joined hands and jumped.

Death, as it always comes to those we love, the voice spoke again.

Everything went black and he turned over in bed.

The unlinked visions continued.

A brightness came upon his subconscious, then a darkness—much the way an old television screen would come on and off. Then, when light was present, something resembling the grave of Billy Carlton was peaceful one minute, then swirling with dirt a moment later, as if blasted up from underneath the ground.

Something grabbed him by the ankle.

I'm here, Van Allen. I'm in your apartment with you.

Van Allen shook in bed. In his dream there was a cold firm hand on his ankle.

He shook again. His eyes flickered open into the darkness of his bedroom.

Jesus! The hand was *still* on his ankle.

He bolted up from sleep and waved his hands at the foot of the bed. The feeling suddenly lifted, as if the hand had released Van Allen's leg.

He turned the light on and looked through the room. He was alone. Or at least he couldn't see anyone. He felt his heart pump and he was aware of the wetness on his brow.

Then he settled back to try to sleep. He turned the light off. Visions of the Moore case danced before his eyes. He held his eyes open in narrow slits in the darkness of his bedroom and waited to see if any images came to him.

None did. His eyes closed and he drifted again.

Sometime later he felt himself turn suddenly in bed, as if startled. He tried to dream again, more peacefully this time. But now he was transported to some strange field in the moonlight and there were white things all around him—things very familiar that he couldn't place—and he was very ill at ease with it because the white things were moving.

And then he realized again that the hand was on his ankle.

Still here, Van Allen!

He turned in his sleep and was trying to sit up again. But suddenly there was a tremendous force upon his leg, as if a very strong man—an unearthly strong man—now had two hands on Van Allen's ankle, and gave it a tremendous pull.

Van Allen felt himself cry out, as in a nightmare. But the force was as powerful as any man he had ever physically challenged. Van Allen felt himself yanked hard. The lower part of his body lifted several feet into the air. He felt himself pulled halfway off his bed.

Then another sharp yank.

He was pulled by the invisible hands onto the floor, where

he hit hard. Then the force was gone from his leg and he looked up and he was certain—as certain as anything in his life—that he saw before him, hovering in the room, a winged figure identical to the fallen image from San Angelo Cemetery.

A human with wings, one arm extended high, either in peace or in foreboding. But the image was like an acid flash because, as with such images before, it was gone in an instant.

Van Allen barely had time to recover. He rolled across the room and found his automatic pistol and the light switch at the same time.

He threw on the lights. As far as he could see, the room was empty as a tomb.

It contained only one body. His, still living.

He took several minutes to let his heart and nerves settle from this incident. His senses were on full alert the entire time, waiting for something unexpected from the next room.

But the something didn't come. Or at least it didn't come yet. Gradually, Van Allen got to his feet. He held his pistol at his side as he walked to the door and looked into the next room.

He put on the lights. Nothing there, either.

He went to his den and froze again.

His precious green Mont Blanc pen was lying on the blotter in the center of his desk. It had been broken in half, as if by a pair of strong angry hands.

Hands as strong as those that had pulled him from bed.

Van Allen stared at it with anger and disbelief. But he barely dared to touch it.

This was no ordinary night. This was no run-of-the-mill sleeplessness from tension or anxiety or ten cups of coffee.

He sank into the chair across from his desk. He looked back to the desktop and waited for the items upon it to fly in every direction as they had once before.

He sat in the chair, saw the clock that said 3:15 A.M. and

sensed the incredible darkness of the spirit that underpinned almost any night. He understood why the ancients of so many cultures felt that the night belonged to Evil, and that in that darkness spirits rose from decrepit old tombs and walked among the living.

Scaring them. Mocking them.

On his desk there commenced another small moment of terror, designed especially for him.

He breathed heavily as he helplessly watched it.

A pencil. Never had a pencil conveyed so much menace.

But in a single instant, it began to roll.

Van Allen sat perfectly still and broke a violent sweat. He watched the pencil proceed to the edge of the desk, hover slightly at the precipice, and then fall.

It clattered on the floor.

It rolled several inches and stopped. Van Allen kept his eyes trained upon it and expected it to rise in the air. Or perhaps propel itself abruptly at him.

Poltergeist phenomenon, he thought to himself.

Yeah, Van Allen thought, *sure!*

"Who are you?" he asked aloud.

It's me, Ed. It's Billy!

"Sure, Billy," he whispered aloud. "Why don't you show yourself, then?"

Jesus! Bad enough that he lived among the wackos of Southern California. Now he had to have restless spirits, too! The gun that weighed so heavily in his hand seemed as useless as a brick.

He felt his forehead wet with perspiration. He felt one bead of sweat moving slowly down his left temple.

He made a gesture. "Pick up the pencil," Van Allen said to whatever being could hear him.

The pencil didn't move.

"Come on. I'm waiting," Van Allen said.

Still it didn't move.

"Can't pick it up?" he asked, gaining some courage. "You can knock things over but you can't pick them up?"

The Ticonderoga lay on the floor.

Words came to him from somewhere. An idle, terrified thought. "How about Billy Carlton's angel?" Van Allen asked. "You knock that over, too?"

In response there was a rapping somewhere in the apartment. And somewhere distant he thought he heard laughter.

Oh, shit!

Van Allen's heart hammered away within his chest!

That damned banging again. The raps came hard and in apparent response to Van Allen's question. He felt the perspiration thicken on his brow.

More thoughts came to him from somewhere. Now it was as if some other force were guiding his brain, turning his thoughts sharply into reverse, sending the patterns of his conscious mind spiraling backward into his own youth.

Nightmares. The recurrent nightmares of his youth. When he was a kid he had a few of them. Some recurring. He hadn't thought of them for years.

And now the room before him went almost blank. Instead, he could see the terrors of when he was a boy.

He was certain. Whatever was in this room, whatever force that he was facing, it was putting on a display of power. It was so powerful that it could get into his head and guide his thoughts.

"Fuck it," Van Allen said.

He spoke boldly. Inside, he was terrified. He stood and hoped the dislodged spirit couldn't read *all* his thoughts.

But actually, it could.

The first nightmare:

He was a boy again, sleeping in a small comfortable room in Palo Alto. He emerged from bed and ran to the top of the steps in the Van Allen family's rambling old house. He took a

*flying, spinning leap into the air, soared above the staircase
and always woke up before his feet touched the ground . . .*

The second one. Pure terror this time.

*In his dream, he walked through the same childhood house,
feeling abandoned. He searched everywhere for his mother.
Then he found her. She was lying motionless on a sofa in the
library, an old cloth coat pulled up to her chin. She was lifeless. Her head turned toward him and she smiled. Then her
face dissolved into something horrible—the face of a monster,
the face of something inhuman.*

In the chair where he sat, he twisted in anguish.

Then a third dream rose up from an unknown somewhere, a
refinement of the dream he had endured less than an hour earlier:

*He was standing in some sort of burial ground and it was
night. Above him, the stars burned like small torches. The
moon was a ghostly bonfire. His feet were again riveted to the
earth and all around him there were tombstones, which began
to sway. They transmogrified themselves from granite and
marble to something lighter than air, itself, and they became
ghostly presences. Demons perhaps—or* Damn it! *were they
angels?—and they transformed themselves into spirits all
around him.*

*Laughing. Taunting. Same as in his own apartment in
Pasadena right now. A hell of a nightmare from his youth, except—*

His eyes opened. A hell of a nightmare from his youth, except he was certain that this wasn't something out of his
youth, at all. It seemed horribly familiar, but he suspected it
was a vision. A flash forward, not a flashback.

His gaze drifted to the floor again, where the pencil had
come to rest.

"Oh, shit . . ." he muttered. The pencil was gone.

It was back up on top of the desk again. It had lifted itself

back up—that invisible hand again—while Van Allen had
been wrestling with visions from the past and the future.

Van Allen spoke bravely to whatever presence was there.

"I want to see you, goddamn it," Van Allen said. "If
you're here, I want to see you."

A beat. Nothing happened. He waited.

A moment of tension and anticipation dissolved into nothing. The only sound Van Allen was aware of was the rhythmic
thumping of his heart in his chest.

His eyes raged with fatigue. They burned the way skin
burns against a Valley sun. He closed his eyes for a moment
and brought his hand to his face.

Van Allen rubbed his face. Then something else happened
in the room. His eyes were closed so he didn't see it, but he
knew he felt it. It was as if he were surrounded by a crowd of
people and they were all staring at him and holding their col-
lective breath at once.

It was as if they were waiting to get his attention. He could
almost hear mumbling around him. Distant, disconcerted dis-
cordant voices, like a party going on in a room down the hall.

Even laughter. And a wisp of music from an old player
piano. That's what it sounded like.

Jesus!

Slowly he pulled his wet hand from his face. He could feel
his scalp tightening and the hair rising on the back of his neck.
Now he knew that he was not alone.

He felt himself age ten years on the spot.

"Oh, my good God . . ." he mumbled.

What was confronting him was a ghost, and Van Allen accepted that as the new reality of what was opposing him.

A ghost.

Somewhere in the room with him, except he couldn't see it.
A ghost.

And the worst part about it was that it all seemed so normal.

Within the context of everything else that had transpired, so logical.

A moment passed. A big loud empty nothing. Perspiration burst again from the policeman's forehead, this time as if someone had opened a thousand tiny hoses.

Van Allen wasn't able to speak. There remained a dream-like, surreal quality to all of this—much akin to one of those bad dreams in which one is riveted in place with a great menace approaching, but one is unable to move or scream. Van Allen also felt as if something—some force—had captured him, as if a giant hand were wrapped around him.

Yet, Van Allen knew this *was* real!

"Tell me what you want," the policeman asked.

The ghost laughed. Van Allen was sure, because he knew he heard laughter from somewhere. Laughter that surrounded the policeman. Then the laughing stopped and the ghost moved. But he didn't float or drift. Instead, it rushed directly at Van Allen.

A message arrived as if by telepathy. "I want justice. I want a murderer!" the ghost said.

Van Allen's heart felt as if it were beating like a kettledrum in the back of his throat. From somewhere, he managed to find his voice. It creaked when he tried to use it, but he managed words.

"So do I," he said. "If there's a killer, I want him."

"Then go to the cemetery," the ghost said.

"Which one?"

"There is only one. The Cemetery of the Angels."

"It's the middle of the night."

The protestation must have angered the spirit. Van Allen thought he saw something shimmer or flicker out of the corner of his eye. But when he turned fully toward it, the image was gone. Simultaneously, there was movement on Van Allen's desktop. The Ticonderoga pencil flipped violently into the air and clattered onto the floor again.

"You will be admitted to San Angelo," the ghost said.

"I . . ."

"Go!" the spirit roared.

Then Van Allen picked up the vibration of extreme passion—a sexual energy as well as a consuming anger. His eyes were riveted upon the place in the room where he thought the ghost might have appeared. Then, like dawn purging the shadows of the night, the tone of the room seemed to suddenly change. Van Allen got the impression that the ghost was gone.

For several seconds, Van Allen stood in the room, feeling more alone than he had ever felt in his life. He was stricken with the suspicion: had this really happened? Had he hallucinated?

But as soon as he entertained those ideas there was a sharp rap in the room. A desk drawer shot open and Van Allen again felt the icy fingers caressing the nape of his neck. Whatever this ghost was, wherever it had come from, it had a way of reading Van Allen's thoughts.

That idea terrified him.

He glanced at his desk. The green pen still lay where he had left it, broken in half sitting in a white saucer. A few drops of ink still ran from it, like dark blood from an otherwise-drained corpse.

He saw something at his feet. He leaned over.

He picked up the Ticonderoga pencil. Then he dropped it. It felt like dry ice; it was so cold that it burned his hand. He let it roll off the desk again and again it clattered to the floor, a resonance of sound and a resonance of action. The pencil dropping repeating itself.

From somewhere came the command again, imploring this time, moaning! *"Go . . . !"*

Van Allen reached to his car keys and hefted them in his hand.

"All right," the policeman said softly. "I'm going."

He went to his car. The Pontiac sounded like an irritated

prematurely awakened beast when Van Allen turned over the engine at 3:45 A.M. Moments later, he was on the expressway leading out toward the city and subsequently to Hollywood.

A thousand associations bombarded him as he drove wildly through the Los Angeles night—the way this city's idiosyncrasies unraveled and expanded the same way the Pacific Ocean curled and unfurled against the city's westernmost borders, and the way the desert pressed in from the east. The way every bloody quirk of the landscape and the population had been made familiar to the entire world thanks to television and films. And yet, crunch all of that up and shove it into a basket and it couldn't match what was transpiring this evening when a dead man had risen to call him, to issue him a summons, to request that he, Ed Van Allen, step into their world.

Or so he thought.

He drove like a madman.

Half an hour later, he stood before the gates to San Angelo Cemetery. He placed a hand on the irons bars and pushed. There was give to it. Martinez's chains, however, held the gate firm.

Van Allen stared beyond the gate. The graveyard was enveloped mostly by darkness, but a few tombstones were clear. Solid granite sentries in the night.

Guarding what? he wondered.

He placed his hands along the iron bars of the gate again and felt something strange. The bars grew very cold, as if hit by a strong blast of Arctic air. Van Allen was fascinated with the change in temperature. It seemed to be so greatly localized, and it was happening right before him.

It reminded him of something. Another recent feeling. He thought about it for a moment and then quickly realized: It was cold the way the pencil had been cold. Like dry ice. He pulled his hand away before his skin burned.

Then he recoiled.

The chains, like the books and desk objects in his apartment and, for that matter, like his ankle an hour earlier, were jolted by a force that Van Allen could not see.

The chains pulled backward before his eyes and shook violently. They snapped and broke, falling away.

They hit the ground hard and with a clunk.

Van Allen reached forward and pushed. He was in the Cemetery of Angels.

He moved forward with caution, drawn, he assumed, by forces that he could never understand or explain.

He felt the asphalt and stone of the entrance path beneath his feet, and then the soft wet turf as he stepped onto the grass. As his eyes adjusted to the night within the cemetery yard, tombs and markers emerged more visibly, now looking like sturdy steadfast phantoms guarding their stretch of this world.

He moved forward. He knew exactly where he was headed. Toward the upended headstone of Billy Carlton. The fallen broken angel.

He approached it carefully.

As he neared the fallen marker, his senses sharpened. Once again, he reentered what he thought of as the cold zone which seemed to accompany the presence of the ghost.

He neared the marker, seeking answers to his questions, wondering how this would bring him to a killer, how this would resolve any crime that had crossed his desk.

He didn't know. What he did know, however, was that by the bulky foot of the overturned angel, he began to discern three figures, one large, two small.

They were shimmering, much like beams of light rising from the ground. Van Allen stopped for a moment, steadied himself, then continued to approach.

The three figures took human form. He recognized the first, because he had studied the photograph of Billy Carlton that he had seen in the film encyclopedia. And the smaller two he recognized from the pictures on his desk, as well as hundreds of police fliers and the pictures in Mr. and Mrs. Moore's home at 2136 Topango Gardens.

Van Allen came to within twenty feet and felt that he should stop. If he came too close, they might vanish.

He might have been right. The adult ghost turned to him and smiled. There was something wrong with the adult's eyes. They glowed like a pair of little night-lights.

The children appeared more normal. Patrick Moore raised a hand and waved to the police officer. Karen did the same.

There they were. The Moore children. Dead? Alive? Van Allen didn't know. But they were with their kidnapper.

Then all three fixed their eyes upon Van Allen. They stared at him with expressionless, grave faces, as if quietly to impress upon him the issue of what to do next. And a final bolt of utter terror shot through him as he realized that all three—the two children hand in hand with the ghost—were floating about twelve inches above the ground.

Van Allen stared back. The exchange became timeless, or perhaps lost in time, because later, as he thought back on it, Van Allen could recall that he remained physically frozen, other than to back up and sit upon a small gravestone as he studied the vision.

Eventually, he held out his hand, as if to ask the ghost if he would release the children. In response, the ghost's eyes steamed slightly, resonating with a fierce angry glow, and a message came to Van Allen from somewhere.

The message was clear: *I want the killer.*

"What killer?" Van Allen asked. "Who? Who, damn it, who?"

The ghost turned away again, then looked back. Same with Patrick and Karen. The tableau seemed to freeze and close.

Van Allen's final image was that of watching the three figures until the sky lightened, staying right in that same spot, perched on the convenient tombstone. Then, before his eyes, as dawn arrived, the vision faded and was gone. At that time, Van Allen found himself looking at nothing.

He finally rose. He glanced at his watch. It was twenty minutes to six and he reasoned—if normal reason applied—that he had been in the cemetery for an hour and a half.

He walked to the overturned angel, examined it, and felt the pang in his calf where he had injured himself. He put a toe to the granite to test its mass and found that it was substantial. He tried to see what he could have seen other than a ghost, what bizarre reflection or quirk in the universe might have been there.

But there was nothing. The same as the night when he thought he had seen the intruder in San Angelo, but had been unable to find anyone.

Van Allen turned, consumed by tiredness. He trudged back to the gates. The chain was still on the ground where it had fallen. He left the cemetery and pulled the gates closed, his head awash in erratic, contradictory, fatigue-driven thoughts. He put the broken chain around a couple of the bars. There was no way he could lock it.

Then he found his way to the bench outside Martinez's guardhouse. He sat down. He leaned back and closed his eyes.

He quickly drifted into sleep.

This time the dreams were peaceful.

He was a boy again and his parents were alive and he was in a field playing catch with his father until his father threw a high fly ball in the air and Van Allen ran over, dived for the ball and speared it in the webbing of his Al Kaline baseball glove as he fell. His shoulder hit the ground hard, which caused him to shudder as he dozed. And then a hand was upon that same shoulder, shaking him, just as the hand had grabbed his ankle in the dream earlier that morning.

In the dream, it was his father's hand. When he opened his eyes, however, it was Martinez. The old caretaker looked down on him with kindly eyes.

The old Mexican leaned back slightly, waited, then smiled. He nodded slightly. "Ghost, hmm?" he asked. "You seen a ghost?"

Van Allen, blinking awake, answered. "Yeah. Yes. I did. How did you know?"

"Happen all the time," Martinez said. "All the time. Ghosts all over the damned place."

25

One afternoon later, the man and the woman sat in the downstairs of the home at 2136 Topango Gardens. The man was not her husband.

"I'm trying to understand this," Ed Van Allen said to his former suspect.

"You and me, both," Rebecca said.

"The ghost in this house," Van Allen continued. "You used to call him 'Ronny.' But I think we both know who he is, don't we?"

She nodded.

"The children came up with the name at their blackboard. Wasn't that how you explained it?" he asked.

She said it was. She led the detective through it again. The ghost had come into the kids' rooms one night, pleasant as a private-school boy, to introduce himself. He had Karen write the letters on the board. Then the kids had unscrambled. The ghost had taken great glee, Karen had reported at the time, in throwing the letters into a jumble.

"Another typical poltergeist trick," Rebecca said. "That's what my friend Melissa always said."

Van Allen considered it for a moment. "I wonder," he said. "Could I look at that blackboard again? The one the children had those scrambled letters on?"

Rebecca shrugged slightly. "Why not?" she asked rhetorically. "It's only going to prove what we already know, isn't it?"

"Probably," said Van Allen.

They climbed the stairs and went to Patrick's room. The chalkboard was where they had left it. Exactly.   .

Van Allen took his notepad from his pocket and wrote the letters upon a fresh page. At first, he copied them exactly as they appeared on the board.

R L L I B O T A C L Y N

Then he extracted the ghost's accepted name: Ronny. That left a residue of letters:

L L I B T A C L

He spelled it out phonetically, sort of the way the kids had pronounced it.

RON(N)Y CILBALLT

And then he remixed it and came up with the letters that the ghost had actually intended:

BILLY CARLTON

He eased back from his assignment. Rebecca looked at him and nodded.

"Ever been to a place called 'The Silent Movie'?" Van Allen asked.

She frowned. "What is it?"

"The world's only authentically restored silent movie theater," said Van Allen. "They show restored silents on three evenings a week. It's located on Fairfax Avenue. I asked them to keep me apprised if certain films came around."

"And?" she asked.

"It's my duty to take you to the movies tonight," Van Allen said. "We can use both cars. And you needn't stay for the entire performance. But there's something tonight you will want to see."

Rebecca disappeared to get a light overcoat. The evening was turning damp. As she left the house, there was a noisy creak in the attic.

They drove separately to Fairfax and parked in adjoining meters in front of a rest home. The silent movie theater was located in an old Jewish neighborhood in the western part of the city on Fairfax, just south of Wiltshire. The theater itself was a small jewel of the entertainment world, lovingly restored to the way it looked in the 1920s. The seats were the old fold-down rialto types and there were portraits on the walls of the auditorium of six long-departed stars: Gish, Chaplin, Fairbanks, Keaton, Langdon, and Lloyd. The Silent Movie was both a museum and monument to the early era of the silver screen.

Van Allen led Rebecca in. The program that evening was a cartoon, followed by a Harry Langdon comedy. But it wasn't the great comedian Langdon they were there to see.

The name of the film was *See America Thirst,* a piece of cinematic mischief from 1930 that carried with it a less than favorable opinion of the Volstead Act. Seventeen minutes into the story a young actor came into view in a speakeasy scene and shared the screen with the star.

He was a handsome young man, sandy-haired, classic features, clean-cut in this picture. White shirt, crisp as new snow. Dark slacks. It had been Billy Carlton's last silent feature before he had been murdered. He portrayed a character named Paul Hammond.

Rebecca should have been startled to see him, but she wasn't. Instead, she had an overwhelming sense of admiration for the man. Almost a longing for him. And surely there was affection.

He looked not too different than when he had been her lover seventy years ago, as well as earlier that week. And when Rebecca turned toward the policeman who was sitting next to her, she found that he was staring at her.

Then he turned his attention to the screen.

"I know, I know. Remember, I've seen him, too, now," Van Allen said. "Call me tomorrow. We'll talk further. There's still a matter about your children, I submit."

Rebecca allowed that he was correct. But a strange sense of contentment had come over her. Whether she felt herself protected or simply resigned to her fate, she couldn't tell. But she suspected it was one or the other.

"Can you get home all right?" Van Allen asked.

"I'm a big girl," she said.

"I know that," he said. "That's not what I'm asking."

"I'll be all right," she said.

"I still need to talk to your husband," Van Allen said.

Rebecca nodded and said she understood.

The policeman rose and left the theater. Rebecca Moore stayed and was enthralled by the entire film. When she emerged from The Silent Movie it was close to ten-thirty and the dampness and cold of the night had turned to a steady drizzle.

And as much as Rebecca was conscious of the dangers of city streets after dark, she took no notice of the man in the car across the block and down Fairfax Avenue a hundred feet away from her.

Waiting for her, specifically.

Watching for her, specifically.

It was difficult to see with the precipitation. But she probably would have recognized him anyway, even though his wraparound sunglasses were in his pocket. It was the face that she would remember.

The drizzle intensified, turning into a steady, monotonous rain. But aside from the temperature, which was warmer in Southern California than Connecticut, it might just as well have been a certain horrible evening in February all over again.

And it soon would be.

26

Rebecca was halfway to her car when she heard the footsteps.

They fell like little blows of a hammer on the pavement behind her. First the footsteps were a hundred feet away, then fifty. A sixth sense told her that they were closing in. But when she turned and looked a more tactile fear kicked in.

She knew the shape of her pursuer immediately. She could see his face under a rain hat and, more than anything else, she knew a surge of life-and-death fear when she felt it.

She ran with her heart in her throat, the beat so fast that she could taste it. She screamed, but it was late evening in a deserted LA neighborhood. The few cars that passed kept going.

"Rebecca!" he called after her. "Rebecca, stop!"

But she didn't. And she wondered strangely if he, too—this man who wanted her dead—was a ghost.

She reached her car. A trembling hand held the keys. She wished she had carried Mace. Or a gun.

Or *anything!*

She tried the keys in the door of the car and they wouldn't turn. She whirled and flung her keys at her assailant and ran. Why in God's name had she let the policeman depart? How could she have been so foolish!

She ducked around the car and the man lunged at her, hitting hard on the hood of her vehicle. She swung a fist wildly

and struck him a glancing blow near the eye. She fled across
Fairfax Avenue as a surge of traffic came northward toward
Hollywood. She heard car horns blaring at her and tires
screeching to avoid her.

An angry driver shouted at her, cursing profanely.

"A man's trying to kill me!" she screamed back. But no
one stopped.

She had momentarily evaded her attacker. He hadn't followed her across the street, but he was tracking her—*again,
like a werewolf?*—from the other side.

She ran to a corner at Waring Avenue. She found a telephone. The entire booth had been vandalized. She turned the
corner and fled eastward on Waring. The rain intensified. She
hoped it would hide her. It didn't.

She pressed her body to the side of a building. Her attacker
stopped at the corner and scanned, looking for her. She was
visible in a streetlamp and knew he would see her. She ducked
into the first recessed doorway she could find, that of some
sort of plumbing supply company. And even as the rain fell,
she heard the man's footsteps start to come near her.

Her hand found the doorknob behind her. She tried the
knob. The door was locked.

Her heart thundered. Tears welled in her eyes. Was this her
destiny? Were her children already dead, she wondered, and
now was she to be murdered?

Was this the only manner in which she and her children
would be reunited? Was this the whole intent of this entire
inexplicable involvement with the ghost of Billy Carlton?

A reunion in death?

All of these thoughts shot through her head within a heartbeat. She knew the man was within a few feet of her now on
the sidewalk. Would she burst from hiding and run? Would
she cower and beg that the end would come with merciful
quickness and lack of pain? Her knees began to buckle. Her

back began to sink downward against the locked door. She sobbed uncontrollably.

She was, she knew, as good as dead. In the afterlife, she wondered, would she eventually learn what had happened to her children?

The man's shadow was visible before her. He was only a step or two away. Then the inexplicable happened again. The unlocked door behind her gave way. It opened with a loud clatter and her body fell within the door.

An unseen hand, guiding the lock? she barely had time to wonder.

"Oh, God . . . !" she heard herself say. She regained her balance and gathered herself, stumbling to her feet. She came fully through the door and the last thing she saw—accompanied by her own scream—as she slammed it, was her killer, who turned the corner and rushed after her.

The door relocked.

His shoulder hit it hard. He tried to smash his way in. The impact of his body against the old door was enormous.

He called to her. "Rebecca! Rebecca! I'm trying to protect you! Open this! Open this!"

Protect? Protect!

The assertion was insane. She turned and saw a staircase, illuminated dimly by emergency nighttime lighting.

The man behind her was still walloping the door, banging it harder and harder with his shoulder. She knew that if the door had opened for her, it would open for him. She was soaked with perspiration now as she started to mount the stairs. She could hear the wood of the doorframe start to give.

For a moment there was silence. She was one and a half flights up the stairs. Then she heard a single shot from a pistol, followed by the sound of crunching wood. Her killer had shot his entrance into the building and was again in close pursuit.

She climbed the steps. She could hear the heavy male footsteps coming up the stairs after her. She ran as fast as she could. Each floor she came to was quiet, with dark closed doors facing a dim hall.

She kept climbing.

She came to the top floor. Three doors—1940s style, they looked like something out of a Raymond Chandler movie—faced a small landing. She tried one. Locked. She could hear the steps one floor below her. She tried the steps again. They led to the roof. And the door to the roof, she found seconds later, was unlocked.

She came out onto a tar paper landing which reminded her of tenement rooftops she had known in New York years ago. There was one squarish chimney and a pair of ventilation pipes. Her eyes adjusted from the light of the city around her, but she could already see that this building stood alone. There was no adjoining rooftop to which she might escape.

There was, she saw quickly, no escape at all. She had cornered herself perfectly. The rain continued to fall. It would muffle her cries for help. In this way, too, she had sealed her doom.

She stood very still by the bricks of the old flat chimney tower, her back against it. She heard her assailant come onto the roof. His footsteps ceased. The door to the roof clicked closed behind him.

"Rebecca?" he asked softly. "I know you're here."

He was looking around, she knew. And, obviously, he read the situation perfectly. The chimney was the only place where she could take cover. So he walked toward it.

She heard his steps growing louder. She could almost *feel* his footsteps coming closer.

He was ten feet away, then five. Then he turned the corner to the chimney. His huge shape hulked into view right in front of her, eclipsing her vision of the city.

He stood in front of her. A horrible, scarred male face. The face of a convict. A murderer.

She looked into his eyes, and he into hers.

His eyes were mean and sharp. Brutal, though with little emotion. In his soul, she saw something horrible, something morally unredeemable.

"Please," she gasped softly. "Let me go."

He shook his head. Almost a smile came to his thick lips. "No, Rebecca. I'm not going to do that."

"Why?" she asked.

"I was hired."

"Why?"

"Don't know," he said. "Don't care. You're a job."

He raised a hand and took her wrist.

"Who?" she asked. "Who hired you?"

"Your husband."

"What?"

"You're in his way."

"What?" She was crying harder now, close to a wail.

"My children . . . ?" she finally pleaded. "Where are—?"

"Don't know. Don't care."

"Did he—?"

"He doesn't know where your brats are. Doesn't know. Doesn't care."

"But—!"

"Look, I'll do you fast. I'll do you painless," the murderer said. "That's my only favor."

The pressure of his hand on her wrist tightened like a vise. At first, she reacted with a tremor of resistance, then she fought wildly. Then he slapped her hard across the face. The force of the blow shook her and knocked half the fight out of her. When she continued to struggle, he hit her again, harder this time. And the fight from her was gone. She sobbed uncontrollably.

"You're going to commit suicide," he said. "You're distraught over the children. You're going to jump off a rooftop."

He pulled her.

Then a third voice intruded. "Here?"

The killer froze. He looked around. Rebecca thought she was hallucinating.

"What's that?" the killer asked.

The voice came again.

"Are you there?" the voice asked.

The killer looked in the direction of the voice.

He pushed Rebecca to the ground and again pulled his weapon from his belt. "Who the fuck's here?" he asked. "Where are you?"

The voice was soft. Silken on the rain, muted with the night. A voice like black crushed velvet, traversing years.

"I'm here," it said.

Rebecca raised her eyes and saw a vision. At the same time, her assassin turned and thought he saw the flickering figure of a man at the edge of the roof, much like an image of an old film from a projector, if there were no screen. The image seemed to hang in the air, then it was gone.

"What are you doing?" came the velvety voice from the edge of the roof.

The assassin faced that direction. "None of your business," the killer answered, trying to find the speaker.

"Are you hurting this woman?"

The killer's eyes narrowed into little mean slits. He glared in the direction of an unwelcome witness. But he couldn't find anyone.

"Where are you?" the killer asked. The killer thought quickly and pulled a rope from his coat. He tied Rebecca's wrists.

"I don't like what you're doing," the voice answered.

"Yeah? Well, you don't have to!" the assailant snapped. He raised his automatic pistol and brandished it. But he appeared frightened.

The killer gagged Rebecca and pushed her roughly to the

tar paper. He turned toward his taunter and still couldn't see him.

"Where the hell—?" the man blurted out.

The killer looked in every direction. Then he thought he saw another flickering movement in a shadow. He squinted and peered at it.

"I'm here," the voice said.

The killer turned back to the spot where he had first seen the vision. Nothing again. The killer wondered how he could have missed him.

"What are you doing to that woman?" the voice asked.

"Same as I'm going to do to you," the assailant said. "I'm going to kill her."

Rebecca lay on the tar paper, helpless, as events unfolded. Her attacker finally had her.

"What's your name, pal?" the killer asked the empty rooftop.

From somewhere, "Hammond, Paul Hammond."

"You're going to die, Paul Hammond."

"You're going to shoot me?"

"Double suicide. The two of you go over the ledge."

"You have to find me first."

Again, the figure of a man shimmered near the ledge of the roof. The quivering nature of the figure unnerved the assassin, but attracted him at the same time.

Then the flickering figure started to move. And again, the killer was given pause. The figure seemed to glide, as if it were on casters rather than moving on its feet.

"Okay. Hold it there!" the killer said.

"If you want me," the voice said, "come get me."

"I'll do that."

The killer thought he saw another image. He approached and cornered it. The attacker was much bigger than his victim, taller, wider, and sturdier. It should be an easy task to propel him over the side of the building, the killer thought. Four flights down, straight onto concrete. Neither body would be found until morning, when all life would be out of them.

It appeared as close to perfect as it could.

"Then come get me, Francis," said the victim. "If you're man enough, come get me."

"How did you know my name?"

"I know that your grave is waiting for you."

Angrily, indignantly, the killer stepped forward.

He was within twenty feet of a vision that he still couldn't see well enough to describe. Then ten. But to Rebecca's attacker, it still seemed as if there were something odd about the light that reflected upward from the parking lot. The unwanted witness seemed to approach and recede at the same time. At one moment, it appeared that this unwelcome witness glided right through a small ventilation pipe on the roof.

Rebecca watched with wide eyes as this bizarre endgame played out in the rain and darkness.

Well, he must have gone *around* the vent pipe, the killer thought. He must have, because otherwise he couldn't believe what he was seeing. What was in front of him was not making sense.

The killer moved to within a few feet of the ledge. And he could see a little better now. This strange man whom he faced was lean, with tousled hair and a very white shirt. Just one good push, the killer thought, and over the ledge he would go.

The killer followed him. The vision continued to move erratically. The killer paid no mind. He trailed his first victim to the edge of the rooftop. Two feet. One foot. He squinted. *Damn this light,* he thought to himself. It was almost as if he could see right through the man.

"Going to push me over the side?" Billy Carlton asked.

"Yes, I am."

"I'll help."

Billy Carlton took a step backward. Sheer suicide. One foot, then the other.

The killer looked at him without comprehension. Carlton didn't fall. He stood before him, big as life, substantial as any man he had ever seen, suspended in the air.

Failing to take the plunge.

"What the—?"

The killer's eyes went wide with terror. He stared and stared and stared at Billy Carlton's feet, planted firmly upon nothing, supported by some abject defiance of all natural laws.

A bolt of fear shot through the killer unlike anything he had ever previously experienced.

Then Billy Carlton faded into nothing. He was there one second and gone the next. But there was no impact below. No sound of death. No scream, no yell, no plunge into oblivion.

Just nothing.

"What the fuck—?" the killer began again.

Disoriented, he turned. Then his eyes went wide with an even greater terror, an even greater shock. The ghost was now on the other side of the killer, just a foot away, trapping him between the ledge and safety. And somehow, as the assassin now looked at him, the killer finally understood the terror that lurked before him.

For he was looking *through* his unnatural adversary. The body next to his was shimmering, yet substantial. Formidable, yet from another plane of existence.

The killer swiped at the specter and an extra level of fear raced through him. His arm passed through a frigid field and continued. Then the man confronting him smiled.

Cold contented eyes. Eyes not of a killer, but eyes of a man who was already at peace with his own death.

Then the ghost put up his own hands and thrust them forward. Something with the force of an express train hit the killer in the center of the chest. He screamed as if his life depended on it—which it did—and he fought madly for his balance.

But the fight was futile. The ghost's force propelled him straight backward and over the side of the ledge. The plunge to the asphalt below lasted less than two seconds.

It was followed by impact and pain.

His body broken and draining of life, he endured a final image in the two agonizing minutes that it took him to die. He saw an old-time movie actor standing over him, looking down with empty, mocking, vengeful eyes, eyes that pitied him but condemned him at the same time.

And in the final few moments of his life, the man hired to kill Rebecca heard something strange. It wasn't a chorus of angels and it wasn't his own heartbeat. It was instead a strange tune played on an old piano.

The tune made no sense. Yet it made all the sense in the world.

On the rooftop, Billy Carlton knelt by Rebecca's side. He unbound her with a gentle touch of his hands. She looked at him imploringly.

"Why?" she asked. "I don't understand."

"You want to know?" the ghost asked. "You're ready to know? Ready to accept?"

She looked up. His face was in shadows, but as she latched upon his eyes, she again felt their pull. It was again as if she had known those eyes for more than a lifetime.

"I'm ready," she said.

"Then come with me," Billy Carlton said.

He placed his hands on her shoulders, then raised them slowly until her face was in his hands. He cradled her head. He knelt forward and brought his brow to hers.

She closed her eyes. She felt a little tremor of fear and then felt very reassured by what was happening. Her mind intersected with Carlton's. She traveled with him.

First there was an incredible darkness, as if she were tumbling through the blackest of nights. This seemed to last forever. But then a brightness beckoned.

More images spun before her. It resembled her hour under hypnosis, but this was more intense. Visions flashed in her mind, all of them horrifying, exactly what her lover Billy wanted her to see.

A time in North Carolina, when her husband completed a transaction for a pound of hashish. The receiver was the man in the wraparound sunglasses, the man who would attempt to kill her . . .

A time in Connecticut this past February, when the man who had tried to kill her met with Bill Moore, and her husband paid him even though he had failed to complete her execution . . .

A time in California when her husband met with her executioner again, bragged of the huge insurance policy he held on his wife, and again handed over money in prepayment of a long-overdue, long-desired murder . . .

And a time that same evening, practically time present, when her husband sat at home and typed out a suicide note in his wife's name, to be presented to the police when she was found dead the next morning . . .

She held her tearful eyes as tightly closed as possible. But when the ghost kissed her on her forehead, she felt her eyes come open again into the darkness of the rainy night, and in the bleakness of the death scene on the roof of a warehouse.

"It's all right now," Billy Carlton said. "It's almost over. Bring your husband to me."

"Where?" she asked.

"There's only one place," he said. "San Angelo."

Then, before her eyes, he again disappeared.

27

"Becca?"

"Uh-huh," she said.

Bill Moore stepped out of his car in front of the gates to San Angelo Cemetery. His wife was seated on the bench before the burial ground. Her clothes were wet. She looked as if she had been waiting for a while. She had telephoned him twenty minutes earlier.

"What in God's name is going on, Rebecca?" he asked. He looked at her quizzically. "I thought you were going to a movie."

"I was. I did."

"So why are you here?" He looked her up and down. And, yes, she decided, he was looking for evidence that she had been attacked. As she searched his eyes, she saw the same expression as she had seen that night in Connecticut nine months earlier. He was shocked that she was alive. He was shocked because he had paid good money to have her killed.

"I have a new insight," she said. "I called Detective Van Allen also. He should be here shortly, too."

"So what? He's a pain in the ass. He treats us like suspects."

"Maybe he's half-right."

"What's that mean?"

"I know where Patrick and Karen are."

"Would you mind sharing it with me instead of making melodramatic gestures?" he snapped.

She didn't answer. He looked at the cemetery gates. "This place gives me the creeps," he said.

"It should."

He looked back at his wife. "Where *are* the children?" he asked.

"Protective custody. Someone took them and hid them so that they and their mother wouldn't be harmed."

"Rebecca, you're acting like you're crazy," he said. "Can we go home?"

"I can. You can't," she said.

"Becca!" he snapped, losing all patience. "Would you make some sense, damn it!"

"I'll make a lot of sense," she said. "I'm finally surrounded by friends."

"What the—?"

He never finished his question, though in his mind the question was never answered. The chains slid free of the cemetery gates and clanked onto the brick driveway. Rebecca walked to the gates and pulled free the bar that kept the gates shut. Then she pushed and the left gate opened enough to admit them.

She walked in. Her husband hesitated.

"Rebecca?" he asked.

"Come on along, Bill," she said. "You owe it to me."

"Goddamn it! You're acting like a madwoman!" he yelled.

She waited just within the portal.

"Are you coming or not?" she demanded.

She held out her hand to beckon her husband. Finally, he joined her. There was still a drizzle in the air, but a half-moon was visible over them. The clouds broke, as if on cue. The slight clearing in the sky allowed enough light to illuminate their path.

Rebecca was more than at home with what followed.

She followed the path that led toward the central burial ground of San Angelo. Her steps led directly toward the overturned marker of Billy Carlton.

She passed it. She led Bill Moore on the same path. He walked quickly behind her. Her vision was lowered, fixed upon the ground, just as Billy Carlton had asked her. And as she walked, she began to sense what Carlton had promised.

At each of the markers, at the fringe of her perception, she began to see something. Or perhaps, she knew they were there, more than she actually physically saw them.

First there was one winged figure. Then another. And not from every tomb, only from some. Carlton's friends. In death as in life.

Angels. Or something very much resembling them. Rebecca didn't care which.

She kept walking. As her eyes adjusted to the darkness there were more of them. They were in every direction. Risen—or descended?—from God knew where. Returned on a mission. A mission of vengeance or mercy, or mercy combined with vengeance.

She was deep in the cemetery. She passed the fallen marker and she quickened her pace. Her husband ran after her until he reached for her arm. But she pulled her arm away and wouldn't stop.

"Rebecca!" he called. "Rebecca!" He chased her.

"Look around you, Bill," she said. "Look around you and tell me that you didn't attempt to have me killed. And God knows what you were planning with Karen and Patrick!"

There was something large, oblong, and dark sitting upon the earth where Billy Carlton's grave had been. It was right near the big gaping hole that had remained in the earth since the coffin had been brought up.

Rebecca reached the spot and turned. Bill Moore had stopped several feet behind her. She stared at him.

"This is insane," he said breathlessly. "This isn't really happening."

"Yes, it is," she said.

He shook his head. Then he looked around. The same vision that brought her such tranquillity and reassurance brought him a terror that no man could ever measure. There were more whitened figures than anyone could count. An army of them. An armada. Shimmering. Opaque. Gliding forward. Small images reflecting the grand angel on Billy Carlton's marker.

Billy's friends. Rebecca's allies.

They surrounded Bill Moore. The expression on his face was twisted with horror.

"I want to get out of here," he said.

He looked beyond her and his horror doubled. The large object near the grave was the unearthed coffin, returned from the medical examiner's office.

The lid was open. The interior was waiting.

"You're staying here," Rebecca said. "It's the only way. And it's what you brought upon yourself."

Bill Moore shook his head. But when he tried to move, he realized that there was some strange field of force around him. His feet wouldn't obey. He was fixed in place.

A moment later, Rebecca felt something in her hand. It was warm and reassuring. Bill Moore's eyes widened a final time when Billy Carlton came into focus next to her.

Billy Carlton. Dead sixty-odd years. More substantial than the other angels, but a ghost nonetheless.

Rebecca's eyes shifted. Beyond the gates shone the headlights of a motor vehicle. She recognized the car as belonging to the policeman. She turned and looked at Billy Carlton.

He nodded.

Rebecca let go of Carlton's hand. The ghost released her and receded. She walked past Bill Moore as Moore screamed obscenely at her.

She lowered her head and walked through the angels. They formed a protective corridor and allowed her to pass.

Ahead of her she saw Ed Van Allen slipping through the open gates, proceeding with caution into the cemetery. She wondered how much he could see.

Van Allen stopped several feet onto the path. Obviously, he could see her approaching. And he could hear Bill Moore screaming. But Van Allen, she knew, was wise enough not to interfere.

She felt a pulsation behind her, a growing sense of shock that built with incredible suddenness. She kept her head down and walked toward the policeman.

She dared not look.

Behind her, it happened. It was like an explosion that took place in her head and in another dimension. But she felt that it was a tremendous roaring sound and as she neared Van Allen, she saw him avert his eyes, too, the way a man looks away from the flashpoint of an explosion to prevent being blinded.

Van Allen's face was white, reflecting some strange light from somewhere, and there was also a tremendous sound of earth being moved and disrupted.

She met the policeman. He opened his arms and held her. Neither looked. The disturbance in the atmosphere was so strong that both their bodies shuddered and pulsated. But they stayed standing and they waited.

There was no way to measure the time. But it must have been over within a few seconds.

Suddenly everything was very still. Rebecca wanted to look backward but Van Allen stopped her.

"No," he said. "Not yet. Just wait."

Then, after another half minute, they were both visited by a thought. It was all right to look. In fact, they *should* look.

The graveyard beyond them was dark. And they dared not venture into it. But they waited upon the path. Van Allen held Rebecca's hand for support.

She looked into the darkness and two small figures began to take shape.

"Oh, my God," she said softly. "Oh, my God . . ."

"Go get them," Van Allen said. "Go get them before anything else happens."

But she was gone long before he finished his second sentence.

Two small voices. Two small human forms.

"Mommy?"

"Mom?"

Rebecca rushed forward and embraced her son and daughter. They were warm as life, spattered here and there with dirt and wearing the same clothes in which she had last seen them.

But they were alive.

"Where are we?"

"What happened?"

She couldn't explain even if she had wanted to. She cried uncontrollably, this time with joy. And she embraced them as she had never embraced them before.

Van Allen's eyes meanwhile began to settle into the darkness and his gaze traveled far into the Cemetery of Angels.

He broke a cold sweat when he saw what had transpired. Billy Carlton's grave was sealed again, the earth back in place. The big oblong shape that had been near the grave was gone. So was Bill Moore.

And the huge, hulking, granite angel, Billy's tombstone, was back in place, its seraph wings wide, its head proud, its one arm raised in greeting.

Or warning.

Van Allen blew out a breath. He led Rebecca and her children from the yard. And he knew that as long as he lived, he would never be able to describe the events that he had just witnessed.

28

Ed Van Allen sat on a bench in Santa Monica, overlooking the Pacific Ocean, trying to put the proper spin on his life and, to a lesser degree, the events surrounding the various incidents at the Cemetery of Angels.

Three weeks had passed since the reappearance of the Moore children. The same amount of time had passed since the disappearance of Bill Moore. And once again, Van Allen was looking at contradictions, contradictions as vast as the ocean in front of him.

There were no answers. Only speculation and haunting suspicions, theories of the occult and supernatural that he could mention to no one. Then there were the frequent reawakenings each night from an uneasy sleep, and a scanning of his room to reassure himself that he was alone.

That he had seen a ghost and had interacted with one, he had no question. Exactly what explanation lay beneath that encounter, he had no way of knowing. His previous life experience had no way of interpreting it, nor did his religion. Christianity and spiritualism were at loggerheads, though perhaps they shouldn't have been.

He watched the ocean water before him. Christmas was coming. More contradiction. The weather in the Southland was warm. Low seventies. He thought of the Christmas card images of the Anglo-German-American concept of Christmas—snow on fir trees, Santa with a sleigh, holiday shoppers in heavy coats in northern cities—and a smile came to his lips. He was watching girls in shorts rollerblade. Christmas in California.

Oh, well, he thought to himself. If he didn't appreciate the lifestyle just a little, he would have moved away two decades ago. He knew that he lived here, belonged here, and would die here.

Of course, then what? After death, what?

Seeing Billy Carlton, meeting a ghost, being yanked out of bed by one, was both the best thing that could have happened to him as well as the worst.

On the one hand, the existence of the ghost suggested the euphoric notion of a spiritual life transcending death. And yet on the other hand, it called into question everything he had ever believed. He sighed. More contradiction. That's all life was: contradiction. His ex-wife had even phoned him that morning. She wanted to have lunch with him, and wondered if he would accompany her to a social event. But she wanted to remain divorced, also.

Did anything, anywhere, he wondered, make any sense?

A few small parts of the puzzle began to take shape for him. The Cemetery of Angels was some sort of enchanted place, he reasoned, one of those quirky places in the universe where the accepted norm does not apply. That Billy Carlton could have risen from a grave and performed the role of a latter-day guardian angel did not necessarily contradict Van Allen's own spin on his Christian beliefs. On a darker note, that Bill Moore could have plotted to murder his wife and stepchildren did not necessarily run against the grain of the worst cases of human behavior that Van Allen had witnessed in twenty years as a cop.

That Billy Carlton had interceded and protected Rebecca's children tested even Van Allen's new orthodoxy. However, if he believed that Carlton's spirit was real and tactile, then he had to make the logical leap to believe that an angel could have become the protector of Patrick and Karen.

Other issues nagged him:

What about the explosion of the grave several weeks earlier? The disappearance of the coffin from the medical examiner's warehouse? The restoration of Carlton's tomb, with the granite angel returned to its proper position? The steadfast insistence of both Karen and Patrick that they could not recall where they had been for five weeks, and Van Allen's every inquiry being met by a headshake or a "no"? It was as if, they said, they had been in a very pleasant dream which, once they were awakened, they could not remember.

And what of Rebecca Moore's willingness to take a final polygraph? During it, she had described the events following the silent movie, and had described this bizarre encounter with angels in the cemetery. She passed her second polygraph so perfectly that Van Allen had wondered if an invisible hand had been guiding the needle.

In his mind, events spiraled. The effect of all the past weeks' events settled upon him as a melancholy haze. Through it, he tried to find some light, some illumination to guide the rest of his life. He figured it might take years, if ever, before he would make that discovery.

A gentle breeze from the Pacific caressed Van Allen's forehead as he sat in perfect physical comfort on the bench. A final contradiction: on the desk in his office, the Moore case and the San Angelo desecration had remained open. In his mind, both affairs were closed.

A woman's voice intruded, jostling him slightly from his reverie. "I thought I might find you here," she said.

Van Allen looked up and shielded his eyes from the sun. Rebecca stood before him.

"I called your office," Rebecca said. "Alice said you'd be spending time down here. So I took a chance."

He smiled. "A good chance," Van Allen said.

"I wanted to speak with you. Off the record. Know what I mean?" she asked.

"I know what you mean."

"You don't mind?"

"Not at all," the detective answered.

She sat down on the far edge of a bench. "We never really had that much time to talk, you and I. First the case was closed. Then the children were back." She shrugged. "The press keeps badgering me. I get offers to sell my story. I don't even know what my story is."

"Well, let's see," he said. "There's the official version. Your husband was into assorted criminal deeds. He had your children hidden somewhere. They were released. He's a fugitive." Van Allen shrugged. "A nice, neat, unclear, wide-open ending to an otherwise thoroughly unlikely story."

She smiled.

"The tabloids should be pumping it for a week or two, till something better comes along," he said.

"Are you going to have the coffin raised?" she asked. She chose her words carefully. "The 'Billy Carlton' coffin?"

He shook his head. "Whatever's down there stays down there," he said. "At least as long as I have anything to do with it."

"Let the dead stay dead?" she asked with irony. "Is that it?"

He appreciated her phraseology. "I'm not sure that's what I mean," he said. "I'm not sure that's what always happens."

For a moment she had a faraway look in her eyes. Her gaze traveled the surface of the water, then returned to the detective. "What do you think we'd discover if we opened the coffin now?" she asked.

"I think we'd discover more questions than we would ever be able to answer," he said. "That's why that box stays down there. Those questions are not for us to answer."

She nodded. "Delicately put," she said.

"It's the best I can do."

"Your best," she said, "is pretty good. Thanks for everything."

He nodded. "Some weeks I earn my check," he said. "These past few were among them."

"Stop over sometime," she suggested.

He nodded. "I'll do that." He knew he wouldn't. She leaned to him and kissed him on the right cheek. In response, he wrapped an arm around her and gave her a hug of friendship.

Rebecca got to her feet and bade him good-bye.

She turned on the walkway and started back toward the pier. She raised one hand and signaled to her two children, who had been playing on the beach. They ran to her and joined her, one on each side.

Van Allen watched her go, walking slowly a hundred, two hundred feet down the promenade. Thereupon, she was joined by a man.

Van Allen squinted.

"Damn," he said to himself. Even with glasses, his eyesight wasn't as sharp as it used to be. He would have liked a closer look at Rebecca's companion.

From the distance, all he could see was that the man had dark brown hair. He wore a white shirt and dark slacks. But it could have been anyone.

Van Allen glanced away for a moment and then looked back. He couldn't pick them out of the crowd anymore. They were gone.

Never again would Van Allen pass by 2136 Topango Gardens and never again would he run into Rebecca Moore. Nor would he ever hear that infernal piano music again.

Nor was there ever another poltergeist manifestation in his home.

Except for one.

Van Allen had kept the broken pieces of the green Mont Blanc pen, the family heirloom. He had packed them in a small box and stashed them in a drawer in his desk.

Several months after the Moore case had been otherwise resolved, Van Allen came to his desk one morning and found the top drawer wide open.

He did not remember leaving it that way. On further inspection, he found that the box containing the pen had been disturbed.

Opening the box, he was shocked to discover the Mont Blanc restored completely. It was intact and in perfect working order, as if an expert craftsman had put the writing utensil back together with the greatest care.

Or as if a friend had come by during the night to say he was sorry and to set matters right. The mystery surrounding the pen was only the last of several events which Van Allen would never understand.

What he did know, however, was that with the repair of the pen, he could finally emotionally accept that the Moore case was closed, as much as it would ever be. And if somewhere out there an angel might be watching over his own interests in ways large or small, so it would have to be.

Not that this was anything he could ever share with anyone. With the exception of Rebecca, and possibly old Martinez, there were few souls in the world who would have believed any bit of it.

But he did make a mental note to carry the pen with him at all times. It would serve as a reminder of what in the world was real, what wasn't, and of the vast area that lay in between.

CHILLING ACCOUNTS OF
TRUE CRIME CASES

BORN BAD   (0-7860-0274-3, $5.99)
by Bill G. Cox
Excerpts from author's personal "death diaries"!
On a lonely backroad in Waxahachie, Texas, the body of 13-year-old
Christina Benjamin is discovered, head and hands missing. She had
been mutilated, disemboweled . . . and then raped. Just a few feet away
was the badly decomposed corpse of 14-year-old James King who had
been shot to death and dumped in a ditch. All his life, good-looking
Jason Massey had a craving he needed to satisfy. His heroes were Henry
Lee Lucas and Ted Bundy and he fantasized about eating the flesh of
his classmates. One sweltering summer night in 1993, Jason became
the country's most celebrated serial killer.

SAVAGE VENGEANCE   (0-7860-0251-4, $5.99)
by Gary C. King and Don Lasseter
12 pages of shocking, never-before-published, photos!
On a sunny day in December, 1974, Charles Campbell came to rural
Clearview, Washington. He attacked Renae Ahlers Wicklund, brutally
raping her in her own home in front of her two-month-old daughter.
Sentenced to 30 years for the crime, Campbell was out on the streets
only eight years later. He'd been set free by an incompetent criminal
justice system that failed to inform Renae of his early release. Now,
she would pay the ultimate price . . .

THE EYEBALL KILLER   (0-7860-0242-5, $5.99)
by John Matthews and Christine Wickers
12 pages of never-before-published photos!
In this chilling true crime, investigative cop John Matthews exposes
the private demons that turned one man's sick fantasies into one of the
most apalling murder sprees in the annals of Texas crime. In December
1990, prostitute Mary Lou Pratt was found brutally murdered—with
her eyes cut out. And in the ensuing months, more prostitutes became
the victims of this twisted killer. The murderer was Charles Albright,
a 57-year-old devoted husband, teacher, and football coach from Dallas.
But beneath Albright's charming demeanor was a savage mutilator ob-
sessed with the eyes of beautiful women.

*Available wherever paperbacks are sold, or order direct from the
Publisher. Send cover price plus 50¢ per copy for mailing and handling to Penguin USA, P.O. Box 999, c/o Dept. 17109, Bergen-
field, NJ 07621. Residents of New York and Tennessee must
include sales tax. DO NOT SEND CASH.*

GREAT GIFT IDEAS FOR THAT
SPECIAL SOMEONE!

DEAR GRANDMA, THANK YOU FOR . . . (0-7860-0253-0, $5.99)
by Scott Matthews and Tamara Nikuradse
Hundreds of heartwarming, funny, loving reasons to thank Grandma
for being there in her special way. This sweet book will say it all, ex-
pressing appreciation for Grandma's care. You can thank her for letting
you break the rules, telling stories about Mom, always saving you the
last piece of cake, and of course, for her gentle laughter and wisdom.

THE BRIDE'S LITTLE   (0-7860-0149-6, $4.99)
INSTRUCTION BOOK
by Barbara Alpert & Gail Holbrook
Forget the bridal registry or that casserole dish. Give her something that
she'll be able to use before and after the wedding. This nifty little treasure
trove of lighthearted and heartwarming tips will make her laugh when
she needs it most: while making the wedding plans.

DAD'S LITTLE INSTRUCTION BOOK   (0-7860-0150-X, $4.99)
by Annie Pigeon
This funny and insightful look at fatherhood is from the author of the
popular Mom's Little Instruction Book (0009-0, $4.99). From "learn
how to make balloon animals" to "know when to stop tickling," and
"it's okay to cry when you walk your daughter down the aisle" to "it's
also okay to cry when you get the catering bill," here's lots of wise and
witty advice for fathers of all ages.

MORE FROM LOVE'S   (0-7860-0107-0, $4.99)
LITTLE INSTRUCTION BOOK
by Annie Pigeon
Just like the previously published LOVE'S LITTLE INSTRUCTION
BOOK (774-4, $4.99), this delightful little book is filled with romantic
hints—one for every day of the year—to liven up your life and make
you and your lover smile. Discover amusing tips to making your lover
happy such as—ask her mother to dance—have his car washed—take
turns being irrational.

*Available wherever paperbacks are sold, or order direct from the
Publisher. Send cover price plus 50¢ per copy for mailing and
handling to Penguin USA, P.O. Box 999, c/o Dept. 17109, Ber-
genfield, NJ 07621. Residents of New York and Tennessee must
include sales tax. DO NOT SEND CASH.*

PINNACLE BOOKS HAS
SOMETHING FOR EVERYONE—

MAGICIANS, EXPLORERS, WITCHES AND CATS

THE HANDYMAN (377-3, $3.95/$4.95)
He is a magician who likes hands. He likes their comfortable shape and weight and size. He likes the portability of the hands once they are severed from the rest of the ponderous body. Detective Lanark must discover who The Handyman is before more handless bodies appear.

PASSAGE TO EDEN (538-5, $4.95/$5.95)
Set in a world of prehistoric beauty, here is the epic story of a courageous seafarer whose wanderings lead him to the ends of the old world—and to the discovery of a new world in the rugged, untamed wilderness of northwestern America.

BLACK BODY (505-9, $5.95/$6.95)
An extraordinary chronicle, this is the diary of a witch, a journal of the secrets of her race kept in return for not being burned for her "sin." It is the story of Alba, that rarest of creatures, a white witch: beautiful and able to walk in the human world undetected.

THE WHITE PUMA (532-6, $4.95/NCR)
The white puma has recognized the men who deprived him of his family. Now, like other predators before him, he has become a man-hater. This story is a fitting tribute to this magnificent animal that stands for all living creatures that have become, through man's carelessness, close to disappearing forever from the face of the earth.